The Moon Hunters

By Anya Pavelle

chandra

TABLE OF CONTENTS

DEDICATION

This book is dedicated to my husband, Mike.

ACKNOWLEDGEMENTS

This book wouldn't have been possible without the contributions of many people. First of all, I'd like to thank my publisher Chandra Press, and specifically Erik Evans, for helping me make this book publication-ready and for believing in the project. I'd also like to thank editors who helped me polish earlier versions of the book, namely Cara Flannery, Sarah Isaacson, and Jerrie Del Vecchio. Thank you also to Deborah, Peggy, Courtney, and Barbara for reading early drafts of the book. Finally, I'd like to thank my husband for his support during my typing sprees.

Ani Island

Sheer Cliff

Gaiae

Criminals' Compound

Central Village

Village of Lehom

CHAPTER ONE

I*t is better that one die than violate the natural order of things. Both flames and ruin flashed in our father, Gerald Ani's, eyes when he met our mother, Lillian. Violating a true woman's nature, Lillian abandoned her husband and three children. Father thus left Holy Wood of the Angels, with its rocky mountains and omnipresent smell of combusting fuels and smog, for a lush island he purchased from a failing government. Even though Gerald did not know of Lehom, this purchase was preordained. While the rest of the world submits to the Pestilence, this blessed island provides us with safety from the Old World and its infectious monsters.*

In order to best preserve our souls, Lehom has established natural roles for the sexes. Unlike Lillian Ani, women of virtue are not selfish, wanton, or independent of spirit. They should instead model themselves after the Ethereal Queen of Lehom, who is quiet, diminutive, graceful, and competent in a way that does not detract from the natural superiority of men.

-Rekin Ani in *The Book of Lehom*

~~~

DEANNE

MARCH 15ᵀᴴ, 2065 13:52 HST, ABOARD *KENTUCKY MARU*

As the H.M.S. *Kentucky Maru* glided quietly on the calm blue seas of the Pacific, the doctor held an old journal in her hand. She traced her fingers over the soft pages. Dr. Deanne Ambagu had been unable to get this book out of her mind since she pulled it from the bag that belonged to the two strange people they'd rescued from the sea. Thanks to a handwritten label on the inside cover, she at least knew it belonged to someone named Samsara Ani. The last name sounded like that of a long-dead actor whose movies she once watched on a classic movie streaming channel. Also inside the bag were two purple dresses made from a soft, shiny material, a wooden case with the word *Leilani* carved on its top, an old diving mask, and a coconut. Deanne and the scientists also found an assemblage of tools on the boat, including a small machete.

"Doc?" her nurse, Tomas, interrupted. "You should go rest. It's been a long week."

That's an understatement, Deanne mused. She yawned and tossed Tomas a grateful look. "I know, but aren't you curious about our refugees? I've never met any before. What made them leave?" She had that faraway look in her eyes—the one that sparkled over the prospect of a puzzle.

"We'll have to ask them when they wake up." Tomas pointed to the journal. "Any clues in there?"

Deanne yawned again. "I've only just started reading it. We've been so busy. Would you terribly mind fetching me some coffee?"

"Roger that. I'll be right back." He closed the hatch behind him, leaving her to her mystery.

A week ago, a norovirus spread through the *Kentucky Maru* and struck down half the boat's marine biologists with a vengeance. It spared only a few, the captain and Deanne included. Very lucky indeed, for as the only physician of the ship's many doctors, Deanne was responsible for supervising the crew's decontamination procedures. They were on their way westward to measure the effects of the recent Pacific earthquake on the local dolphin populations when the virus struck. While half of the crew quarantined themselves in their quarters, the doldrums of the past week's holding pattern anchored Deanne's spirits in with the filth of the sick. This was no mystery. She knew their fates and could only make them comfortable. Thankfully, the last sick crew member just nearly recovered. So the odd book and the Viking boat's inhabitants provided a welcome respite from her week of sanitation efforts.

The world primarily focused efforts on monitoring human populations, balancing geopolitics in an ever-changing climate, and strengthening economies. However, something had changed. Deanne didn't know why, just that it had, and that was enough for her. Thanks to the jointly-financed venture between Great Britain, the United States, and Japan, she had the luxury of paying attention to creatures other than humans, a sign that the world's recovery was moving beyond its usual grinding pace. In all her years in medicine, Deanne believed one thing. That through time, all things right themselves just as these dolphins seemed to have weathered the earthquake and subsequent tsunami safely.

Then, two hours ago, the *Kentucky Maru* came across a small bamboo Viking ship bobbing in the middle of the Pacific. With two unconscious and dehydrated people on board, no less. Although this had initially shocked Deanne, the captain explained that he came across refugees from Kiribati every few months. Unfortunately, a nasty dictator ruled those islands, and people left in whatever makeshift vessels they could construct.

But why a *Viking* ship? That was Deanne's best estimation of the boat. It wasn't much larger than one of the *Kentucky Maru's* lifeboats, but the polished wood gleamed in the bright sun. The little ship's curved edges tapered sharply at the stern and gracefully terminated at a dragon figurehead someone had secured to the bow. The dragon's lips curled into a mysterious smile instead of the snarl she'd seen on the illustrated dragons from her childhood fantasy books. Whoever built this boat had spent time lovingly crafting it. That she could tell. But why the Viking theme? Such a strange thing.

Nevermind the boat, everything about these two young strangers was odd.

Deanne studied the young woman resting comfortably in the bed. Thankfully, she looked much more peaceful than when they'd found her and the young man. The crew members who'd hauled them aboard had had to carefully pry the young couple apart from their tight, seemingly desperate, embrace.

The girl's tan skin contrasted with her salt-crusted red hair that hung to her waist. Deanne figured she was no older than twenty, and when the crew hauled her aboard, she'd been wearing a shiny purple robe, a filigree gold bracelet, and a wooden moon-shaped necklace. When Deanne had removed the robe to assess the girl's condition, though, she'd noticed the seven faint scars that traced across the girl's upper back.

Another mystery. Or was it? Did Kiribati's dictator punish people by whipping them? Deanne's heart pounded. What kind of horrible place could the girl possibly come from? The doctor gently rocked the bed with her foot, hoping to rouse the girl to satisfy her curiosity. She didn't move.

The doctor sighed, slumped into the bedside chair, and occupied herself with the book. She carefully flipped through the pages and saw handwriting from three different people as well as signatures from authors named Samsara, Samilla, and Leilani. Thinking it best to start at the beginning, Deanne focused on an excerpt. The date listed on the top right corner read: *Year of the Pestilence 1, Month of Yaxkin, Day 15.*

Yaxkin? *What?* That didn't sound like any calendrical system that Deanne knew. Year of the Pestilence? She shook her head.

It's been nearly three years since my friends and I came back to Father's island to set up our village, Gaiae. We wanted to live in peace. Well, that's ended. Ever since the world went mad, I've been recording things beyond our crop yields and births in Gaiae. Then, Chanson and Rekin came on Rekin's ship with his followers.

Chanson is sane, and he thankfully brought his factory workers, machinery parts, tools, building materials, seeds, food, a menagerie of livestock, rust-proof tools, and enough medical supplies to last us a few years. He's building around Father's mansion and making it the new administration building of "Central Village," his settlement. However, Rekin's completely insane. The only good thing he did was allow Chanson and his followers to ride along on the ship.

At least I know they don't carry the plague since they were at sea for five days. Radio reports indicate the bacterium sickens its victims within forty-eight hours of exposure. These reports are growing fainter, quieter, like the fading heartbeats of the ones left on the mainlands of the world. Rekin lives in direct opposition to me and Chanson. So far he's abided by his decision to set up his "Village of Lehom" on the other side of the island from our settlements. Three distinct villages: Village of Lehom, Central Village, and Gaiae. All on one isolated island. Can we actually manage to coexist without killing one another? Time will tell.

Deanne stopped reading.

Sickness? Plague? Was this journal referring to the pandemic that had killed a fifth of the world's population 52 years ago? Heart pumping, she jumped up and ran to her desk to examine the meager items she'd collected from the small boat. Their pile of clothes and the other items looked so... *primitive.* Yes, Kiribati was remote, but Kiribatians, if that's what they were called, had technology and modern clothes. Why didn't *these* two people have a long-range mobile communicator or even a navigation system on board the ship?

Then, with growing horror, Deanne dropped the journal on the desk with a thump.

Shit.

These refugees weren't from Kiribati.

And what if they'd been isolated from the world since the plague? She hadn't even thought to follow the World Health Organization's standard quarantine procedures! Why would she? Those measures had been dispensed with thirty years ago because the world had, through those same procedures and a new bacteriophage, rid itself of the antibiotic-resistant bacterium that had killed so many. All survivors had *seemed* accounted for. Plus, the *Kentucky Maru's* captain hadn't been worried.

But then she remembered the story of a Japanese soldier, who, after World War Two, became stranded alone on a Pacific island for almost thirty years. He didn't even know the war had ended. What if these people had stayed hidden, too? They might not know the plague was long gone from the mainland.

Deanne looked down at the couple, horror striking into her bones. If these people carried a mutated strain, they could kill everyone on this ship. What had they brought aboard?

The sheets rustled from one of the beds, so she turned to see the young woman's brow furrow in either pain or confusion.

Was she waking?

Wasting no time, the doctor grabbed the book and bolted from the room, hoping it wasn't too late.

CHAPTER TWO

Not counting Chanson and his unholy people, six families accompanied me on my ship. These six righteous families were renamed by Lehom as the Misu, Simi, Uya, Eno, Oru, and Cona. With the Ani, the Village of Lehom now has seven founding families. The most worthy male member of each family shall have the title of prince. I am the first King of Lehom, but every ten years, the princes will elect one from among them to be a new king. The king's power is absolute because he is a living embodiment of Lehom, and Lehom is infallible.

-Rekin Ani, excerpt from *The Book of Lehom*

~~~

DEANNE

Clad in a thick yellow biohazard suit, Deanne stared through the small glass window on the door to her infirmary. Red hazard lights, activated by the captain on her orders, flashed throughout the whole ship and made everything glow as if on fire. Tomas stood next to her. Through the glass faceplate of his own protective helmet, Deanne saw beads of sweat gathering on his brow, likely not just from his trapped body heat.

"Will these suits really help?" Tomas asked. Dampened by the helmet, his voice came out raspy.

Deanne squinted and focused back on the girl in the bed, who remained asleep even though she tossed restlessly under her sheet. Deanne wanted to reassure her nurse, tell him the two strangers for sure hadn't contaminated the ship. But that would be a lie, and Deanne hated lying. Not only had she and Tomas been exposed to the rescuees for hours now, but the crew members who'd hauled them aboard had, too. Deanne sighed in frustration. "Probably not. But let's keep them on just in case."

Tomas whimpered beside her. "I guess. Maybe you should read more of that book. To find out what we're dealing with, mutant bacterium or no."

Taking the potentially contaminated book from the infirmary had been a gamble, but Deanne agreed with Tomas. They'd also taken reasonable precautions to keep them safe from then on. The rest of the crew would stay away from her and Tomas, and both of them now had the suits for protection. The best-laid plans under the circumstances. Deanne carefully flipped through the book's pages, a cumbersome task in her impermeable rubber gloves. The answers she sought were probably toward the end of the book, written by the final author, Leilani, the same name inscribed on the wooden chest. She knew she'd made the right choice when she came upon Leilani's first entry. It began, "To whoever may read this, in case of our death, please send food, seeds, and cattle to Ani Island. Nearly a thousand lives are at stake."

***

To whoever may read this, in case of our deaths, please send food, seeds, and cattle to Ani Island. Nearly a thousand lives are at stake. Although I don't know how to direct you the island with coordinates, I hope the following details, as well as my descriptions of our villages, will help you find it. My island home is about three miles long and a mile at its widest point. It's a verdant shade of green from the beaches that form most of its perimeter to the mountain that rises up sharply from the shore about a quarter of a mile from the waves. At the bases of the island's waterfalls that bisect the green and black craggy cliffs, freshwater pools smell faintly of the nearby hibiscus flowers. Next to the sea caves of Gaiae, there's a chink in the mountain, a cleft that regresses back from the beach we departed from. The waterfall in the center of this crevasse got smaller as the boat carried us further out to sea. As the crashing of waves on the shore became quieter, my home departed into a misty dreamscape as it often does when the rain clouds descend and conceal it.

Most importantly, the island is far away from any of the world's mainlands. *Isolation breeds health. Congestion breeds death.* I used to accept these laws without question. We had what we needed. We measured time by the sun's progress across the sky, the sea's tides, the moon, a sundial in the center of the village, and moments of work, singing, and, more infrequently, laughter. We also used a calendar that Samsara had created when she established Gaiae, one more appropriate for us than the Old World's. As I grew older, however, I realized the Old World utterly haunted us. Its rhythms still guided our thoughts and actions even if we believed we moved in deliberate opposition to them. People marveled at its inventions, things we didn't have. The problem was, anyone who attempted to leave the island would break our most serious law. The penalty for that was death.

My mother always warned me that outside the safe cocoon of our home, the night was dangerous and full of the angry ghosts who Lehom damned to an eternity outside the Eternal Spirit Garden. She, like most people in my home village, hated night and what it concealed. But I loved darkness for its ability to shroud me in beautiful lies. The sun was always my true enemy. It's no different on our boat, where I've been praying for rain, even a torrential gale that could sink us. Anything except this…this nothing. We've now been listless in the ocean for two days after the trade winds died, yet we've still been spending these days at sea with the sails drawn outward to catch the absent breezes. Far from home and with my mental infrastructure in flux, I don't know where in the world I am for the first time in my life. Without the tradewinds, our little ship remains still, suspended on a sea of glass that reflects the blazing sun. My husband and I've almost consumed the last of our water. Lying under the sky's myriad constellations in the cooler nights, I've listened to his parched singing and savored our respite from the blinding heat. Love makes everything bearable and precious.

As I write this, my stomach feels hollow. That's also how my heart feels, too, from its weighty layers of grief. In case you're curious, my reader, about how we ended up stranded in this boat, it all began one fateful day back on the island, when my fall from daughter of a prince to criminal began. That was only about three months ago, but it feels like an eternity. I remember most the images of shattered pottery littering the dirt floor of my family's cooking pavilion, my best friend Dirmisu's tears, and a nasty bruise on my arm.

Before daylight sullied my mood that morning, I imagined myself as a mermaid under the sea, piercing the water's surface under a full moon and sky of stars. Dawn appeared as a fusion of pink sunrise and blue moontrap, the lamps fueled by iridescent plankton, that we used at night. In the world of sun and sand, my surroundings glowed pink as the sun's rays reflected off the inlaid mother of pearl carvings on the support beams of my room. My cocoon hummed with birdsong, and a sea breeze crept through the large fabric-covered window that dominated the wall across from my bed. That light, while beautiful to the eye, exposed all the things wrong with my life: broken dishes, temper tantrums, and bruises. Night's darkness was beautiful because it made the impossible possible by obscuring my life's ugliness.

My youngest brother Gisnen's voice barreled into my room, startling me awake. "Leilani," he whined as he banged on my bedroom door. "Dirmisu needs help with breakfast!"

Groaning, I rolled on my mattress of woven palm leaves and cotilk, a fabric Samsara had created from infusing the old cotton plant with silk-like strength and iridescence. "I'm coming!" I yelled back.

Just make it through breakfast. You'll be at the library soon. That's what I told myself every morning as I got ready for my twin brother Irin's scrutiny. Women's assets musn't tempt men, so I bound my breasts before tying my iridescent persimmon sarong. I completed my morning routine by brushing my teeth, gathering my hair in a chignon, applying light cosmetics, and placing the key to the spice cabinet around my neck.

Taking a deep breath, I walked down the hallway, past the home's three other bedrooms, the women's bathing room, and the men's bathing room, until I reached our back covered porch, which opened onto our family's ancestral spirit garden, where our dead rested in the ground. My family also ate meals in this sacred space. As usual, my family members, who were seated around the table, didn't even look up as I passed by. My two brothers discussed male-world topics, and my grandmother looked blankly at her favorite gold bracelet. They didn't need me, but Dirmisu did, so I headed to the detached cooking pavilion. There, my best friend and servant frowned at an array of four eggs, two sliced mangoes, milk of coconut, honey, and quinoa flour, the goods that the food distributor had brought to our kitchen that morning.

My friend's eyes lit up when I approached. "You look like a fiery barracuda in that persimmon robe."

"I wish I had a barracuda's power," I said, feeling guilty because my finery contrasted so vividly with her simple gray robe. "Well, dare we hope *today* my brother doesn't throw a tantrum about your cooking?"

Dirmisu's face fell, and her voice became but a whisper. "Yes, lets. Speaking of, I know I can make cakes with this stuff, but what about the spices? I can't make another mistake."

I shuddered. Yesterday, Irin had thrown Dirmisu's food on the ground because the spices were off. And, oh did he yell. When he wasn't satisfied with the food, my twin berated Dirmisu until she cried. Irin didn't understand that tasting cinnamon's fiery tang and nutmeg's nutty flavor in breakfast cakes, for example, was the only way to truly discover their proper proportions in the batter. And Dirmisu's family never got spices for food, only as medicine. All this because my father had been a prince, but hers hadn't.

Resolved to avert disaster today, I handed her a spoon and used my key to gather the appropriate spices from our locked spice cabinet. "Place half the honey in the batter to sweeten it, and add some cinnamon and nutmeg. I'll drizzle the remainder over the top."

She threw in the ground spices, which stood out against the light batter. "I'd give anything to taste spices every day."

My family remained oblivious to us, so I handed her some cinnamon in a bag and said, "Take some with you."

Dirmisu made sure no one saw her hide the illicit package between her bosoms. "I owe you so much already."

No, my poor friend was mistaken. *I* owed her for all her work. "You can return the favor one day," I joked back to lighten the mood.

She sighed. "But you're the great-granddaughter of the First King of Lehom. You'll marry a prince and be queen someday. Why would you need a favor from me?"

"Just because my grandmother was queen doesn't mean I will. Lineage isn't everything," I countered. Little did my friend know how much I loathed my world's trappings.

Ignoring me at first, Dirmisu bent down to check the heat of the solar cooking stone and rested a metal frying surface over it. She next began whipping the breakfast cake batter so it had the consistency of a feather, her clavicles jutting out prominently as she hunched over the ceramic mixing bowl. The rhythmic thumps of the spoon against the mixing bowl formed the drumbeat of her life. Finally, she poured the batter for the first cake on the frying pan. As it hissed against the hot metal, sweet cinnamon and nutmeg scented the air around us.

"Leilani," she said, her green eyes sparkling with determination. "Don't be ridiculous. You have everything, including indoor plumbing and an easy job in the Central Village library. And me? My house has only two rooms, I have to queue for the public cook house and bathhouse, and when not serving *you*, I work hard at the weaving house. Lineage is *everything*. Please don't patronize me."

My heart sank. Patronize her? Ethereal Queen preserve me. That hadn't been my intention at all! I rested my hand on her shoulder. Honestly, back then, I believed Dirmisu *could* rise if she became a virtue, one of the seven women who embodied the seven heavenly virtues of the Ethereal Queen. Patience, Obedience, Elegance, Beauty, Compassion, Quietude, and Resourcefulness were the Queen's companions. "I just meant you'd make the perfect virtue."

My friend shook off my hand. "No. Common girls like *me* have only been made virtues twice. Daughters or princes become virtues. Like *you*." Her words came out sharply.

Not willing to give up, I placed my hand on her shoulder again and assured Dirmisu, "But you're beautiful." She had full lips, chestnut brown hair, and a straight nose. With her tiny frame, my friend was just like the Ethereal Queen. Delicate and unobtrusive. Her bony back also made her more alluring to the men in the village, who for some reason found a woman's back to be her most erotic part. I, on the other hand, stood four inches taller than Dirmisu, and my arms and legs were toned rather than slight.

This time, Dirmisu relented and nestled into my touch. "Except when I'm as clumsy as an egret that's had too much to drink in the Central Village public house. I don't have your poise."

I laughed at this. "Well, not naturally! I've just had time to practice being elegant. It's not your fault you haven't. But, you *are* the Ethereal Queen's goodness personified," I said with a wink and a devilish smile.

My friend rolled her eyes. "Well, we've only been told to 'be good' at least one hundred times per day since birth, but blood's still more important than goodness. I insist."

"Then if I'm one day queen, I'll make sure you marry well," I promised. We'd been best friends ever since our first day at school. Most other girls of my rank only talked about their clothes and embroidery, things that bored me, but Dirmisu and I had bonded easily over making fun of these pursuits. And even when my mother forced me to interact with other daughters of princes, I maintained my friendship with Dirmisu by threatening to run through the village naked unless my mother dropped the subject.

Dirmisu's face grew dreamy for a moment, almost as if her desired future hung right within her reach. "I should finish," she finally said, gesturing to the remaining cake batter. "I don't want to get screamed at again."

Well, neither did I, so as Dirmisu continued to fry the cakes, I began my job. Required to make the food aesthetically appealing for my brothers, I arranged the mango slices into a pinwheel on each of the cakes and finally drizzled some honey, cinnamon, and nutmeg atop it all. "Behold, Mango Sunrise, a fitting name for the Ani prince's breakfast, for whom the consumption of food is an aesthetic experience," I said with mock seriousness.

She actually giggled despite the tension of the moment, and I joined in.

Unfortunately, our levity was short-lived. Reality, in the form of my brother's voice, intruded. "Leilani, have the servant bring the food," beckoned Irin from the table with a quick flick of his hand.

Yes, Irin. Yes, yes, yes, I thought. A daughter of a prince can say nothing else.

Dirmisu blanched. "I suppose I'll bring over the sunny mango cakes in a minute. And a broom in case he throws everything down again."

"Oh, no, it's 'Mango Sunrise," I cautioned. "'Sunny Mango Cakes' sounds like something a toddler would say. Not appropriate for the Ani prince."

This time, an ashen-faced Dirmisu didn't laugh at my joke. "But what if he doesn't like it again?" she asked in a quiet voice. Quiet. Diminutive. Meek. Perfect for a woman.

Curses to my brother. He'd been head of the family since the King made him prince after our parents died last year, and he'd been taking liberties with this power ever since. What had happened to the boy who loved to tease me by leaving tree frogs in my room? Shaking my head in disgust, I said, "Drop off the cakes quickly and go back to the kitchen. I'll handle Irin."

I took a second to look at the garden and draw strength from my mother, who we'd buried not three feet from the cooking pavilion. She was perfect and would've known what to say, so I prayed for her ghost to rise up as a misty haze and guide me or placate Irin.

I waited.

But nothing. Her bones kept silent, leaving me alone to handle my brother with my own meager wits.

When I reached the table, I discovered Irin still waited for his coffee to be poured. What a graceful dance I did as I took the carafe my grandmother had brought to the table before my arrival and poured four mugs of the beverage, making sure to serve Irin first, Gisnen second, Grandmother third, and then, finally, myself. As I gently secured my sarong under my legs and sat on my chair, Irin grabbed the mug of coffee without thanking me.

"Administration of island resources by the princes is the most important of jobs," Irin explained to Gisnen as he took the first sip.

I contained a sigh. But just barely. My brother copied the King's staunch, formal tone. "I thought the King has the most important job," Gisnen replied. My younger brother was still learning to appreciate the taste and power of coffee, so he scrunched his face in distaste after his first sip.

"It is," admitted Irin. "The king's the moral arbiter of our people, but the princes are the ones who enact the king's will. And therefore Lehom's will."

Dirmisu brought over the fried cakes on a ceramic platter and left them in the middle of our table before scurrying back to the cookhouse. Gisnen grabbed one before Irin could, a mistake since Irin ranked higher than he, and began eating it. The most virtuous son, the one most like Lehom, usually succeeded as prince of the family. However, the newly elected king likely chose Irin last year because he was then 18 to Gisnen's mere 11.

Irin held up one of the cakes and appraised it. "What are these called?"

"Mango Sunrise," I replied, waiting for Irin's permission to eat.

Irin took a small bite and nodded in approval. "The simultaneous sweetness and tartness of the mango does make me think of the complexity of a sunrise. You may have one now."

Thank the Ethereal Queen he didn't throw his food down today. Breathing a sigh of relief, I bit into one of Dirmisu's cakes and appreciated its spongy texture. She'd make an excellent virtue based on her cooking skills alone.

Irin frowned. "You should've thanked me for permission before eating."

I stopped chewing and put the cake down, swallowing the now leaden bite. Finally. Here it came. The daily corrective meant to keep me virtuous. "Of course. How silly of me."

My magnanimous brother Irin finally looked me in the eyes. "I'm sure you'll remember next time. Anyway, I have some good news."

This day was only getting worse. True, my brother did secure me my scribe's position last year after our parents died, but everything else from him brought nothing but grief. "Good news" at my age usually meant one of two things. A virtue's position or marriage, neither of which I wanted right then. I took a dainty sip of coffee and tried to sound nonchalant. "For me?"

"Virtue Elegance is Elegance no longer. You'll take her place," Irin said with a proud smile on his face.

No. *No!*

This was the worst possible news. I didn't care about court, embroidering, or learning how to apply makeup perfectly, all things virtues did. A crash from the cooking pavilion broke me from my reverie. Dirmisu had broken something. Today, apparently, *was* a day for spilled food and broken dishes. I'd also just been proven vastly wrong about our earlier conversation, and to make useless amends, I jumped up to help her, but Irin grabbed my wrist. "No. Stay here. Let the clumsy servant handle that."

His grip felt hard enough to leave a bruise, again. I suppose I should've considered myself lucky to have earned just one. After all, Irin had the right to discipline me as he wanted within reason. All heads of family did. In my village, we could tell a woman had been reprimanded if she hobbled or had bruises. Men couldn't maim or kill because that would make the other villages intervene, but they had explicit permission to physically discipline wayward women within the confines of the village.

"Irin," my grandmother hissed, slamming down her coffee cup. "That's enough." Her eyes were fierce. Penetrating. And honed right in on my powerful brother.

A wide-eyed Irin abruptly dropped my hand. Although he technically ranked higher than her, Irin hadn't quite yet worked up the nerve to defy her. My grandmother usually didn't notice his tantrums, but today was unique. She'd actually intervened on my behalf. Not willing to risk Irin's anger again, I sat down and asked respectfully, "Why isn't Meguya still Elegance?"

In addition to being Elegance, Meguya Uya was the sister of the current queen and therefore also sister-in-law to the King. Virtues remained virtues until they married an upcoming prince or were, very rarely, dismissed for being unsuitable. However, Meguya hadn't been married, and her position should've been safe due to her family connections.

"She's been retired," Irin replied, finding his voice after our grandmother's rebuke. "You'll meet with the Queen today to begin your transition to court."

"But what about my job? I love being a scribe." That was my truest truth, then. The woody scent of books, the feeling of lampblack pen being dragged across smooth paper. The knowledge, albeit fragmentary, of the Old World. Those precious things were all in the Central Village library.

I'd evidently asked something stupid because Irin gave me a scornful look. "You'll give it up, of course. As the head of this family, my connections allowed you to become a scribe in the first place to fulfill your work quota. *Temporarily*. Being a virtue is far better. You'll be among our holy people instead of that degenerate village. Where's your gratitude?"

I studied my twin, someone only older than me by a sheer two minutes. Although we had the same dark eyes, olive skin, and red hair, our power within the family unit was oceans apart. Yes, he'd used his connections to get me this job, but he didn't really have much choice when I thought about it. All people my age needed a job, and the only other open position appropriate for my social position was as an embroiderer. However, given my clumsy hand at embroidery, the embroiderers didn't want me. Thankfully, I had excellent handwriting, so a scribe's position it was. My brother primarily secured me the job to save face. Obliged to obey my brother's commands, I looked down at my cake with its lonely bite and replied, "Yes, Irin. Thank you. This is unexpected."

"You might as well go help the servant. I can't stand your ungratefulness right now."

How lovely. He'd given me the blessed dismissal I needed.

He couldn't stand my ungratefulness? Well, I couldn't stand him at all. I gathered my skirt and ran back to the cooking pavilion. That's where I saw Dirmisu glaring at me, the remaining cake batter and broken pieces of crockery scattered on the floor. My best friend hated me. Why else look at me like I'd just killed her mother?

As Dirmisu bent down to pick up the broken pieces of the mixing bowl, I knelt on the dirt floor and reached out my hands to comfort her, but she pushed them away quickly, tears streaming down her face. "See? You're on the path to queen. Virtue to princess to queen."

Her caustic words caused me more agony than the loss of my job. I picked up one jagged piece of crockery and placed it on the cooking table. "Please don't be upset. I don't even want this."

Her beautiful Cupid's bow lips pursed together in anger as she sputtered out, "But you still got it, just like everything else."

"You want what's fair." I sat down, not caring if I got dirt on the persimmon robe she loved so much. "So do I, but you know I have to obey Irin. Blaming me isn't fair either."

After a moment, the storm in her green eyes, probably inherited from her Uya mother, began to retreat as she sat down to me and sighed in defeat. "You're right, but my life's so hard. I just want to relax."

As Dirmisu studied the shattered pottery, I took her hands in mine, hoping to comfort her. Even though my village's laws prohibited me from hugging my brothers, I could have physical contact with family members and close friends of the same sex. "You'll have the chance when another position becomes available."

"How?" Dirmisu asked quietly as she stared at the ruins of her hopes resting on the floor.

I then reaffirmed my promise, something I'd later come to regret in spades. "I'll promote you, even if I have to bribe the Queen with some Sunny Mango Cakes."

At the mention of the childish food name, Dirmisu gave me a weak smile, and she resumed picking up the broken dish. Relieved that she'd recovered, I returned to the porch and saw my grandmother staring at me. She still looked somewhat alert.

Lady Samilla Ani was a woman of two faces, one properly regal and the other girlishly spontaneous and, dare I say, even bold. During her aloof and dignified phases, she lived in her own world. Former queens often spent most of their days lost in thought, so I only brought up important topics of conversation when she was lucid and engaged.

Since Irin and Gisnen had by then left, I joined her at the table and finally took another bite of my now-cold breakfast cake, noting again the pleasing blend of cinnamon and nutmeg as I drank my coffee and waited for her to speak. The din of early morning surrounded us. The ancestral family houses were close together, and the gardens abutted each other with only bamboo fences to separate them. We could hear our neighbors' servants gossip among themselves as they cleaned up from the morning meal. As my grandmother wrung her intricate gold bracelet against the delicate bones of her wrist, she said, "How surreal my life's become in its twists and turns from Calabasas to here."

"Where's Calabasas?" I ventured the question even though she rarely spoke of her life before the island. Only after the death of my parents last year did fragments of information emerge when she let her guard down. I relished this distraction from the disappointment over my lost job.

My grandmother gazed at the lush family garden when she spoke. "A place of arid hills, malls, and horses. I had a beautiful horse named Lucky Charm, who we brought here on the ship. Father made him a work animal after we arrived. I never rode him again because Father said it was unladylike."

The longing in her voice echoed my own misery at the loss of my scribe's position. Life wasn't fair. And women were powerless to keep the things they loved. Without thinking, I lashed out at our religion's holiest person. "What a cruel man!"

My grandmother clenched her fist around her coffee cup and took a sip. "Leilani. He was the holiest man in the world as well as our king. I had to please my kings just as you'll need to please this king as a virtue."

"But kings have nothing to do with such womanly concerns," I protested. "Virtues please their queen."

She shook her head, causing her beautiful earrings to jingle. She always managed to look impeccable. "No. *No.* A queen is beholden to a king more than anyone else. So, you must please both the King and Queen in equal measure. Please one too much, and you'll displease the other. It's why Meguya failed..."

Wondering why her voice trailed off at such an important moment, I followed her gaze to the garden. From her vantage point, she could see our largest tree, a wide and tall banyan that offered shade to us on even the island's most sweltering days. This tree was unique, however, because it had grown around a now-dead palm tree. After a few minutes, she pointed to the tree. "That palm tree once offered this family coconuts. It certainly looked majestic when my father built this house, but then I married your grandfather. He planted that banyan too close to the palm tree, thereby choking it. Living creatures are overcome and then destroyed by slow-moving dangers that only hindsight reveals as dangerous."

"My grandfather was like that banyan?" There were so many ways I could read into her story. People as trees? Trees as a symbol of power? My scant memories of him held a stern but not unkind man, just one who didn't have a penchant for indulging a young girl's inclinations.

"In many ways, yes," she admitted. "When your grandfather became King, he became an embodiment of Lehom. Living gods can't but help stifle the mere humans around them."

This made more sense. Nodding, I took another bite of my breakfast and contemplated this idea, realizing that as a virtue, I'd feel the same. Stifled. "Like the banyan."

She finished her last bite of cake and daintily patted her lips with a napkin, not even disturbing her white foundation and pink lip stain. "Exactly. I gained a forcibly-placid countenance in my marriage. Both my father and my husband put me on a pedestal, but your grandfather left me with a rhythm of nothing to fill my days. Come with me."

We walked through the bamboo hallway to her room, where by now, plenty of sunlight diffused through the cotilk wall, making the polished bamboo interior shine like gold. I watched, perplexed, as she knelt on the floor in a corner and pulled up one of the segmented bamboo floorboards. My grandmother reached into the void created by the missing board. "I expect you didn't know this house has two layers of flooring with a gap in between them to allow for better air circulation. It's the perfect hiding place." She then pulled out a small bag the size of an orange. A clinking sound emerged as she removed a handful of tokens, the currency we used in all three villages to facilitate trade. She returned them to the bag and handed it to me. "Hide them in your room. In the same place."

"Where'd you get them?" In the Village of Lehom, men usually held the money, and while they may give a female family member money to shop in the Central Market, women never kept the money for themselves.

The fine lines around my grandmother's eyes cracked with mirth. "Why, from your grandfather of course. I saved them over the years from my trips to the market. Few women marry with a light and happy heart, so I want you to use them to buy yourself some happiness."

Considering all the lessons she'd told me about how being virtuous brings a good marriage, this struck me as odd. "But, you've always told me that marriage brings perfect love."

She winced at this. "It was for your own good, then, at least under the old king. It's true that there'll be fewer chores if you marry a prince, and you'll have access to better food and leisure if you become queen. Whether you'll find love or not, though, I can't say."

Ah, the mystery of the hour. "How *does* one find love then?"

Her eyes clouded with the remembrance of something deeply hidden. "Both inside yourself and in another. In the midst of the Lord of the Deep, or Lady Moon."

"What?" She'd mentioned Gaiae's deities instead of Lehom and the Ethereal Queen, something treasonous and heretical.

She shrugged. "All the sacred fruits I had when I was queen have obscured my reality. My prejudices clouding your vision could lead you to Meguya's fate, but remember that this king is also like that banyan tree." Her voice sounded listless, then, as if our encounter had drained her of all her energy.

"So, I must avoid becoming the palm tree," I said even though I had no idea how to heed her warning at court.

She moved to her bed and laid down slowly so she wouldn't jar her ancient limbs. "I'm going to rest now. This day has been trying, and I've only been awake for an hour."

We left each other alone in our respective states of uncertainty.

My grandmother's illicit tokens, the broken crockery, and Dirmisu's angry face, all potent memories of that day, flit through my brain. I think I should stop writing now and rest. I've become weary.

***

"Doc! I think she's waking up for real this time," an excited Tomas said, breaking Deanne's concentration.

She lowered the journal a bit, enough so she could see through the window of the infirmary. The girl moved restlessly beneath the sheets, and the doctor thought she saw her squint. "You're right," Deanne replied.

"Did you find out anything?" the nurse asked.

Deanne shook her head, probably a humorous looking gesture in her gargantuan suit. "Not about a bacterium, but it seems like these people were forced to flee their island for some reason. Hopefully not from some type of outbreak."

Tomas pointed to the bed. "You might as well ask the girl. She's gonna freak out in there alone."

"She'll freak out from this *suit*," Deanne corrected him. "But I don't have a choice for now. Go tell the captain she's waking up. I'm going in."

And with that, the doctor took a deep breath of stale air and rested her hand on the doorknob, hoping she wasn't making a big mistake.

CHAPTER THREE

YEAR OF THE PESTILENCE 1, MONTH OF YAXKIN, DAY 30

I *recently went to Rekin's village to give my niece, who I haven't seen in three years, my mother's bracelet, but Rekin said I couldn't visit Samilla until I accepted Lehom as my god. Standing behind her father, Samilla appeared statuesque in her flowing robes, elaborate updo, and platform sandals. At the mention of her name, Samilla's dark eyes lit up, but fear enshrouded this eight-year-old version of my niece.*

"I can't believe in a god who hates women," I replied.

"Lehom protects them from the world and themselves," he insisted.

Stifling is not protecting. Poor Freja, my beautiful but daft Icelandic sister-in-law, barely spoke. Resigned, I said, "Well, I've brought her mother's bracelet."

At the word "bracelet," his face twisted into something menacing. He dismissed me with the words, "Never pollute her with that slut's things."

I held "that slut's" gold bracelet and watched the red and white-hot flames from Rekin's torches dance upon its delicate filigree pattern. Our mother brought this bracelet from Shanghai when she moved to the U.S. with a dream of becoming a star. However, she divorced her first husband for Father and, later, she divorced Father and abandoned us. Rekin has reason to hate her, and this animosity toward her had, evidently, transferred to her jewelry.

How different my brothers and I are. Why? Father brought us here to the island after Mother left, and we all had the same upbringing. We all went to college in the States when we came of age. It's after Father died that our differences fractured us apart. Before I moved back here and became a modern hippie, I genetically engineered plants. Chanson makes sustainable living products in a factory and finds hippies silly. And Rekin became a cult leader. I should be glad about something. Rekin purchased this ship before the pandemic so he and his followers could live their lives on international waters free from government intrusion. If he hadn't had done so, he and Chanson probably wouldn't have made it to this island. They would have died from the plague. Rekin hadn't wanted to bring Chanson's group at all, but I'd insisted. We three Ani siblings live lives of tenuous compromise.

Rekin insists this is all Lehom's doing, but Father's luck in the stock market and his purchase of this island, not the blessing of a misogynistic volcano deity, provided us with a refuge. And to think of it, Father's job as an actor really funded this place. It's where he earned the money to invest in the first place. Father must've wanted us to support one another because he left this island to all three of us. He thought legacy was important. I'll find a way to give this heirloom to Samilla when she's older.

-Excerpt from *The Journal of Samsara Ani*

~~~

LEILANI

MARCH 15, 2065, 14:30 HST, ABOARD *KENTUCKY MARU*

Before the lights awoke me from the ether of sleep, I was dreaming of our beautiful home. I clearly wasn't there anymore. My gold bracelet dangled from my wrist, and my moon necklace still hung around my neck. Those familiar things anchored me. I was lying in a bed. A bed with a metal headboard that reflected this unholy light. I looked to my right, and relief flooded through my body when I saw my husband lying in the bed next to mine, his chest moving up and down with deep, placid breaths. I wouldn't have wanted to survive this ordeal if he hadn't.

The colors here were all wrong. Wherever *here* was. Red. Red was an intimately familiar color, whether it be in a sunset, hibiscus petals, my favorite crimson lip stain, or blood. The flashing lights coming from the ceiling, however, shouldn't have been red. What made lights red? Electricity? I'd never seen electricity.

Everything about my surroundings, not just the odd placement of colors, felt wrong, from the cool, stale air that pricked my skin, to the pungent citrus smell that permeated the room. And I lay completely naked beneath my blankets. We were alone save for a series of strange hums that whirled through the air. Scanning my surroundings, I saw one wall with five circular windows that held back the blazing sapphire sky. Blue. That's a color I also knew well. Ocean, my grandmother's sapphire wedding robe, and the lips of drowned people. Those things were all various shades of blue. Shivering from the cold air, I noticed some cabinets and a desk. On the desk were more familiar things. My satchel. His bag.

The only way out, it seemed, was through a metal door with a small window in it. Wherever we were, I needed to be near my husband, to touch his soft skin with my lips. As I pulled back my covers to join him, the door began to shake and crack open.

I shrank back on the bed, not quite believing the scene unfolding before my eyes.

A yellow monster with no face came through that door. Instead, it had a head-like mass with a mirror where its eyes should've been. Yellow. Bananas, Meguya's hair, and sunrises. Those things were normally yellow. The monster also had four bulky appendages where legs and arms would be on a human. Strangely, that thing was also clutching Samsara's journal.

As it lumbered toward the beds, my skin grew colder from terror, just like when the King tried to trap me. The same feeling I had when I ran for my life up the mountain. My life had too much terror in it. We weren't safe here either. We'd been wrong to leave the island. Because I was awake, I decided to stand between that monster and my husband. I started to jump out of bed, only to be snapped back into place as fire coursed through my veins.

I looked down to see that a clear rubbery snake, which was anchored in the top of my hand, tethered my wrist to a metal tower near the bed. These creatures had restrained me with some type of torture device. I needed to get it off. Gritting my teeth against the horrible pain, I yanked on the snake. Drops of blood gathered on the meager white blanket that covered me. It's strange that at that moment, I took solace in the fact that this blood was red. That, at least, made sense here.

"No!" the monster yelled in a muffled voice. "Don't pull that out!"

My eyes darted from the droplets of blood on the blanket to the monster's face. It must've once been a human because it spoke in a language I could understand. But I certainly didn't trust it. "Stay away," I shouted back, my voice hoarse and weak. "Or I'll kill you."

I stopped and looked back at my blood. Then at the monster. Kill it with *what*? My necklace? My husband's machete? That weapon was far away in his bag on that desk, and this monster would kill me before I could reach it.

Talking with it seemed like my only option. I'd reasoned with monsters before when I had my wits about me, but now I was tired. So tired. Too tired to fight. Somehow, in the midst of my resignation to fate, I noticed how my lips still felt parched and crusted with invisible salt from the days at sea.

"I'm not going to hurt you," the creature said, resting the journal on a table. It then extended its arms above its head and pulled.

My eyes had to have been failing me because the monster's head came off, only to reveal the face of a middle-aged blonde woman with kind eyes. Kind *blue* eyes like the calm shallows of the island. Eyes. People have eyes. Eyes are normal things. Human and not monstrous. She spoke with measured calm. "I've already been around you for two hours without this suit, so I supposed a little longer won't hurt."

She didn't plan on harming us. At least, I didn't think so. "Who are you?" I asked, collapsing on the bed now that my immediate panic had ceased. I noticed the crisp cool feeling of the sheets, unencumbered by a heavy humidity, now that I was calm enough to truly absorb my surroundings. I reluctantly tested my limbs and felt their soreness, but they still had more levity than they had on our boat.

"I'm the ship's doctor, Dr. Deanne Ambagu, and I need to know something." She still remained a cautious distance away from us as she rested her hat on the desk. "How long has it been since your people have been sick from the plague, as you call it in your book?"

My book? She must've been referring to Samsara's journal. I shrugged. "No one's ever been sick from it."

"Really?" The red flashing lights augmented the look of disbelief on her face. "It killed a fifth of the world's population back then."

"We found safety from the world before that happened," I said, confused. Surely she wasn't afraid *we* carried the sickness. My Lehom ancestors called the Pestilence *the bringer of all good things* and the *gift of Lehom* since it formed our culture. There were many worship days where I listened to the King discuss this event as the cleanser of evil. The Old World had special medicines that could cure many diseases, but doctors abused these medicines by giving them to people who didn't need them. They subsequently stopped working. Then, a sickness came from the shadows and spread across the Old World quickly since people in those days could fly to distant lands in the blink of an eye. "On our island. Fifty-two years ago. We haven't had contact with the world since. Does the Pestilence still live here?"

Her expression relaxed as she approached the bed. "No. We found a cure for that bacterium, called a bacteriophage, about fifty years ago. We've forgotten about that horrible time and rebuilt. Things have been stable, politically speaking, for thirty years." Gesturing to the metal tower before me, the doctor said, "I'll take this out now. We gave you intravenous fluids to rehydrate you."

Bacterium, I knew. It was an organism too small to see with the naked eye. But bacterio*phage* was a new word. Even though she assured me we were safe, when the doctor reached the bed, my heart quickened thanks to all the conditioning I'd received growing up. She came from the Old World, an allegedly dangerous place, so I scrutinized her movements as she deftly removed the rubber snake from my hand and covered the resulting small hole with an adhesive cloth. With my body finally free, I shrank back and covered myself with my blanket. Although I apparently owed this doctor my life, I couldn't stand to be so exposed now, so out of control. I wasn't ready to let her see my scarred back. Then again, she probably already had. "I need my clothes back. Now," I demanded, my voice sounding more unkind that I intended.

"Okay, okay," Deanne said quickly as she got up and walked across the room to the cabinet, where she pulled out some blue clothing. "We're going to wash your clothes as soon as we figure out what material they are. But for now, here's a clean ship-issued hoodie and some scrub pants."

Hoodie? Pants? Old World names. I took the bundle from her and unfurled the shirt, which read, *Kentucky Maru*. "What does it mean?"

"It's the name of this ship," she replied as she turned around to grant me some privacy, a wonderful thing since no amount of time in Gaiae could completely erase the nearly twenty years of religious conditioning I'd received in my home village, the Village of Lehom, where they'd condemned nakedness.

A ship. We were on a ship. I knew what ships were. And boats. Ships and boats were normal things.

I slipped on the clothing and marveled at its strange shape, of the predetermined holes for various appendages, and at its utter simplicity, so unlike the iridescent robes I was accustomed to. As I settled back on the bed, I relished the feeling of the outfit's soft fabric on my skin, especially since these garments covered my shivering arms and legs. "How did we get here?" I asked, still unsure, my voice cracking.

The doctor gave a patient nod. "I'll explain. Promise. But first, let me get those lights turned off. I flashed them to alert everyone in case you were both contagious. You probably also want some water, too."

She left the room, and a few seconds later, when the lights stopped flashing, the room became less chaotic. The doctor soon returned with a glass in hand. She had also removed her frightening yellow suit and instead wore a simple blue uniform. "Here you go."

I grabbed the glass and almost dropped it. *Cold, this must be what cold is.* The air around me was cool, but the sensation this glass gave off felt much more extreme. I then noticed clear cubes floating in the water. "What is this?"

"Just water."

"No, I mean the floating things."

"Ice…" The doctor cocked her head as if I were a curious specimen of bird or bug.

"Ah. Solid water. Like snow. I didn't know it came in cubes." I only remembered the description of snow from my grandmother's story, how it both trapped and blanketed the lady in the tower until her escape. And, then, I had escaped too. I hadn't been the nightingale.

"Do you want crushed instead?" she asked.

It wasn't the shape that puzzled me, but the entire existence of water in an unfamiliar state. I ventured an explanation. "Cubes are fine. I've just never seen ice before. Our island is too hot, and we don't have refrigeration. No means to power it." I sipped the water and savored how its wetness removed the sandiness from my throat.

She nodded in understanding. "I see. How about some food, then?"

It was so long since we'd eaten that the thought of some coconut cakes or grilled chicken made my stomach growl. I needed to resume slowly, though. "After I drink some more water and let my thoughts settle." Taking a long sip of the gloriously cool water, I drained the glass of its liquid contents.

"Of course," she said as I handed her the glass, the ice cubes clinking against it. The doctor took her seat next to me again. She looked intent. Focused on getting answers to her questions. "So, let's start with the basics. Are you Leilani?"

"Yes," I replied. Suddenly, with my immediate needs taken care of, I remembered the reason we left in the first place. My voice urgent, I blurted out, "Our people need food and supplies, or they'll die."

"I know. I read that in your book," the doctor said. "How soon?"

"Within three or four months," I replied.

Deanne walked over to the desk and retrieved a large map, unfolding it on top of my blanket and pointing to an unmarked spot in a vast space of blue. "We're here. Can you show me where your island is?"

"I can't," I whispered as I scanned the confounding thing. Most maps of the area surrounding our island, save for a single crude one, had been destroyed decades ago. But, that single remaining map had coordinates and landmasses without detailed coastlines or even accurate proportions. What would we do if she couldn't help? Or *wouldn't* help? I knew nothing about her world's protocol. Were her people generous? Militant? "Are you going to cast us back in the sea?" I asked, suddenly feeling helpless.

My words jolted her attention from the map to me. "Why would you ask that?"

I shrugged and thought of my original home, the Village of Lehom. "People withdraw favors all the time."

As soon as I uttered those words, which tasted of betrayal, the tension that had been gathering inside me broke to the surface in a flurry of tears. Of sobs. Of grief. I lifted the blanket to my face and shuddered. I couldn't breathe, only gasp in the clean scent of this foreign material. Then, I felt the doctor's hand caress my shoulder.

"Breathe," Deanne gently commanded. "*Breathe.* We'll figure out a way to help your people. If we don't bring supplies ourselves, I'm sure someone will. We have some time. And we're certainly not going to put you back in the sea in *that* boat."

That boat? She sounded so dismissive about that wonderful boat, the one that had saved us. This doctor, who'd apparently seen much of the world since she sailed upon it in this great boat, couldn't know what our smaller vessel meant to us. At home, people could only borrow boats with permission from their respective village's leadership. The lucky few were usually fishermen who went, equipped with no more than two days' worth of food and water rations, briefly into our waters. As a child, I once asked one of these fishermen if he saw anything beyond the waters surrounding our island. He said no, that there was nothing but death outside our sanctum. True, some people used boats for pleasure cruises, but like the fishermen, they had to return the vessel within the prescribed time. Such ventures could also lead to death. That's how it went for my parents, anyway. Because of the island's restrictions about seacraft, this boat took so much effort to make. I even had to lie to my mentor in order to get permission to copy the plans for an ancient Viking ship called a *knarr* when working in the Central Village library. I uncovered my face and looked the doctor squarely in the eyes. "Don't condemn that boat. My husband made it." I nodded toward him in the other bed. The fact that he hadn't yet woken up worried me. "Will he be fine?"

"He's okay. Just tired, so we're letting him rest," Deanne assured me. "The fluids we gave both of you brought you out of danger. I promise."

Out of danger…was that too good to be true? I had to trust her. Everything was so confusing, and I needed an anchor in this world, especially since my husband still slept. "This is all just so strange."

"Well, you have to understand how odd this is for me, too. For that reason, I need to know more about where you're from." Deanne got up, pulled out a glass bottle filled with amber liquid from her desk, and poured some into a glass. She took a long sip before gesturing to the bottle. "I have a feeling I'm gonna need this. I'd offer you some, but I'm too curious to risk you passing out drunk."

"Like from palm wine?" It was the only point of reference I had for drunkenness.

Deanne finished her liquid. "It's bourbon. I think it's stronger than palm wine. Anyway. I'm assuming that since you don't know what ice is, you come from a very different world than this one. Tell me about it."

I stared at the bourbon eagerly as Deanne poured herself another drink. "I don't even know where to start," I said, feeling completely and utterly lost.

"What do you know about our world? Let's start with that," the doctor suggested.

In truth, barely anything, just fragmentary knowledge that had been gathered from books, stories, and cautionary legends. "I can tell you about Viking ships, Norman castles, snow, horses, nightingales, and Calabasas. That's where we were going for help. Calabasas."

"The Calabasas in California?" Deanne asked.

Well, that I didn't know. "It's near a city called Holy Wood of the Angels."

"Holy Wood of the Angels," Deanne muttered. "I'm guessing that's Hollywood in Los Angeles. What else do you know?"

"Even though I don't believe it anymore, my old religion taught me the plague was punishment for humanity's wickedness," I said. "The people of the Old World worshipped false idols and allowed women to govern."

Deanne almost spit out some of her drink. "Punishment for women in power? But that's crazy. No bloody wonder you were desperate to leave that island."

Desperate? Oh yes. Despite Ani Island's beauty, some horrible people with even worse beliefs lived there. I closed my eyes and recalled how endlessly blue the ocean looked from the white sand beaches of the Gaiae section of the island. I often felt both awe and longing when looking at the infinite sea. Before I left, I'd only known the limited space of our home island, where the sea laps up onto the land, and explored its immediate shallows, mild depths, and protected reefs. I could swim very well compared to the others from the Village of Lehom, but I only once ventured out beyond the point where the turquoise waters turned deep blue. When I swam for my freedom. I kept that to myself for the moment, though, and kept my answer simple. "Yes. We were desperate to leave for many reasons. My world went mad."

"That's a line from the journal," Deanne said, nodding in appreciation and appraising me from the chair. "But how? Specifically?"

A tidal wave of dread swept over me as I remembered how my days first turned to anxious shadow, and my eyes filled with tears. "I don't know how to start."

Deanne's expression instantly became sympathetic. "Simply start at the beginning. Right after your asshole of a brother forced to give up your job. I've read that far."

I hadn't heard the term asshole before, but I understood its meaning. It definitely described Irin at that point in time. "I'll do that," I replied. "But could I have some of that stuff first?"

Deanne reluctantly poured me a glass of my own, and I let the liquid slide down my throat, savoring how this liquid fire sequestered the pain of remembrance, of violent waves, of screams, and of death, to oblivion.

CHAPTER FOUR

Lehom first created the Old World as a garden. Humans defiled it, so Lehom and his queen moved to the Eternal Spirit Garden, where the righteous will join them after death. For now, behind the Temple of Lehom, we have the earthly Eternal Spirit Garden. It exists in the same place but on a different plane than the heavenly one. Each founding family in the village will also construct its own spirit garden, a place to bury their ancestors and where the living may partake of them by eating the garden's fruit.

The end of the Old World came about because people disturbed the cycle of life established by Lehom. They forgot their natural places in life, so Lehom smote them with the Pestilence. Our world, the New World, is a gift, but all gifts must end if we are to experience the Eternal Spirit Garden. When the natural cycles of life have again been broken, the New World will die.

It will be a time of shadows. Be ready.

-The Book of Lehom

~~~

LEILANI

So, the day my asshole brother told me to quit my job. I'll arrive back at that story soon, but I should explain a bit about why his command upset me so. And why our villages had such vastly different rules, cultures even. All three villages forbid us to leave Ani Island, but their similarities ended there. For example, the Village of Lehom repressed women, but Central Village and Gaiae didn't. Also, while the highest-ranking people in the Village of Lehom got the best jobs, housing, and food, the other villages portioned out resources more fairly. All three settlements had to work together, though, to ensure everyone's survival. Accordingly, each village was responsible for certain crops. My home village grew cotilk and quinoa. Central Village mainly harvested almonds, coconuts, and fruits such as mangoes. Finally, Gaiae had soya and vegetable crops. All three villages also dried and stored food until it went to Central Village for equal distribution across all villages. This system helped ensure villages didn't fight with one another for resources. That's not to say people in the Village of Lehom, such as my friend Dirmisu, didn't resent the inequalities.

It's amazing that while some life events are formative for people, others coalesce into a collective mental background noise. Born privileged in the Village of Lehom, I emerged from a milieu of firm boundaries. And also from the domain of ghosts. We believed our ancestors came to visit us in our sacred gardens, and, conversely, that the night jungles were haunted by the damned dead. Thankfully, though, my job as a scribe in Central Village saved me from being completely brainwashed by my upbringing. Well, Gaiae was responsible, too. Up until age nineteen, I'd only been there once, at ten years old. And how absolutely formative that single event turned out to be. After my grandfather died, my grandmother took me there to visit the newly erected monument to her aunt Samsara. Adjacent to her grave, the village built a temple to Lady Moon and the Lord of the Deep, the goddess and god Gaiae worshipped.

I remember most the view of the sea there. The scent and sound of the waves assimilated with my vision to produce a vista of absolute tranquility. The way the sea moved, glistening like blue diamonds under the sun, I knew it had to be alive. Vital and so unlike Lehom's silent, faceless statue. The ocean, then, infused itself in my veins. While my grandmother communed alone with her aunt's bones, I clasped my arms around one of the temple's pillars. Closing my eyes, I felt the stones, which were somehow cool in the tropical heat. Then, I heard the faint sounds of crying layered onto the wind's whistle, so I looked around and saw a boy, close to my age, huddled at the base of a column.

"Why're you so sad?" I asked.

"My parents died," he replied.

"There's really nothing to say to make it better. Mine might as well be too," I admitted, thinking of how my own father and mother preferred to spend time with the King and Queen, their closest friends, instead of me.

"So, you understand." He smiled and took my hand. It was warm and moist with the blazing sea air. In his other hand, he fiddled with a wooden dolphin pendant that hung around his neck.

"I love this temple," I told him. "The columns make the roof look like it's floating."

His eyes lit up at my use of architectural terms. "You like buildings? I want to create them when I'm older. I'm studying right now." I savored the next moments, happy that someone shared my interests. Then, he asked, "Can you stay here?"

I felt the knobby bones of his knuckles interlaced with mine and whispered back, "They won't let me come too often. I'm the daughter of a prince."

He gave me a curious look. "Is that really a big deal?"

I thought for a moment and then shook my head. "No. I'll try to come."

"You can always find me here," he replied.

So, there we were, children from different villages on different sides of the island, each finding comfort from one another until my grandmother came to fetch me. I remembered his eyes the most, blue with flecks of aquamarine and fluid like the sea itself. These mere figments of a person sustained me in the frequent maelstroms of my natal village. Only separated from him by the mountain that ran down the center of the island, I often wondered how he grew up because my grandmother never took me to Gaiae again. I think she grew afraid I wouldn't marry well if people thought I'd been tainted by that place and its unholy people. Well, that place did corrupt me, and I'm glad for it despite that visit's ultimate cost. I think my grandmother felt the same. Even until the end of it all. The day Irin told me I'd become Elegance was also a year after the King's coronation. During that time, our village had been living under the previous king's rules. New kings created their own laws a year and two weeks after they ascended. No one said so out loud, but this was a stressful time. None of us knew what rules King Marit Simi of the Simi family would soon set forth.

After I secured my grandmother's tokens between my bosoms, I turned into the hallway and almost bumped into a flush-faced Gisnen. Hoping he hadn't seen the token pouch, I asked, "What's wrong?"

He wiped some sweat from his brow. "Nothing. I was climbing the palm tree in the garden and saw Meguya waiting outside the front door."

Climbing trees. How full of innocent mischief. At least one of my siblings had a redeeming quality. "You must've been high up if you saw her over the house's roofline, Little Monkey," I teased.

"It's good exercise!" He jutted out his chin and glared at me. "I have time before school, so don't call me Little Monkey!"

My poor brother hated the six hours per day he had to attend school until the age of sixteen. Whatever other problems my village had, they *did* educate both sexes to the same age, a concession Rekin's siblings had demanded for our village's girls. Still, Gisnen would've much rather been climbing his way through the jungle. I held up my hands in mock surrender. "Whoa, whoa, exercise it is. Is Meguya still waiting outside? Tell me where she is, and then go climb all you want. Don't spy on us, though."

Gisnen's features twisted into an exaggerated expression of disgust. "Of course I didn't leave her standing outside. That's rude. She's on the back porch. And why would I want to spy on you? Girls are boring. You're just gonna talk about marrying princes and weaving."

Well, given that it was Meguya, he was probably right! I tried to contain my laughter as Gisnen scampered off, and I went to meet Meguya.

She sat at our table, looking paler than usual, which was saying something since her skin was the color of Gaiae's white sand beaches. Like me, she wore a brilliantly colored robe, hers the emerald green of the manicured grass from our gardens to match her eyes. She stared down at the shimmering folds of her garment, tracing the fabric through her fingers.

At my approach, Meguya's desperate eyes shot up to meet mine. "You've heard, I gather. Is your grandmother here?"

Meguya's voice was hollow with the loss of her position, something I now unwittingly possessed. "She's resting, but I can go get her." It was a feeble offer compelled by my guilt.

"You needn't bother," she said, her shoulders hunched.

This didn't sound like the proud Meguya I knew. We'd never been good friends even though she was only two years older than me, but I had nothing against her. "Do you want some tea?" I asked awkwardly. "It's the least I can do. Or, you can have my prettiest robe."

"Goodness, no," she scoffed. "Keep your robes. Ethereal Queen knows I have enough. But tea sounds nice. Could you make mine with parsley?"

Parsley? As a garnish, fine, but as a tea? Even as I choked on that idea, I wasn't about to argue with her. "If that's what you want, sure. But let me add other herbs, or you'll vomit from the taste."

She tucked an errant hair behind her ear. "Whatever. As long as it's strong on the parsley."

I walked over to the solar stone, heated some water, and retrieved our best tea, a blue lotus and lavender combination, from the cabinet. I grudgingly added two heaping spoonfuls of parsley to Meguya's mug, and as the tea steeped, I avoided conversation and stared into the darkening liquid. When the tea reached its optimal concentration, I brought the two mugs over to the table.

She peered over her mug and gazed at the blue flowers floating in the water, her elegant neck curved like an egret. "Remember that time we tried to divine the future with these? On one of those days when your mother forced you to play with me instead of Dirmisu?"

Oh, the hubris of little girls who believe they can predict their fates. "Yes. I suggested it because I didn't want to talk about embroidery."

"How prepared I was to be the perfect princess." Meguya dipped her index finger into the steaming liquid and sent the floating blue lotus flowers to the bottom. After her finger emerged with a thick coating of loose parsley, I watched her lick it off her fingers. "I never would've divined my failure back then."

"It's ungrateful of me, but I don't even want this," I said as I watched my own flowers swirl to the bottom in the whirlpool of tea. "I have to give up my scribe's position."

Meguya blew on her tea and took a sip, wincing for a moment, perhaps from the taste or the heat of the liquid. It was a few moments before she spoke, her eyes lost in the nebulous depths of her mug. "You and your books. That's how I felt about being a virtue."

I didn't know what to say, so I remained quiet. Faint birdsong filled the air, then, rifling through the porch on the warm breeze. Amidst the pitter patter of beaks echoing against the trunks of the palm trees in the garden, Meguya's façade cracked, causing tears to stream down her face and ruin her makeup. "But I failed. My sister dismissed me."

This made no sense for the Meguya I knew, the proud girl who preened in front of mirrors, cascaded through the village with bright, vibrant eyes, and played her flute in the perfect pose of submission. "Impossible."

Then, she covered her face with her hands, thereby muffling her words. "Be careful of him, my brother-in-law."

Be careful of the King? First my grandmother and then Meguya? Criticizing or doubting the King was unthinkable. Still, I continued into forbidden territory and asked, "What do you mean?"

"He'll deny it. Are you *sure* you want to hear my truth?" She studied my face, waiting to see how I'd react.

The intensity burning in Meguya's eyes told me she hid an ugly secret, one about our holiest and most powerful person. I felt the tension of that moment, such as when a major storm is about to break. I wanted to know, but dare I? Although there was no coming back from this knowledge, I needed to understand what had gone wrong since I'd be taking her place at court. "You can tell me," I said evenly.

Eyes vacant, she confessed, "He's improper with women. With me."

I took a long sip of my tea, and since I forgot to blow it, the hot liquid nearly scorched my tongue. Doubts burned inside me. Banyan trees can slowly stifle, but can they take bold, quick initiative? Holy people such as the King shouldn't violate Lehom's rule, and Lehom explicitly said that touching the opposite sex outside of marriage was forbidden. "Did you try to stop him?" I asked.

As soon as the words escaped, I realized my mistake. Meguya had been gripping her mug firmly when I asked the question, about to take another sip, but she thumped it against the table instead, sending droplets of tea and clumps of wet parsley flying in all directions. "Of course I did! But not always successfully! I don't know why I came. You probably just think I'm jealous."

Panicking, I jumped in quickly, "It's not that. I believe *you*, but if you're right, then the King's wrong, and we've been told that kings are never wrong. The whole thought is maddening."

"We're *not* wrong," she insisted. "*He* is, but he doesn't think he is."

Seeing a flaw in this logic, I asked, "But does that make him right since he's King? And if he's right even though he's technically wrong, does that make us wrong?"

Delicate, proper Meguya gave me a quizzical look and then burst into raucous, but also desperate, laughter. "Oh, Ethereal Queen bless us, I don't even know who these pronouns are referring to anymore," she said as she dried her tears. "Serves us right. My brother would say we're getting too philosophical for women."

I couldn't help but laugh with her at this ridiculous conversation. The dark clouds receded a bit from the room, but the ultimate questions remained unanswered. If the King was wrong in this, did it make him wrong in other things? Conversely, if he was right, did it make Meguya wrong for declining him? "Maybe we should talk about embroidery," I joked.

"No, no. Then I'd be boring you, Miss Bookface. I haven't told anyone else, so don't say anything. I'll deny…" Her voice trailed off as she looked at the Ani Spirit Garden.

"I won't," I promised, shifting my position. We sat for a moment in silence, and I decided to change the subject. "What will you do now?"

Incredibly, Meguya blushed. "My brother wants me to marry the upcoming Cona prince."

Earlier troubles aside, it seemed that she'd emerged from her ordeal none the worse. "Well, that's good! Your brother can convince the King to consent?"

Meguya laughed bitterly and drained her cup of the remaining liquid. "Oh, I'm sure. Let's just say that, for the reasons I mentioned, the King has reason to make me happy."

"I see." That stale air intruded again, seeping in from the shadows of the jungle. Wanting to change the subject, I nodded towards her cup. "What do you see in there?"

Meguya rolled her eyes but focused on the bottom of the mug. With an exaggerated flourish, she said, "Why, drowned flowers, of course. What about you?"

I finished the sweet earthy liquid and then gazed at the abstract form of the clumped tea leaves that rested in my own cup. "A dolphin, I think."

"Soggy flowers and cetaceans. What a pair we make. It's time for me to go," she said as she stood up. "Can I have some more parsley for later?"

"If you want." I walked back over to the spice cabinet and handed her the rest of our supply.

Meguya smiled gratefully as I handed her the package. She stood up to leave but gave her mug with the drowned flowers a final glance. Suddenly, tears filled her eyes again. Meguya threw the mug with such ferocity that the ceramic shattered and ricocheted across the polished floor. As she stared at the broken mug, her face changed from angry to aghast. "I'm sorry! I hate flowers now because the king gave so many to me. Let me help you clean up."

Unfortunately, today really was a day for broken dishes. "No," I assured her. "It's fine."

"Remember. Tell no one. Please," were her final words to me.

Looking back, I made so many promises that manifested an equal number of regrets. At that moment, though, I promised Meguya my silence, and she disappeared down our long hallway with her delicate spine peeking out the back of her robes. With trembling hands, I carefully picked up the ceramic shards. We all covet our secrets, and I was no exception. My back wasn't as delicate as Dirmisu's or even Meguya's, but it was strong. For, you see, I loved swimming in the sea during my brief amount of free time after breakfast and before my work quota. We bathed in the sea because it saved us from using the fresh water from our cisterns for showers too often. Many women, however, didn't *swim*.

Then again, I was not most women. I felt a fantastic pull from the unbridled elements of the natural world, the ones beyond the manicured grounds of my home village. I often wished for a room with a view of the sea since both the serene and mercurial elements of nature seemed to appear within it. The water turned teal, crystalline turquoise, white, and deeper blue as the clouds passed overhead.

After my conversation with Meguya, I went back to my room. Because I promised my grandmother, I jostled open the equivalent floorboard in my room, truly a convenient location to stow contraband, and hid her tokens inside. I then went to my rosewood chest, the place where I kept an ancient diving mask, a relic from the Old World that my grandmother gave me when she taught me to swim in another fit of unladylike lucidity. Even though the rubber strap had long since broken, I'd fashioned a new one with braided cotilk. But, thankfully, the glass faceplate and its plastic seal were still in working order. I placed this treasured gift from her in a bamboo basket and headed down to the Village of Lehom's beaches.

Such were my limited remaining days among the unfettered winds, Deanne.

I walked down the women's beach, noting the large pile of rocks that secluded us from the men's beach preserved our modesty. Others were often busy after breakfast and preferred to bathe in the evening, so I usually had the beach to myself. When I arrived at the deserted, windswept shoreline, I hung my clothing on a banyan near the beach's glimmering tidal pools. I felt the warm white sand on my feet and the tepid ocean water on my ankles as I moved deeper into the sea. The sea glistened like a brilliant turquoise jewel near the shore, but as the eye moved closer to the horizon, the color became sapphire blue.

Most women in the village stayed near the shore, never straying out beyond where their feet could touch. Although the water was relatively calm because of the offshore reef that broke the incoming waves, my grandmother had told me as a child that danger lurked in the deep. Then, after my parents drowned, she changed her mind about the water and taught me to swim when we were alone. I became a strong swimmer, pushing myself until I could make it out to the reef itself. From there, I would gaze at the sapphire line, the depths of the sea beyond the reef. I'd go to the point where I could just make out the looming form of my great-grandfather's massive ship, which he himself had sunk beneath the waves after he stripped it of all of its treasures.

My mask also allowed me to witness life beneath the waves in all of its purity and beauty. In the shallows, the watercolor turned the wave-rippled white sand a light turquoise that was filtered by gold ribbons of sunlight. Tropical fish glistened around me, darting in and out among the coral reef. My soul breathed beneath the surface even if my physical body could not.

That morning, after Meguya's news, I watched a clownfish hide amid the coral, waiting to pounce on a smaller fish. True, it hunted as nature intended, but it didn't do so with the King's malice. He was a predator who hid in the deepest depths of the sea, out where the sapphire color turns a frigid black. Where I've read the dead, eyeless things dwell.

My shoulders and back had developed muscle definition from my sojourns among these creatures, something that kept it from remaining delicate like Dirmisu's. That morning under the water, I realized how hard it would be to swim alone from now on since virtues usually bathed with the Queen. Entertaining her was essentially my new job.

In those moments, I mourned the loss of the job I loved, where I was ensconced in the library among its many books. Just as Meguya craved beauty and Dirmisu luxury, I delighted in acquiring information, especially bits about the Old World from the library's books.

Yet, lest it corrupt me, Irin instructed me to only copy the words instead of absorbing this content. Girls like me were accompanied by chaperones outside the village to both to protect our reputations and to ensure that we weren't tempted by the unholy influences outside our community. An elderly, virtuous lady named Nereno was both my chaperone and also poor Meguya's grandmother.

After I emerged from the sea on my last day as a scribe, I returned home to read our *Book of Lehom* in a sunny space of our garden while I let my hair dry. I hoped to find some tidbit I could use to convince Irin to let me keep my position at the library.

Instead, the words validated Irin's whims, no matter how arbitrary and capricious.

Teach your women what they need to be industrious and virtuous, manage their homes, and to keep their minds occupied in lieu of tempting distractions. But teach them not things that would tempt them outside of the faith. Sons of Lehom, control the women of your family, for they are prone to ruinous fancy if not properly guided.

I dashed the book down on the grass, watching in pleasure as my throw forced its pages askew. It wasn't fair. Why couldn't I be both scribe and virtue? My hands felt leaden as I stood before my mirror and once again applied my light makeup.

The library, the sea, and my bedroom were the only places I felt cushioned and safe from the outside world, my contrived world with its many regulations and expectations, the place that wanted me to hold myself above people like Dirmisu. Then, the unspent tears in my eyes threatened to spill and ruin my efforts at disguising my face.

CHAPTER FIVE

YEAR OF THE PESTILENCE 10, MONTH OF NISAN, DAY 8

Samilla's getting married today. At eighteen. In this new world, I can see the practical reasons for marrying young. At least her fiancé appears to cherish her, and he's a much better option than the Simi prince. Samilla told me he watches her every move. I suppose, then, that Cleman Ani is the least terrible choice out of a host of terrible choices. Another reason I won't protest this marriage is because Rekin actually consented to me being there. I should gift her this book. I'm not afraid if Rekin objects to its content. My brother's nearly blind from cataracts, and Freja's had way too much "sacred fruit" to care. I'd call it poetic justice if it didn't make me sound like a vengeful bitch.

-The Journal of Samsara Ani

~~~

"I can't believe how little your village trusted women," Deanne said, her voice tinged with disgust. "Samsara had to wait until Samilla's father went blind to give her the journal. And you had a *chaperone?*"

From my vantage point on the bed, the sky was gray instead of searing cobalt, the color of the blinding heat that had nearly choked us on the boat. I got up, walked to one of the infirmary's windows, and pressed my face against the glass, savoring its coolness. "We're expecting rain."

"You're changing the topic. Is this uncomfortable for you?" Deanne asked.

"No, no. It's just that the rain brought me the right things," I assured her as I walked back to the bed and got comfortable again, amused at the questions threatening to erupt out of her skin. Thankfully, at that moment, my stomach let off a low growl, causing Deanne to blush.

"I'm so sorry," she said. "You need to eat instead of blathering on. I'll be right back."

How right she was. Although I was lightheaded from hunger, I smiled at the doctor's unrelenting curiosity, revenge for all the times I'd peppered my mother and grandmother with my questions. In a few minutes, she returned with two small paper packages, handing one to me and then taking a seat next to the bed. I watched as she opened hers and took a bite of the square piece of food inside. I did the same and discovered the food's outer layers were spongy, much like Dirmisu's coconut cakes. Inside were chunks of a meat that tasted like chicken, covered by a hot, tangy sauce with notes of garlic.

Deanne must've mistaken the look of pleasure on my face for pain because she asked, "Is the sandwich too spicy?"

I stopped chewing and asked with a full mouth, "There's *sand* in this bread?" My poor teeth!

At this, Deanne suddenly started coughing, and her face became red. Alarmed, the nurse who'd been checking over my husband ran over and slapped the doctor's back.

I swallowed the food and asked, "Are you alright?"

It took a few moments, but Deanne's breathing slowly returned to normal in spite of the tears of laughter that still ran down her cheeks. "I'm fine. That was hilarious. A sandwich is just two pieces of bread with any filling. It's named after a place in England, my country's protector. There's no real sand in it!"

Even though I felt ridiculous for my error, I wasn't about to look a gift parrot in the beak because of pride. "Well, I like it, so thank you."

"I'm glad," Deanne replied, taking another bite of her sandwich without sand. "Now that you've been bribed, after you swallow your food so you don't choke on me, explain why your village's women have their family name as part of their first name."

I contemplated this as I finished chewing. Despite the burden imposed by names in my home village, a name did save me once. But, they were also instruments of power and deceit. Such as the name Lehom. I recalled my surprise when I finally read Samsara's journal and discovered an entry where she'd written Lehom and L'homme right next to each other. L'homme, which means "the man" in a language called French, was very similar to the god's name that Rekin heard during some hallucinatory stupor. I didn't tell Deanne all this or how Rekin made his followers change their first and family names while he kept his. I kept my answer simple. "So their original family name is still with them after marriage. My grandmother, Samilla, is the exception. As Rekin's only heir, she got to keep her first and last names. Her husband even changed his to Ani when Rekin adopted him."

Deanne let out a low whistle. "That's also a great way to mark women as family property."

Swallowing my last bite of food, I nodded in appreciation at her understanding. "People think they're protecting their *property*, but they often end up stifling it instead. Anyway. My chaperone, Nereno. She was there to protect my virtue." I looked back out at the overcast sky and smiled before continuing with my story, happy to finally relay a happy part.

***

I pulled myself together that morning and prepared to leave for the library. I found Nereno waiting for me on the front porch as usual, paper parasol in hand to protect her skin from the sun.

She gracefully bowed when I emerged from the house. Nereno was just as dignified as my grandmother in her immaculate robe and perfectly applied cosmetics. "I think we should send a servant to the library with a message and head right to court ourselves."

Unable to bear having someone else deliver this bad news, I said, quickly, "No. That wouldn't be right."

She opened her mouth to argue, but then shrugged. "Well, I suppose the walk will do my old bones some good."

After I grabbed my own parasol, we set out on the one-mile walk to Central Village, a trip I dreaded under the circumstances. As the sound of our sandals crunching the sun-bleached coral pavement filled the air around us, I daydreamed about the library. And about book-making, a process I found fascinating given our limited resources on Ani Island. The pages of the original manuscripts were protected from the humid sea air with a plastic laminate, something my ancestors had coated these books with when they still lived in the Old World. We, on the other hand, had to make our books from materials found on the island, so I wrote on paper made from the pulp of palm leaves and used a bamboo quill to inscribe the words. Words took on holy proportions in my mind, and I felt proud to create such precious objects. Irin's order to quit my job killed not only my joy but also threatened my sense of self.

I remembered the day when the librarian, Lucina, asked me to copy a book about Norman Castles. Nereno had been sitting at a nearby table reading a book of recipes, thankfully engrossed in its content so she couldn't overhear my conversation.

"Those books give you a partial history of the Old World," Lucina had said to me when she came to inspect my work.

"Why'd they bring these books and not others?" I asked, puzzled as to why she'd given me something that seemed useless here. Castles of stone? We had no need for such things.

"They couldn't bring everything from the Old World on the ship, so people selected what was important to them," Lucina explained. "This book on Norman architecture belonged to a historian from Central Village. He probably wanted to keep a record of old civilization."

"I'm glad he did," I replied because things from the Old World fascinated me. I didn't have access to such books at home. In the Village of Lehom, each family had a copy of the *Book of Lehom*, and the library held religious texts. Holy things were important to them, not obscure, dead cultures. The schoolhouse also had books on practical subjects such as grammar, mathematics, basic science, cooking and nutrition, the architecture of bamboo, cultivation, weaving, and civic sanitary standards. Strangely, we also had twelve volumes of poetry and courtly romance in the schoolhouse for the girls. I think because these stories instilled submission in girls. Romantic notions of passivity.

Lucina flipped through the pages until she reached the map of a land called Europe and pointed to Normandy, a region in a place labeled "France." Although we had maps of the world's faraway places, we had none of our immediate area, nothing that could allow someone to navigate away on a stolen boat. Back then, I couldn't have imagined that an inverted courtly tale would provide the key to a hidden map.

Eventually, as my thoughts continued wandering, Nereno took the initiative and began a conversation. Twisting her parasol so it obscured her face from me, she asked in a neutral tone, "Did Meguya give you any details about her dismissal when she came to see you this morning?

"None," I lied. "But I honestly can't picture Meguya as anything *but* elegant."

All I could see of Nereno's face was her delicate chin and painted lips as she continued, "When Veluya summoned Meguya to court, the birds outside my morning window sounded all the sweeter."

The oil of clove and eucalyptus that Nereno used to help soothe her aches wafted through the morning hibiscus. Although never a queen herself, Nereno *was* the dowager princess of the Uya clan, and she'd helped mold her daughters and granddaughters for success since their births. Now, growing old interfered with her duties.

We remained quiet as we walked through the densest jungle between the villages, something neither cultivated nor culled, but only cut back from the road by our low-class agricultural workers and criminals. The morning sun had begun to raise steam from the damp earth. "They're twelve years apart, right?" I asked, hoping to fill the silence. "That's a lot."

"Veluya can be picky," Nereno confessed on this jungle path far from the village's ears. "She simply declared Meguya inelegant. There's more to it, I'm sure, but it's best to let sleeping eels lie. I'm not going to pry into this affair of sisters."

An affair of sisters. Sisters are simultaneously companions and rivals, for as with sons of princes, usually only one daughter of a prince, the most virtuous one, ended up marrying a prince herself. When Veluya married Marit Simi, then prince of the Simi clan, she made it more difficult for Meguya to secure a princely marriage. That'd changed when Veluya the queen installed her sister in court as a virtue. Instead of bonding the sisters, however, Maguya's entrance to court catapulted them apart. The King poisoned their relationship and left both of them feeling betrayed. How awful. I couldn't bear for something like that to happen between me and Dirmisu, my essential sister in the world.

I pushed away that fear as Central Village's marble administration building, my great-great-grandfather Gerald's former mansion, emerged from behind the trees at the bend in the road. The village's largest structure, it stood two-stories tall and had five rooms on each floor. It was also a place for commerce and where the Central Authority, the inter-village governing body, met to discuss inter-village disputes and governance. Today, food and clothing vendors had set up kiosks under the two-story portico at the entrance and were announcing their wares.

The entire Central Village itself, really, hummed with activity. As the lively sounds of the village's apothecary, hospital, clothing and food vendors, school, cobbler's store, and the public house, where people consumed intoxicating drinks and played music, flooded our senses, Nereno's features twisted in displeasure. This place had a beautiful vivacity that we lacked in the Village of Lehom, which didn't have a public house or anything nearly as boisterous.

People here moved quickly and laughed freely, things as elusive and as impermanent to me as the rainbows that form in mountains after it rains. Public laughter and merriment could be unladylike in even casual circumstances, and, of course, the music emerging from the public house was highly improper. At home we were permitted flutes, and beautiful though that instrument's sound was, it captured a limited range of human experiences, solely the meditative and solitary elements of nature. But what about joy, laughter, and all that's unbridled?

Nereno also hated how much skin people revealed here and in Gaiae. Some men wore sarongs around their waists and left their chests bare, as did some women! Most girls, though, secured their wraps around their chests, but this still left their calves and sometimes lower thighs visible.

My chaperone chastised me for staring too long at anyone, so I focused my attention on the houses along the village's perimeter. Not wanting to clear the land of its majestic banyans, Chanson Ani had installed living spaces in the Central Village's trees, some as high as four levels. About three hundred people lived here, the same as the Village of Lehom. The people of Central Village, however, didn't hierarchize their sections as we did.

We finally reached the library, a large, airy single-story bamboo structure that rambled pleasantly among the surrounding trees that shaded it. This place usually triggered excitement at the temporary freedom it granted me, but now I felt dread because walking inside would signal the end of that precious freedom.

"You don't need me to come inside." Nereno collapsed her parasol, adjusted her skirt beneath her, and settled on a bench in the shade provided by a colorful bougainvillea. "So I'll wait here."

Nodding, I struggled to hold back my tears. As I walked inside, the smell of palm paper lingered on the cross breezes that blew in from the open walls. I scanned the reading area for Lucina and saw her talking to a group of Central Village children at a table in the center of the room.

"I've got just the book for you. On Vikings and their ships. They're a fascinating warrior people who sailed the ocean over a thousand years ago," Lucina said as I approached. After she instructed the children to sit quietly, she asked, "Where's your chaperone?"

I studied the patterns in the polished bamboo floor because I couldn't bear to see Lucina's disappointment. "She's waiting outside for me while I say goodbye. I've been summoned to court by Queen Veluya. To become a virtue."

"Oh, for the love of...you *want* that?"

Personal wants? What are those to girls who don't have a valid voice, only the option of obedience? "It makes a princely marriage easier..."

I finally met Lucina's gaze, but instead of anger or disappointment, I found pity, which is worse since there's no hope for the pitiful. "I'll never understand your village's system of kings and queens," she said.

Well, why would she? Every five years, Central Village and Gaiae each held democratic elections for the three people who'd set the local laws and represent their village as a member of the Central Authority. The Village of Lehom also had three members on "The Authority," as we called it, but they weren't democratically elected. The King was one member, and he selected two others to accompany him. The only time people from Central Village or Gaiae interacted with our government was through the Central Authority. However, the Authority didn't usually interfere with the Village of Lehom's daily life but instead had jurisdiction over work quotas, food dispersal, disease prevention and sanitation, and other items agreed on in the *Treaty of Three*, the written accord all three Ani siblings created when Rekin's ship arrived. The Authority believed this rule helped promote harmony between villages. But harmony and dissonance are never too far apart.

Plagued by shame, I comforted myself by rubbing the silky fabric of my robe between my right-hand fingers. Lucina's face softened as she asked me plainly, "What do *you* want, Leilani?"

Such a simple question, really. But how to answer it adequately? I wanted pretty clothes, books, the sea, and a transcendent, true love, all without the guilt I felt when I saw Dirmisu working herself to the bone in my place. But instead of this litany of contradictory wants, I simply said. "I don't want to quit."

"Well, that's fine then. Can't you work here and still attend court?"

If only. Despite my own desires, exercising them was still unthinkable. Irin could punish me however he wanted, and defying him in this would earn me more than a singular bruise.

How lucky Meguya was to get dismissed.

Meguya! I became excited when I realized the answer to my woes dangled right in front of me.

Well, not exactly. I wouldn't want to get dismissed for being improper with the King, whatever that meant, but perhaps I'd be so terrible at being elegant that the Queen would send me away. As I mentally inventoried all of the upcoming princes in my village, I realized that none of them appealed to me. So, why even pursue the status? My heart pounded at the realization that there *was* a way for me to avoid court. Through *failure* of all things. This normally dreadful word rolled pleasantly off my tongue as I silently mouthed it. I had to make sure, though, that my failure didn't look deliberate. Irin would see through that.

I gave Lucina a coy smile. "I'm naturally clumsy, so I'm sure I'll fail. The Queen dismissed the last girl in this position. My brother might send me back if that happens."

At these words, Lucina perked up. "Don't even bother with that. Just move here! I can find you a place to live here or in Gaiae."

There's a duality to promises in that they're both cruel and wonderful. Wonderful because of the possibility of them manifesting, cruel because hope can lead to delusion. Leave the village? For good? At every weekly worship service, the King told us that those outside the Village of Lehom were condemned to an afterlife of eternal torment. Cut off forever from family and paradise. Exile, eternal punishment, and alienation from my grandmother and Gisnen were more than I could bear. At least, I thought so at the time.

But then again, would leaving automatically mean exile, or under certain circumstances could our villagers spread their wings? No one had ever left, so I supposed exile was severely implied. Of course, I fantasized about living elsewhere when growing up, thus getting my view of the sea. This offer from Lucina, coupled with my grandmother's tokens, made living outside the village possible. The day's cascade of disappointments vanished with this beautiful news. I actually had hope of a life beyond my brother's reach.

I needed to think, one step at a time, and find a way to leave without being alienated from family. Otherwise, I could never go back. "Eventually, yes," I replied. "But I can't give up on my family just yet."

Now I saw the expected disappointment on Lucina's face, but she reached out to hug me, something I returned in equal measure. "I understand. Remember. Your place is always here," she said, breaking my embrace.

Lucina then walked back to the group of children and joined in their laughter. Such innocence in that happy din, something my own upbringing had lacked. "What your husband requests, you must do," my mother once told me when we were embroidering cotilk on our back porch. "This, and behaving like the Ethereal Queen, are how you'll prove your worth in life and earn your place in the Eternal Spirit Garden."

I wanted to be a good wife, so I asked, "What if I can't do what he wants?"

My mother looked resplendent that day. Her coppery red hair, the same as Irin's and mine, was shiny and interlaced with flowers. "You're excused if it's something that's impossible according to Lehom's standards. But otherwise, a good woman will find a way to accommodate her husband's desires."

"What *is* impossible, then?" I asked since I was a young girl prone to annoying my mother with frequent questions.

She rolled her eyes at me and stabbed her embroidery, resulting in an unsightly stitch. I seemed to ruin all of my mother's attempts at perfection. "If your husband demands you turn the sky red or to make food in a time of famine, this is impossible according to Lehom. But if he wants you to prepare something according to his liking in a time when resources are scarce, this is possible."

"How's that different from famine?" I still didn't understand.

"If there's no honey to sweeten his food, you could use a mango's juice for this purpose or substitute with spices. *This* is a situation of scarce resources. If all are starving, which has never happened before on this island, *then* you have an excuse from Lehom."

"But, what if my husband believes the impossible to be possible?" I continued.

I could tell my mother's impatience had grown to exasperation because she threw down her embroidery and glared at me as one does a fly. "Then convince him otherwise without arguing with him. That *is* possible for a good woman. I'm headed to court."

She strode out of the room, her robes sashaying behind her. Would things have been any different for me or Meguya if our parents hadn't died? Perhaps the universe had spun off its intended course all because of the boating accident that killed all four of them last year. Taking a small craft out for pleasure purposes rarely happened since it required the King's permission. On the day of his coronation, however, the King granted his consent to Meguya's and my parents, who were great friends of his. There was no storm responsible for the party's demise. Rather, the culprit was probably a current that brought them far out to sea, where a whale likely sank the boat. We assume that's what happened because the boat never returned and none of them could swim. Stupid, really, for island life.

Outside, I saw that Nereno still rested languidly under the tree. She was only four years younger than my grandmother, old enough to feel the pains of age in her bones, but young enough to have completely forgotten the Old World. She sat up as heard me approach. "How did it go?"

I told her the truth, less the details of my plan. "Lucina accepted my resignation."

"Well, of course, she did. It's not like there's any choice in the matter," Nereno said as she stood up warily. "Now, I suggest we stop idling our time away and head to the palace."

I held out my hand to steady her. "We might as well."

As we both turned back in the direction of our village, I heard the rumble of thunder. The heat from the sky had waned, and as the rain clouds made their way over the mountain, the sky let forth its tears.

"Oh, Great Pestilence curse us," Nereno cried. "It hasn't rained in a week! I thought the sun parasol would be fine."

"We could go back to the library and wait," I suggested. Our island usually experienced daily showers, an absolute blessing for our crops. We often traveled with waterproof umbrellas made from oiled cotilk and bamboo. However, because of the unusually dry weather of the past week, Nereno and I had brought our flimsy paper parasol. All because they were less cumbersome to carry.

"You can't be late today, Leilani," she grumbled as she opened up her parasol.

I copied this futile gesture but then heard larger raindrops batter my parasol. "We could walk back and then change our clothes at home," I suggested.

Nereno shook her head. "It would take forever to get you looking proper again. Veluya will think me incompetent."

Improper…how wonderful! Perhaps looking a drowned mess would make the Queen reject me. All thanks to our useless parasols. I was about to suggest we brave the storm, but then I stopped. Nereno would be suspicious. Instead, I played the part of a dutiful girl and searched around for options. Finally, I saw the kiosks under the mansion's portico. "Let's see if any of the vendors in the administration building have some extra umbrellas."

Noticing that our parasols were sodden, she finally relented. "My servant has the tokens today, but it seems like the best idea."

Nereno and I quickly scuttled across the village's main thoroughfare and settled under the portico. By the time we reached cover, the rain poured down even more fiercely and collected in puddles at the base of the mansion. Even though our paper shields were beginning to break down from the onslaught of water, our robes were only slightly damp at the bottom.

As I shook off the umbrella at the base of one of the portico's strong stone columns, I heard a male voice behind me say, "You made it. And none the worse for wear."

I spun around and saw that the voice belonged to the clothing vendor. He was around my age but not of my home, for he'd secured his sarong around his waist rather than tied over one shoulder as men did in my village. I had no complaints since this exposed his toned chest and shoulders, which were lightly tanned from the sun. My eyes traced from his chest and up to his arms, focusing then on the tendons in his arm and his strong shoulders.

And then I saw his face. Staring at men was an unseemly thing to do in my village, but stare I did at his brown hair, blue eyes, and chiseled features. My eyes then lingered on his strong jaw before jostling themselves back down to his taut forearms, which were rested against the edge of his kiosk as if waiting to pounce into action. I next moved back to his eyes. They were bluish, almost aquamarine. Looking into them triggered a warmth to move from my chest to my fingers, much like when taking a bite of our sacred fruit.

Those eyes.

My heartbeat quickened. Could he be related to the boy from Gaiae I'd connected with as a child? Or even the boy himself? Likely not, as he'd wanted to be an architect instead of a salesman. He also wasn't wearing the dolphin necklace.

I couldn't ask this question directly, so I returned his smile but then looked down at the ground lest I appear flirtatious. "Barely, but yes. We've surrendered our parasols to this rain."

Nereno stepped between us and asked, "Do you have umbrellas for sale?"

"Of course, ma'am." He laughed and gestured to the umbrellas stacked near the other clothes in the kiosk. "I'm assuming you want two?"

"Please. We can't pay for them now, but later today I'll have someone from the Village of Lehom bring you what we owe plus some extra for your troubles," Nereno offered.

"Not necessary." He rested two waterproof umbrellas on the kiosk's counter. "Just tell me your name, and I'll let you have them."

Nereno picked up one of the umbrellas and opened it, nodding and acknowledging its quality. "I'm Lady Nereno Uya of the Uya clan."

He leaned a bit to the right, removing Nereno as a barrier so he could see me directly. With a dazzling smile, he bowed and said, "I was talking to the pretty scribe."

"Leilani Ani," I replied quickly, meeting his eyes and smiling. The warmth returned, and I felt my chest flush a light pink. *How did he know I was a scribe?* I wondered.

"Leilani!" Nereno spun around, her eyes wide with shock. "Hold these umbrellas and be quiet."

"I'm sorry, Lady Nereno." I grabbed the new umbrellas, which, like this young man, smelled of sandalwood oil, handed her my destroyed one, and studied the pattern my wet sandals made against the marble floor of the portico as they darkened the veins of the stone. Always looking away from the eyes of men were we, the Daughters of Lehom.

Despite her delicate stature, Nereno appeared to grow five feet with indignation. "And you, young man, are *not* supposed to flirt with our girls. She's going to court today to help eventually secure a marriage to a prince if she doesn't ruin her chances with the likes of an umbrella salesman."

How quickly the weather on his face changed, from that of a sunny, zephyr-scented day to the sky of a young thunderstorm. He took a few seconds to collect himself. Finally, he gave Nereno a deep bow. "I'm Jenay Lo of Gaiae, lowly umbrella salesman but also bamboo architect. And I'd never ruin anything for this lady."

Nereno wasn't going to force me to be rude, so I stepped forward and returned his bow. "It's a pleasure to meet you. Thanks for the umbrellas."

At that moment, his other words hit me.

Gaiae! Architect!

I studied Jenay's eyes for a moment and scrutinized them this time. Were they as aquamarine as that boy's had been? I stupidly hadn't asked his name all those many years ago. Surely more than one person from that village had bluish eyes. But, then, as his eyes met mine again, the years between our childhood encounter and this moment collapsed into nothing. I was nearly sure he was the same boy. After all, he could've lost the necklace or grown tired of it.

"We'll have the tokens sent to you, Jenay Lo, of Gaiae," Nereno said as she handed him the destroyed parasols. "Leilani's not about to prostitute her affections for want of two umbrellas. Will you be here at this kiosk the rest of the day?"

"I will," he replied, frowning at Nereno's words. "But prostitute her affections? I assure you again I had no bad intentions…"

"And how much do we owe you?" Nereno cut him off.

He looked aghast as he said, "Two five-piece tokens."

"You'll have three of them by the end of the day, an extra for your trouble." She then turned to me. "We're leaving."

No! Was she insane? Lucina's offer of a place here in the village became all the more tempting. I wondered what would happen if I simply ran back to the library and refused to leave.

Jenay pointed upward. "The columns make this roof look like it's floating."

With that line, I couldn't move even though I could feel Nereno dragging me away with her glare. He was the boy! Who else would know my childhood observations about Gaiae's temple? I had to let him know I remembered, so I added, "The place where you can always be found."

His eyes crinkled with happiness. "Then until next time, Lady Scribe."

Now, thunder accompanied the rain, and I felt Nereno grab my arm. "There will *not* be a next time. What's wrong with you? We're leaving now."

And with that, Nereno dragged me towards the Village of Lehom and my alleged destiny. To my shame, I followed her. The rain pattered harmlessly on our new umbrellas, and my delight made me nearly drunk. He'd called me pretty! I felt like collapsing into happy giggles and rolling around in the mud puddles at my feet. I'd never felt so deliriously happy.

Although Nereno had dropped my arm by then, I didn't dare look back at him, so I forged ahead, one foot in front of the other. To steady my excited heartbeat, I took some deep breaths and noticed the rain smelled sweet, like earth and flowers in the sunshine. After we'd been walking for about fifteen minutes, the rain waned, then ceased, and finally, the sky emerged from the clouds. I watched Nereno gracefully twirl her umbrella to remove the excess water before closing it. I followed suit so the bottom of my robe could dry in the sun. As my sandals crunched on the road, muddy from the rain, my thoughts went back to Jenay. Why had I felt that warmth? That lightheadedness? Simply because I found his features and mind pleasing? Or, was it the brief connection we'd made as children? Unless I got dismissed from court, we wouldn't get another chance to see each other.

Suddenly, with the sun beating down on us and the insects humming in the foliage on either side of the road, Nereno stopped walking. "Leilani, that was foolish."

"Talking to Jenay?"

"The lot of it."

I tried the innocent approach. "I've talked to vendors before, and it wasn't a big issue then."

I could see the disappointment on her face when she insisted, "Your brazenness was. You should've said, *not that you have a need to know it, but my name is Leilani.*"

"But that would've been unfriendly. I don't understand how women can be both friendly and aloof. Compassion is one of the Ethereal Queen's virtues!"

"Compassionate and friendly to our own people, yes. But those from the Central Village and Gaiae aren't our people. You should still be superficially polite to them, but not too friendly, or they'll tempt you to their ways. Their *unholy* ways."

"I don't understand how being friendly could tempt me," I insisted. Although my grandmother's views seemed to be evolving, apparently Lady Nereno's weren't.

"Being at court will be good for you. That's all I have to say. Come on, let's go," she commanded as she resumed walking. Again, to my shame, I followed her to a village that isolated itself out of fear and hate for those different from us.

CHAPTER SIX

I was born at a time when the world's machines had already rendered human usefulness fallow. This, like other things, angered Lehom so much so that the Earth shook with his displeasure. He revealed himself to me during an actor friend's frivolous party. We were all sitting on the floor and feeling our alienation so profoundly our bones ached with it. The ground shook, my senses jostled, and the word "Lehom" came to me at the same time, replacing my longing with bliss. Something eternal was within my grasp. Lehom presented himself to me as strong, faceless, and eternal God. He moves the Earth's terrain through fire and rock, spewing forth the seeds of his creation from mountaintops around the planet.

He also revealed to me a vision of his consort, called the Ethereal Queen, who is one of elegant disposition. Where he is iron, she is silk. The Queen wore layered robes of this silk, and she had a white face, red lips, and eyes accented with kohl. I couldn't see her eyes because she gazed demurely at Lehom's feet. Where my mother had been brash, brazen and seductive, Lehom's Queen possessed the virtues of Beauty, Compassion, Elegance, Quietude, Resourcefulness, Patience, and Obedience. The Ethereal Queen is all of these in perfect proportion, as important as Lehom but subservient. This was the way the world once was and should again be.

Lehom has always been guiding me. My wife, Freja, was the exact image of the Ethereal Queen, and we met years before Lehom's revelation to me. She comes from a land of ice, trembling earth, and of Lehom's molten seed, so when Lehom revealed himself to me years later, Freja took me in her arms

and said she believed in me. She, like the Ethereal Queen, is perfect. Women, model yourselves after the Ethereal Queen and obey your husbands since they know your best path. Husbands, protect your wives and keep them pure.
  Rekin Ani -*The Book of Lehom*

~~~

"So, *now* I see why you like the rain," Deanne said with a knowing smile. "But why didn't you just run back to the library and stay?"

I took a sip of the tea that she'd given me, relishing the caffeine that awakened my senses. Even thousands of miles from Ani Island, I still remembered the beautiful sensations of that day, the rain splashing on my toes, Jenay's grin cracking in front of my eyes, and the first twinges of love springing from my heart. I experienced it all again and savored it from my hospital bed. But not even all those wonderful things could make me immediately forsake my family. Of course, I treasured my freedom when I got it, but it came at a huge price. How obvious it must have seemed to her, a woman with endless choices and a firm knowledge of her place in the world that my sacrifices were effortless. "Letting go of the familiar and emerging into uncertainty are never painless. I knew I had to eventually act, but I still loved my grandmother, Dirmisu, and Gisnen enough to try getting dismissed from court without being exiled from my family. Little did I know that I'd soon pray for simple exile."

The doctor frowned. "Well, that sounds ominous."

"You're not entirely wrong," I said, resolved to find the right words to explain how tightly family ties can bind one to a place. They're as powerful as a snake's coil and the thickest of jungle vines.

***

Think of me as a baby bird first breaking out of its shell, of its tentativeness as it pecks from its protective shelter. Rebellions are rarely sudden because their seeds take long to sprout. For this comparison to make sense, I should explain exactly what exile meant to my people. They believe the souls of the blessed enter the Eternal Spirit Garden after death and live for eternity in bliss, without hunger or sadness, in a place where the leaves and flowers sparkle like gems. The villagers accept this false reality since they saw it once per week.

Those in exile from the community, however, remain outside the garden after death in an eternal state of pain and longing. Unable to enter the village or its family spirit gardens, these angry ghosts haunt the jungle surrounding the village. I was taught they could harm the living who dared wander among the trees at night. As a result, people rarely strayed off the beaten path when the sun departed. The people in my village think that's *my* fate. Well, the ones left alive at least. These same villagers believe it was my own self-destructiveness that exiled me, but that's because of their limited perspective. How much power anyone who's been brainwashed has to deviate from such a course is debatable, but, thankfully, I managed to escape. Eventually, that is.

Until then, I followed orders. On that surface, at least. About a half an hour after my conversation with Jenay, Nereno and I arrived back at the village and headed towards the royal complex that held the palace and temple. One story tall, the palace sprawled across the flat grassy terrain of the village's center. Rekin Ani had built this palace for daytime use when he was King, but he slept in the Ani family home at night. As the next king, my grandfather did the same. The third King of Lehom, however, began the tradition of making the palace his official quarters and appointing a temporary prince to occupy the ancestral home. Temporary princes were other brothers, like Gisnen, who would act as prince and head of the family while the official prince reigned as king. After ten years, temporary princes retired to their own section of the village. Their homes there weren't as grand as the ancestral homes I grew up in, but they were much better than Dirmisu's.

Nereno and I entered the palace through the main entrance, which led to the King's audience hall, and made a right-hand turn through a door to the Queen's audience hall. Like in my home, the palace segregated living spaces according to sex. I wondered where the King could've had the opportunity to be improper with Meguya away from the Queen's eyes.

The ambiance shifted as soon as we stepped into the Queen's audience hall and saw Queen Veluya Simi. She was shrouded in a veil of light cardamom incense and poised in front of her altar, which held a statue of the Ethereal Queen. As the Queen glided across her domain, her arms and legs moved delicately but surely to the flute music played by Compassion. Obedience, patience, elegance, compassion, resourcefulness, beauty, and quietude were the virtues that made the Ethereal Queen perfect. Like this goddess, Veluya Simi was supposed to embody all seven virtues in equal measure.

Well, that's how I thought of her then, but now I know how easily people can construct an artifice when their only obligation in life is to maintain it. She must've heard us shuffle in, for as she held up her hand, Compassion's flute music ceased. She greeted us with a melodious, "Welcome."

Like Meguya, Veluya had fair skin, blonde hair, and eyes as green as the jungle's foliage, features many men in our village considered ideal. Nereno inclined her head slightly. "My Queen."

Veluya laughed at Nereno's deference. "Please, Grandmother, I don't need such formality from you." Veluya then turned to me and said, "Welcome. Your mother was a great friend, so if you're anything like her, you'll do well as Elegance."

Well, I wasn't like my mother. At all. And she'd always let me know it. Hopefully, this would work in my favor and get me dismissed all the more quickly. Still, I needed to construct my own artifice of initiative, so I gave her a respectful bow and lied. "I'll do my best."

Then, to add to an already surreal day, Veluya walked across the room to a low table and rested herself on a large bamboo-leaf stuffed pillow, reclining back so her ankles peeked delicately from under her robes. The six virtues followed suit, and a plainly dressed woman emerged with a tray, setting down seven cups of tea. Once the Queen took a sip, the others did as well. As I wondered if the virtues did anything on their own, I heard a squawk like one that normally comes from the jungle.

I looked for the source of this sound, and saw, in a cage hanging suspended from a tall stand, a parrot. This was no ordinary bird. It wore bamboo inlaid mother of pearl jewelry. Well, that sight rendered me speechless. Why bedeck a poor creature like that? It looked miserable.

"That's Ethereal. My pet. The virtues take turns making jewelry for him and rather turn it into a contest," the Queen explained as she put down her tea. "You may return here tomorrow after your family's breakfast is prepared. I'll contact the weaving room and have some appropriate robes sent over to flatter your coloring. It wouldn't do to have you wear my sister's former virtue's robes. What a curse."

The Queen then turned to the other six virtues. "Welcome your new sister."

The other virtues, who'd been waiting for the Queen to instruct them to speak, inclined their heads slightly and said in unison, "Welcome, sister Elegance."

All six of them moved as one unit, sipping their tea and smiling to one another like a shiny-scaled school of fish. They were transcendent in their elegant robes, which were hammered with mother of pearl like mine. Only much more glamorous. With every movement, they manifested the glimmer of the stars, even while mundanely sipping tea. Having grown up with these girls, I knew them all. Two were even my cousins! But there, surrounding the Queen in her audience hall, they'd subdued their original identities.

"Thank you for the welcome," I said, suppressing my distaste for the whole charade.

The Queen gave me a radiant smile before turning her virtues. And with that, my formal introduction to court was complete. It left me perturbed. And full of dread. Those are the best words to describe my feelings. You see, Deanne, a woman's highest purpose in my home village is to emulate the Ethereal Queen, become perfect like her because that's how men prefer it. That commandment never seemed right to me, though. I always had the nagging suspicion that whatever deities created humans crafted me from different clay than other women I grew up with. During my island nights, I often experienced a recurring dream where I was a bodiless spirit, an incorporeal mist in a sky of stars, that gazed down upon myself as Elegance. Her face was still and serene, and layers of cosmetics covered her face, exactly like the Ethereal Queen. She knelt, pointing herself east, in the direction of the Old World that the Pestilence allegedly destroyed. Next, I saw a blast of light come from outside the room, and her eyes cracked open and reflected the red glint of fire. From above, I observed as a gust of torrential smoke blew her away. Powder flitted off and exposed her skeleton, which itself subsequently turned to dust. There was no sound. No heat. Just the light. I felt peace after the wind carried her away and as the sky turned dark.

After this dream, I'd awaken in my birdsong-filled room and gaze upon the statue of the Ethereal Queen near my bed. This queen allegedly inspires peace, harmony, and growth. The statue's eyes were closed. The ceramic lines of her robes were smooth and contiguous, lapping over one another before finally pooling at her feet. In her right hand, she held a scroll. It's said that the destiny of each person upon this planet, such as whether they'll be allowed into the Eternal Spirit Garden or eternally condemned outside its gates, is etched on this scroll. I used to ask her what my future was, who I was beyond the flesh. I never received an answer, though. Perhaps that's why I eventually turned my hopes to Lady Moon, an act unworthy of a Daughter of Lehom.

That dream told me I'd been damned to fail as a virtue since the day I was born, and my introduction to the court confirmed that notion with spectacular clarity. After Nereno returned me home, I had an afternoon to myself, likely the last I'd have in a while. I went to the back porch and stared at the garden, thinking of my tea divination earlier in the day. I'd seen a dolphin. Was that significant? My grandmother believed that the Ethereal Queen would sometimes communicate with people through nature. During her own reign as queen, she established tea reading as a permissible activity for women. After all, we spent so much time cultivating tea and serving it to ourselves and to others that it would be practical for the Ethereal Queen to communicate with us in this way if any at all. Preparing and drinking tea was beautiful. Tranquil. Just like Lehom's consort. Of that morning with Meguya, I remembered how the mist rose up from the boiling water and how the flowers danced like seagrass in calm waves. That is, until Meguya and I had drunk ours. The dancing flowers then wilted to finally reveal that dolphin for me and the drowned flowers for Meguya.

As I stared at the tea, I also remembered a tale from Gaiae, one that my grandmother told me in a moment of lucidity when I was a child. She whispered that on the night when the moon was at its fullest, *Out among the dancing waves live the mermen, the earthly representations of the Lord of the Deep. If you, as a physical manifestation of Lady Moon, wish to summon one of them to you, stand in the shallows of the sea when the sea is blue with the light of the full moon. Wear your most serene face, and emblazon in your eyes pure desire. Don't wait until the moon begins to wane to enact your summoning. If he comes, be ready to leave the world of sun and sand, for only one that dances among the sea herself will make him a ready companion in his kingdom within the ocean's depths. The dolphins are the harbingers of the merman. Find them and you'll be on your path to his kingdom beneath the sea. The sound of your loved one's singing will let you know you've found him at last.*

So, if I could believe my reading, the sea must be in my future. And maybe Jenay, too, if his dolphin necklace was any indication. Not all was lost. Resolved, I decided to summon my destiny instead of spending my days making jewelry for parrots.

CHAPTER SEVEN

L ehom created this Earth by spewing forth his fire. Other men ignored the signs and ascribed Lehom's wonder to mere physical phenomena, but I heard Lehom's rumble for what it was: a simultaneous call to the righteous and battle cry against the wicked. Even before Lehom's revelation to me, I chose Freja Guðjónsdottir to be my wife. Freja, herself from a land that spews Lehom's fire, is the first physical manifestation of the Ethereal Queen of Lehom. Freja Ani, thus renamed after our marriage, embodies all seven virtues of the Ethereal Queen of Lehom. The Queen is elegant, compassionate, beautiful, patient, quiet, obedient, and resourceful. She illuminates the King of Lehom but never steals his inherent light. To mold the Village's young women properly, she will name one young woman to embody each virtue.

-Rekin Ani, *The Book of Lehom*

~~~

"Wait, what? Jewelry for parrots?" Deanne asked with an incredulous look on her face. "Granted, people dress their dogs in clothes sometimes, but I've never heard of jewelry for birds."

At the mention of dogs, my heart melted. I'd seen pictures of the furry little creatures in books at the library. They looked like such friendly companions. "I've never met a dog," I said.

"Well, that's a pity." The doctor walked over to her desk and retrieved a small black rectangle thing. I knew that object wasn't a dog and wondered what it had to do with our conversation. Deanne next pressed a button and, to my absolute delight, an image of a dog manifested right in the center of that rectangle.

I gaped at Deanne, marveling at the contraption that allowed me to look at the adorable little animal. The device had an internal light source, making it so different than a laminated photograph in a book. Finally, my eyes rested back on the dog. "What is it called?" I asked.

"A phone," Deanne explained.

"Phone," I repeated. "A nice name for a dog. Is it yours?"

Deanne looked confused for a moment but then broke into laughter and patted my shoulder. "No. A phone is a piece of technology. The dog's name is Winston, and yes, he's mine. He's a schnauzer."

My cheeks burned as, I imagined, a furious blush spread across them. I didn't ask what a schnauzer was, but I assumed it was a specific type of dog. I knew many types existed. Winston, phones, schnauzers. I repeated those precious new words in my brain so I'd remember them. I needed to learn as much as I could about this strange new world. I gave the doctor a wishful smile. "I'd like to own a dog someday. Can I see Winston again?"

The doctor complied, and I spent my time imagining how it would feel to pet Winston. Perhaps its fur would be like the hair of a cow or horse, mostly soft and smelling of hay and earth. Ani Island had both those animals, but no one kept them as pets, not when we needed them for work. "Winston isn't wearing clothes," I observed.

"Some people dress their dogs. Others don't," Deanne said.

I nodded, understanding that at least in some ways, Ani Island was similar to Deanne's home. "Queen Veluya was the only person I knew who dressed her parrot. I found it odd, honestly."

"Did you end up making jewelry?" the doctor asked.

My lips curled into distaste at that thought. "Thankfully, no. The Queen had other worries on her mind. And so did I after court became a dangerous place."

"How so?" Deanne prodded. She held my gaze, her curiosity etched plainly on her face. "Forgive me, but your culture's foreign to me. How were you in danger?"

***

When I first arrived at the palace, I underestimated just how precarious my situation was as someone wanting to sabotage her place. My entry into court was like the eye of a seasonal typhoon, quiet and unassuming at first, but explosive as soon as I let my guard down. Like the palm tree ensconced our garden's banyan, the palace complex anchored the virtues inside the beautiful enclosed space of carved and polished bamboo. Compassion would play her flute music to fill the Queen's reception area, casting a penumbra against the birdsong that filtered in from the Spirit Garden outside. My new work quota was to entertain the Queen and, with the other virtues, to look stunning for the King and his court when they paid us audience. All my life, my grandmother warned me about letting men devour me with their eyes, but at the palace, these glances became a matter of course.

There used to be a snapshot, a tangible picture, of when I first knew Meguya spoke the truth. It's since been destroyed, but it encapsulated the first moment I felt dread about my situation at court. That picture, taken by King Marit, featured me as Elegance. Each village had a camera obscura. The King held ours, so his eyes ultimately determined the composition. My surroundings were reduced to an overexposed black and white landscape, a lonely place with the patterned tropical foliage of the Eternal Spirit Garden, a bright sun, and burning blue sky that are left to your imagination to reconstruct in color. I stood wearing the beautiful robes of Elegance with my face covered in white foundation and crimson lip stain, a complicated updo decorated with flowers, and, though you must imagine it since I faced the camera's lens, an unscarred back. His gaze was that of the camera's, and I became simultaneously undressed and put away from the view of others. In that picture, I stood as vulnerable and alone as when I was branded a criminal not much later. And as alone as Meguya had been after her dismissal. He took that picture a week after I arrived at court, an event I'll get to soon. But first, let me tell you about my first day there. And, more importantly, about the lesson my grandmother imparted to me through a story about a lady and her useless knight.

On my first official morning at court, the day after my life turned upside down, the normal birdsong lulled me out of a sleep that'd been sweetened by the scent of newly falling rain and the embrace of a faceless man. How I hated waking up from that dream. An inner sense of the world being in flux, and a pit of hollowness at my core, heralded that something disturbing hovered on the horizon. I heard a knock on my door and expected Gisnen to be standing there and complaining about his breakfast.

"It's me," came my grandmother's voice from the other side. "Are you decent?"

What a fundamental question. I thought I was a decent person, generally speaking, but after my allegedly *indecent* display yesterday, Lady Nereno probably thought I strut around my room naked, perhaps plastering my nude body against my cotilk window screen for all the village boys to see. Had she told my grandmother about what happened?

I opened the door and replied, "Yes, of course."

"It's time to get you ready," she grumbled as she entered my room with a bamboo basket in her hands.

Noting her slouched posture, I was surprised by how irritable and resigned she seemed. "What's wrong?"

My grandmother shrugged. "I have something for you."

"From Queen Veluya?" Although she'd promise me some uncursed robes, I knew any gift she gave me would be laden with Meguya's sorrow. And mine, considering how little I wanted any of this.

My grandmother nodded at the burden in her hands. "She sent you an under robe, but the outer robe is from me." She placed the basket on my rosewood chest, uncovered it, and pulled out two pieces of cloth. The larger one was an iridescent blue that scintillated in the morning light. She held this one up first. It was the color of the deep ocean, far beyond where I would dare swim on my own, and of a radiant sapphire. The sun made the robe shimmer with hints of pink, light green, a lighter blue, purple, and silver.

"Where did this come from?" I asked, transfixed by the beauty of the colors as they changed in the light.

"I wore it for my wedding," my grandmother said, handing it to me. "It's been protected in my trunk ever since."

My hands also marveled at the softness of the weave. "It's so exquisite."

"No doubt. All fancy cotilk has mother of pearl hammered into it, but this one also has silver threaded into the weave."

I nodded in understanding. "And we don't have any remaining silver to make more." The only precious metals from the Old World were ones that came with us. Families usually held onto these objects, but some of these metals had also gone to make the tokens we used as our standard currency.

My grandmother looked pleased that I appreciated its beauty. "It's for you. To keep."

Although I wanted to wear this beautiful garment for sentimental reasons, a tangible connection to my grandmother that it was, it felt deceptive to enjoy the robe's beauty when I planned to sabotage my position. I couldn't reject the gift outright, so I caressed the fabric and assured her, "I'll take good care of it. Thank you so much."

"I know you will. Now, let's look at the one the Queen sent for you." She held up the other, a pale purple under robe, interlaced with silver embroidery, that would rest against my skin tightly.

I studied the complex foliate pattern that someone, perhaps even Meguya, had stitched into it. Somehow, though, *this* robe's obligations stifled its beauty. "What a beautiful pattern," was the only unenthusiastic observation I could muster.

"Let's get the under robe on you first," my grandmother said as I removed my sleeping sarong and slid into the soft purple fabric. While our regular robes were easy to put on and secure, the under robes worn by virtues and the Queen had to be cinched in the back with tightly secured laces.

I felt my ribs constrict as my grandmother pulled the strings tightly. In response to my wince, she said, "You'll get used to it. Eventually."

Next, I slid, somewhat stiffly, into the outer robe. My grandmother then arranged the outer robe so that the under robe, and thus the contours of my body, would peek through when I moved. In this way, my ensemble was both modest and alluring, depending upon the angle of the viewer. What pressure from these contradictory values. How could I be alluring enough to deserve notice but modest enough not to cross the threshold into indecency?

Not wanting to criticize my grandmother's efforts, I commented on the dynamic combination of colors. "The colors work so well together. I look like a barracuda."

She grimaced in response. "You'll need to behave like one if you're to survive this. Now go and sit on your chest while I finish getting you ready."

When I was seated, she took out some cosmetics, a wooden comb, mother of pearl sticks, and a black pearl necklace from her basket. She began by applying three layers of white powder to my face. After the foundation dried, she ran a stick of black liner over my eyelids and finished my makeup by staining my lips crimson. It all felt much heavier than the lighter layers I usually applied. My grandmother next brushed my hair and arranged it into a complicated updo, which she secured with mother of pearl sticks. Finally, she clasped the pearl beads around my neck. My grandmother appraised her handiwork with an expression that was both admiring and sad. Finally, she said, "Turn around and see yourself in the mirror."

I stood and saw my first glimpse of myself as Elegance. She appeared taller with the updo, and her face was formed from the smoothest porcelain. This white facade didn't extend down onto her neck, so her slightly tanned skin and piercing dark eyes provided some contrast against the white canvas of her face. Due to the mirror's age, there were slight cracks around its perimeter, and they splintered the perfect white mask when I moved my face around. This revenant of myself haunted me the entire time I was at court.

You may think it strange that we created frivolous things such as cosmetics on our island. However, for women such as Dirmisu, who only made herself up minimally on worship days or for very special occasions, cosmetics were investments in a better social position. Quinoa flour and ground coral formed the foundation, cotilk resin was used to line the eyes, and the pigment from various flowers made excellent lip stain.

"I look beautiful," I told my amazed reflection, which, thanks to the contrast between the cool, dark blue sheen of the cotilk robe and my fiery red hair, emanated an eerie energy. "Is that it?"

"Well, you'll get some shoes at the palace. But yes, that's all." My grandmother's eyes then became wistful, but I'm not sure if it was for Calabasas, Lucky Charm, or for the Old World itself. "Let me tell you a story. When you understand its deeper meaning, you'll be ready to successfully navigate court."

As she gestured for me to sit on the bed, I sensed this was going to be a long story. My bed creaked under our combined weight. "I'm reporting to court today, though."

"True enough. Do you remember the tales of knights and ladies from the Old World I used to tell you?"

"Yes, of course." All village girls were told the romantic stories of knights and damsels.

My grandmother began, "This is the story of a married lady of high birth and strong wits. Candlelight infused her castle with warmth. She peered out at the snowy weather from the cross-hatched glass in front of her table, codices spread out in front of her, and held in her hand a quill. As usual, the Lord of the castle, named Fels, was away on conquest. He'd, unfortunately, locked her securely in the tower with his other spoils of war.

The Lord, however, was kind in his own way. He provided the Lady with one hundred books to occupy her time since she loathed weaving and sewing. Still, the books didn't satisfy all her needs. Seeing the white powder fall to the ground, she wished she could run outside among the flakes and into the woods that covered the tall, steep hills.

A pebble tapped against the window, and the Lady's heart leapt as she heard this sound. She rushed down the stairs to the base of the tower. Through the locked gate, she could see a knight standing on its outer side, his tunic covered in snow. 'I saw the light of your candles in the upper chamber,' he said.

'My Laustic, it's good to see you! Curse this locked gate,' she lamented.

'I've brought you this to show my love.' He handed her a slim volume through the bars. 'The book merchant claims the exit from this tower is hidden in a cipher among the words. I know you can find it.'

She was taken with his confidence in her. 'Thank you. I'll search for this cipher immediately.'

'I'd better leave, lest one of the villagers see me here. Until later, my Lady.' He turned and walked away, a snow-drift at his back.

The Lady held the book in her hands and stared outside the gate for a few moments, watching Laustic's footprints fill in with snow. She walked back up the steps to her chamber, where the light was soft. Although she longed to run away with Laustic, she still savored the comfort of the room. She took the new book and lay in her warm bed, sinking comfortably into the mattress.

The book gave an audible crack as she opened it, and she stared at the words, hoping the path that led out of the tower would make itself clear. The volume only had a few pages, though. The words described a village called *Coeur*, a place that means "heart," which was located on the shore of the blue sea.

One week later, the book revealed its secrets. The Lady noticed that some of the letters on the first page were tilted slightly to the right. She wrote these letters on a separate sheet of paper, and they read, *Behind the bloody tapestry lies your freedom.* Could it be referring to the tapestry in her Lord's room?

His room was under hers, so she went inside and examined the tapestry that depicted the bloody battle that had made her Lord famous. She lifted the heavy fabric and saw a small door, which opened easily and yielded to a dark corridor. The Lady felt her way down the spiral stairs with a candle as the only light to guide her. After a few minutes of walking, she came upon a loose stone. A crack of light shined behind it. She pushed back the stone and, through a hole big enough for a small person to fit through, saw the snow-covered ground outside.

Freedom! The Lady closed the door and went back upstairs, careful to leave things as they were. With her means of exit secured, the Lady decided she'd wait for Laustic to return.

Three full weeks after receiving Laustic's gift, the Lady lay in her bed with the book. Then, she felt something irregular under the cover of the book, so she ripped open the cover and, to her surprise, a map leapt out and rested itself upon her coverlet. On the pale velum, she noticed roughly-rendered buildings and geographical features. The Lady studied the landscape with intensity and saw her Lord's castle, Laustic's town, and beyond it, 'Coeur.'

Then, she heard the familiar ping at the window, so she flew down the stairs as quickly as her gown would allow and stood at the bottom of the tower before the gate. As predicted, it was Laustic.

'I've found the exit,' she said breathlessly.

'That's good, my Lady. I come bearing you a gift,' the knight replied. He held this gift, a nightingale in a cage, in front of him.

'Of what use is this bird in the snow?' asked the Lady. 'I much appreciate your courtly gesture towards me, but the bird will only hinder us during our escape.'

'We can't leave now,' he protested. 'My family's relying on me to barter our fief's crop for an imported fabric from the East. I'll whisk you away after."

'But if my husband returns, I won't be able to leave. The exit's in his chamber,' explained the Lady, who was, by all accounts, trying to remain calm and ladylike in the face of such distressing news.

'Don't worry about that now. I've brought you this bird so you won't be lonely while I finish conducting my business.'

Laustic handed her the bird through the bars and promised he'd return soon, but she wasn't comforted by his words. The Lady patiently bided her time in her chamber alone with the nightingale. A week later, she heard the herald announce her Lord's return, and heaviness overcame her heart. Thinking quickly, the Lady grabbed the book, the map, and her warmest cape. She looked at her chamber for the last time and surrendered it to the nightingale as she escaped by means of the passage behind the tapestry.

When the Lord discovered that she was gone, he flew into a rage and searched the castle, looking under beds and in chests, anywhere a person could presumably hide. He tore down curtains and tapestries alike in his rage, but did not touch the tapestry depicting his exploits, so strong was his pride of that event. Additionally, the Lord never discovered her means of escape because the architect who constructed the tower had decorated the interior before the Lord's arrival and had neglected to tell him of the secret passage. Finding no trace of the Lady, the Lord killed the nightingale before leaving to search for her in the forest.

Because of her cunning, the Lady remained in the passage until the Lord left to search for her. She used the map to find Coeur, where she made a place for herself.

And what of Laustic, the daft lover? Before the Lord returned to his tower, Laustic snuck into the Lady's chamber. He found the crushed bird and did the courtly thing. With a portion of the money he earned from his transaction, he commissioned a hollow orb to be made of silver to hold the remains of the nightingale."

"And?" I asked. "Please continue."

"That's the end of the story."

How amazing. And wonderful. This daring lady took control by leaving the safety of her warm enclosure for the cold, dark unknown. I shivered as I conjured the feeling of snowflakes melting on my lashes and of walking with snow-encrusted feet. She'd had no light to guide her. My predestined future in this village fell cold upon the piles of ashes we used to make soap, yet a life outside this place glistened and dazzled me. "Could I emulate her?" I asked quietly.

My grandmother nodded. "Long ago, at my wedding, Samsara told me this story as she handed me a special gift. She claimed the story's lesson might be useful one day. So, now I offer you this: whatever you do, don't be like the nightingale. Gain control of your destiny. And, if *you* end up being happy at court, consign this entire conversation to the rantings of an old, feeble woman."

How shocking this advice was coming from a former queen, especially the daughter of Lehom's emissary! Would she actually support my desire to live life on my own terms? "I think I would have loved Samsara," I said, getting up and walking to the cotilk window that overlooked the garden. "Grandmother, with that in mind, court isn't the place for me."

Instead of yelling, she joined me at the window. We listened to the uncaged birds sing in the garden. Eventually, she whispered, "The palace is full of nightingales."

And then I let go the dangerous words, "What can I do to avoid becoming that cursed bird?"

My grandmother left the window and sat down on the floor. "I don't know. You either have to work inside or outside our village's laws. Inside, it's complicated. Our system can't sustain itself. The princes and virtues can only marry one another for this generation before we'll all be related. We have to branch out to the other villages, but they don't want to live by our ideals, and our laws prevent us from mingling with them."

I sat down next to her with a huff. That *was* decidedly complicated. "Does King Marit know?"

An expression of disgust crossed my grandmother's face. "Yes. I overheard Irin discussing it with the temporary Simi prince last week when they were figuring out how each virtue could be matched to a non-relative prince. You'd be matched with the upcoming Eno prince."

Ugh. At that distasteful news, my skin bristled even in the humid tropical air. Leppi Eno. Or, as I called him, "Eel-boy Eno," who slithered and skulked around the girls at our weekly worship service. Only fifteen, he was also the only son of the current Eno Prince and therefore the heir. Any such marriage would, of course, be postponed until both parties were at minimum eighteen years of age, but still! Horrified, I cried, "I'm not going to marry Memeno's brother, nor anyone else in this village!"

I wasn't thinking, uttering it aloud as I did. I braced myself for an Irin-like scathing condemnation, but my confession actually earned a laugh. "After what Nereno told me, I didn't think so."

Well, then, apparently she knew about Jenay. I had to ask, "Why aren't you upset?"

Her smile faded. "A year ago, I would've been, but not after what I know now. Not with *this* king."

Perhaps she also knew about Meguya's true reasons for failure, but I couldn't confirm it without breaking Meguya's trust. "What can I do? Plan-wise and without metaphors?"

"I gave you the tokens so you could leave the village if necessary."

I felt weak for a moment. "Leave? Lucina did offer me a place, but wouldn't I be exiled?"

Although I could hear the sadness in her voice, she also sounded at peace as she answered, "Probably."

"But, I don't want to be separated from you or Gisnen. Especially forever." I leaned over and rested my head on my grandmother's shoulder, savoring her orange blossom perfume. "I also want my old job back and to get to know Jenay. Talk about an incompatible combination of desires."

My grandmother sounded so lucid, so controlled as she explained my options. "Well, you have two choices. The first is to leave the village immediately and be exiled. Work *outside* the system. The second is to get dismissed from court for something minor, in which case Irin might let you be a scribe again. I think he'd prefer that to you laboring for your work quota. Like Meguya, you wouldn't be exiled for your failure. Perhaps, then, if you aren't marriageable material by our standards, you could branch out to your young man." She stopped and shook her head. "Well, realistically speaking, the last part's unlikely."

I felt a rush of love for my grandmother. She was the mother who'd raised me, so I couldn't stand the thought of being separated from her forever. "For now, I just want to sabotage my place at court. I've decided to unleash my clumsy side there."

She gave me an appraising look. "That's good, then. You're also stronger than court's traditional conventions, and while I've always thought of strength as an asset rather than a liability, our men like helpless, emaciated birds. Subtly assert your strength, physically and mentally speaking. Be the *opposite* of elegant at moments, but don't make your sabotage obvious."

In other words, I had to maintain a delicate balance between showing my true self and being Elegance. "Any other suggestions?"

She looked down at her delicate, fragile arms. "You'll find that virtues leave much of their food untouched since the sacred fruit abates hunger. Don't deny yourself nourishment for an ideal."

"I'd have the sacred fruit every day if I stayed. That'd be nice at least," I said.

The sacred fruit was, well, sacred. Holy. And rare. It only grew in the Earthly Eternal Spirit Garden behind the temple. This fruit enabled us to cut through the veil that separated the physical plane from the spiritual one, enabling us to see facets of the heavenly Eternal Spirit Garden, where Lehom and the Ethereal Queen live. This is where the holy were thought to go when they died. While regular villagers received a single sliver each week during the worship service, virtues consumed some daily, which allowed them to spend their days ensconced in bliss while contemplating the Ethereal Queen's essence. When one ate it, the leaves of the trees and petals of the flowers shined with evanescence. The happiness one felt when swimming above a coral reef or glancing at a beloved magnified itself and burst from the heart, through the body, and to the ends of the fingertips. No one, therefore, dared disparage this gift.

For that reason, I jumped in surprise when my grandmother said, bitterly, "Without that fruit, there's no Eternal Spirit Garden."

What a strange thing to say. She grasped my hand and sat next to me in companionable quietude. But then, the outside world intruded when I heard Gisnen yelling for Dirmisu to pour him some coffee.

"Can I join you for breakfast?" I asked as I helped her stand.

"No. You're eating at court with the Queen from now on."

Of course. And on that note, I handed her the key to the spice cabinet, a rather uneven exchange for the pearl necklace and robe she'd just given me. With my plans of sabotage percolating in my brain, I followed my grandmother out of my room and left the house with my new waterproof umbrella, a memento from Jenay that I could keep close without arousing suspicion.

Soon, I arrived at the palace and temple complex in the center of the village's princely section. Rekin Ani had chosen the location well. The sharply rising mountain that formed the spine of the island functioned as a backdrop for the royal buildings. The Eternal Spirit Garden also surrounded the entire back sections of the palace and temple, where the banyan, palm, and live oak trees formed a canopy that cooled and cushioned those in its midst.

When I reached the palace entrance, a guard with brown hair and sharp features narrowed his eyes and pointed me in the direction of the Queen's audience chamber. I gave him a smile of thanks, but his unsettling expression remained firmly planted.

Why? Had I offended him somehow? It was the Queen I wanted to displease, not him. I didn't even know his name. I found Veluya Simi and the virtues were all eating breakfast around the table that overlooked, through transparent curtains, the Eternal Spirit Garden.

"Elegance, come join us for breakfast." The Queen gestured for me to approach the table, where some servant had arranged food on small mats of woven palm leaves.

"It appears I'm late. My apologies," I said as I sat at the open spot across from the Queen.

"No matter. Please help yourself." Her voice was light and carefree as she appraised me, moving her eyes up and down my frame. "You look as elegant as your grandmother."

"Thank you." I hungrily eyed the beautifully arranged spread of fruits, egg custard cups, and a type of tart that covered the table. Grouped arrangements of flowers complemented the food's colors, creating a visually exquisite, curated dining experience.

"Cameno," the Queen commanded the girl standing at attention near the table, the one who'd served her tea yesterday, "please bring Elegance some coffee and a plate."

Cameno, a minor daughter of the Eno family, bowed at the queen's request and carried over a tray with a cup of coffee and a wooden plate. I lifted the delicate ceramic cup to my lips and let the rich, smoky coffee roll over my tongue. This brew was a grade above what I had in my home, vastly better than what Dirmisu drank, and had a sweet, sultry taste from the added honey and cinnamon.

As the virtues mimicked the Queen and took delicate nibbles of their food, afterward discreetly wiping their hands on their napkins, I took two egg cups, seasoned with nutmeg and coconut, as well as a tart made with a light almond paste crust. I tried the tart first, and the fruit in the center of the pastry exploded on my tongue, tasting exactly like a sweetened version of the sacred fruit. Baking that holy food in a tart would be too decadent, even for the Queen's entourage. "What's *in* this?"

"The sacred fruit, of course," Beauty said before covering her mouth to smother her giggles.

No wonder everyone was so carefree and happy this morning. They were simply intoxicated, and I would soon be, too. Every week when we received the fruit, Dirmisu and I preferred to await the fruit's bliss near the fountain in the garden, close to the temple. There, I could usually tell that the spirit world was entering this realm when the fountain's flowing water became dappled with nuggets of gold among the lily pads and koi. Just like the crystalline blue shallows of the sea. That's when the warmth would start to spread from the core of my being to my fingers and the tips of my toes, infusing me with a subtle wave of bliss that I knew would grow to a body-shaking infusion of eternal love. I would then lay down among the plants that surrounded the fountain, where my senses would become hidden in the jungle's tangle, twisting into old Celtic knots like the ones I'd seen in the laminated facsimile of an old manuscript.

I expected a similar experience that day with the Queen and her virtues. However, amidst everyone's carefree on that morning at breakfast, the sacred fruit brought something different than its usual melting-into-nature feeling. The warmth and beginning of bliss were the same, but combined with the coffee, I also felt giddy, causing my doubts about court to melt as the night does with the coming of daybreak.

I also became more bold, more confident. I joked to Compassion, "I should smuggle some of these tarts home with me tonight." This was ordinarily no laughing matter, for taking the sacred fruit without permission would condemn the thief to weeks in the village's Criminals' Compound.

Compassion stopped chewing her food and stared at me for a moment. But, then she asked casually, "And just *how* would you accomplish that? Stash them illicitly beneath your robes?"

"*Far* beneath them," I replied with unladylike aplomb.

And that's how the refined audience hall of the Queen of Lehom transformed, however fleetingly, into the public house from Central Village. In other words, everyone broke into simultaneous laughter, making court seem like a wonderful place to be after all.

"She has wit!" the red-faced queen exclaimed between gasps for air. "Thank the Ethereal Queen. We mustn't have a boring court."

Beauty raised her coffee mug in the air. "Well, to wit!"

We all cheered in unison, "To wit!"

As the warmth waxed in magnitude, I felt my hunger wane to the point of nothingness. Is this why the spines of the virtues were so prominent? Even though I didn't feel the need for it, I ate the two egg cups on my plate. The smooth, slightly sweet texture made them pleasurable to consume even if my body didn't demand them.

"Thank you so much for the robe," I said to the Queen.

She acknowledged the compliment with a smile. "I'll send you another set tomorrow so you can wear robes while your servant launders the other. Virtues must look immaculate at all times." Suddenly, the Queen's smile faded. "And I certainly couldn't curse you with my sister's castoffs."

"I'm beginning to see Paradise..." I trailed off, forgetting about Meguya and her accusations against the King as the veil between the physical and eternal worlds receded from my eyes. The bamboo wood of the Queen's audience hall began glowing as the temporal palace converged with its eternal counterpart. Looking out the window, I also saw the trees transform into sparkling emeralds and peridots. The chaos of banyan tree vines became ropes of braided silver, and the chatter of eternal animals filled my ears while the birdsong rose to a melodious cadence. I closed my eyes and heard heavenly chimes and flute music. Who played such instruments in the beyond? The Ethereal Queen or some of my long-dead ancestors? "I can hear it too," I whispered to no one in particular.

After a few minutes of otherworldly music, the laughter of the virtues brought me back to the audience hall, and when I opened my eyes, I saw them all talking amongst one another. I should perhaps introduce the other virtues to you and tell you their family names. Compassion was Tolsimi of the Simi clan. The Misu family, which my dear friend Dirmisu came from, yielded Vinmisu as Beauty, and Kimsimi, the Queen's daughter, was Obedience. Memeno from the Eno clan was Patience, and Niloru from the Oru family, and my cousin on my mother's side, was Quietude. The final virtue, Rencona, was Resourcefulness. She was my least favorite, as you'll soon see.

CHAPTER EIGHT

*T*he sacred fruit binds us together in holiness. When you have doubts, remember Lehom grants you this gift in return for your loyalty and trust. You will know when you need to partake of the fruit again, for the loneliness of eternity outside of the Eternal Spirit Garden will begin to make its way into your soul. First, it will start with a troubling pang, and if neglected will become all-consuming. Only Lehom's gift can restore you.
 -The Book of Lehom

~~~

"Wait. Stop for a minute. As good as it is to know about the other virtues, tell me, what the hell was in this fruit?" Deanne asked. "It made you see things? *Supernatural* things?"

I shifted on the bed and sighed, a bit annoyed she'd interrupted my story just as I was about to launch into a blistering description about Resourcefulness. Perhaps it was best, though. I didn't want to jump too far ahead and confuse the doctor with events she wouldn't yet understand. Considering I had no idea how her world conceived of that which lies beyond our immediate senses, I started with the simple answer. "At the time, I thought so, yes."

Deanne pulled out the coconut from my satchel. "Is this from that garden?"

I lay back on my pillows and laughed. "No, the sacred fruit is a small berry that tastes like honey. That's a coconut from the Ani family garden. I'm going to plant it wherever I settle. It's my one remaining connection to my ancestors."

Deanne's face grew sympathetic, probably because I sounded melancholy as I spoke about my family. Yes, that coconut was important to me. More than she knew. Deanne poured another glass of amber fire and held it out to me. "Want some more? I have a feeling that what's coming is going to be difficult for you."

"Yes, please," I said as I mentally scanned through the remainder of events in my tale. With all its death and betrayal, I required an anesthetic. *It's better to look ahead, not back*, my fearful side warned me. *Tell your story in honor of the dead*, my courageous self argued back.

Deanne handed me the glass. "So, I'm curious about something. Did the Queen know about her sister's accusations against the King?"

I swallowed the liquid and savored its bite. "Yes, but she didn't believe them."

The good doctor sat down beside the bed. "How did you manage under those conditions? I'd be on edge every second."

I took another liberal sip of bourbon and smiled weakly. "I *was* terrified. As for how I managed? Just as the Queen did. With the fruit."

***

All our activities at court revolved around entertaining the Queen and consuming the fruit that dissolved away our troubles. In the morning, after breakfast, we practiced our dancing routines, ones we'd eventually perform during special worship ceremonies. Following dance, we ate a light lunch, usually something such as lime flavored chicken, sacred fruit slices on salad, and herb-infused water. Normally after lunch, the King required the virtues to sit in his audience hall so the court could enjoy looking at us. I'm unfortunately serious. That's why I was surprised when I didn't see the King during my first week at court. Irin told me King Marit had to spend all his time crafting his new laws.

Instead, in the afternoons, the Queen gave us more fruit. We virtues then practiced our flute music, lounged in the garden, and played mahjong, the Queen's favorite game. In our quieter moments, we would all relax in the open space of the Queen's hall and meditate upon the Ethereal Queen.

I let all those doses of fruit melt away my anxieties about the King and his intentions. The palace was the King's corner of the world, *his* domain more so than the Queen's. That's why his absence was a relief. A blessed relief considering how wary Meguya's accusations made me of the King. Unfortunately, though, I knew I couldn't avoid him forever.

On a leisurely morning exactly a week after my arrival at court, the Queen tapped my shoulder with her foot as I reclined on the polished bamboo floor and stared at the intricately carved, star-studded ceiling of the Queen's audience hall with the other virtues. We were blissed out of our senes, of course.

"You have an audience with the King," the Queen announced. "He wants to see you alone."

The King.

With her announcement, my feelings of ecstasy departed as my head dizzied in remembrance of ravenous banyan trees and crushed nightingales. I also felt completely flummoxed, not only from the sacred fruit. To avoid accusations of impropriety, men and women from different families didn't usually speak beyond formalities, so this audience with the King was unique. And, as far as I knew, only I believed Meguya's accusations. That knowledge itself made me nervous for this visit.

I eased myself upright and asked, "Alone? Me? Why?"

"It's merely a formality," she said tersely. "I'm sure you'll be fine. Have another fruit tart. And follow me."

I obeyed her and hoped more fruit would quell my nervousness. The Queen stopped in front of a large wooden chest, pulled out the same tall sandals that she and the virtues wore, and handed them to me, saying, "I should've had you practice in these earlier, before your audience with my husband, but this meeting came as a complete surprise."

Despite their ridiculous height, I secured the sandals on my feet and crossed back and forth across the audience hall until I gained my balance. The Queen then walked around me in a circle, scrutinizing me from every angle. Finally, she nodded with what looked like resignation. "You'll be fine once this definition in your shoulders fades. It'll make your spine all the more alluring."

My grandmother's words spilled out of me. "I've always thought of strength as an asset." Because they were much too bold for a virtue, I hoped they'd show the Queen I was wrong for this position.

Surprise flashed in the Queen's eyes, but she quickly contained her emotions. "Well, now quietude and grace are your assets. As is *elegance*, as you should know. You won't be able to move enough to keep this shoulder definition, thankfully."

Very true since the virtues' clothing was designed for exactly that. It would be impossible to do anything remotely boisterous in this tight ensemble. The under robe, clinging so tightly to the skin, also made me hotter than I would otherwise be in my looser sarong robes, definitely too hot to expend much effort.

I followed her through a door into the King's audience chamber. This space, like the Queen's audience hall, also opened onto the Eternal Spirit Garden since the back wall was merely a row of cotilk curtains. Despite its airy dimensions, however, the King's reception room felt oppressive, most likely because of the massive throne King Marit Simi sat upon. I later realized the King liked to surround himself in darkness whenever possible. To limit daylight, for example, the curtains had been dyed a deep purple. He also held worship services at dusk and into the night, which gave his sharp features an even more menacing power when they stood out from the shadowed plains of his face.

That morning, his chief valet had arranged the King's morning breakfast of coffee, fruit tarts, and beef kebabs on a wooden table inlaid with gold. We rarely slaughtered cows for meat, so we only ate beef approximately once every two months. However, the King was having it for his breakfast. Whatever he wanted, he got.

Or, what he lacked he also demanded.

The King took a nimble bite of the kebab, but his look of pleasure abruptly transformed into anger. He threw the remaining beef back onto the plate with such force that the dish flew off the table and shattered at his feet. What in the world had set him on this precipice of violence? Did Irin pick up his habit of throwing food from the King?

"Not nearly enough lime but entirely too much salt. Have Cameno season this again," he commanded the servant. With downcast eyes, this same valet picked up the broken pieces of plate and the offensive food without uttering a word. The King's scowl disappeared when he saw us. "Elegance, welcome. Forgive my servant's unsightly display."

Veluya bowed to her husband respectfully, and I followed suit.

"You may leave us," Marit Simi said to his wife while focusing his attention on me.

Absent the confident posture I'd witnessed earlier, the Queen muttered a quiet, "Of course," before retreating back across the threshold into her domain.

I was now alone with him. Just as Meguya had been.

Narrowing my eyes, I studied King Marit in the dim light. He wasn't conventionally handsome, nor even good looking, but he did project both an imposing figure and a controlled menace. King Marit had sharp facial features, dark curly hair, and a beard that hid the slight jowls of his face. The man apparently enjoyed the most sumptuous foods, and the evidence of his body's indulgence was covered in three layers of dark robes that'd been embroidered with silver and gold threads. Of course, the patterns on this wardrobe were the most intricate in the village. In the morning light that filtered into his audience hall, he looked like an overstuffed barracuda, one still threatening but also more lumbering than his sleek counterpart of the sea.

Perhaps he seemed imposing to me because of his absolute power. You see, the only way to strike down a king's edict was if all seven princes vote in favor of such. This had never been done because striking against a king without cause was the same as striking against Lehom. What a conundrum. After all, the King is Lehom's emissary, so how could the princes then prove their claim? Only by making the impossible possible again.

"Thank you for the welcome," I said automatically. By then, my wits, and therefore, cognizance of my plan had returned. In order to make my sabotage believable, I had to make him believe I'd do my best.

"Come here," he gestured, his lips glimmering with oil from the unfortunate beef. "Approach the throne."

As I glided towards him slowly, I was thankful the skirts of my robes constrained my movement. Anything to keep me as far away from him as possible. I stopped about three feet from the throne.

He frowned. "Did I give you permission to stop?"

This village controlled every aspect of my life. My clothing. My friendships. My job. Even my body and personal space! Reluctantly, I approached another foot and hoped the hatred radiating out of every pore of my being wasn't noticeable. It wouldn't help to appear defiant, for defiance would be quashed at my expense. With that extra foot of closeness, I wasn't close enough to touch him, but his proximity made Meguya's words ring all the more true. What had he done to her exactly? She hadn't specified but only said he'd been improper, and impropriety covered a wide range of unsavory activities.

"Keep coming," he whispered softly.

I inhaled the stale air of the space between us. As I moved a smidgen closer, he smacked his lips, allowing me to smell both the beef kebab and coffee emanating from his mouth.

"Who is the Ethereal Queen to you, Leilani Ani?" he asked.

I was repulsed and nervous, so my reply had the annoying upspeak of an insecure girl. "T-the ultimate queen, of course, who I should aspire to be?"

He took another sip of coffee and appraised me from his eyrie. "There is that. But as Elegance, you must come to learn your own definition of this virtue, inspired by the Ethereal Queen, of course. Only after mastering her essence will you embody this virtue."

Hoping he wouldn't notice, I glided one small step back. "I'll meditate on her, then."

He swirled his right index finger in a circle and commanded, "Turn around, please."

Not knowing what else to do, I complied and gathered my distractions where I could by closing my eyes and listening to the birdsong from the Eternal Spirit Garden. I still had enough sacred fruit in me to afford a little bit of escape, so I also focused on the smells of earth, fresh sunshine, and flowers. For a time, it worked.

Then, the throne creaked. I never really believed angry ghosts haunted our jungle, but at that moment, I understood how those unfortunate believers feel when they sense something lurking among the shadows. The anticipation made my body quake with dread, so I sought something, anything really, to fill that void between me and *it*.

My efforts were somewhat unsuccessful because suddenly, I felt his moist hand on my back. It reeked of beef oil. Then, he grabbed my outer robe, thereby exposing more of my back, and I felt his terrible closeness as he exhaled onto my bare shoulder. "Too strong, but we can fix that."

My breathing ceased, and my peripheral world turned gray like the horizon of a thunder-ridden sky. Men shouldn't be this close to women, thus commanded Lehom. Meguya's warning pounded through my skull. What was coming next? That terrible suspense, that unknowing, made me want to surrender to the fruit's gift and detach from my body. Would it matter what he did to me if I couldn't feel it, couldn't remember it?

In those moments *before* something terrible could happen, I longed for Jenay. For my books. I prayed for the *after*, the time when everything would be over. Without thinking, I jerked my body a foot to the right and huddled away from him.

I anticipated that he'd next grab me back into place and pull down my robes. It was the next logical step. The way he dismissed the Queen, I'm sure she wouldn't return uninvited. We were alone. Truly alone. I now had my answer about where and how his improprieties occurred.

But, only silence surrounded me until I heard a gasp of surprise from the King, an exhale signaling I'd done something unexpected. Quiet. Quiet came once more save for the hum of insects from the garden, a blessed distracting hum. Then, as quickly as that dark energy had appeared, it departed like the jungle ghosts allegedly do at the first hint of sunrise.

He must've backed off. What other explanation was there?

Still facing away from him, I heard him command, "Follow me out into the garden." His voice sounded gruff, indicating his displeasure. But I didn't care, then. I'd worry about that later.

There's more space in the garden, I thought in relief as I relished the increasing distance between us. I uncurled my arms from around my torso, turned around, and saw him standing in the Eternal Spirit Garden.

Camera obscura in hand, he gestured for me to stand in the sun. "Smile," he commanded.

Really? After that charade? Not wanting to anger him to action, I walked outside and forced my mouth into a smile, causing my jaw to stiffen. This sudden exposure to the bright sun forced my eyes into a hopefully unflattering squint. He examined me through the viewfinder, capturing that moment and ensnaring my essence in that tiny box for him to later covet. "Good. Go stand in front of the throne again."

No. Not that cursed place.

I tried to come up with some excuse, any excuse to leave. I wanted nothing more than to run away and tell my grandmother everything that happened. Then, I heard noises emerging from the throne room. I wouldn't be alone with the King, which meant I was likely safe, at least for now. So, I followed the King into the throne room, where the servant had returned with the newly seasoned kebabs and a scroll. Standing there in front of the throne, I watched as the King delved his teeth into the tender meat. Apparently, Cameno was successful this time, for the King swallowed quickly. The valet left, and the King stared straight into my eyes as he took a sip of coffee and wiped his oily hands on a napkin. His penetrating black gaze made my skin break out in a sweat. "Your words are but mist compared to mine," he whispered.

For a brief second, my heart almost stopped beating at that shrouded threat. In that village, women's words held all the might of water vapor. But as I thought about it, one thing the King hadn't thought of when making that analogy was that mist rises into the sky. No one can capture and hold it against its will. He'd meant his warning to scare me, but instead, it strengthened my resolve. "I understand," I replied, vowing to tell my grandmother about all the day's events as soon as I got home after that night's worship service.

A garish smile spread across his face. He thought he'd won. "Very well," he said, shifting his focus to the contents of the scroll. "I need to continue my preparation for next week's worship ceremony. And the announcement of my new laws. Veluya will explain my expectations."

Whatever play he directed, whatever role he wished for me to embody, I wanted to escape. At least I had his permission to do so now that he'd blessed me with his inattention. Taking a few deep breaths to steady my shaking hands, I made my way back to the Queen's realm, with its welcoming sunlight, tranquil flute music, and pleasant-smelling incense. There I found the Queen, who sat at her table with her virtues artfully arranged around her.

Sunlight refracted off her rings as she fed her parrot some bits of dried fruit. So focused was she on the bird that she didn't even look at me. "So, how was your private audience with my husband?" she asked in a cool voice.

Oh no. She suspects something, I thought. I frantically searched my brain for an essence of truth. If I confessed, she'd blame *me* for tempting the King. True, I would be dismissed, but getting let go for this reason would also cause problems with my family, which I wanted to avoid if possible. Finally, remembering the unfortunate kebabs, I laughed. "Well, as you saw, he didn't like his beef."

That earned me a wry grin. "How hard it is to find decent help," she said between the bird's bites of food. "But *surely* you discussed more."

It appeared my humor could only conceal so much, so I decided to go with the other truth. "He told me you'd help me find my own understanding of elegance."

By now, the Queen had finished feeding her parrot, so she turned to face me. Her lips tightened as she noticed my slightly askew outer robe. "Did he ask to see your back?"

I shrugged, hoping to deflect the perception. "He took a picture, I assume to show the future prince I hope to marry. He also said I was too strong. You were right on that count."

The Queen's internal battle between her duty and her instincts flashed in her eyes. A storm at first, and then nothing. Placid and muted. Shrugging, she turned to Compassion, or Tolsimi, her niece-in-law. "Let's show Elegance how we dance. Patience, please play *Ocean Waves.*"

As commanded, Compassion began moving her thin arms slowly to the music, holding still when the flute ceased. Virtues embodied stillness during quiet moments and moved only to the music itself. The Queen asked, "Elegance, how are we like the ocean?"

I thought for a moment. This could be a chance to sabotage, so I said, with absolute bravado, "The essence of chaos, of course, since the sea can also be violent."

She grimaced at this answer. "Oh no. Certainly not *our* waves. Even amidst the tumult, we're always graceful just as the Ethereal Queen is consistently virtuous. Notice she never complains. She remains blessedly calm. *Always.*"

That last word resounded in my ears. I'd just seen evidence of how Queen Veluya suppressed her anger, and I had the feeling she'd one day explode. Woe to anyone nearby.

CHAPTER NINE

A *ll three villages must quarantine potentially contagious illnesses and only drink water from cisterns equipped with charcoal filters. To avoid getting sick from spoiled food, we all must cook, cure, smoke, or dry everything that can't be plucked immediately from the trees. People must only use bathhouses connected to the sewer system. Its coated bamboo pipes lead to a leach field from which we will extract compost. Nothing must be wasted. Everyone must burn their refuse and save the ashes for soap.*

Isolation breeds health, and congestion breeds death. This law helps contain the filth human civilization can't help but create.

-Excerpt from *The Sanitary Laws of Ani Island*

~~~

I was about to recount how in the week following the King's assault, my heart raced when I heard sounds from his audience hall. And when the breeze tickled my back, I couldn't help but shudder from the shivers of fear that ran up my spine. How I felt polluted and regretful I didn't heed my instincts to flee the village immediately. However, my voice died when I noticed a face peering through the window of the door.

A male face. Its owner wasn't exactly leering at me, but staring? Oh, yes, he was just as plainly as water is clear. I drew the covers closer to my body and pointed to the door. "Who *is* that? And what's he doing?"

Deanne frowned and followed my gaze to the door, her expression easing when she saw the man in the window. "Oh, that's Tomas, my head nurse. He's curious about you. The whole ship is. They only know what I've told them when I stepped out to turn off the lights and get your sandwich. Mainly, that you're not a threat to us."

The doctor's news made me smile. "Lady doctors and male nurses. I like that."

"Let me guess. They don't like women doctors in your village? Too masculine an occupation?" she asked.

"The Ethereal Queen would never presume to order a man around," I replied, looking again at the curious man in the window, this Tomas. He didn't have the King's hard, challenging stare. Instead, his eyes held kindness and curiosity, nothing the least bit threatening. "Does he want to come inside?"

"He would, but only if you don't mind. You have control over who you talk to for now," Deanne reassured me.

How refreshing to have choices. I thought about it for a moment and then gave Deanne a nod of assent. The only other person from the Old World I'd met thus far was Deanne's lady nurse, and that woman had barely acknowledged me as she'd checked over my husband. Deannae had probably allowed her entry because she'd been so quiet and non-threatening. After my doctor friend opened the door, Tomas ambled in and took a seat in a chair near Deanne's desk. He had a broad, friendly grin on his face. "I'm Tomas."

"Leilani," I replied, returning his smile.

Unsure what to say next, I looked to Deanne for guidance, wondering if I should resume where I'd left off. I hoped beyond hope Tomas didn't expect me to begin my story again. I felt too tired to even entertain that idea. Thankfully, she picked up on my cues and asked, "Did you tell anyone about what the King did? Like your grandmother?"

I shook my head. "At first, I didn't have the chance. My grandmother was sick for almost an entire week after the King's assault. Withdrawal from the sacred fruit."

"That's right," Deanne replied. "I remember you telling me she stopped taking it. So how did you cope?"

Indeed, how did I? I looked at Tomas and noticed his eager expression. Although I felt weary and drained, I took a deep breath and resumed my tale, hoping I'd provide enough details to satisfy this newcomer.

***

Under normal circumstances, I would have coped just as anyone does in the face of fear. By being aware of my surroundings and plotting an escape from unsavory circumstances. Unfortunately, the fruit dulled my wits, so I simply kept close to other virtue so I wouldn't find myself alone with the King. Thankfully, the King remained busy doing legal research, so I had minimal contact with him the week following our meeting. I first saw him briefly several hours after he made his overtures, at that night's worship service. I ignored him as best as I could, and the entire village acted as a buffer between me and him that night. After that service, I didn't see him again until the following week's service. It was the night he announced his new edicts, a horrible night if there ever was one.

As the Queen of Lehom, Veluya Simi's job, first and foremost, was to embody the Ethereal Queen and serve as an exemplar to other women, especially the virtues. On the surface of things, she modeled her spiritual counterpart well. That is, at least until she felt her place in her husband's life threatened. The visible cracks in Queen Veluya's façade first appeared the night of her husband's announcement. I had been lounging in the Queen's audience hall with her and the other virtues when the hollow, portentous sound of the gong interrupted our solitude. Time for the evening worship service. The Queen smiled, arose, and gestured for us to follow her into the temple, which was attached to the palace by means of a covered walkway. I stood with her and the other virtues instead of with the villagers as I had before coming to court. I watched as people, dressed in their finest robes, gathered inside the temple space. Dirmisu filtered in with her family and gave me a smile, but my grandmother stood at the back section, whispering to Meguya, who helped support her. I remember feeling happy that my grandmother was up and about. And relieved I could finally speak to her about what the King had tried a week ago.

 Before its destruction, the temple was simple, architecturally speaking, forming a large hypostyle hall with three uncovered walls so the interior space flowed directly into the Eternal Spirit Garden. At the back of the temple, up against the only section with a solid wall, were the life-sized statues of Lehom and the Ethereal Queen. But while the Ethereal Queen looked human, albeit regal, Lehom's statue didn't have a face. Lehom's body was that of a strong, young, and virile man, but he had only a featureless sphere for his head.

He's everyman but no man, I remember Irin once telling me. Just like the Ethereal Queen was for women.

In front of Lehom's statue, the King stood silently in his formal worship robes, waiting for the nervous chatter of his congregants to settle. When the people saw him staring at them, the whispering ceased. Everyone wanted to hear his new laws. New kings sometimes sought the advice of the recently retired one, but Marit Simi's predecessor, a member of the Cona family, had passed away a month after King Marit's ascension.

He intoned, "Brothers and Sisters, the Children of Lehom. We have gathered here today to learn of Lehom's will for us. Let us silently reflect for a few moments on the past year, let go of it, and ready ourselves for the one ahead."

Before and after that pivotal moment, that point of no return existed as two distinct moods in my mind.

Before. Thick incense permeated everything. The dwindling birdsong that comes with dusk filled our silence, and flickering candles mixed their warm light with the cool blue hue cast by the moontrap. While everyone waited for the King's pronouncements, I began to daydream about gliding under the sea. My ability to escape within my imagination and detach from the world caused my physical surroundings to melt away. In this state, I transported myself to the temple of Lady Moon and the Lord of the Deep, where I rested quietly against Jenay's chest. I smelled his sandalwood oil in this vision, and then, as his lips were about to touch mine, my immediate senses came rushing back.

Because it was *after*.

After was something I'd missed at first. I only perceived low exhales of air en mass and a soft gasp of excitement from the Queen, who stood next to me with the other virtues. These sounds initially defined my understanding of *after*.

What had he said? Curses to my wandering mind.

"I say to you again." The King stared at us, his eyes darkening in the retreating light of day. "Lehom has asked me to remain King until the time of my death or until I retire and appoint a new successor. There won't be another election in nine years. Rekin Ani was correct in the beginning. Lehom wanted a new king every ten years to promote harmony and trust among the seven families. But now, with days of shadow fast approaching, our strength is in our permanence and stability."

As nervous chatter from the villagers filled the temple, five of the seven princes, including Veluya's brother, looked to one another for their next move, their faces uncertain. Would any of them speak out? King Marit's brother, Temporary Prince Addys Simi, was especially quiet after the announcement. Well, I suppose that he was the permanent prince of the Simi clan now. With no brother to reclaim the princehood in nine years, would he be happy to remain prince for the rest of his life? I watched a half smile grow on his face and knew, then, that there was no reason for him to vote against his brother's edict. Aside from Prince Addys, only Irin wore a pleased and steady expression. That perplexed me all the more.

But the King hadn't yet finished. "Lehom has also commanded me to make concubines of the virtues who cannot marry princes. In another generation, the seven families will be thoroughly mixed. I would not deprive three of our virtues of a good marriage, so they'll become a part of my household."

At that moment, Veluya's excitement at being queen for the rest of her life vanished. Her features, buried beneath her layers of white makeup, grew dark. She grabbed my arm with her trembling hand, and her eyes filled with the poison that grows in the cassava plant's leaves.

"I must channel the Ethereal Queen," she whispered to Compassion, who also stood close to her.

"Can he do that? What's a concubine?" Compassion asked me.

"I don't know what concubines are, but he's the King. Only the princes can overrule him. Maybe my brother will," I whispered back.

The King raised his hand to silence the chatter. "This is also the time to announce one of the marriages sanctioned by Lehom. Prince Irin Ani will wed my daughter."

Well, there went my hope for that vote.

The rest of the service passed in a blur of anxiety and despair. I wasn't the only one who felt that way. I must give the Queen credit for remaining graceful while passing out the sacred fruit after the King's news. She'd looked at the Ethereal Queen for serenity all her life and had successfully embodied her for much of that time. In the privacy of her audience hall after the worship service, though, Veluya remained bereft of any serenity. As the fruit's magic waned, the colors of the garden grew dimmer, and the night sky lost its crystalline appearance. Kimsimi had disappeared to her room after the service, so the six of us remaining virtues comforted her. But little comfort we were. After all, the morbid hastens the morbid.

"She's only seventeen," Queen Veluya said, her hands shaking as Beauty brought her some herb-infused waters. "Too young!"

I understood her worries. Marriage meant marriage congress, which led to babies. Even though Kimsimi was only a year younger than the minimum age for marriage, that extra time increased a woman's chances of surviving childbirth.

"Maybe they'll have a long betrothal," I said. I hoped so even though my feelings on the matter counted as much as the vaporous morning dew is permanent.

"Did you know? About Irin?" Veluya asked me suddenly. The crackled white powder at the corners of her pursed lips hinted at my betrayal.

"No. Honestly," I replied quickly.

The King's voice emerged from the shadows. "They'll be married next week, but they won't consummate the union until Kimsimi turns eighteen,"

"Husband!" Queen Veluya cast her eyes downward in shame as the King walked into the audience hall. "Forgive my doubt in your wisdom."

The soft edges of his face were made sharper by the audience hall's moontrap, and his finely embroidered cotilk robe gleamed eerily in the hazy blue light. The King moved closer to Veluya, almost as if he could gauge her loyalty with his scrutiny. "We need the blood of Lehom's emissary to merge with ours through this union. If he's worthy, Irin Ani will be my successor, and his first male child with Kimsimi his. I forgive your momentary doubt. Such is the way of women." His voice was cool. Smooth. And, most of all, expectant.

You may ask why she accepted such demeaning words from the King. Well, there are no easy answers. I was only about five years old when they were married, so I remember but snippets and flashes, mostly my excitement at the lovely robe I'd get to wear for the occasion. But, as a daughter of a prince, I have insight into Veluya's early life. She'd also grown up privileged and sheltered from the eyes of men, without much excitement beyond beautiful clothes.

Then, something different happened.

And everything changed.

For young Veluya Uya, that catalyzing force was Marit Simi with his youthful vigor, brooding confidence, and ambition. Handsome when young, he paid her attention and let the then-King know he was interested in her hand. Marit's affections introduced a beautiful alien light to her world. The familiar cacoon she once loved transformed into a dark, scary thing in relation to this light. You see, the Daughters of Lehom are desperate for affection and love, so they gladly accept piecemeal and tainted scraps where they can get them lest they be cast back into that darkness.

Perhaps because she remembered the early years at that moment, the mask of Queen Veluya's face became almost whimsical. "That's quite sensible, husband."

All of this drama made me want to leave the village tonight, but I had promised to help Dirmisu. After two weeks at court, I still had no idea how to get her placed here. Would my friend still even want to come? I prayed not, but I'd have to ask her the next day. Until then, I'd play the role I'd been assigned, now that of a dutiful sister. "I'll make her my sister. Kimsimi can share my room."

Both frowned at my outburst as if they were shocked that others were present. They shouldn't have been. Six of us stood right near them, but I suppose virtues are mere figureheads who shouldn't speak unless prompted to.

Spontaneity. Another fault of mine, which I'm sure Nereno would attest to.

"You're generous, Elegance, but that won't be necessary," the King finally said. "The virtues will all be moving to the palace."

Suddenly, with her concerns for her daughter quelled, the Queen remembered her husband's other edict. She bowed respectfully. "My Dear, as always, I applaud your wisdom. But where will all seven of them live? In Kimsimi's room? They won't comfortably fit."

Sighing as if dealing with a petulant child, King Marit sat down on a chair that'd been designed for a Daughter of Lehom. It creaked under his weight as he glared at his wife. "You're still doubting me, my dear." He then turned to Patience. "Get her a fruit tart. Now."

The Queen opened her mouth to protest, but the King shushed her. "*Five girls, Veluya*. Tolsimi is exempt from this since she's my niece. For the five remaining, there are marriages to princes to arrange and concubines to select, so they need to be here at the palace for me to make those decisions wisely."

At the word "concubine," the Queen wilted like a parched flower in the hot tropical sun. When Patience returned with the fruit tart, Queen Veluya bowed her head, dutifully bit off a corner of the fruit tart, and swallowed it. Then, in a honey-smooth voice only a bit louder than her usual hummingbird volume, she said, "Please enlighten me, a mere woman, as to the details of this plan. Without them, I'm unable to ensure that the palace runs as it should, according to your wishes."

She was demure and resigned, the perfect disposition for the Ethereal Queen but a horrible one for maintaining individual happiness.

I didn't want her fate, Ethereal Queen be damned.

Ethereal squawked from his cage, and the King asked, "Why must you neglect this creature, Veluya?" Before she could answer, he got up from the chair, causing it to groan in pleasure at being relieved of its burden, and gave the bird a piece of dried banana. "I'm having an annex built for the virtues. Attached to the palace but also in the garden. You'll have them close."

And so will you, I thought, remembering both Meguya's warning and his advances toward me during my private audience.

"Girls," the King said as he secured the latch on the birdcage's door, "You're moving to the palace. The ones not married to upcoming princes will join my royal household."

"What's a concubine?" Beauty asked. "Is it like a wife?"

Resourcefulness chimed in next. "Because Queen Veluya's your wife."

King Marit placed a hand around Resourcefulness's shoulder. "That's true. But Lehom himself commanded that I take the unmarried virtues into my protection and provide them with the lives they deserve."

What we deserved.

What did anyone really *deserve*? I'd always been told that our system was a meritocracy. The sordid rationalizations went like this...Because goodness was hereditary, upcoming princes were, naturally, selected from the sons of princes themselves, and the most virtuous daughters of princes made the best virtues. In essence, merit became solidified in blood. The cyclical privilege of the upper class, therefore, continued as a natural law. But none of this seemed *deserved* to me. Well, none of it was *earned*. People can deserve things according to various forms of twisted logic, but it's harder to pervert the concept of earning.

Rekin Ani once wrote that Lehom came to him in a "poignant moment of clarity." This moment was one such moment for me. My understanding of the world, with its princely homes, stately gardens, and complex social hierarchy now had fully tilted off its familiar axis as I flushed with sweat under my many layers of makeup and robes. You see, I realized the King was gathering us for his own pleasure, not solely to keep families from becoming too inbred. This also meant Meguya was undoubtedly right and that the King was wrong. I further extrapolated that either Lehom didn't exist or he wasn't benevolent. I couldn't say anything aloud, however, because as a woman, I had no voice outside that of an echo of male intent.

"Husband, I have confidence in your wisdom, but I'm still confused," Veluya said in a languid voice. Even though the fruit tart was taking effect, her words were still far too bold. "Wouldn't the taking of concubines intermesh the seven families all the more?"

"Not in the least. You women focus too much on minutiae, without the intellectual means to parse them. That does not diminish your beauty, though." An insult followed by a compliment. Piecemeal scraps.

"I'm *beautiful*," the Queen happily parroted back as she melted into a smile.

"But, to answer your question, they are for me to admire with my eyes, not hands. The time of shadows is coming, Veluya, and the Ethereal concubines will make this realm beautiful in order to bring about eternity for all of us." The King's logic twisted about us like a snake from the island's jungle. He manipulated the Children of Lehom's belief that when this physical world ends, the Eternal Spirit Garden will manifest here for the righteous to enjoy.

"But-you…you just said *I* was beautiful," she spat out, her eyes gathering tears.

The King stroked his wife's cheek. "Of course you are. But I also need youth right now, Veluya, and young you are not." He then turned to us. "Ladies, concubines will have a royal status as a member of my own family, only under Veluya and myself."

The corners of Resourcefulness's mouth curled into a self-satisfied smile. Her demeanor contrasted with the frightened pitter patter of my heart. She genuinely wanted this.

But not me. And certainly not Meguya.

What had the King done to her exactly? Only look? Was that enough to make her as upset as I'd seen her? But then I remembered the King's hot breath on my shoulder, how close he'd stood to me in the confines of his audience hall. What sordid actions had I averted by moving away and blocking him? I had an idea but didn't have any evidence. Probably only Meguya knew what he was truly capable of. I'd have to ask her in the morning. For the last two weeks, I had worked hard to avoid her considering how upset her dismissal made her. If she confirmed my worst suspicions, his promise of not touching must simply have been a lie for the devastated Queen's ears.

My grandmother's story rang in my ears. The King would lock these concubines in castles of his own making, remarkably like nightingales waiting to be crushed. If their surroundings become similarly unbearable, people must venture into a dark, snowy night in pursuit of their freedom. In other words, they need to brave exile from the familiar for the potential of something better.

What a world of shadows. From the limited vantage point of someone living in this place, the outside world looked unfamiliar and perilous. Danger lurked here and in my future if I didn't leave. It was as if the people in this village had been lashed to rocks on our shores. As the tide grew higher, only the airless slumber of death would await them.

I searched for an alternative, looking through the jungle and beyond the tangled confines of this village. Beautiful things, such as the library in Central Village and the floating houses of Gaiae, lay outside the Village of Lehom's boundaries. I felt myself lying on the calm, warm sand, breathing unencumbered and in the arms of someone that I loved. These delightful things were within my grasp, but I needed to act. And soon. But, of course, we all make sacrifices to get what we want. My concession was the knowledge that I'd be exiled.

I realized, then, that I was willing to give up my family. Strangely, this moment of clarity brought me comfort. I'd be sad to leave them, but I didn't have to hide my feelings anymore. Dirmisu was the only reason I couldn't pack my things and leave immediately after I got home. I prayed to Lady Moon that she no longer wanted to be a virtue after hearing the King's words. Great Pestilence curse it, I'd take her with me when I left if it'd help free her of her dangerous wants. I mentally added her to my list of people to have important conversations with tomorrow.

"When will you select these concubines?" Resourcefulness asked, still plotting her rise in the world.

The King replied, "In twenty-five days, thus says Lehom. You see, five virtues will move to the palace, and from them, I'll choose two concubines. Five squared is twenty-five. Before that auspicious day, you, Quietude, Elegance, Beauty, and Patience will join me and the Queen here."

As I pondered the insanity of the King's fascination with numerology, Veluya asked, "Can you really build this Annex that quickly?" Doubt, the Queen's alleged vice and enemy, came back to see her, for every virtue has its vice. Elegance has Baseness, Quietude is negated by Garrulousness, the opposite of Obedience is Insubordination, Patience contends with Eagerness, Beauty can be negated by Ugliness, Resourcefulness can be canceled out by Wastefulness, and Compassion's opposite is Malice.

"Yes. The best builders in all three villages will be here tomorrow. Ready the girls for the move, Veluya," he said before leaving us all in an uncomfortable silence.

The Queen walked up to the statue of the Ethereal Queen and knelt before it, allowing the darkness to conceal her tears. "Please go home," she whispered to the night, "we'll talk about this tomorrow."

We each shuffled away in our tall shoes and left her to her nighttime solitude. The moon shone brightly that night. It hovered high over the banyan and palm trees of the Eternal Spirit Garden, and this blue light mixed with the yellow fire of the torches that lit the paths from the Palace complex to the princely homes. As the silhouettes of bats crossed the moon, I imagined the angry ghosts hovering along the periphery of the village, rustling the trees, and luring the living to them. The cool ocean breeze whirled the bottom of my robes, and in less than a minute, even in my tall shoes, I reached my home. Weighed down by fatigue, I removed my platform sandals at the house's entrance so the dead from our family spirit garden wouldn't arise from the noise. At first, I planned on heading to my room, but then I noticed the faint light of moontrap at the end of the hallway coming from our back porch. I moved silently towards that light in my bare feet, hoping my grandmother was awake. She'd be able to offer advice and consolation.

But, no. Irin, the last person I wanted to see, sat at our table. My instincts compelled me to run back to my room, but that would arouse his ire since it was my job to serve him if needed. But what did my wants signify to him?

Nothing. *Piecemeal scraps.*

Irin finally acknowledged me with a lopsided grin. "Sister. Aren't you going to congratulate me on my impending nuptials?" His face was faint blue from the lights of the iridescent plankton, the same color as our drowned parents' skin. Apropos since their bodies were buried in the garden that abutted this porch.

I uttered something genuine in return. "Congratulations. Kimsimi will be a wonderful sister." I couldn't help but wonder what she thought about the matter, but she'd dashed to her room and hid before I had the chance to embrace her into the family.

He gestured to the empty chair next to him. "Please join me."

Resigned, I planted myself on a chair and noticed a familiar food in front of him. "Fruit tarts?" I asked in disbelief.

"An early wedding present, compliments of the King. Would you like one?" he asked, his voice sarcastic and intoxicated.

"No. I've had too many today as it is." Even though the bliss of these tarts tempted me, I needed a clear head tonight. There were important plans to make. Escapes to execute.

"Suit yourself." He shrugged and took another bite, letting crumbs gather and scatter on the table.

"I'll retire now," I said as I began to rise. "It's been a trying day."

Irin raised his hand. "Not yet, Leilani."

I thudded back down and rolled my eyes, safely concealed in the darkness as I was. "What can I do for you?"

"For one thing, thank me for making you virtue so you can become a concubine or princess."

Well, what else was new. His gifts pressed down upon my already too-developed shoulders with expectations and intrigue. I was much too tired to indulge my brother's whims, so I said, "How unappealing."

"Why? If you're selected, you'd be established for life." He put down his remaining bit of tart and looked at me expectantly.

I thought for a moment before speaking. My earlier moment of clarity fueled my confidence, so I went with the truth. "How do they say it in Central Village when something turns out differently than expected? It's not what I signed up for? Yes, that's it."

"The King is nothing if not practical. There aren't enough future princes to go around for all of the virtues. Do you want to risk getting stuck in a marriage with an agricultural laborer?" he asked.

I relaxed my stance by sitting back in the chair and staried him down in the semi-light. "Is that really all that this is about?"

He conceded my point with a nod. "There's more, of course. King Marit wants stability, and this edict puts a stop to the endless competition for decade-long kingship, an end to the bribes and competition between the heads of the families that happen right before these elections. Unity will be needed in the days to come." Irin had such bravado for someone so young, almost as if the King were speaking through his voice.

For once, I let my annoyance with my brother escape in his presence. "For *what*? The time of shadows? What does that even mean?"

Even in the dim light, I could see Irin's shock at my outburst. He threw down the piece of tart that had been suspended in his fingertips. "Yes, the time of shadows! Lehom will reveal details when he wants, but for now, the King's edict prepares us."

Irin had always been the impulsive one, the son to act when others persuaded him, only never by his own initiative or with any internal examination. I shot back, "This doesn't exactly promote stability. I'm sure the princes are furious. At everything."

With a cocksure expression on his face, Irin waved his hand dismissively. "They'll get over it."

I fumed as I thought about how the King had purchased the power of my brother's vote with a betrothal to his daughter. What a traitor, not just to me but also the other princes. "I've underestimated your mercenary side. That is, until tonight."

Irin stood and loomed over me. "You don't understand. I'm not just doing this for me. Our family needs to unite with his. Permanently. If you become his concubine, this union would be even stronger than with just me and Kimsimi."

I uttered a wry laugh. "I won't be his concubine." *There. I said it.*

"You have no idea what pressure I'm under, the constant pressure to be a perfect man, firm and righteous. A guardian for you. A righteous man ensures the women in his charge obey." He sat down again, and in a tone that brooked no argument, he said, "Leilani, you'll comply fully with the King's wishes."

I studied his confident demeanor. He was so sure I'd respect his authority as head of the Ani family. Being assertive wasn't working, so I lowered my voice and tried to reason with my twin, to soothe his anger. "I've always respected your decisions, Irin, but something's wrong with this king."

"You sound like his doubtful wife," he said with the King's vitriol.

I envisioned Queen Veluya's quaking voice, her bent shoulders, and her oceans of hidden tears. "Better that than blind obedience," I retorted.

"Such audacity," Irin shouted. "You *will* obey the decisions he makes. If not, I'll get permission from the King to beat you within an inch of your life." He sprung out of his chair, mouthed the remaining bit of fruit tart, and stormed down the hallway to his room, leaving his dirty, empty plate for me to clean up.

Looking back, Deanne, that confrontation with Irin is more evidence I should've taken my things and run right then. I, at least, should have shut my mouth instead of fighting with him. However, because I wanted to be a noble friend to Dirmisu, I didn't leave. I only mentally damned my promise to her. After Irin's fit, I stared numbly at the ghostless night around me and then walked to the garden, the night grass cool against my feet. Amidst the hum of cicadas and crickets, I realized I needed someone to help me unlace my tight under robe if I wanted to breathe. During my grandmother's illness the past week, I'd corralled Dirmisu into lacing the blasted thing in the morning and untying it in the evening. That night, I was alone in that confining costume I'd come to loathe, and my grandmother was asleep. I couldn't justify waking her after a worship service like that night's.

The grass felt blessedly cool, so I laid down and stretched my body over the soft ground that held the bones of my ancestors. As always, they remained silent despite my need for their comfort. I looked at the moon and asked it to bring me reassurance in an otherwise still and vacant night.

CHAPTER TEN

YEAR OF THE PESTILENCE 30, MONTH OF NISAN, DAY 23

*A*unt Samsara is dead. Despite my husband's grumbling, I attended her funeral. I hadn't visited her in an eternity, it seemed. As they set her body into the ground, they said a prayer to Lady Moon. I hope she's the same as our Ethereal Queen. I like to envision the world as a single jewel with many facets rather than a divided lot of treasure.*

Speaking of treasure, my aunt's surviving partner, Emmaline, gave me Samsara's gold bracelet after the service. Sadness clutched me as I fingered the gold filigree pattern. It had looked so beautiful on her wrist. I don't care if it's cursed. My husband doesn't know its significance, so I'll wear it in remembrance of her.

I really think we make our own legacies. Because of this, I'll add to Samsara's journal. I haven't touched it since she gave it to me at the wedding. I sometimes think she was the only sane person I knew. Who else do I have? My parents are dead. My strict husband, though kind to me, is busy. I'm no longer queen, and I don't have a court to entertain me. Although my son is distant from me, at least he's set to marry Bisoru Oru, daughter of the Oru prince. Maybe she'll be a friend to me, someone to pass on this journal and the bracelet to. Legacy both haunts and comforts.

-Samilla Ani, addendum to The Journal of Samsara Ani

~~~

"So, was your mother a friend to your grandmother?" Deanne asked from behind her desk, where she typed notes for her medical log on something called a computer.

I wish that had been the case. "Unfortunately not. I'd say women in my village often end up more as foes than friends."

The doctor nodded. "I can see concubines being competitive. And oppressed. It's so hard to imagine because the women I know have power over our own lives."

I hoped she wasn't planning on judging the Daughters of Lehom too harshly, we who came from a world unembossed with our valor. But, the island also had strong women, the ones from my village who disobeyed the King as well as those who lived outside his jurisdiction. "Well, women had control in Gaiae and Central Village," I explained.

"That's a relief." Deanne tapped her fingers on the keyboard. Suddenly, she stopped typing and looked at me. "I just realized something. You both need vaccines before you disembark."

"Vaccines? Injections that prevent against contagious disease?"

She broke into laughter at my formal definition. "Good. At least you know what they are."

"We know of them but didn't have them." No syringes, no means to make them.

"Tomas, would you please get me two rounds of a comprehensive vaccine?" Deanne asked.

"Right away," her nurse said as he sprung up from his seat and dutifully left the room. A few minutes later, Tomas returned with a small syringe.

Deanne sat on the chair next to my bed and rolled up my sleeve. "While I do this, tell me what happened next."

I felt the cool evaporation of alcohol followed by a quick prick on my upper arm. "I will, but after that, I need a rest." I actually felt comfortable asserting my wants in this strange world.

The doctor met my eyes as she rolled down my sleeve. "I promise."

***

The morning after my fight with Irin, I awoke to the last embers of sleep warm upon my eyelids and my new robes soaked with morning dew. The scent of roasting meat tinged my nostrils.

The King's beef.

Even now, the smell of roasting beef, its toughness turning to tenderness, occasionally makes my throat lurch for the smallest fraction of a moment. But why should I deny myself something so tasty? For the ghost of some unpleasant memory? No, giving in to that would be a tragedy.

Anyway, I was jolted out of my half-sleep by the wails of an older woman. Another voice joined in, "I'm so sorry... I can't believe it."

What in the *world*?

I winced to block out the dim light of the morning sun and saw Gisnen standing on the porch. Looking forlorn, he stared into the shadowy void of the hallway. Hearing me stir in the grass, he turned and asked, "Did you fall asleep there?"

"It appears I did." I stood up and steadied my bare feet on the damp grass. "What's going on? Who's crying?"

"Grandmother and Lady Nereno." He looked very young as his eyes filled with tears. "Meguya died."

Deanne, do you ever have those moments when words are reduced to muttered nonsense in your ears? Of course, I understood the words "Meguya died" at their elemental level, but I didn't believe them to be true. She and I'd just had tea, what, two weeks ago now? "Huh? How?"

"They found her dead on the women's beach," he said, lacking his earlier masculine bravado about girls and their stupidity.

Shrugging off my disbelief, I rushed to my grandmother's room, where I found Nereno prostrate on the ground, her head resting against my grandmother's shoulder. I sat down beside them and took Nereno's trembling hand in mine, but before I could offer my condolences, Dirmisu shadowed the doorway to ask about breakfast. Of course, Irin expected his meal on time and prepared according to his expectations despite the circumstances. Shaking her head in disgust, my grandmother removed a sobbing Nereno from her shoulder so she could remove the key to the spice cabinet from around her neck.

I took the key and surrendered it to my friend. "Make the same thing as yesterday."

She gave me a weak smile and assured me, "I'll handle Irin."

It took about a third of an hour for Nereno to calm herself enough to describe the horrible scene they'd encountered on the beach. Wanting to break their usual routine of bathing in the evening, just after daybreak, when morning light dusted the sand a beautiful pink, Nereno and Grandmother headed to the women's beach. Grandmother noticed a dark form floating in a tidal pool at the shore, and thinking it a stranded animal, they moved toward it to help send it back into its home.

But, as soon as they saw a familiar emerald robe gleaming in the creeping sun, they realized it was Meguya rather than an animal resting in that pool. A completely still Meguya, floating face-down in the water. Her hair fanned out around her body and moved in concert with the tidal pool's minuscule waves.

A drowned flower.

How I loathed that prophetic tea reading. Was Lehom punishing us for trying to divine our destiny? Do we herald our fates simply by trying to know them? No, no, this tragedy had a more mundane cause. The angry red mark on her forehead suggested that she'd somehow tripped, hit her head on the rocks at one end of the pool's boundary, and then drowned in three feet of water while unconscious. Nereno and my grandmother ran back to the village, screaming for help. Only once assured that the palace guards would fetch Meguya's body did they return to my home to mourn.

Nereno burst into tears after she finished this tale, so my grandmother pulled her back into an embrace and whispered, "See if Dirmisu needs help with breakfast."

I felt relieved leaving that room. I didn't really believe in ghosts, but I couldn't shrug off the feeling that some remnant of Meguya was hovering over her grandmother's shoulder and begging to be seen. None of this tragedy yet seemed real.

By the time I reached the kitchen, Dirmisu was cleaning up the cooking dishes. "It's terrible," she said.

I nodded in agreement. "Drowned just like her parents and mine."

"Such bad luck." Dirmisu shuddered as she removed the key to the spice cabinet from around her neck, and she paused before continuing. As if weighing her next words. "So, are you excited about maybe becoming a concubine?"

"*What*?" I asked, gaping at her in horror, for I only felt sadness.

My friend scanned our surroundings, perhaps afraid people would judge her personal ambition at this inopportune moment, and whispered tersely, "Come now, you must be. Being part of the royal family? Think of the luxury!"

"Dirmisu!" I balked at her bad timing. For the past two weeks, every second we spent together, Dirmisu asked me again and again what the virtues did at court. I repeated until my own breath left me that we ate the sacred fruit in tarts and then meditated on the Ethereal Queen's essence. I hadn't said a word of what the King tried, of course.

"Admit it. You're happy about moving to the palace." Dirmisu's eyes gleamed as she rubbed her calloused hands together as if wishing away the evidence of her hard labor. "I don't care what it takes. I want to be a virtue. Or even better, a concubine."

I struggled to suppress my irritation then. She wouldn't have such lofty impressions if she knew what Meguya had been through. Then again, I didn't even know the details of Meguya's sordid truth. After my own unpleasant encounter with the King, I suspected he would have taken liberties with me if I'd permitted it, but I had no solid proof of that. Certainly nothing that I could use to convince Dirmisu to give up her most precious wish. Now, with Meguya dead, Dirmisu would quickly dismiss my concerns for lack of evidence. I couldn't even warn my best friend. She'd think me spoiled and ungrateful for dismissing that which she coveted the most. Instead, I attempted to paint a boring picture. "Being a concubine would mean sitting around all day. Embroidering or entertaining the court. That's no fun!"

"Relaxing all day sounds perfect to *me*," Dirmisu insisted. "And all the beautiful clothes? What's wrong with you? Don't you *want* to be a concubine?"

What a loaded question, one I needed to deflect given my plans to leave. Then, I remembered the King's other announcement, that Kimsimi would soon marry Irin. With resignation, I admitted to myself that the sooner Dirmisu was installed in court as the new Obedience, the sooner I could leave. "I can recommend you to take Kimsimi's place if you want."

Dirmisu threw down the towel she'd used to dry the dishes and grabbed me in her arms. "Are you sure it's not too soon?"

Shrugging, I replied, "I think the Queen will want someone to fill her daughter's place. But are you *sure* you want this?"

Dirmisu broke our embrace, and her face fell at my incredulous tone. "*Anything* is better than the life I lead. I'd go through anything to escape it, Leilani. *Anything!*"

In the face of my friend's earnest wishes, I had no choice but to fulfill my promise. "I'm sorry. It's just that the King is so…disgusting. Like a beef-scented barracuda!"

Dirmisu burst into laughter, her tension fading. "For a life of luxury, I'll easily put up with the King. Remember he's our *king*, though. Don't make fun."

How strange it is the concessions we choose to make. Did the King's power make him attractive enough to endure? Now, I'm not saying that the

King's physical appearance was a reason to reject him right off, but his manipulative personality is what made him revolting in my mind. Beauty is not something that lives solely on the surface. If he'd been dashing and handsome, I'd still find Dirmisu's wishes disgusting. I said the only thing I could, "Then, I'll put in a good word."

Smiling triumphantly, she handed me a cake on a bamboo platter. "Try some of the cakes I made this morning. I added some ground fennel to the batter."

I took a bite, and the sweet, flavorful fennel added volume to the overall flavor profile. "This is excellent. And original!"

My friend blushed. "That means a lot coming from you."

How far Dirmisu's cooking had evolved. She deserved recognition for her innovation, and I thought about how I could parlay her talent. "I know…why don't I bring some of these to the Queen? If she doesn't accept you as a virtue outright, you can come to court and cook. Get in her good graces. She loves to surround herself with talented people."

"If you think that'll help." Dirmisu wrapped the remaining cake in cotilk and placed them in a basket. She then nudged me toward the breakfast table. "Anyway, Irin's glaring at you."

"We had words last night," I explained, giving Dirmisu a dramatic eye roll before heading over to my brothers.

Gisnen scampered off to climb the trees in the garden as I approached, his face still streaked with dried tears. At least one brother had a heart. But Irin. Irin scowled at me when I reached the table. "Your robes are wrinkled."

Well, no wonder considering last night's events. "I slept in this," I explained. "I plan on changing before I go."

"And remember to fix your hair and makeup," he said with contempt. "The King can't see you looking so sloppy."

I was merely a currency to barter for his own gain. Our argument from last night fresh in my mind, I opened my mouth to protest but then stopped myself. I needed to play my subservient role until Dirmisu was installed. For the first time that morning, I noticed the rich scent of coffee, the more distant hint of seawater, hibiscus from the garden, and other good things. *Patience, Leilani, patience,* I told myself. I took in another breath of sweet island air, letting its floral delicacy infuse my voice, "You're right, Irin. How silly of me."

His face softened in surprise. "Carry on then, Sister."

Two weeks.

It had only been two weeks since my world shifted off its axis. And, hopefully, it wouldn't be too much longer until I could leave it all behind forever. As I walked toward my room to apply my makeup for court, I saw Nereno exit my grandmother's room. She swished past me without a word or glance, so all-consuming was her grief.

"Poor Nereno's headed home to prepare Meguya's body for burial," my grandmother said as she emerged from her room, cosmetics case and comb in hand. "Come on, let's get you ready for today."

We went into my bedroom, and I washed my face clean so my grandmother could decorate me for court. Do promises to the dead still count as promises? I pondered that as my grandmother laced me into a clean under robe. By the time I was ready for my makeup, I decided to tell poor Meguya's secret. Using as few facial muscles as possible so I wouldn't disturb my grandmother's handiwork, of course. "The day Nereno introduced me to court, Meguya said the King behaved improperly with her. That she tried to fight, not always successfully."

My grandmother barely batted an eye at this news, continuing to powder my face to a porcelain white. "And the Queen dismissed her for being less than elegant. What a euphemism. I wonder how much Veluya knew."

I thought back to the Queen's harsh words about her sister. "I think she knew enough and then blamed Meguya rather than the King."

"Women are always blamed," she said as she applied kohl to my eyelids and arranged my hair. "She came here to tell you this?"

"No, she came here to see you." I then recalled her bizarre tea request. "It was strange. She wanted to ask you for some parsley. You were asleep, so I made her some tea with some."

My grandmother had been about to add a hair ornament, but she dropped it suddenly. "Parsley? Oh no."

"What's wrong?"

Picking up the ornament, she whispered, "It's worse than I thought. Parsley can be used to prevent pregnancy," Then, she looked at me, horrified. "Did he do anything to you?"

No wonder poor Meguya wanted to drink that awful herb in a tea. I suppose that meant the King had forced himself on her and she was unable to repel him. Nausea built up in my own throat at the memory of being forced to draw closer to him, yet Meguya's encounters had been much, much worse. My voice shaking, I replied, "He pulled my outer robe down a bit to expose my back before taking a picture, but nothing beyond that. I moved away and blocked him before he could."

With my toilette complete, my grandmother sat next to me on the bed. "He'll take liberty after liberty. Just like his father. That one tried to touch me before I was married. I told my own father, and that was the end of that."

I stared at Elegance and Queen Samilla Ani, the allegedly perfect versions of us, in the mirror across from my bed. "I don't want to go back there," I told my reflection, my voice defiant.

"That's it, then. You have to leave the village." Despite the implications of these words, she sounded resolved. Strong.

I said aloud the consequences we both knew to be true. "I'd be exiled."

We silently acknowledged that moment of sadness. Finally, my grandmother summoned some hope. "I don't think we'd be separated in the afterlife. I haven't taken the sacred fruit for weeks, and since it's left my body, my thinking's become clearer. Great Pestilence curse it, I'll even brave exile myself to visit you."

That warmed my heart. As long as I could see her, I'd bear the separation from my brothers. Thankfully, I doubted the King would dare exile my grandmother for trying to see me. She was the daughter of the emissary, after all. "Lucina said she'd arrange it," I offered.

"No one's ever left here, so we need to figure out the best procedure. The *Treaty of Three* allows anyone to switch villages, but only if that person isn't a criminal."

"Why does that matter?" I asked, not seeing the problem. "I'm not a criminal."

"Not *yet*," she cautioned. "However, I'm worried that the King may try to label you as one in order to keep you from leaving."

"That's ridiculous," I countered. "Surely I'm not that important to him."

"You're connected to the emissary directly by blood. But more than anything, Marit Simi doesn't like to lose." Suddenly, her voice perked up. "He can't label you a criminal if he doesn't know your plans. You should leave today. We'll both go on an errand to Central Village. I'd be your chaperone."

"And by the time he finds out, it'll be too late," I complete her thought. What a tempting prospect! It was such a simple solution, really. I felt free. Unburdened, until I remembered Dirmisu and that stupid promise I now regretted. "But I can't leave until I get Dirmisu in as Obedience."

My grandmother looked at me as if I'd said I liked caged nightingales. "With this king? I thought she was your friend!"

I let out a short, despondent laugh. "It's what she *wants*. She'd even be his concubine if it meant an easier life."

She shook her head. "Poor Dirmisu. Do what you think's best, I suppose, but comfort Veluya, too. She'll pretend to be unaffected. That'll be the greatest farce of her life. And, most importantly, don't be alone with the King!"

I stared down my revenant in the mirror, daring her to challenge my plans. "Well, I've already been saying bold things to the Queen, hoping to sabotage my place. I'll just continue."

"That can't hurt." My grandmother patted me on the knee. "But if things start to go wrong, excuse yourself and come back here. Immediately."

I promised her I would. As if promises can always be kept.

After my grandmother left, I applied some lip stain. Finally, ready for court with a deceptive facade shellacked to my face and Dirmisu's cakes in hand, I walked out of the house towards the palace and temple complex. I'd come to think of the palace as a fortress because its only access point from the village was the main entrance, which usually had at least one unarmed guard controlling entry. Today, though, I found the sentry posts empty. As I walked past them undeterred, I wondered if the guards could still be collecting Meguya's body.

I found the palace strangely quiet as I crossed the threshold of the Queen's audience hall. Had she and the virtues gone to the Uya home to prepare Meguya's body for burial? Instead of the virtues' chatter, a male's beautiful singing voice permeated the air. Puzzled, I followed the melodic voice and, as I got closer to its source, heard it meld seamlessly with the hollow sound of mallets striking bamboo.

Since the Queen's curtains were open, I saw movement in the Eternal Spirit Garden, where construction of the Virtues' Annex had apparently begun. The vertical posts that would eventually support the bamboo flooring poked up from the ground, and a series of these unanchored bamboo piling rested against the palace wall. One man struck a mallet and drove the piling into the ground while another, the one singing, held the wood support steady.

And one day the realm of the deep shall her bring
The one who she's heard these same verses sing
Away from the world of sun and sand
Goes Lady Moon to the sea with her man.

Even though he faced away from me, something about the man holding the piling looked familiar. Those arms were the same ones that handed Nereno and I umbrellas only two weeks before.

It was Jenay!

Only about fifty feet away...

Lighthearted and dizzy with excitement, I took a step forward, my platform shoes clambering against the audience hall's floor. This scuffling interrupted his song, and Jenay let go of the piling, turned around, and peered into the shadows from where I viewed his exquisite form. I realized he must've been a talented architect if he was allowed in the palace complex and garden. Outsiders were never invited to this sacred ground. And something hung around his neck. A dolphin necklace.

I must've come into focus because Jenay asked, "Leilani?"

I walked into the Eternal Spirit Garden myself, balancing my weight and navigating the plush grass in my sandals. My hands were shaking, so much so that the grass almost ate Dirmisu's cakes instead of the Queen. "I'm surprised you recognize me under all this makeup."

The other man gave Jenay a knowing smile as he walked a few feet away towards the temple. That meant, I supposed with delight, that Jenay had spoken about me to others. Did that indicate his interest?

"You made quite the impression, Lady Scribe," Jenay said with a playful smile on his face.

Here I was, Deanne, finally alone with the boy I'd conversed with so easily as a child. I'd known what to say then to comfort him, but now, my words abandoned me. I squeaked out, "The umbrella held up well," and instantly felt like an idiot.

Jenay gave me a mock bow and answered neutrally, "I hope it brings you what you want. A prince, is it?"

I was about to answer when I heard a voice behind me say, "Elegance?"

That deep, horrid voice belonged to the King.

I'd been so enchanted with Jenay that I hadn't heard Marit Simi approach, likely from his own audience hall. If you remember, Deanne, the garden was also accessible from there. I turned around and immediately armed myself with the look of someone in mourning. In my most obsequious voice, I said, "I'm so glad you're here. I've been looking for the Queen. Her poor sister."

"Well, as you can see, she's not here," he replied, probing with his eyes the little space between me and Jenay. "What business do you have with this architect?"

In my village, the smarter women are, the more suspicious others become of them. Only the daft inspire trust, so I adopted the blankest expression I could. "Well, he was the only one I could find. The guards are even gone."

His frown eased at my feminine bewilderment. "I can see why you were confused. I've asked them to bury Meguya's body in the Uya family garden immediately. To prevent putrefaction. The funeral rites will take place in three days."

"So that's where I'll find the Queen?"

"No. She and the other virtues are in Kimsimi's room. Gathering together her trousseau, I believe. You can join them there."

I looked down at the grass and traced a circular furrow in it with my right sandal, trying to stall my departure. The King had dismissed me, but I couldn't leave without saying goodbye to Jenay, who'd been quietly observing this exchange. Even though it would make the King suspicious, I looked Jenay in the eye. "The answer to your question is no."

Of course, this got the King's attention. He demanded, "*What* question?"

"He wanted to know if I knew anything about architecture," I said, gesturing to the stacked pilings.

The King burst into laughter. "You? That's hardly a pastime for a virtue."

"You're right." I giggled like a silly girl as I focused my attention back on the garden's grass. "What would I know about it?"

The King said to Jenay, amusement in his voice, "Not that you'd know, Young Man, but our women aren't authorities on such subjects. To keep them righteous, they learn about things pertaining to the home." The King paused and then looked me up and down before continuing, "And about how to stay beautiful for their men."

From Jenay's clenched jaw, I could tell his anger was quickening, much like a gathering storm. I prayed to Lady Moon that he wouldn't say something that would damn us both.

But then, something miraculous happened.

Marit Simi's eyes suddenly darted to the temple, where Jenay's helper had run to while we were performing our awkward little drama. "Young man," shouted the King as he ran after him. "Stay away from there!"

I seized the opportunity and whispered to Jenay, "Please tell Lucina to hold my scribe's position and to find me a place at Gaiae."

A relieved smile broke out on his face, one that melted me on the spot. "Of course I will. You have no idea how happy that news makes me."

I remember feeling lightheaded at this news, so much so I had to steady myself in those tall shoes to avoid falling over. "Really?" I asked, the basket trembling in my hand. "You don't know anything about me, though."

Jenay's face reddened. "I know enough, from when we were children, and from the library." His blush spread deeper, migrating down his neck. "I've seen you there, copying your books. Looking beautiful and intelligent."

I glanced at the temple and saw that Jenay's friend was still arguing with the King. The opportunity wouldn't last long, so I mustered all my bravery. "When I escape, I want to see you."

During our encounter at the kiosk, thanks to Nereno's scrutiny, I didn't have the chance to fully savor Jenay's eyes and how they glinted with merriment, freedom, and ease. But now I looked directly into them, holding his gaze as they showed me true happiness.

"So do I," he reassured me. "So do I. When can you leave?"

When indeed! Now more than ever, I regretted my promise to Dirmisu. "As soon as I get my friend a place here. I promised her. A couple of weeks?"

After making sure the King wasn't looking, Jenay took my free hand in his and brought it to his lips. The sensation was as if I'd touched an electric eel from the coral reef. "I'll be waiting, Lady Scribe," he said as he returned my hand. "By the way, that's my friend Baril, and he's definitely distracting the King on purpose."

"Well, thank Baril for me." But then I heard a bee in the garden, and its drone reminded me of my immediate surroundings, my temporary cage. "I need to go before he gets suspicious."

Jenay gave me a reluctant nod, and I blew him a kiss before slowly turning away. The promise of his words, that he was happy I wanted to leave, dragged my heart toward him even as my feet hauled my body unwillingly. How hard it is to be of body and heart divided.

The mallet's echo resumed behind me as I headed to Kimsimi's room. Knocking on the door, I heard laughter emerging from within. Compassion opened the door. "You're finally here! The King sent us in here so that the men working on our new annex wouldn't gawk at us. They're not Brothers of Lehom."

What reason for this merriment under the shadow of Meguya's accident? Compassion gestured for me to come inside, where the air was thick with bergamot incense. The other virtues were nestled among the room's fixtures, giggling languidly while the Queen sat with Kimsimi on her bed. Both of them were looking into a rosewood trunk with mother of pearl inlay in the shape of glistening flowers that covered most of its surface.

"See, Darling, what beautiful things I've set aside for you?" The Queen pulled out an iridescent white gold robe. It must've also been infused with actual metal, much like the one my grandmother gave me.

Kimsimi remained sullen, a contrast from the nearly drunk exuberance of the others. Her eyes brightened, though, when she saw me. As she rushed to hug me, she jostled the basket of cakes that hung from my arm. "My new sister!"

A sister. The only good to come out of the King's plans. "I've always wanted a sister," I whispered in her ear as I returned her embrace. How unfortunate I wouldn't stay to be her sister forever.

The Queen cleared her throat. "Well, I hope you're good to one another."

I moved to the edge of the bed and bowed on my knees, letting the basket rest beside me. "I'm sorry about Meguya."

Veluya's beautiful face crinkled in disgust. "Your pity's misplaced, Elegance. My sister's been punished by Lehom." With those words, she dispelled all that was proper and winsome about her character. Did she even know her sister had been trying to avoid pregnancy at the time of her death? I shuddered as Veluya touched my arm. "Have some sacred fruit."

To my surprise, Kimsimi contradicted her mother. "Well, *I'll* miss her. She was my aunt, and father's having her buried before I can even say goodbye. That's not fair! We should postpone the wedding until after the traditional month-long mourning period."

"No," the Queen gasped at her daughter's defiance. "We will *not*. A month is far too long, but I'll see if your father will grant you two weeks. Will you behave, then?"

Kimsimi nodded as she wiped away the tears streaking down her face.

Veluya rolled her eyes. "Thank the Ethereal Queen. Now, eat some fruit to lift your spirits. Crying will make your complexion splotchy!"

How quickly Veluya seemed to have forgotten about her initial reservations towards this union. This fruit strengthened the capacity for denial, something I didn't want, but I couldn't refuse the Queen right before I was about to endorse Dirmisu. When Resourcefulness brought me a fruit tart, I dutifully swallowed a piece, ready for the warmth to come but also determined to keep my wits at the forefront.

I then remembered Dirmisu's gift. The sooner I could get her to court, the sooner I could leave. As I unwrapped the cakes, the bold fennel filled the air around us. I held one out to the Queen. "A present from Dirmisu, friend and servant of my house. Her own unique concoction and perfect complement to these tarts."

"Ah, yes, I know Dirmisu. Her mother's my cousin." Veluya examined the cake, inhaled its scent, and smiled. "How lovely. I'm not usually hungry after partaking of the fruit, but I must try these."

"I promise it's worth it."

The Queen bit the cake and rolled her eyes back happily. "Quite. How's her character? You'd know better than me."

"She's delicate, graceful, and obedient," I replied with honesty.

Queen Veluya nodded. "How fortuitous that we'll be needing another Obedience soon. Do you think Dirmisu would be a good fit?"

The thick incense hung in the air. This was the moment I'd been waiting for. I sensed Veluya's hesitation, for girls of Dirmisu's class normally didn't become virtues. I, therefore, decided to highlight Dirmisus's cooking ability. "She's the most obedient person I know. Perhaps if she came to court to cook you could see for yourself."

A little flicker in the Queen's eyes told me the proposition appealed to her. "A good suggestion. She's not of noble birth, but I'm not sure that means so much these days. Just look at my sister's behavior. *She* was highborn but traitorous." The Queen scowled and threw her hands in the air before turning to Compassion and yelling, "Get me my creams! We'll show my husband who's lacking in youth."

I felt lightheaded then, both from my fruit and my apparent victory. Quite intoxicated, I watched Compassion apply a pink cream, made of ground hibiscus and sea anemone venom, to the Queen's face. Was the Queen amenable to Dirmisu simply because they were related? Or, perhaps she thought my friend would be so grateful for the position that she'd remain loyal. A loyal virtue, even if made concubine, would still keep her queen's interests at heart. Dirmisu would certainly be more loyal than Resourcefulness, who oozed ambition.

As I felt the fruit's warmth spread through my body, I joined the other virtues, who were lounging on the floor on pillows while Kimsimi and her mother packed her trousseau. What memories I have of that day are fuzzy. I believe the fruit may have been stronger than usual. But we all still managed to make it through the afternoon and gracefully dance in front of the court. I even looked presentable once the Queen had me change into a new set of robes. I do remember my senses coming back to me strongly by early evening, the time we all headed home to have dinners with our families. That was the last week we'd do so before moving into the Virtues' Annex.

That evening, Irin was as confident as ever, Gisnen as youthful, and my grandmother ever as quiet. Only Dirmisu was different. She barely contained her glee as she brought over our coconut and chicken salads. I'd, of course, told her about the Queen's desire to see her at court and had promised her my persimmon robe for her presentation to the Queen.

After dinner, when darkness fell over the beach where Meguya had died, my grandmother summoned me into her room. She went to her hiding place, pulled out a book I'd never seen before, and handed it to me gently. "It's time you read this."

I opened it to the first page, where someone had written *The Journal of Samsara Ani*. My hands shook. My great-great-aunt's book! "Where did you get it?" I whispered, shocked.

My grandmother sounded wistful as she said, "It was my wedding present from Samsara herself. She thought it would help me, but it was too late to do any good. I already had permanent obligations. But you don't…" her voice trailed off with unspoken possibilities.

Sensing my grandmother needed to be alone with her thoughts, I thanked her and took the book back to my room. I opened it to a random page and read the words, *My mad brother is drugging his people with the alleged sacred fruit.*

CHAPTER ELEVEN

YEAR OF THE PESTILENCE 1, MONTH OF TAMMUZ, DAY 2

H*ow wrong my experiment's gone. The honeyberry, a pain reliever meant for the terminally ill, turns out to be a poison for the living. Although it kills their pain, the fruit also causes hallucinations and, if taken too long, addiction. Rekin stole this fruit from my medicinal garden as soon as he got here. He claims that one can see his Eternal Spirit Garden after eating it, that it provides a glimpse of eternity. He's using it to control his followers. Who knows what the long-term effects are. What's worse, the Central Authority leaders will do nothing to stop it because all three villages need to co-exist. My mad brother is drugging his people with this alleged 'sacred fruit.'*

-Excerpt from *The Journal of Samsara Ani*

~~~

LEILANI

It had grown dark in Deanne's sickroom, and only my husband's steady breathing and the hum of machines kept me company as I began to drift off to sleep, a sleep of genuine fatigue instead of dehydration or heat stroke. It felt strange to have all my immediate needs met. The dangers that had plagued us on the island and our little boat suddenly didn't exist. That monster lay slain at my feet. I lifted open my heavy eyelids and looked at my husband's bed. How I wanted to crawl in beside him and press my body to his. But not while he was still tethered to the snake that fed him vital nutrients. Instead, I sent him a kiss through the air and whispered my words of love as I drifted off to sleep. I knew Deanne would want more of my story as soon as I woke.

***

"Leilani, is your brother a kind man?" A soft voice asked, plucking me from my mental wanderings under the sea.

A couple of hours before eventide and the air was soft with hibiscus. I'd just nestled my grandmother's wedding robe in among my other belongings in my rosewood chest while the woman, now known as Kimisimi Ani, gazed out the window at the Ani Garden, the place holding my ancestor's ghosts. Was she thinking about Meguya? How strange that so many of life's events occur in the same place as death. Kimsimi's wedding to my brother happened earlier that day. The shadow of Meguya's funeral, itself just eleven days ago in the privacy of the Uya family garden, hovered over her marriage. Kimsimi lost an aunt and gained a husband and sister in just over a week. I used a hairpin to carve discreet little notches in the corner of my wooden chest for each of my days in what felt like captivity. You see, Deanne, it was also fifteen days since the King's announcement and nearly a month since I'd arrived at court. It felt like an absolute eternity, and I wondered if Jenay still waited for me.

I ended up in this predicament, moving to the Virtues' Annex specifically, because I'd failed to make the Queen dismiss me, even though I'd been letting loose some rather brazen characteristics at court over the past few weeks. Instead of gliding gracefully in my elevated sandals, I stumbled as if being tripped by the angry ghosts of the jungle. Perhaps most offending of all, I corrected Leppi Eno. My command of mathematics was better than Leppi's, and when he presented his calculations regarding this month's quinoa yield to the King, I interrupted with the correct answer. Now, Eel-Boy Eno glared at me rather than leer. I didn't dare do anything more scandalous since that could jeopardize Dirmisu's chance at being a virtue. What a delicate line I walked between making myself look undesirable for my position but still a reliable person who could testify to Dirmisu's character.

My efforts on that front hadn't born fruit fast enough either. I couldn't blame Dirmisu for that particular failure. In fact, as soon as my friend cooked for the Queen, she blossomed with all the grace and subservience I'd expect from a blood daughter of a prince. Dirmisu deferred to Veluya's every whim and anticipated her every culinary need, all with the hope she'd one day possess the riches surrounding her. Dirmisu's eyes glowed covetously at every shimmering robe that swished by, and I once saw her reclining on Resourcefulness's favorite pillow, her body positioned just like that ambitious girl. I wouldn't have minded the change in my best friend if I hadn't seen something more alarming. Dirmisu actually began ordering around Camuna, the Queen's regular servant, with an entitled tone that made me shudder.

Thankfully, I still saw occasional glimpses of the friend I knew underneath this new person's shell, but they emerged less frequently the longer Dirmisu worked at the palace. I tried to bring up these concerns at my home, during the times she still worked for my family, but Dirmisu brushed them off. Deanne, the funny thing is, Dirmisu and I used to make fun of prissy daughters of princes. In fact, if you remember, those jokes cemented our initial bond. Court certainly changed my best friend for the worse, and the Queen hadn't even elevated her from servant to virtue.

I couldn't help what I couldn't control, though, so I buried my sadness by focusing on my new sister, Kimsimi. "I think he'll be good to you," I replied evenly, trying to be charitable.

Kimsimi twisted her beautiful gold wedding necklace, an heirloom of her mother's family, with her fingers. "I'm sure of that, but is he *kind*?"

Despite my brother's harsh threats the night the King announced his new laws, I had considered what he'd confessed about being under immense pressure. Irin became a prince too early in his life. True, women in the village are oppressed, but men are forced to apply this pressure lest they themselves be judged as weak and incompetent. Irin had always been stodgy, but his recent cruel streak only emerged after he became head of the family. I had to be honest. "He *can* be when his kindness isn't tempered by his duties."

Kimsimi nodded in agreement. "He's still young for all of these responsibilities," she said as a blush spread across her cheeks. "He's also handsome, so I look forward to next year when we can..." her voice trailed off.

My mouth hung open in shock. Where had this unabashed girl come from, one who'd apparently gotten over her reservations about marrying my brother? Was she referring to marriage congress? I burst into laughter and dropped the lid of the chest, which subsequently closed with a loud thud. "*Well* then! And here I'd thought you were a demure flower!"

"Well, I *am* demure." Kimsimi gave me a pleading look. "I'm supposed to be, at least. The Ethereal Queen is sensual for her husband's purposes but not brazen enough to own these desires herself. Is it bad that I have my own wants?"

"No, it's not bad," I assured her. Actually, it brought me relief to know Kimsimi wasn't solely her mother's shadow.

"I wish you could stay here with me, Leilani," my sister said, looking around the room that had been stripped of my belongings and replaced with hers. "I feel like I can talk with you. Frankly."

Happy days exist even in times of great uncertainty, and the day of Kimsimi's marriage to Irin qualifies as one. You see, Kimsimi was kind. And charitable. And wonderful. My sister's status as an upcoming princess, and the daughter of a king no less, entitled her to a fancy, day-long celebration filled with sacred fruit, flutists, and a procession of small gifts from the village's families great and humble alike. Kimsimi, however, insisted that she only wanted a quick ceremony and an hour-long celebration that focused on providing refreshments for the villagers.

The whole affair began in the Temple. Kimsimi and Irin, both shining in their robes, stood under Lehom's faceless statue. The King gave the blessing, and everyone partook of sacred fruit, honey candies, and coconut water. After these events, Irin brought back Kimsimi's trousseau, and it was then my job to acquaint her with her new home. Now, she was Lady of the House. My fondness for Kimsimi cast a small, niggling shadow on my plans to leave. My grandmother had assured me she'd defy orders to come visit me outside the village if I were exiled, but I couldn't expect the same from my new sister.

"I'd like that, too," I said as I stroked the top of my carved box. Inside was the inventory of my life: my cotilk robes, a cosmetic case, my *Book of Lehom*, a few pieces of jewelry, and some hair ornaments. I almost packed Samsara's journal, my grandmother's tokens, and the diving mask, but I couldn't rely on privacy in my new quarters. The only other solution was to leave them here. But, if I did, I'd have to tell Kimsimi. Trusting her was a gamble. I studied my sister's face and ventured, "Could I ask a favor?"

Kimsimi nodded eagerly. "Of course. What is it?"

I tried to remain nonchalant as I asked, "Could I keep some things here? Things that women usually don't own?"

Kimsimi hesitated, her enthusiasm to help me probably battling with her cautious nature. "What things?"

"Nothing bad," I said quickly. "My grandmother gave me her aunt's journal, some tokens, and a diving mask that I use when swimming."

My request must've seemed benign because I saw her face relax. "Oh. Of course. Women don't usually have tokens or diving masks, but they're technically not forbidden. And, certainly, the journal's fine."

"It's Samsara Ani's..." I left the implication hanging in the air.

"Ah. I see. Gaiae's founder." Kimsimi thought for a moment and then shrugged. "Well, she's still your ancestor."

"Thank you so much." I moved to the edge of the room, pulled up a bamboo floorboard, and showed her the space. "They're in here. If you're ever curious, you can read the journal. And please spend the tokens if you want."

"No need. I won't tell Irin, either. There should be some secrets among sisters."

"He doesn't even know they exist, so you won't be lying to him." I replaced the floorboard just as we heard the creak of the door opening behind us.

We turned to see my twin enter. I hoped he'd remember to knock when Kimsimi was here alone. Even though he was her husband, he still had to respect the rules of propriety until she reached maturity. Irin walked over to his new wife and asked sweetly, "How're you settling in?"

Well, then. At least he *was* treating her respectfully.

"Perfectly," she replied. "Leilani's been so kind."

"As I expected her to be." He kissed his wife on the forehead, one of the few gestures of affection he'd be permitted until next year. I noticed Kimsimi almost swoon under his kiss. Most shockingly, Irin looked something different than….well, eternally grim. Like a human being. Was she actually softening up his sharp edges? Perhaps this would be a good match after all!

"I've packed everything of mine," I announced, patting my chest.

"Good," Irin replied in an annoyingly upbeat voice. "There's a cart waiting outside to take it to the annex. You'll love it there. Your new room is bigger than this one."

I barely contained my displeasure at being confined in the palace near that lecherous king. Even more alarmingly, the King planned to announce the names of his new concubines in another ten days. I took one more look around my former room, which now glowed white gold as the late afternoon sun hummed off the mother of pearl inlay decorations. And while I breathed in the sweet air of the garden, the breaths of my ancestors, I didn't revel in sentimentality, for this room, this house, and this family would lead me down a suffocating path.

For better or worse, this place was Kimsimi's now. "I'll say goodbye to Grandmother. Then we can go," I told my brother.

Irin ushered me towards the door. "She's at the annex, ready to help you settle in."

"She wants to make sure you'll be happy," Kimsimi said as she hugged me goodbye.

Irin took Kimsimi's hand in his. "Darling, I'll be back soon. Make yourself at home."

Kimsimi gave a little bow and then stated, in the sweetest voice possible, "I'd like to fill this place with flowers."

Irin looked at her blankly for a minute. She'd articulated her own desires instead of asking his opinion first. But, then he broke into a smile in response to the sparkle of excitement in Kimsimi's emerald eyes. He gave her a nod of approval. "Of course."

How cunning Kimsimi was! She'd gotten her wish *and* made Irin happy. If his current treatment of her was any indication of the future, he'd be considerate and patient. Hopefully not one to leave her bruised as so many other husbands in the village did.

As I exited the room, Gisnen rushed down the hall and hugged me. I returned the embrace. "Hey, Little Monkey. I'm just moving next door."

Irin rolled his eyes but didn't chastise my brother for breaking the taboo that forbids such contact. Instead, he supervised two men, lower-ranking members of the Ani family, who'd come inside to grab my wooden chest. It was strange to watch my brother, who was the youngest by far of the three of them, issue orders to hoist my chest onto their cart and haul it to the Virtues' Annex. How my blasted cart creaked and groaned as they dragged it along. I've read that in the Old World, people were executed for crimes against humanity. On the long walk to their executions, the world would contract before their eyes. I put one foot in front of the other during my own walk towards the death of my freedom. On that path, the village and its buildings swayed as if rendered amiss by an earthquake when the realization hit me that I should've snuck out when I had the chance.

But, it was too late. I let Irin shepherd me in through the palace doors, where we were greeted by incense thick enough to stifle my breathing. We continued into the King's audience chamber and walked up to where it met the Eternal Spirit Garden. And, there among the trees stood the Virtues' Annex. Only one story high, the structure had seven distinct sections along the facade, and each of these partitions also had a door that slid open into the garden itself, giving each occupant, and perhaps the King himself, a point of entry that wouldn't disturb others. Thankfully, though, this building was also visible from the Queen's audience hall. I had a feeling Veluya would be very watchful of the Garden from now on.

As we crossed the threshold of the annex, Irin asked, "Well, how do you like it?"

I pondered this question as I let my eyes roam around the space. Irin was correct. My new home was a little bigger, but it featured a bed twice as large as my own, an unnecessary luxury with sordid implications. I was still, however, impressed by how the wooden bamboo gleamed. I also admired how the surfaces of the walls had both decorated and sparse sections, creating a beautiful symphony of balanced wood hues. Looking up, I saw light streaming in through a cotilk clerestory level. Although I didn't want to stay here, I had to admit that Baril and Jenay had done well. I feigned a smile for my brother. "You're right. The room is bigger."

Irin frowned at my lackluster answer, but before he could speak, the two Ani family members heaved my trunk into the room through the open door. My brother hadn't expressed any gratitude, so I thanked them as they left.

Irin shot me a curious look. "They're merely doing their job."

My brother seemed to mistake kindness with weakness, something I wanted to point out to him, but the pitter-patter of high sandals interrupted me as the Queen and my grandmother stepped into the room. For some reason, Veluya's face had a pinkish cast to it, even below her layers of white makeup. Was this an effect of the creams she'd been wearing in order to appear younger for the King? I couldn't imagine she'd allow herself to get burned by the sun. Before I arrived at court, I'd admired the Queen even though she intimidated me. After? I saw her as a snake, exactly like the one in the parable of the fisherman and the coral snake. In this story, a fisherman returned to shore one day with a treasure load of fish. As he reached the mangroves near his dock, he came upon an injured coral snake. Taking pity on it, the fisherman brought the serpent into his boat. When the boat reached the dock, the snake bit the fisherman. The fisherman felt betrayed and asked the snake why he committed this horrible act. While the venom worked its lethal magic, the snake explained that biting was in his nature.

Well, when the Queen set her eyes on Irin, they contained the venom of that very same coral snake. And her voice? It had a healthy dose of ice. "We'll attend to your sister now. Go see your bride."

"H-have I done something to offend?" Irin asked, at a loss like that poor fisherman.

In the pink-gold light that rained in through the windows, the Queen remained as poised as a statue, so my grandmother spoke. "It's been a long day."

What I take from the snake parable isn't that people can't change their nature but instead that when people are cornered, their true natures shine through. This queen, trapped by her husband's edicts, focused her wrath on my brother, a logical thing because he'd committed sins of his own. Part of me relished seeing Irin get a taste of what he gave me, but then my heart melted a little bit for him. We were both so young. Neither of us felt confident enough to change the world. Yet, we still could make informed choices, one reason I couldn't break my promise to Dirmisu even though I felt cornered by the King. And, I hoped that when the time came, my brother's true inner self would show itself to be good. "Go see Kimsimi," I said kindly.

He actually gave me a grateful nod. How amazing. Maybe there was some good left in my twin brother.

As he departed, Veluya's eyes tracked him out the door. "My dear Lady Samilla," she said to my grandmother, "that boy had better leave my daughter intact until her eighteenth birthday."

My grandmother let go a light chuckle as she sat on the bed. "Irin may be young and foolish in his own way, but he's determined to prove himself worthy of his position. He'll respect Kimsimi. I'm also not yet dead. I'll supervise the two of them."

"Speaking of supervision, Elegance," the Queen continued, suddenly sounding animated, "we have a surprise for you. The King and I made Dirmisu the new Obedience as of this morning. She's in the room next to yours. I'm sure you'll help supervise her transition."

Dirmisu. Why hadn't anyone told me? I could've left the village before coming to this enclosure! "Of c-course," I stuttered both from shock and anger.

"I can see you're surprised. The King and I wanted to keep it a secret since our daughter deserves to shine without any distractions on her wedding day," Queen Veluya explained as she got up from the bed. "In any case, let's go visit Dirmisu. That girl still needs polishing. I leave that task to you."

I could have left. I could have left. Curses to the Queen, I thought as I followed the Queen. So great was my anger, I tripped and planted my forehead on the polished bamboo floor. Pain shot through my temples, my eyes blurred, and then I felt a steady hand lift me upright and into a seated position.

Expecting to see the Queen, I blinked to clear my vision.

But clarity wasn't what I found. Even though I was of sound mind, the sacred fruit I'd had at the wedding must've been making me hallucinate. Because I saw Jenay kneeling next to me and looking as handsome as ever.

"Oh, th-thank you," my voice faltered as Jenay helped me up.

Could my blissful shock be mistaken for clumsiness? I prayed the Queen wouldn't detect my attraction for him on my face. My grandmother gaped at this tableau from the bed, but the Queen had zeroed in her focus on Jenay.

Of course, he wore his sarong secured around his waist, which left his chest bare. I certainly didn't mind, but the Queen pulled her own robes tighter to hide herself from a cursed unbeliever. "Who are you? Why are you here?" she demanded.

Jenay let go of my shoulder and bowed. "I'm the architect of this annex. The King wanted me to see if the ladies find their spaces satisfactory."

"It's lovely," I said, somehow finding my voice. "Quite lovely."

My grandmother stood and held out her hand to Jenay. "I'm Lady Samilla Ani, Leilani's grandmother."

"The pleasure's all mine." Jenay brought her hand to his lips, an action directly from the courtly stories of knights and ladies she told me in my youth.

My grandmother beamed. "Well, how very sweet of you. And here I was expecting a mere handshake!"

The Queen interrupted, "Elegance, if everything's satisfactory, let's send him on his way and visit Obedience."

I needed to talk to him alone before he left, so I asked, in my most naïve voice, "Before we do that, I need some help figuring out the plumbing work in the bathing area."

"Fine, fine," Veluya said dismissively. "Quickly, please. It's been a trying day."

Jenay held out his arm as if to escort me, and as I rested mine on his, my grandmother's eyes widened in alarm. I should've heeded her warning, but, in my hubris, I didn't. I followed him.

"Here," he said in normal volume as he led me through a small sliding door on the wall opposite of the room's entrance, "is your own wooden tub, shower, with fresh cistern rainwater."

"How does the cistern work?" I asked, again loud enough for the Queen to hear.

Then, since the door to the main room was still open, he whispered, "Lucina told me she's keeping your job for you. And I've found you a place at Gaiae."

He smelled of sandalwood and sea, making my legs weaken on my stilted shoes. With those words, the impossible had just become possible. How I savored his hand in mine as I looked longingly up at the sky through the clerestory level, at the birds flying freely aloft. Those flimsy cotilk panels were the only barriers holding back the limitless sky. "Thank you. I just found out my friend got the position here. I can leave any time."

Taking advantage of the distance between us and the prying eyes of the Queen, he took one hand and stroked my face. "Just walk away with me now."

How simple he made it sound. I wanted to, oh how I wanted to. But along with that desire, what ran through me was fear. Not fear of Jenay or a future with him, but fear of what the King would do to stop me. Would he hurt Jenay if I tried to leave with him? We wouldn't be able to avoid detection. The Eternal Spirit Garden was secured by a tall bamboo fence and only accessible through the audience halls of the palace itself. Guards were always stationed at the entrance to the palace, ostensibly to make sure those outside of the village didn't invade this sacred space. But, like many things, that which keeps undesirables out also undesirably confines others in.

I let my face melt into his fingers. Gossamer, that's what his touch was. Gossamer, so much so that I wanted more. In that cocooned space, I envisioned my hands running across his chest, our legs and hips interlocked as we reclined on a bed. I imagined us engaged in all the forbidden things, wonderfully forbidden things. I restrained myself, though, and simply nestled my forehead against his. The perspiration on his skin, with hints of sandalwood, traced upon my own. "That's what I want more than anything, but I need to sneak away. I'll do it tonight if possible. My grandmother will figure something out."

I could see the glimmer of disappointment in his eyes, but he nodded. "All right, then. You know best." His lips came closer to mine, and he kissed me lightly on the cheek. Only a few millimeters more and our lips would lock. Instead, he hesitated, aimed upward, and kissed my temple. "Soon. I'll kiss you when your smudged makeup won't give us away. But for now, remember me with this," he said, holding out a piece of wood carved into the shape of a moon.

"Lady Moon! To match your dolphin for the Lord of the Deep! Thank you." I took the gift and caressed its polished surface, noticing the hole drilled in its top so I could fashion a necklace. I then knew the magnitude of his affection for me. Why else give something that symbolized the sacred marriage of Gaiae's deities? "When they leave, I'll weave it into my hair so it's hidden from view," I said as I secured it against my bosoms.

I saw softness in his eyes, something so different from the resolute hardness and detachment customary to my home village's men. Maybe they had to steel themselves against their women in order to emulate Lehom. But not Jenay, who looked at me with nothing but kindness. "I'll be waiting. Until then, I suppose we'd better get back."

We adopted impassive expressions before Jenay escorted me out of the bathing area with merely a hand upon mine. "Thanks for showing me how everything works," I said in what I hoped was a detached but grateful voice.

Veluya was leaning against the outside door when we returned. "I'm glad you didn't fall into the toilet, Elegance, considering how long it took you."

"I couldn't figure out how to access the cistern water." I shrugged helplessly, praying she bought my ruse. "So many levers."

"And you're clear now about how things work?" the Queen asked. I could tell her patience was running thin.

"I am." I smiled once more at Jenay. "Thank you. For everything."

He released my arm and bowed to the Queen. As he departed through the door, he neglected to look back at me, probably a good thing given the Queen's scrutiny.

As she watched him leave, Veluya straightened the imaginary flyaways in her elaborate updo. "What an odd man. I can't believe he had the nerve to show up here half naked. Well, let's visit Obedience. Finally."

"Could I have a few moments with Elegance alone first?" my grandmother asked. "I have some final words of advice."

The Queen sighed dramatically but nodded. "If you must. I suppose I'll just send Obedience in here, then. I need to rest before tonight's meal. All you virtues are dining with me and the King. He says it'll help him become better acquainted with you."

My grandmother gave the Queen a sympathetic look, which changed to one of annoyance once Veluya Simi was safely outside the room.

I gestured for my grandmother to join me closer to the bathroom entrance, hopefully far from any prying ears. "I don't have to wait for Dirmisu anymore, and I have a place in Gaiae. I can sneak out tonight. I'll scale the fence." The jungle at night, despite its alleged angry ghosts, lured me in with its promise.

My grandmother vetoed this idea with a vigorous shake of her head. "But the jungle ghosts!"

"Aren't real," I insisted. "They're meant to scare us."

"The vines and snakes, then," she said, exasperation in her voice. "That's even if you get past the guards."

I was about to protest but stopped as I looked out onto the garden. She had a point. At night, I could easily trip and hurt myself among the jungle plants. "What do I do? I'm trapped in here."

"Being maudlin won't do you any good," my grandmother warned. "Tomorrow we'll pretend to go on an errand, and you'll continue on to Gaiae. Tonight, you're simply dining with him. In the company of many. In case he does attempt something untoward, say you have your moon curse. The King won't do anything improper after if he believes this to be true. "

How smart she was. It was the perfect solution since men thought women unclean during that time. Only one day until I'd be free. I felt myself choking up and could only nod and bite my lip to keep my tears in check. She pulled me into an embrace, where her robe muffled my dry sobs. After a few moments, my grandmother pulled away but rested her hands firmly on my shoulders. Her final words were, "Hold on until tomorrow. And by the way, he's a handsome gentleman. I'm happy for you, Leilani."

After she left, I tried to feel Jenay's redolent energy. I went to the door that opened to the bathing suite and thought about how he'd been there with me only moments before. Despite the room's airy dimensions, a humid miasma made it hard to breathe. Alone in this space, it became stifling. I recalled the Lady in the Tower and realized this place was my equivalent prison. Who was the nightingale in this scenario? Hopefully not me!

Water. I needed water, so I staggered to the sink and let the tepid liquid run over my hands, splashing it over my face to wash off the heavy makeup I'd worn to my brother's wedding, for it had begun to cake. Would my grandmother's plan actually work? What future would Jenay and I have with only our brief meetings? I let the despair that accompanies uncertainty delude me for a moment, but then I decided it didn't matter what eventually became of Jenay and I. My freedom would be enough.

Tap. Tap.

A knock on the frame of the outside door snapped me out of my trace. I walked into the main room and saw Dirmisu standing at the door, taller than usual, her body draped in an iridescent pink virtue's robe. Almost tripping over her own shoes, she rushed inside and embraced me. "Leilani, isn't it wonderful?"

I forced myself to return her hug, my body again betraying my heart. I pulled back and looked into her ecstatic face, gorgeous in her new makeup. "Why didn't you say anything?" I wanted to scream that question at her. If not for her, I could've left!

"The Queen told me not to." She noticed my trunk near the bed where the men had left it. "Do you need help unpacking? I only brought a small satchel because most of my stuff was too lowly to bring here. Can you believe the Queen is giving me all the new things I need? It's like a dream! She told me to give her servant the recipe for my fennel cakes. Your plan actually worked, you wonderful friend."

"You can help me unpack," I said, relishing in her happy chatter despite my annoyance. Dirmisu continued to describe the beautiful furnishings in her room as we hung my clothes in the wardrobe. I never knew she had the capacity for such a buoyant personality.

"Can I put on your makeup for dinner tonight? Resourcefulness did mine for me, so I need the practice," she admitted, suddenly insecure from the burden of all these new responsibilities. "Face the mirror so you can instruct me if needed."

Although my fresh face lasted barely a smidgen, I smiled at her and sat in the vanity chair before the mirror. "Of course."

"A mirror," my friend muttered as she arranged my cosmetics on the vanity. "From the original ship. I didn't have one at home."

Mirrors. Mirrors told both truths and lies.

Facing mine, I saw all of Dirmisu's movements through this unreal space, a reflection of what was. She applied the white powder base, obscuring the real me. Feeling disgusted, I remained quiet as she finished my face powder and rimmed my eyes with kohl. "You're doing well, Dirmisu," I said. My voice sounded dead.

"No, it's Obedience now." Having finished her work, my friend sat down on the bed, the only place to rest aside from the vanity stool. She asked me in a quiet voice, "What will the concubines do?"

My revenant's makeup was complete save for her lips. "I have no idea," I mouthed. I was sick of pretending for my best friend, someone I shouldn't have secrets from. Then, something strange and unbidden took control of my senses. The words, "I don't want to find out," emerged before I thought about the consequences of saying them aloud.

Dirmisu sat up straighter on the bed and frowned. "Why?"

I looked back at the mirror, at the unreal me, rather than meeting her eyes. "For me, this king is like a snake. But that doesn't mean you shouldn't enjoy palace life."

My friend seemed to ponder this seriously. She asked evenly, "You want to be married to a prince instead, then? I can see you wanting your own home after how you've grown up."

I blushed beneath my white powder. "None of these princes."

"You want to be a scribe again?" she asked, aghast.

My silence said it all.

Dirmisu's beautiful face became crestfallen, and her eyes, which were gathering tears, narrowed as I said, "Yes."

"That can't be all." She got up from the bed and towered over me. "You like books, but not enough to marry an agricultural worker."

Her voice was rising, which wasn't good at all. I needed to make sure she quieted down. *Surely she'll support me if she knows the real reason*, I thought, hoping she'd repay me in kind for getting her this position. "I met someone," I gambled. "From Gaiae. I'm in love."

"What?" The vitriol of her reaction let me know I'd miscalculated badly. She spat out, "Don't be ridiculous! Our kind can't marry outside of the village! You'll be exiled! For what, your whims?"

"You don't understand," I insisted. "I *love* him."

By now, orange-gold light from the sun poured in the windows, inflaming Dirmisu's face with Lehom's fiery essence. "If you get dismissed, exiled even, for this impurity, the Queen will send me away! She told me she made me Obedience because she trusts your judgment!"

My heart lurched as Dirmisu's condemnations spilled from her. "I'm so sor-"

"No," she interrupted my apology as she started towards the door, "you don't get to destroy my plans."

In a panic, I jumped up and gathered her into my arms, hoping that gesture could placate her until my escape. "I take everything back!"

Dirmisu shoved me away, tears now spilling down her cheeks and ruining her makeup. "I'm not your servant anymore. I won't let you ruin my plans," she whispered fiercely. "Forget this madness!"

"I promise," I assured her desperately.

"I'm going to get ready for dinner," she said as she tried to gather her robes with her shaking hands. "I need to look my best,."

"Do you need help?" I offered, panicked to let her leave while she was still this upset.

An angry ghost, a nearly perfect replica of a young Vellua Uya, glared back at me from beneath my friend's streaked white foundation. "I'm not the one who needs help."

And with that last word, she glided out of the room without falling.

CHAPTER TWELVE

*W*hat is impurity but the betrayal of vows to one's self, one's
family, or one's community? Lillian Ani's initial betrayal was to
her first husband when she had an affair with Gerald Ani, her
new costar. She also broke a sacred vow when she left Gerald, who was by
then her second husband, and her children. Lillian Ani was impure, and
Lehom smote her for it by forever isolating her from her family. She exists in
the netherworld now as an angry ghost who roams the jungle at night. You'll
hear her tortured breathing if you venture among the trees after the sun sets.
Women must model themselves after the Ethereal Queen in order to avoid
the fate of Lillian Ani. Sisters of Lehom, be tempted not by the impurities of
the world. Impurity of thought or of action, for both are equally horrible.
    -The Book of Lehom

~~~

Golden morning light streamed in through the circular window Deanne had
called a "porthole." The doctor placed a fresh cup of coffee and a plate
containing scrambled eggs, a meat called bacon that comes from a pig, and
a few pieces of strange looking fruit in front of me. My stomach rumbled, so
I inched my chair closer to her desk so I could partake of this delicious-
smelling feast. She'd offered to take me to a place called a cafeteria to eat
and speak her crew members, but I wanted to stay close to my husband in
case he woke up. The only time I left him alone was when I took a brief

shower in the adjacent bathing room. Thankfully, when I'd returned, he still slept.

"So, did your grandmother's plan work?" Deanne asked.

I took a sip of coffee and let the warm liquid slide down my throat before answering. "Unfortunately, not. King Marit said all the virtues had to stay at the palace until he selected his concubines. He thought outside influences would corrupt us while he assessed our characters."

The doctor balked at this. "What? He thought your grandmother would corrupt you? But you said her father was Lehom's emissary."

"I'll explain more after I eat my breakfast," I said, hungrily eyeing the food in front of me.

Deanne was as eager for information as I was for food, but that didn't excuse her impatience. I'd told her about my move to the palace and my confrontation with Dirmisu as soon as I woke up, but I wasn't about to relay the next part before I finished eating, especially not with blood on the menu. In response to my firm, steely expression, the doctor gave me a sheepish grin and nodded. "Of course. Forgive me."

Forgiveness is a funny thing. People beg for it for the tiniest of things, offenses forgotten in the blink of an eye. But those who cause genuine harm? It often takes them longer to realize the damage their errors cause, if they come to that realization at all. I pondered that truth as I finished my plate of food.

***

Because my grandmother's plan failed, I carved another ten notches into the corner of my wooden chest to mark the passage of days I remained trapped in the palace compound. I'd lied to the Queen, told her I had my moon curse, hoping the news reached the King's ears. Thankfully, though, the King didn't make advances on anyone during those days. At least, not to my knowledge. The night of King Marit's ceremony, the one when he'd announce the names of his concubines, finally came. During that ceremony, I breathed in and out, thinking of my great-grandfather's ghost ship beneath the sea, which was a prison. Just like this temple and the Virtues' Annex. As my eyes focused on the bamboo floor, I could make out boat-like patterns amidst the fibers in the wood. I breathed in and wondered how it would be to swim inside the ship and explore its rooms, long ago robbed of their treasure. That sunken vessel was our only means of escape, a useless one. Just like a covert escape from the palace compound was futile with King Marit's stoic guards standing constant sentry at the only entrance. In the blackest moments of my first night at the Annex, I'd tried to inch my arm through the bamboo fence that enclosed the garden. That desperate act earned me nothing but a few scratches because of how tightly the builders of that fence had set their posts. And scaling the fence? An impossible feat due to all the polish on the bamboo.

Then, a rumble came from the distance, from thunderclouds that hovered over the sea. The King's voice plunged through the incense and the candlelight, intruding into my thoughts. He said, "Brothers and Sisters of Lehom, the time has come for me to announce the new members of my royal house."

I stood among the virtues, all of us next to the Queen, my body humming from the sacred fruit the Queen had handed me earlier. *Please not me*, I silently mouthed to the Ethereal Queen's statue as a flash of blue-white light illuminated her features. Normally, the room's candlelight kept her statue cast in shadow.

"Resourcefulness and Obedience," he said.

Not me...thank you, I thought towards the Ethereal Queen. And Lady Moon. And the Lord of the Deep. Thank you, whoever.

I'd been dutifully watching Dirmisu's face, and she'd been frowning all evening. In fact, ever since she'd stormed out of my room when I confessed my feelings for Jenay, she'd ignored me with fierce resolution. Although she hadn't betrayed my secret, I knew she was still angry at me. At the King's news, however, Dirmisu's eyes brightened, and she and Resourcefulness jumped and hugged one another.

"Ladies, *do* remember your decorum!" the Queen hissed at her new rivals. After this reprimand, Dirmisu looked truly contrite while Resourcefulness merely appeared coy.

I almost felt bad for Veluya, especially as the King stared at his new concubines as a jungle cat does upon its prey. He continued, "The remaining virtues will be married to upcoming princes."

Well, not me, I thought to myself. King Marit had said he'd permit the virtues to leave the palace compound for appropriate reasons after he selected his concubines. My grandmother probably planned to come get me in the morning. I didn't feel like waiting, though, so I'd contrived a plan of my own. To get past the palace guards, I'd say that I needed my moon curse supplies, which I'd left in my old room at the Ani house. If the King insisted on an escort, that was fine. A guard could accompany me to my family compound, and my grandmother would pick up on my cues and say she'd escort me back. Then, I'd slip away, melt into the jungle, and be on my way to Central Village, only about a mile away. I didn't fear the jungle ghosts. As children, we'd been told that because these ghosts were deprived of company and earthly pleasures, they'd tempt the living to step among the night jungle's inky, moonless trees. I'd come to realize, however, that they were merely another illusion Rekin had created to control his followers.

We were all prisoners of the emissary's illusions, and they tainted everyone just as the dead poison the earth around us with their rotting corpses. My poor Dirmisu was also a victim of these lies. Feeling sad for my beloved friend, I gave her a resigned smile of congratulations. But instead of returning my grin, she frowned yet again and stared at the floor. I thought I saw her mouth the words, "I'm sorry," but I couldn't be sure, for at that moment lightning flared again, and the scattered light of the flash distorted her words. I realized, then, that something was horribly wrong. My skin grew clammy despite the tropical heat.

The King's lips also moved, but his voice became lost in the ensuing thunder, the rumbling of which brought me to increasing degrees of panic.

Of dread. The sea storm must have arrived, thunder and lightning shouting together. He waited until the thunder ceased before speaking again. "This storm is fortuitous. It exposes the tension that lies beneath the surface of things, purges the rot. Brothers and sisters of Lehom, there's corruption in our midst, corruption of the most impure kind."

At that moment, his eyes locked on me, and instead of moving on to the virtue next to me, his niece Compassion, he remained focused on my face. "And I, like this storm can root up a tree, will root out that which Lehom loathes." He hesitated and said, "Leilani Ani, please approach."

I remember being detached, unsure he had actually uttered my name, my real one instead of my virtue's name. My mouth became dry as my heart beat faster, yet all I could hear was the thunder in my ear. And then my feet wouldn't work, instead keeping me stuck in place on the bamboo floor. Why was he talking about me after this speech about corruption?

Our eyes still connected, I saw him gesture me forward with his right hand, and he uttered, "Yes, please come forward."

My body moved unsteadily from its trembling, but I forced one foot to move. The other dragged reluctantly behind me. Still, though, I somehow managed not to collapse. Rain began to fall outside, pounding fiercely against the roof of the temple. Could I escape through the garden and use this downpour as cover? As I crept unsteadily toward the King, I scanned the space around me. Nearly all three hundred of the villagers filled the covered temple space, and they'd gladly swarm me in an instant. There was no way out.

Rumble went the thunder. I tried to summon strength from the water above, perhaps the only action of my own accord. That didn't work. So I teetered forward until I stood in front of the King.

"Turn and face your fellow villagers," he commanded me.

Pressed by fear, I obeyed and saw my grandmother watching this scene with terror in her eyes. Nereno stood at her right and Gisnen to her left. A kind-faced Kimsimi rested against Irin. My brother, however, glared at me, his eyes nearly as ferocious as the King's. Was I finally being dismissed? Wasn't something like that usually handled in private? The lightning flashed once more, but then the thunder ceased, leaving only the sound of the rain and my heart pounding in my head to fill the absent thunder's vacuum. What a strange storm it was.

Facing my fellow brothers and sisters, I heard the King's voice once more. "I won't belabor the point. Leilani Ani, formerly Elegance, has betrayed her people."

The words "former" and "virtue" together should've brought me comfort. It's what I'd been waiting for, but something here was wrong. Failing as a virtue shouldn't constitute betrayal. I turned around and saw Dirmisu, who looked at me with tears in her eyes, again mouthing, *I'm sorry*. This time her words were unobscured.

What did you do? I mouthed back. If she'd told the King that I'd fallen for someone outside the village, all my plans would be laid to waste. The thunder returned, resonating loudly throughout the temple hall and echoing the hate that was building up inside of me. Had my best friend *betrayed* me?

"Virtues should live up to their names," the King began when the sky quieted enough for us to hear his words. "Our new Obedience has done just that when she informed me of Leilani's betrayal. Do you want to know this betrayal, Brothers and Sisters of Lehom?"

"Yes!" they yelled as one chorus.

I stared into the crowd, the people I'd known all my life, and saw a sea of menace, of dangerous coral outcroppings ready to break a ship. Only my grandmother, Nereno, Gisnen, and Kimsimi were looking down. From this distance of time, I'd like to forgive my fellow brothers and sisters. Oppressed people lash out when given the opportunity to do so, especially when these actions are free of any personal consequences. In their own way, though, they also loved this king slavishly despite any abuse he doled out through his laws.

Piecemeal scraps.

At that moment, however, I couldn't forgive. Especially not Dirmisu, who'd betrayed me. How could she have done this? I only stayed here as a favor to her! More importantly, what did she say exactly? That question resounded through my head. I didn't want to confess to more than she's said!

The King continued, his voice and outrage rising, "It's a Time of Shadows. This former virtue has defiled herself with an outsider. The natural cycle of life has been disrupted, and it is my duty as Lehom's representative on Earth to restore his order."

My legs almost failed me at these words. Dirmisu had been specific, deliberate even, because he evidently knew about Jenay. Not the details, perhaps, but enough.

I was sunk just like my great-grandfather's ship.

The King's voice dropped as he stood at my side. Marit Simi was so close that his putrid aura infected mine, filling me with so much revulsion that it quelled my fear. He asked, his breath menacing my cheek, "Do you deny it, Leilani Ani?"

Perhaps I could have gotten away with lying, but what would that accomplish? I knew there was no point in being dishonest because then I'd be in the same position as before, stuck, and expending my energy on maintaining a flimsy sandcastle against the ocean's tides. "I don't deny it." I stared at the King, somehow unafraid to meet his gaze for that very brief moment. "But I didn't defile myself with him. With anyone, really."

The King shook his head, almost pityingly. "Your desire itself defiles you."

"It does *not*," I insisted as the villagers remained silent for our little drama.

He thwacked his barracuda hand onto my shoulder. "I'm nothing if not merciful. I offer you this chance here: become my concubine and rehabilitate yourself through prayer, and you'll be forgiven."

No. No chance. I knew the King would never trust me again. I'd be guarded against leaving, prevented from thinking, and kept trapped in confines like the Lady's tower. So, I replied in the only way that I could, "No, thank you."

He shook his head with exaggerated pity. "This grieves me, but if you're sure."

"I'm sure." My words had lost their swagger, though, as the uncertainty of what was to come made my heart beat in my head.

Marit Simi stepped back. "Hold her!" he commanded the two guards.

No, no, no. What was happening? Could I take everything back? *No, no. Too late,* said the kernel of bravery that lived in my heart. With nothing left to do, I surrendered and let myself go slack just as I felt the guards prop up my body.

"I've never had to use this before," the King said as he grabbed a small whip that had been hidden behind Lehom's statue, evidence he'd been planning my punishment.

My eyes widen in terror, and I tried to fight against the guards who were holding me. However, my body, which was drenched in sweat, slid around uselessly in the guards' vice-like grip.

Ghost ship. Jungle ghosts. Nothing is right. Dirmisu betrayed me. What is wrong this storm? This can't be real, thus spun my thoughts.

Marit Simi gave his queen a delighted smile. "My Dear, please help me."

Queen Veluya stood behind me and pulled back my outer robe. After one of the guards handed her a small knife, she slashed the binding of my tight inner robe, exposing my back. I felt the humid island air upon my skin mingle with her moist breath as she whispered in my ear, "Struggle if you want. It won't do you any good."

"I apologize for ruining this robe, but it can't be helped," the King said to the Queen as he raised the whip above my back.

Was he really going to do this? Flinching before the whip even hit, I closed my eyes and thought of the sea and of Jenay as if conjuring pleasant things could protect me. I knew I'd failed when the first lash sent fire through my back. The pain was fiercest upon contact and only slightly receded until the next blow. And the next. Somehow, despite the temple's roof that shielded us from the rain, I felt wetness on my skin. I flew above the island's mountain as does the sun when it traces the contours of the mountain's spine, I swam beneath the calm waves, and I stood in the soft rain as it hit the jungle.

Four.

Five.

Six.

Seven.

There are always seven of everything: princes, virtues, founding families, rewards, and punishments.

And then, like all things in this world, the lashes eventually stopped. I forced myself back into my body, my back stinging as if a jellyfish had laid its arms across me. Then, despite my unsteadiness, I stared down the King. Looking back, I like to believe that I glared at him defiantly, but any fierceness was likely diluted by the pain.

He shook his head in disgust. "No one will want you now defiled as you are."

I looked at my grandmother and saw that Irin and Nereno were holding her up. My twin refused to look at me, and Gisnen shot daggers at the King. Kimsimi, my true sister, held Gisnen's hand and smiled at me through her tears. By then, my head was light from the pain, and I relaxed into the arms of the palace guards, slumping down and seeing a few drops of blood on the bamboo floor of the temple. "I defile you," I whispered to Lehom's statue. "With my own blood, I truly defile you now."

"Take her away," King Marit commanded the palace guards. "She needs the doctor first. Then send her to stay with the other village criminals."

A criminal. I had been branded, quite literally, a criminal. Would Gaiae take me now? I wondered this as the guards dragged me from the temple. As the rain cooled my burning back, a small amount of my blood washed away, nestled itself in the soil of the Eternal Spirit Garden, and became the only fragment of myself to remain with my ancestors in their vision of eternity.

Soon, I slipped into the welcoming darkness, one dominated by Dirmisu's treacherous face. In that quiet space between unconsciousness and the wakeful world of sound, I dreamt that I stood in the center of my village's temple. We were surrounded by multicolor lights and moontrap flashes. Light that blessed them but condemned me. My only movements were through my tears. Not tears from the pain, but tears for what Dirmisu had done. They poured out and bathed my trembling jaw before finally assimilating into a puddle of water at my feet. My former friend mouthed the words, *I'm sorry*, over and over, which eventually transformed into a vision of the King's mouth uttering, *You deserve this*.

I remained paralyzed as Dirmisu took the whip herself and lashed my back with her own hands. In that nightmare, I lingered on a paranoid precipice where the hours and minutes were confused. Then, however, a seed of strength that I'd kept hidden deep inside revealed itself to me, and I surrendered to it. Huddled in the tiny moontrap and candle-lit medical room, my temporary cocoon, I finally rested. Chaos, paroxysm, silence. That's my summary of those strange moments after being whipped.

The first thing I sensed when awakening in the doctor's office was the pain, a feeling made sharper by someone cleaning my back. I also smelled blood, so strange a smell, metallic and a bit earthy, blending with the astringent tang of witch hazel and incense.

Firefly lights swirled in front of my closed eyes as a voice cautioned, "Hold still."

I cracked open my eyes. In the humming candlelight, I saw our village's doctor, the brother of the Cona prince, sitting beside my bed and huddled over my back. Sterile cotilk pads in hand, he said in a hushed voice, "Please don't move."

Would that I could. He'd laid me out on my stomach. My entire back was exposed to him because my blood-stained under robe remained coiled around my waist. "Is it bad?" I asked hoarsely.

From my awkward vantage point, I saw him shake his head. Half of his features remained obscured in shadow, the others illuminated by flickering gold. "You won't get an infection. Light scarring, yes, but infection, no."

The King thought he'd ruined me with a scarred back, but little did he know that he'd cemented my resolve. "I'll live, then." I tried to smile back at him but managed only a pained expression.

I felt the cool astringent and soft cloth trace my skin, numbing the wounds slightly. He finally finished by adhering a piece of cotilk to my skin with pitch. "You might not believe this, but you're lucky. You have more muscle than other girls of your class, and this made the lashes much less damaging."

That tidbit made me genuinely smile. Things would've been worse had I let my muscles waste away as the Queen had wanted. "How long do I need to stay here?"

"Until tomorrow morning." The doctor got up, and I heard water dripping into a hollow basin behind me. "The guards plan on moving you to the home for female criminals."

The guards were here? Not that I was in any condition to leave, but it would've been nice to have had a chance. "How long will I stay there?"

"There's someone here who can better explain that to you," he replied before moving on to another patient.

I heard the clack of sandals on the floor and watched as Queen Veluya sat down in his former chair, her face stern as she surveyed my covered wounds. Through pursed lips, she said, "Well, then. You're awake."

"I'm sorry I didn't want to be a virtue." That, at least, I could apologize for. Whatever enmity passed between us, the remaining fragment of the brainwashed little girl I'd once been felt bad about disappointing her. At some minuscule level, that was.

She ignored my apology. "I can't believe you sacrificed everything for a heathen architect."

I stretched on the bed and let my cheekbone rest against the wooden bed frame, savoring its slight coolness in the humid night. "How'd you know it was him? I never told Dirmisu."

As the Queen shook her head in disappointment, candlelight glimmered off her mother of pearl jewelry, casting her as both menacing and beautiful. "Lady Nereno, the King, and I all witnessed your little interactions with this architect. We put everything together after Obedience told us of your betrayal. How stupid."

We'd never agree on that point. Never. So, I asked at this impasse, "How long do I stay with the criminals?"

"Until you repent and the King forgives you." She continued with sadistic pleasure. "I suppose you thought we'd send you away from here. No one leaves, though, especially not when it would be a reward for bad behavior."

I studied her unhappy face, one lacking the smallest trace of compassion or beauty, to see if it gave any hints about what had made her so angry. Veluya Simi embodied nothing of the Ethereal Queen. At that moment, my belief in the Ethereal Queen died. How could someone who claimed to embody her so completely end up like this? I reasoned that either the Ethereal Queen inspired hate or she didn't exist at all. Queen Veluya was only ethereal through her cruelty. "Why does this make you so happy?"

Candlelight reflected in her pale eyes, echoing Lehom's fire. "You tried to seduce my husband during your private audience with him. Why wouldn't your downfall bring me joy?"

So *that* was it. What a lying piece of rotten barracuda he was, accusing me of the same thing as Meguya. Of course, the Queen wouldn't believe it. She required the title of queen just like she did the air itself. Come to think of it, no privileged person from my village ever protested. Their titles, meaningless words to everyone outside their isolated bubble, assigned them status. If they lost that, they'd lose their identities. Kings and queens were highest, princes and princesses next. Virtues could become princesses while the title of "Lady" gave status to dowager princesses and queens. No one wanted to be a "criminal." So, everyone competed so that their lives meant something. Good deeds or a kind heart meant nothing to one bereft of a prestigious title.

Despite my awkward vantage point, I met her eyes. "Not that you'll believe me, but he's lying. He tried to touch *me*. And Meguya warned me about him. She was trying to avoid a pregnancy from him."

Veluya's eyes narrowed at my words, but her training allowed her to bury the truth under an impenetrable armor. She arose in a flurry of expensive jewelry and gleaming robes. "I pity you, Leilani. Because I'm compassionate, I've brought you some things. Two basic robes, your toothbrush, comb, and sandals. You can keep your soiled virtue's robes since they're ruined, but Kimsimi gets your other possessions. You no longer deserve them."

I silently pleaded with Kimsimi to keep my precious objects hidden but said aloud, "I'm happy she'll have them. Is my grandmother well?"

"What do *you* think?" she shot back. "She's taken to her bed!"

My poor grandmother. I closed my eyes to keep my tears at bay, but all I could see was her crumpling form as she witnessed my punishment. I had to make it up to her. "Please tell her I'll come visit her soon."

"No. *She'll* come see *you* when the King permits it. You're no longer welcome in the Ani home."

"Then, give her my love. Whatever you think of me, the Ethereal Queen would want you to bring *her* compassion." I was surprised at how strong my own voice sounded.

The Queen hesitated and weighed her next words, finally giving me a brief nod. "There's no need for Lady Samilla to suffer, so I will. What a fool you are," were her final words to me as she clacked away on her weighty pedestal. How strange that despite the cruelty of men towards women, women could be just as vicious to their sisters, especially if pitted against one another by these same men.

That's one way they controlled the Daughters of Lehom.

Lying there alone, save for the doctor who attended to another patient, my grandmother's story came back to me, the one about the Lady locked in her tower. Was I her, trapped by my equivalent of a Lord named Fels? Fels...what an odd name. With little else to do, I mentally rearranged the letters. Slef, Elfs, Self.

Self!

The keeper of the Lady's prison was herself. *Self.* Did this mean I was free? Well, not quite yet. The palace guards could keep me in here, perhaps lock me in my new home, but the King hadn't successfully claimed me. Because I rejected his offer to maintain my truth, I hadn't been crushed like the nightingale, a courtly trifle with no significance, or smothered like the palm tree within a malignant banyan. I was like the Lady, poised to escape at the proper time. I had claimed myself with my truth. And I would one day escape like she did to a place called Coeur. *Heart.*

CHAPTER THIRTEEN

"So, that's how you got the scars on your back. I was wondering," Deanne said.

"But you thought it impolite to ask?" Because my back twinged after recounting that part of the story, I readjusted the pillows that propped me up in the bed. I'd retired there after finishing my breakfast, for a fresh wave of fatigue had washed over me. Thankfully, Deanne had assured me it was normal.

"I figured you'd tell me in your own good time if you wanted to." Deanne paused for a moment before continuing. "I'm still confused, though. What exactly was your crime?"

"The King later argued that according to Lehom's laws, my crime was adultery," I said, wondering what rules governed Deanne's world. "Are women in your country punished for such things?"

Deanne looked horrified. "No, thank God! In some countries, yes, unfortunately, but very few nowadays."

It made me both happy and sad to hear this news. Deanne apparently lived in a more enlightened part of the world. However, I badly for the women living in harsher sections. "I'd like to hear about these places when I finish my story."

"I can do you one better. You can see them. In film," she said. In response to my confused stare, Deanne added, "Moving pictures."

My curiosity about how these pictures moved gave me the energy to tell her the next segment of my tale. "I'd like that. I'll continue where I left off."

***

The customary *trill trill tweet* of birdsong woke me that next morning, and I opened my eyes and squinted against the light pouring in through the windows. How I hated mornings, the world of reality. Especially this new reality where I'd lost my family, Jenay, and my freedom. Grimacing at the pain shooting through my back, I slowly sat up and studied my surroundings. There were three beds in this small medical house, and the only other patient, a young boy, still slept.

Hearing me rise, the doctor's wife, who also worked as his nurse, emerged from an adjacent room with a sour look on her face. "So, you're awake. I suppose you'll want a bath."

Indeed, I thought, ignoring her rude tone. "Is it safe to wash my back?"

She shrugged with indifference and pointed to the bathing room. "Start your bath so that you get out of here sooner. I'll come in to redress your wounds."

Why did she have so much hate in her voice? I carried the satchel the Queen had left, gingerly walked to the bathing area, and stood in front of the mirror as the tub filled. I looked as dreadful as I felt, with my streaked makeup, red eyes, and disheveled updo.

But, unfortunately, that wasn't the worst of things.

Wincing, I removed the tattered cotilk robes and let them fall to my feet. The torn and bloody under robe was a loss. But my grandmother's wedding robe only had two small tears where the guards had grabbed me, and the dark color obscured any bloodstains. I didn't care about the robe from the Queen, but my grandmother's was priceless, the only tangible thing I had of hers now. How grateful I was for the fact I'd worn it that fateful night and for the imperfections that let me keep it.

I tried to examine my back, but a square of white cotilk cloth, laced with seven red stripes, covered the wounds. I'd have to check the damage later. In the meantime, however, I stepped into the earth-scented water and used lavender and melaleuca soap to cleanse my body of the King's defilement.

How strange, how freeing it felt as the soap washed away the weighty obligations I'd been saddled with. Virtues, perfection, a princely marriage, and naming breakfast cakes were all things I didn't have to worry about anymore. Still, what a strange notion of freedom, feeling relieved even though I was still technically a prisoner. I wondered if I'd gone mad.

One thing I couldn't wash away, though, was my devastation at Dirmisu's betrayal. I couldn't help it. Tears ran down my face in that bath. So long to my temporary feelings of peace. How could she? After everything I did for her? I could've escaped without being labeled as a criminal! By keeping my promise to her I'd also damned myself, so I vowed to never again make myself a victim. Did that make me a good person or a bad person? I didn't care then because I tallied not leaving when I had the chance among my many failures.

Curses to Dirmisu. I prayed, then, for the angry ghosts to be real because then she could end up as one of them for her deceit. The nurse's footsteps roused me from my mental wanderings, and I quickly stifled my tears. I wouldn't give them the satisfaction of seeing me upset. Instead, I'd let anger fuel my resolve.

"I'll use water to loosen the cloth," the nurse said as she sat next to the tub. "But it'll still hurt."

I felt a trickle of water, a gentle tug, and then multiple prongs of sharp pain. Through gritted teeth, I replied, "It's fine."

"I once wanted to be a doctor." Her voice was businesslike but lacked its earlier rudeness as she tended to me. There was something about that moment where she felt in control, felt useful. This, somehow, made her kind.

"But women can't be doctors here," I added, hoping she'd sympathize with me. Instead, she pressed down on my wounds with such force that I clenched my hands on the edge of the wooden tub.

In response to my ragged breath, she insisted, "Our way of life isn't wrong. *You* are."

Not wanting to aggravate her further, I remained quiet. In a cold voice, she continued, "You've stopped bleeding. The doctor insists you come back every day to have your wounds cleaned."

"I'll do that. Thank you," I replied.

She continued to apply some witch hazel and fresh cotilk in silence, the scent of blood between us. Finally, when finished, the anger returned to her voice. "Don't thank me. The King ordered us to tend to you. Now get dressed, and come have a quick breakfast before you join the other criminals. Doctor's orders."

Ah, that was it, I thought as she left.

As I sat in this water that had turned pink from my dissolved blood, I realized she was battling with herself, her true desires and her conditioning roiling in fierce contest with one another. That was no excuse to treat me badly, though. To spite her, I decided to spend time washing my hair instead of finishing quickly. I loosened my updo and felt Jenay's carved gift slip into my hand, which made me thankful I'd taken the time to weave it in with a cotilk string after my confrontation with Dirmisu. A rush of warmth filled me. I might've been alone in this prison, but I wasn't alone in this world.

I still felt Jenay with me.

Finally, the water lost its appeal, so I dried off and put on the gray robe that Queen Veluya had left me. It was made of coarse unrefined cotilk, exactly the same as Dirmisu's old one. But it was clean and therefore much appreciated. Since Queen Veluya had taken my expensive accessories, I again wove Jenay's charm into my hair and secured it in an updo with my remaining bamboo pins. One thing my ensemble didn't do was disguise the marks on my back. No doubt the King wanted me to serve as an example to others. What he failed to realize is that the unashamed can't be made to feel sorry, so I emerged with my dignity intact.

I packed my meager possessions in the Queen's castoff satchel and went to the porch, where the nurse had left me coffee, a boiled egg, and some quinoa toast on a table. Without my brothers clamoring for my attention, I sat down and savored the quiet, staring at the jungle at the edge of the village. The lush green foliage continued up most of the mountain, save for a few rough paths that led to ledges, themselves hovering judgmentally above the village. Who had forged those paths and cleared the ledges? The foliage also hadn't grown back, so whoever originally cleared that jungle must've also salted the earth to prevent regrowth. More importantly, I wondered *why* someone did this. No one ever went up the mountain. I searched my memories for information, but I only recalled that my grandmother had once told me they were escape routes. To escape from the village? That didn't make sense. These paths only went part way up the mountain. In other words, they were useless to me as escape routes unless I continued the rest of the way up through the jungle and over the mountain's peak. That included scaling rocky terrain, something I wasn't equipped to do. I don't think anyone had ever done that!

I closed my eyes and felt a breeze on my skin that sent a shiver coursing through my body just like Jenay's touch had done only, what, eleven days ago?

Eleven days. So far in distance yet so close in time. I could almost smell sandalwood, the perfumed oil he always wore. My sightless senses were working overtime, for I could almost hear him say my name, *Leilani.* He uttered it so softly, so kindly, without the commanding, overbearing tone my brother used. My real name had been discouraged when I'd become Elegance, so it felt so good to hear it once again even if only in my own head. I vowed to find a way to him, to my freedom. I wouldn't let promises to others stand in my way. Even if it made me a bad person, I'd put myself first the next time it counted.

Despite my resolve and optimism, I felt a longing, a hollow need so deep that it caused my teeth to clench. I opened my eyes and stared at the great obstacle before me and wondered again if I could climb the mountain, make my way through its tangle of vines and earth-scented mist. Gaiae was just on the other side. How hard could it really be?

"I know what you're thinking," a gruff voice interrupted.

"What?" I asked, turning around to see one of the guards who'd held me during the whipping last night.

I flinched back as he sat down in the seat across from me at the table, put his hands behind his head, and reclined backward in the chair. The guard nodded smugly at the jungle. "You're planning an escape."

"Wrong." I looked at him steadily, pushing my true intentions far down within me as I took my last sip of coffee. The clank of the cup on the table echoed my firm voice. "I'm in no condition to go traipsing through the jungle. I was merely admiring the foliage."

"Of *course* you were," he mocked. This man had cruel blue eyes, so different from Jenay's warm aquamarine ones. "Forget about escaping. The King's posted guards on the road leading out of the village. And this might interest you the most. He's had traps set in the jungle."

With those words, the jungle vines I'd just contemplated running through tightened around my neck. I could almost feel my mother's ghost, infused with expensive pikake flower perfume and courtly manners, trapping me here. I don't know why I thought of her then, as a mechanism of restraint rather than a source of comfort. I tried laughing to diffuse my nervousness. "Traps? I can't imagine he'd go through the effort."

"*I* set them." The guard spoke in an animated voice as he described his idol's means of control. "The King says we're in a time of shadows. He's also stationed guards on the road to make sure no woman leaves the village without a chaperone and that no unescorted foreigners enter the village." He hesitated a moment, emphasizing the next words, "Isolation breeds health."

Those from Gaiae and the Central Village were foreigners now? For the love of Lady Moon, the relations between us were disintegrating quickly.

"My name's Nimec. Nimec Cona. And it was my honor to help punish you for your sins last night," he continued with sadistic glee. "You deserved it for your attitude and unholy ways."

He enjoyed punishing me? Had he really just said that? I looked at him and disbelief, searching his face for a logical reason for this hatred.

Great Pestilence, curse it! This was the same guard who'd given me a dirty look on my first day as Elegance, and I'd ignored him when I had status. *That* was why he hated me. I opened my mouth to retort. What did I have to lose? But at that moment, the nurse came outside and prevented me from condemning this idiot guard. The morning sun illuminated her face, and I noticed how slate-gray her eyes were in this light. Was this the color of the ocean in Normandy? Cold and drained of all blue pigment when under the snowy winter sky at midday? She nodded at my empty plate. "It's time for you to head out. He's your escort."

Looking back, I'm happy she stopped me from contradicting Nimec. He later revealed himself to be a brutish character who would've used my words as ammunition to make my life even more miserable. I took a second to cool my temper and then stood up to meet her gaze, my belongings in hand. My voice was cool but dignified as I said, "I'll see you tomorrow to have my wounds checked."

"As the doctor demands," were her final words.

I gave the nurse a little bow and followed Nimec. He guided me through the section of the village where I'd once lived. Next, Nimec took me past the medium-sized houses of the former temporary princes and finally through the section where Dirmisu, my erstwhile friend, used to live, with its tiny, cramped homes. All classes of villagers averted their eyes when I passed.

I'd become a pariah. Even though I'd planned on abandoning my home, my gut clenched when I experienced people's reaction to me.

Nimec and I continued on to the section that housed the village's criminals. I'd never been here before. The obviously-named "Criminals' Compound" was located in a small clearing near the village's agricultural fields and consisted only of three buildings. A large pavilion sat in the center of the clearing, and it was flanked by two small buildings. These smaller structures had cotilk screens instead of walls and covered porches near their entrances. I didn't notice much activity when we arrived, only two women working under the pavilion. Another guard stood outside the structure, but he drew circles in the dirt with one of his sandals instead of watching the women.

"*This* is your new home," Nimec said with an exaggerated flourish as we stopped in front of one of the small buildings. "Women sleep here, and men stay in the other."

"I see." It was a humble structure, but at least the cotilk walls were dyed black for privacy.

As I studied the building, Nimec continued, "You'll always be guarded by at least one person here. Two at night." He then walked over to a bored looking guard, who was large, muscular, and had light blonde, almost white, hair, and pointed at me, saying, "Uralin, that's the new one."

The new one. I preferred Leilani, but I didn't feel up to arguing. I needed to save my strength and wits for my eventual escape, a difficult task with both of the guards hovering over us. Well, Nimec looked like the scrutinizing type while Uralin appeared disinterested. Maybe he could be distracted.

I stepped inside my new home and saw ten small woven pallets, arranged in two rows of five, spread over the unpolished bamboo floor. Rough-hewn boxes rested at the head of each primitive bed. I refused to submit to desperation, however, because desperation kills logical thought. Being optimistic and deliberate was impossible if I panicked, so I focused on the positive things before me. Although it lacked the privacy of my former quarters, the space was clean and came with a palette to cushion me from the hard floor. A blessing. And, most importantly, I knew the King wouldn't sully his eyes by coming here.

I knew deep in my bones, too, I'd eventually find my way to Gaiae. Until then, I would make the best of my situation.

"Well, hello, new criminal," I heard a smooth voice behind me say.

I turned and saw one of the women from the pavilion had joined me inside. She wore a plain robe similar to mine, and she had hair the color of night with eyes to match. Although quite pretty, her face had a slightly skeletal cast to it, a visage augmented by prominent shadows under her eyes. Those tenacious eyes scanned me up and down a few times. I realized then that I didn't even know her name. Nor the other woman's. I'd seen them around at worship and in the village, of course, but we'd never interacted with one another.

"I'm Leilani," I said, holding my hand out to shake hers. As I took it, I felt her calloused hands clash with my smooth ones. "And you are?"

"I'm Belsimi, and the girl working outside is Limcona." She dropped my hand and pointed to the pallets. "Anyway, with you here, it'll be just the three of us. Have your pick of any unoccupied bed, and then come help us with today's work. Did you eat this morning?"

I nodded. "At the doctor's."

"That's good. We don't get to eat again until our guards say we can. It'll be at least four hours." As we headed to the covered pavilion where this Limcona was working, Belsimi continued, "We all saw the whipping. Very harsh."

I knew why I was here, but I wondered what she and the other woman had done. "Can I ask you something?"

Belsimi gave me a knowing look. "You want to know what I did to get sent here?"

I shrugged. "If you don't mind."

"Disobeying my husband. He's an agricultural worker from the Cona family and very rough during marriage congress. Five months ago, I fought back and got sent here for 'rehabilitation.' I can go back to our hovel when I repent. Which I refuse to do."

"You don't introduce yourself as Belsimi Cona," I observed.

She snorted. "Well, I don't consider myself to be his. I leave off the Cona name."

How wonderful. Belsimi seemed like a kindred spirit, unlike my treacherous Dirmisu. "I think we'll get along well."

By then we reached the pavilion, and Limcona, who was grinding what appeared to be mother of pearl, looked up as we entered. She must've heard our conversation, because she said, in her quiet voice, "Well, I'm here because two weeks ago, the Eno princess claimed I stole her bracelet. They always blame the servants."

"And *you* have to stay here until she gets it back or you can afford to replace it, which means both of us are stuck here for a while," Belsimi added. She then swept her arm as if to give me a grand tour of the space. "This is where we grind anything that's too delicate to process in our food and cotilk mills."

"Where should I start?" I asked, seating myself next to the alleged bracelet thief, determined to earn their trust and pull my weight.

"What was your old job?" Belsimi asked.

"A scribe in the Central Village Library. I copied texts for about five hours a day."

"Oh dear." Limcona pushed her light brown braid behind her sagging shoulders. "We work for at least ten hours each day or we don't eat. And you're still sore from last night, I take it?"

I moved my neck from side to side, my skin stinging as the wounds stretched. "I am, but I'll manage."

"At least you look stronger than those puny non-disgraced daughters-of-princes," Belsimi said as she appraised my shoulder definition. "Let's start you with spices on account of your injuries. That requires finesse instead of brute strength."

As Belsimi handed me a turmeric root, I held it to my face and inhaled, remembering the savory soup I'd once had Dirmisu create, a memory that sent pains throughout my core. "I love the smell. It's great in soup."

Belsimi raised her eyebrow in disbelief. "The doctor's stuff? But it's medicinal!"

"With the right ingredients, it's also very tasty in food," I insisted.

"Ethereal Queen bless you and your strange tastes." Limcona pointed to Uralin, who was standing by himself outside the pavilion, and cautioned, "Don't eat it, though. He usually watches us so we don't steal anything, and Nimec, the other, roams around and checks on the men in the fields. The criminal men work there about sixteen hours per day, so we don't see them much."

I sat down and grabbed a mortar and pestle. Then, I began to grind. Over the drumbeat of our activity, I asked, "What spices are we allowed?"

"Spices? Us?" Belsimi asked, sounding incredulous. "We don't get spices unless they fall on the ground. Our food's pretty meager. For breakfast, we get some soybeans. At the midday meal, some quinoa. For the evening meal, some more quinoa."

"No eggs or fruit?" Even the lowest classes got those!

Belsimi's clavicles, made more prominent by her grinding motion, jutted out from her ribcage. "No eggs. We occasionally get a coconut. But we only get fruit if we find it on the ground. It's enough to keep us alive," she explained. "But there's no variety, and we're always hungry." Well, that explained her skeletal figure. I wondered if she'd end up submitting to her husband out of desperation.

Limcona put down her mortar. "The guards get better food. We have to prepare it for all of them. Not being able to eat it drives me crazy."

What a destitute place the King had sent me to. Although our sleeping quarters were clean, the scent of smoke and burning rubbish from the ash heaps infused every part of the compound. Even more problematic, the village had more than enough food to give us eggs and fruit, some occasional meat even, but we were only allocated enough to survive.

Then, I had an idea.

I dropped the bowl that held the turmeric I was grinding, and some of it spilled onto the pavilion's floor, painting the drab color a brilliant burnt orange. "Oh no, how clumsy of me!" I cried.

My alarm roused Uralin from his stupor, and he came over to survey the damage. His eyes moved from the orange pile on the floor to me and back again. His only words were, "Worthless idiot!"

"I'm sorry," I said, trying my best to look repentant. "My injuries."

"That's no excuse." The guard paused and seemed to consider what to do next as punishment. "We can't waste it, but the doctor's not going to want that now. You're going to have to use it in your food. It tastes terrible, just so you know."

I turned away so he wouldn't see my eyes crinkled in mirth. "I suppose that's an appropriate punishment."

Both Belsimi and Limcona tried to appear busy as I scooped up the fallen turmeric and placed it on a banana leaf. For the next few hours, we continued to grind, sort, grind, sort, and grind. My arms ached. My back was also on fire by the time that midday rolled around and we were allowed to stop for a food break. Uralin had brought over our lunch provisions, and I was delighted to see a coconut among them. Of course, he and Nimec got chicken and pineapple.

Because we had no solar stones here, Belsimi built a fire under a small covered cooking area, and while she attended to the guards' lunch, I added some coconut milk and then, finally, my legitimately pilfered spice into the quinoa we'd been given. I stirred it until it was creamy and spooned out three equal portions for us three girls. Thankfully, we were the only ones being "punished" with eating this concoction because the criminal men ate their own portable lunch in the agricultural fields.

"I promise that the coconut milk will sweeten the spice," I said.

As Belsimi gave me a skeptical look, Nimec came over, bowl in hand. "What do you say?" he asked her.

Limcona stepped in front of Belsimi and knelt in from of Nimec, touching her forehead to the ground. Quietly, she asked, "Nimec, the powerful one, may we eat our food?"

Although Belsimi looked away, I watched this scene wide-eyed. What a humiliating power play on his part. Nimec lorded over Limcona for a moment, but he finally said, "You may. But hand me my food first."

Limcona lowered her eyes and handed Nimec his bowl of savory food, and Uralin accepted his immediately after. With that, both guards left us in peace.

Aghast, I asked, "He does that before every meal?"

Belsimi nodded. "I vomit right after eating if I'm forced to do that. It hurts being so pitiful, so lovely Limcona volunteered to take the brunt."

"You won't throw this up. It's wonderful!" Limcona exclaimed after her first bite of my concoction.

We finished eating and then worked together for another seven hours, only pausing when we needed water. By the end of the day, my body screamed for a respite. I was thrilled to learn we each got to shower in our own bathhouse since I felt rank after a full day of work and no access to perfumed oil. At least we didn't have to wait for a spot in one of the village's communal bathhouses. Being a spiritual contaminant to others *did* have its unique advantages, I supposed.

CHAPTER FOURTEEN

Everything went downhill for my family when Mother's first husband blackballed her and father from Hollywood after their affair. She tried to be happy, but we three kids weren't enough. Why else would she have abandoned us for a new life in Milan as a model? I made peace with her absence by connecting to the natural beauty of our island home, my Gaiae, where I can feel Lady Moon's spirit. This Lehom, however, gives Rekin a conduit for his rage and permission to control women for fear they'll turn into Lillian Ani if given freedom. I think our absent mother inspired the Ethereal Queen since her statue looks exactly like that of our mother's statue of Kwan Yin, the Goddess of Mercy. Come to think of it, our Chinese and Irish mother would look like that statue if she dressed the part. Even more fucked up, he has his upper-class women put on makeup modeled after ancient Chinese Imperial courtiers. Women were controlled then.

I wish Chanson and I could intervene on behalf of the women in Rekin's Village, but then I remember the importance of the Treaty of Three, the agreement that all three of us came to when Rekin and Chanson first landed on the island. Although some laws bind all three villages together, we cannot interfere in matters of daily life. I hope it's not too late for poor Samilla. I've instructed my partner, Emmaline, to give her mother's gold bracelet if I die first. It's important for her to have connections to her past. No matter how complicated the legacy giver.

-The Journal of Samsara Ani

~~~

In essence, the King imprisoned me because I dared fall in love with someone from another village, something he considered adultery. Love, the greatest human emotion in existence. How could that be worthy of punishment? I pondered this as I stared at the box Deanne had handed me.

Moving pictures.

Well, not only moving. They spoke, too. As the doctor had explained it to me, the King's camera obscura produced but one stationary image at a time. However, her world's technology captured picture after picture, and then a contraption smooshed them all together and made them move and speak. This picture series showed a prison in a place called the United Kingdom. Those women had beds, enough food to eat, and even something called a "craft room" to occupy their hands and minds. The pictures showed the women working, assembling something I couldn't identify, but they didn't appear overly fatigued or desperate. What a difference from the Criminals' Compound.

I handed the device back to Deanne after the moving-speaking picture concluded. "My husband will love seeing this contraption."

"I wanted you to see that people in my world treat even their criminals humanely," she replied.

"Well, I found humanity, too," I began.

***

I also found my first sliver of genuine hope after our evening meal on my second night at the Criminals' Compound. Unfortunately, it didn't contain any spices. How appropriate I found it at night, a magical time for me as I've told you. We still relaxed together on the porch of our building and savored our quinoa. "So, I'm curious. Why did Obedience tell the King about your lover?" Belsimi asked. "I don't mean to pry, or maybe I do, but it's been bothering me."

Of course, Belsimi was the one to pose that question so suddenly. Limcona was quieter and more conscious of decorum. I really wanted to forget Dirmisu's betrayal, for all day I'd mentally cursed her name as my back stung with every move. I stayed quiet and focused on the delicate sound of the night's sea breezes ruffling through the palm fronds.

"I'm sorry," Belsimi said. "That's your business."

True, it was, but I couldn't remain angry at Dirmisu forever. Anger distracts, and I needed to divert my energies to escape. Sighing, I replied, "The glamour of court possessed her."

At this, Belsimi nodded and relaxed against one of the porch's support posts, "Is *he* worth all the trouble?"

Another bold question, but this time, one that brought a smile to my lips. "He is. As was being true to myself. Those things are worth giving up all the riches at court."

"Did they let you keep anything at all?" Limcona asked, joining the conversation.

Nothing anyone would consider truly valuable. Only my grandmother's wedding robe and the ruined under robe from the Queen. But that gave me an idea. "I'll be right back," I told them as I ran inside our building to my satchel.

I pulled out my grandmother's outer robe, setting it aside for me alone, and then grabbed the one the Queen had given me. Returning to the porch, I held it up in the firelight for Limcona and Belsimi. "We can use strips of this to braid through our hair."

This piqued Limcona's interest. "I can weave some bracelets made of this and add some shells. They'll be even more beautiful than the Eno princess's missing bracelet. Stupid crone."

And in the fading light of the evening, with torches instead of moontrap to aid us, we washed and salvaged the fabric for our own purposes. The conversation between us hummed with the cicadas and tree frogs, and I was so involved with the other girls that I didn't notice it was the night of the full moon, nor did I hear Uralin approach the porch.

I dropped the cotilk bracelet I'd been weaving when he interrupted our girlish laughter with his raspy announcement. "Someone's here to see you. Make it quick."

Hoping it wasn't the King, I got up and followed Uralin to the edge of the porch, greeting the darkness with a weak, "Hello?"

Then, from that moonlit night, my grandmother appeared. She embraced me carefully around my waist. "How are you?"

I savored the orangey scent of her perfume as we held each other close. "Enduring."

She pulled back and examined my face for the truth. "Really?"

"Yes," I admitted. "But what about you? The Queen told me you'd taken to bed."

My grandmother laughed. "For a very brief moment. I'm not on my deathbed yet." She reached into her bag and pulled out a small book. "I brought this for you."

As I was about to take it from her, Uralin rushed over and held out his hand to inspect the gift. "What is that? Did the King approve?"

The former queen, my grandmother, emerged just then, regal and commanding but still feminine when she addressed the guard. "It's simply a meditation on the Ethereal Queen that my own mother, the first Queen of Lehom, wrote many years ago. Nothing treasonous, I assure you. Please check it yourself." She then handed him the volume.

Uralin studied the pages for a few moments in the firelight of the torches, scanning the words on the book's few pages. "It looks fine," he said sheepishly before giving it to me.

As I examined the unfamiliar book up close, my grandmother casually rambled. "You wouldn't believe the trouble I went through to get you this. I went all the way to the Central Village Library today to fetch it for you and had to promise your poor brother Gisnen some honey candy to escort me, seeing as I need to do that now. But anyways, a meditation on the Ethereal Queen will help you repent."

Those words made me pause. What? The Central Village library? Impossible. They wouldn't carry religious texts from our village. She was trying to tell me something, but I wasn't yet sure what, so simply said, "I see."

"Leilani." The torchlight magnified the intensity of her expression. "Remember the Lady and the nightingale. The answers you seek are in that story. She remedied her situation through strategic reading and thinking, and so should you."

Frowning, I stared at the volume in my hands, willing it to give me answers. In order to read it strategically, I needed privacy, something I clearly didn't have with Uralin breathing the same air as me. "I understand," I assured her in a voice more confident than I felt.

"It's time to go. I'm off duty now," Uralin interrupted, nodding toward the night-shift guards who'd just arrived at the compound to relieve him and Nimec.

My grandmother, in all of her queenly glory, turned to him and asked, "My boy, before you leave, would you escort us on a quick beach walk?"

Cicadas and night birds filled the silence, but finally, Uralin eyed my grandmother and spoke, "A walk on the beach? I'm finished with my shift."

She responded by pointing to the sky. "The full moon is beautiful tonight. Seeing it spread across the sea would remind my errant granddaughter of the beauty of Lehom's creation." My grandmother reached out her hand to him, and in her palm, three tokens reflected the warmth of the torches. "Would these help?"

Uralin looked into her hand. "Are you trying to bribe me?"

My grandmother laughed dismissively. "Bribe you? Oh, Lehom bless you. Not at all. I'm merely providing compensation for the inconvenience."

"I suppose it's fine." He slowly held out his hand, took the tokens, and examined them in the torchlight. "A quick walk, then."

My grandmother led us towards the compound's beach, only perhaps a hundred yards away. The moonlight peeked through the palm trees and fragmented into diamond patterns from the leaves. As we walked to the edge of the shore where the fisherman launched for the day, the sand glowed blue with the iridescent plankton that fueled our moontrap lamps.

She finally stopped before a tidal pool. "Remember the Lord," she began, followed by the whispered words, *of the Deep*, uttered so softly due to Uralin's proximity.

The Lord of the Deep ritual! She'd remembered.

With my sandals on, I stepped into the tidal pool as the water shimmered to the cadence of the moon. I stood in seawater about one inch deep, where the moon reflected off the light blue sand, and looked at the inky horizon. Its color was so deep a black that I had to imagine the beings that danced along the point where the water met the night sky. With a pure face and heart, I whispered almost silently, *Lord of the Deep, come to me.*

I closed my eyes and meditated for a moment. As I imagined that darkened horizon line in my mind, a merman with a shadowy face approached me.

Then, suddenly, Jenay's face replaced the shadowed one.

My heart quickened. I inhaled the sea air, letting its tropical magic infuse my lungs. *Magic*. Magic was everywhere, even in the Criminals' Compound and under the jurisdiction of such a corrupt king. I felt ready to leave this world of sun and sand.

"Time's up," Uralin said.

Well, no matter. I had what I needed.

Smiling to myself in the darkness, I opened my eyes, stared out at the sea, and walked back toward the compound still covered with moonlight.

"Did that help?" my grandmother asked.

Sensing Uralin's impatience, I embraced her. "It did. Thank you again for coming."

"Remember the lesson of the nightingale." My grandmother threw me a final crafty smile before she allowed Uralin to lead her away into the darkness, to the privileged section of the village.

Still puzzled by what I was supposed to do with this book, I returned to the porch and asked Belsimi and Limcona for a few moments alone to meditate on the book's contents. Both girls said that they'd be happy to make accessories while I read. In the privacy of our sleeping area, I recounted the story of the Lady and the nightingale. She'd found her means of escape hidden in the cover of her book. As I felt my grandmother's volume, I noticed it was too thin to have something hidden in the cover, meaning the message must be in the text itself. With only meager light from a low-hanging torch, after a few minutes of staring at the first page, I noticed that, just like the Lady's book in my grandmother's story, some of the letters were ever so slightly tilted the right. Anyone not explicitly looking for this code would miss it.

It was too dangerous to write these letters somewhere, so I concentrated on forming them into words. My heart thumped as the words formed into sentences, into beautiful sentences that could aid me in my escape. Hidden in the pages of this book was the covert message, *Lucina going to Central Authority. Authority member will visit you soon.*

CHAPTER FIFTEEN

I haven't written in this journal for a long time, but today's occasion demands it. I have grandchildren. Twins, a boy and girl each. My son is happy there's a boy to inherit the Ani prince title. He'll be the one molding the boy into Lehom's image, but given her mother's disinterest, I'll be the one raising the girl. Long ago, back in Calabasas, I wanted to be a businesswoman when I grew up. Little did I know I'd be a queen, albeit temporarily. Even though I've had to bow my head to men, I've had an easy life compared to other women. This girl should grow up to be a queen, too. I'll do my best to make sure it happens. Bisoru at least did a good thing by naming her Leilani. It rolls off the tongue pleasantly.

-Samilla Ani, addendum to *The Journal of Samsara Ani*

~~~

"So, did the Central Authority help you escape?" Tomas asked.

Deanne had reluctantly gone to speak with the captain regarding something about a status report, so the nurse acted as her proxy by recording my story for Deanne in case I needed to rest again. I hadn't believed him at first because he wasn't writing anything down, but then he'd pointed to a small circle contraption and claimed that *it* was capturing my voice. I'd held my breath in amazement when he pressed a button, causing my past words to fly through the air to my ears. Only, the person speaking from that machine sounded different than me. What magic. What fearsome, awesome magic.

"They played their part," I replied. "But I also had other help."

"Please continue," the nurse prompted, nudging the circle machine closer to me.

***

I hadn't realized it on my first day at the compound, but we were close enough to the beach to hear the waves softly pounding on the sand. The ocean's subtle beat lulled me to sleep, a good thing considering how hard my pallet was. My criminal mornings, as I came to call them, consisted of soft sea breezes and the scent of ashes from the nearby ash heap. Then, as soon as the sun began to peek over the mountain, the chatter of men getting ready for the day barreled into our women's space and distracted me from the lovely birdsong that emerged from the jungle. The first few mornings were difficult because I no longer consumed the sacred fruit, something I'd been doing multiple times per day at court. My body felt that lack acutely in the moments when a current of anxiety charged through my veins and made me want to smash in the guards' faces with my fists. Those moments became less frequent, though, as time dragged on. After a week in the compound, I quickly accepted my circumstances, happy I no longer expended energy trying to live a farce, a drama over which I had no control. I wouldn't say that I submitted to fate, though, since I constantly strategized my escape.

I also learned how much work it took for my former lifestyle to appear effortless. This may sound silly, but food used to simply appear at my house right before every meal. I hadn't thought of who brought it to us. I knew, of course, that people were working behind the scenes, but I never imagined the sustained effort it took to keep my class in relative leisure. You see, Belsimi, Limcona, and I had to finish all the work that Dirmisu's former class of women couldn't complete. With Uralin guarding us, I was now one of three women assigned to clean out the chicken coop that provided eggs for the entire village. We also sorted large amounts of food, processed it, and sometimes did laundry that servants for the elite didn't have time to finish.

As the days of work dragged on forever, I began to understand why Dirmisu had hated her old life so much.

My seventh morning among my village's criminals, a humid grey light woke me. It was a dead light, devoid of any warmth even though it came from the sun. Although I'd already opened my eyes that morning, Belsimi was the first one to actually arise from her pallet. I watched as she changed from her sleep sarong to her daytime one and saw her jutting hip bones, concave stomach, and prominent vertebrae. I began to worry about how much longer she could survive here.

As she threaded strands of iridescent cotilk through her hair, Belsimi urged me, "Come on. Don't just lay there. It's time to get up."

Belsimi's voice must've awakened Limcona because she furrowed her closed eyes against the morning light and groaned from her pallet. "Leilani, I'll take care of the laundry if you help Belsimi with the cooking."

"Yes, to both of you," I agreed. I sat up and stretched, causing pain to shoot through my shoulders and hips. Both my wounds and muscles gave me grief in equal measure. Despite these aches, the doctor had pronounced me as healed a few days ago since the lashes had scabbed over. The nurse certainly looked happy when he said I didn't have to return.

Before I left the doctor's office that last time, I finally had a chance to examine my back in the mirror of the bathing room. The marks were still prominent, but they no longer festered. They reached from the base of my neck to my right shoulder, extending only slightly onto my upper left shoulder. *You've survived a tiger*, I told myself. *Bear the marks of that survival proudly.* Still, in my weaker moments, I couldn't help but wonder if Jenay would find me unattractive because of them.

To battle that negativity, I drew strength from my full moon transaction with the sea. Like a lizard basking on the rocks, I savored the warmth I felt from thinking of Jenay and reinvigorated myself by chasing out any cold kernels of desperation. I'd made myself ready for my own Lord of the Deep. Perhaps because I'd grown up comfortable praying to the Ethereal Queen, asking the sea and moon for favors didn't seem too foreign. Some might rebuke me by arguing that only fools believe in magic. Well, I never claimed to be wise. I needed that magic, though, because we all felt fatigued from the lack of food, and our work became harder and harder to complete. I wondered how long until I no longer had the strength or energy to escape.

"Would you tie my sarong?" Limcona asked.

"Of course." I grabbed the strings with my hands which, thanks to the work I'd been doing, were no longer smooth. Despite our work-heavy hands, Limcona and I both loved beautiful things. We found ways to manifest this beauty with ordinary found objects, such as weaving shells into the strips of my ruined under robe to make jewelry. This gleaming fabric, along with flowers from the jungle's edge, also made wonderful decorations for our hair. I'd say we were the prettiest hard laborers on the island. And I, of course, always wore Jenay's pendant woven into my hair lest it be confiscated. I wouldn't say I became fast friends with my fellow lady prisoners, but we did share a camaraderie, working together to make our respective loads easier to bear. We thankfully enjoyed one another's company, too.

When we were ready to greet the day's labor, Limcona scurried off with a large basket of laundry containing our clothes and those of the criminal men. I'm grateful she volunteered for that loathsome task while I could help cook, something I actually enjoyed.

Belsimi started a fire to cook the quinoa, and soon, the water boiled fiercely. I took charge of boiling the eggs for the guards and preparing the coffee for all of us, grumbling, "The men eat first, just like at home."

Stirring the quinoa, Belsimi wiped the steam from her eyes. "Yes, men must come first, unfortunately."

"*Here*, that's true," I whispered as I stared at the jungle and debated what types of traps the King had set among the vines. There was a sadistic medley of options, such as weight-triggered spears, a pit of snakes, and hidden jungle snares.

"Where else is there? The other villages? The King's posted guards on the roads." Belsimi followed my gaze and frowned, nodding toward Uralin. Her voice was almost silent against bubbling water beneath her. "Plus, our *friends* keep us here."

I shrugged and began to slice the mango, which was, of course, also for the guards. "Maybe there's another way."

My cooking partner stopped stirring the quinoa, her cheeks pink from the steam. "You can't mean the jungle," she said no louder than a cicada. "There're traps."

"I know." What I left unsaid was that I'd brave that risk as a last resort. And that I'd do so without her or Limcona. My initial mistake was waiting for Dirmisu, and that had cost me dearly. Even though I liked Belsimi and Limcona, I needed to get away. Telling either one of them about my grandmother's note could put any plans in jeopardy.

When the food was done, Belsimi spooned the quinoa into bowls and poured the coffee into vessels for each of us while I placed a boiled egg in the center of the guards' portion and arranged the mango slices in pinwheels around the perimeter of the egg. Belsimi stopped pouring and gave me an incredulous look. "What in the world do you call that arrangement?"

"Eggy flowers," I said with pride. "My brother Irin would hate that name."

Belsimi laughed as she finished pouring the coffee. "You're strange. But I can appreciate that you want to defy your brother however you can. Even privately."

How right she was. Even meaningless gestures of rebellion helped fuel my resolve to find an escape. I didn't want to end up as an emotionless drone, something the men here had been reduced to. Smelling their cooked breakfast of plain quinoa, the criminal men filtered out of their building. They formed a queue and took the food and coffee we prepared to the porch of their own home. Because they'd been conditioned not to acknowledge us, they didn't utter one word or even look us in the eye.

The guards approached next. Uralin gave me a strange look at the food arrangement while Nimec frowned as he grabbed his portion. Well, Great Pestilence cursed them and their ungratefulness. My body craved protein, and it took great restraint not to gobble down their eggs.

Finally, it was time for us girls to eat. Because of how that spiceless quinoa clumped together in a homogenous mass, I could tell today was going to be a humid scorcher. Belsimi watched me poke at my food and savored a long sip of her brew. "Enjoy this coffee. I made it extra strong because we're sorting cotilk fibers today."

Cotilk was ground in our textile mill, and our strong sea breezes powered the millstone, but our primitive machinery couldn't separate the fine ground cotilk from its husks. Criminals did that. "I can't imagine ground cotilk would be heavy," I said.

"It's not," she admitted, "but separating the fibers from their ground husks takes concentration."

"It's more boring than anything else," Limcona added. "The men pick it, haul it to the mill, and then bring it to us. We sort out the good parts for the weaving room, and the other stuff is burned for soap ashes."

I gulped my coffee, weaker than I was used to, but still discernibly coffee. The powdery dregs were beautifully familiar, bitter but powerful. "Well, I'm ready when you are."

Before I stood up, I heard Uralin lumber onto our porch. "The King wants to see you first," he announced. At least Uralin, though annoying, didn't possess Nimec's cruelty.

And the King. This could either be the best news or the worst news. Did he want to punish me further? Or, had a member of the Central Authority come to my rescue? Although I latched onto that last possibility, my meager breakfast sat heavily in my stomach. "Why does he wish to see me?" I asked with more irritation that I intended.

Uralin froze for a second, frowning at me. Finally, he responded through his clenched jaw, "You think *I* know why? No. So shut your mouth. You're going to find out when you get there."

Indeed I was. For better or worse. Hopefully, better. I wasn't the only one who didn't want me to go. A sullen Limcona pushed the remainder of her breakfast around in her bowl. "How long do you think she'll be gone?" she asked quietly.

At these words, Uralin's mood reversed instantly, and he gave her a patient look. "Don't worry, Limcona. She'll be back soon to help you. Thank you for all of your hard work."

"Of…course," Limcona muttered as her face turned lobster red from the compliment.

Belsimi, who'd been observing this exchange with interest, tried to avoid spitting out her mouthful of coffee. Our perplexed looks mirrored one another. Had Uralin grown fond of Limcona? Shaking her head in wonderment, Belsimi gulped down her remaining beverage and said to me, "Be careful."

"I promise." I gathered my skirt and followed Uralin. Resolved to get this meeting over with, I settled my nerves by latching onto the small chance, albeit a very slim one, that I'd be with Jenay soon.

As we walked along the shore the fishermen departed from each morning, I gazed up at the volcanic mountain that separated me from the other side of the island, from Central Village and Gaiae. However majestic its peaks, I loathed that mountain now since it separated me from Jenay and from my freedom. There were allegedly traps in the jungle around the village, but did that include the *entire* jungle? Like the morning after my whipping, I again noticed how the tree canopy on the mountain was punctuated by rough paths that led up to a series of overlooks. My grandmother had said they were an escape route, and another vague memory hinted they had something to do with the ocean. Still, that didn't make sense. That fragment of memory was useless. Just like the paths themselves.

All the way to the palace, I pondered my escape options as my sandals rasped across the crushed shells beneath my feet. When Uralin and I arrived, I saw that three guards were stationed at the complex's entrance. Strangely, though, all of them now held spears of sharpened wood at their side. We'd never had a need for weapons here on the island.

I took a deep breath and followed Uralin past the stony guards. Inside, the sweet combination of incense and hibiscus from the King's audience hall bombarded me. How long ago it seemed that he'd taken my picture and made his ignoble advances. So much had changed since that horrible event.

As usual, Marit Simi languished on his throne, but now he was flanked by Dirmisu and Resourcefulness, each seated on opulent chairs next to the throne. Both women were beautifully dressed. Well, immaculately dressed to be precise. But something seemed amiss. Dirmisu looked more like a porcelain statue than a person, blanching when she saw me enter. From remorse, perhaps? True, she was free of her old life and relieved of its burdens, but what did she sacrifice in order to achieve it? Seeing her seated near the King, a fragment of my old love for her reemerged.

I realized, then, that even though she'd betrayed me, perhaps I'd also betrayed her by not considering her wants. Shouldn't she have the right to determine her own path? A life of luxury, even if as a concubine to the King, was her choice, one I'd unwittingly jeopardized. A poison to me was a balm to her, and this allowed me to begin to forgive. And to feel sorry for her because she looked truly miserable despite her lofty position.

Resourcefulness, on the other hand, smiled triumphantly at my plain appearance. Straightening my back and narrowing my eyes at that pretentious concubine, I was grateful the accessories that Limcona and I'd made afforded me some dignity. Then, I noticed a woman I'd never seen before, as well as a vaguely familiar man, standing in front of the throne. Was this lady my rescuer? I hoped so. Her knee-length sarong, much like the one Lucina wore, and her confident expression indicated she was an outsider. I focused on her as the King waved me forward with an impatient gesture of his hand. When I finally reached the throne, she rewarded me with a kind smile.

The King crossed his legs and leaned back in his chair. "I suppose you're wondering why I've summoned you here today."

No longer compelled to be deferential, I inclined my neck slightly but kept my eyes fixed on his as I replied, "I am."

"There have been some ridiculous complaints made to the Central Authority about our treatment of you." His face remained grim as he gestured towards the strangers. "We have two representatives from the Authority here, one from Gaiae and the other, Boma, my legal advisor."

Here I was, so close to help, but at the word *complaints*, my tongue remained stuck to the roof of my mouth. Would the King punish me further for this? Should I speak? Stay quiet?

Sensing my hesitancy, the woman from Gaiae stepped forward and introduced herself. "I'm Mimza. It's nice to meet you, Leilani." Her strong presence and kind eyes, green like the foliage in our jungle, emerald-like Meguya's robe at our final meeting before her death, made me like her immediately.

"It's good to meet you, too." I bowed a true bow, showing her the respect I'd just denied the King, and then begged her with my eyes for help. If such a thing were possible.

Mimza gave me a sympathetic nod. "I'll get to the point. I've been told that you were whipped as punishment?"

"Yes," I said, turning to the left so she could see my back.

I heard Mimza gasp. "Oh my word! What was the reason for this? No crime warrants such punishment."

Elevated on his throne, Marit Simi gave Mimza a withering look. "Adultery. She defiled herself with a foreigner from Gaiae. It's against our laws."

No, that wasn't true. I wasn't an adulteress. And if I could convince Mimza of this, maybe she could take me away to Gaiae. "I've never been married," I insisted. "And I *never* defiled myself."

Boma shook his head and thrust the book he was holding at Mimza's face. "In our *Book of Lehom*, we define adultery as either having impure desires or engaging in impure actions."

"But she says she's never even been married, so how is this adultery?" Mimza asked, as she pushed the book away.

The King coughed and cleared his throat. Using the tone of someone speaking to a petulant child, he explained, "Virtues are dedicated to marry princes or join my royal house. She accepted the position, so she's bound by its rules."

In response, Boma retrieved yet another book from a table across the room, scanning its contents excitedly until his finger rested on a specific line of text. "She broke our law, and per the consensus of the Authority since its inception, we can punish our lawbreakers as we see fit."

"*What* exactly are you citing?" Mimza asked. Boma handed her the volume, and after a few seconds, she rolled her eyes. "Oh, Lady Moon preserve me. This is the *Treaty of Three*. All of us know it by heart. Anyway, he's referring to this line, Leilani. *Each village may deal with its criminal as it sees fit, but no village may mistreat one of its prisoners. Criminals may not seek asylum in another village.*"

"So you see, the only question is whether or not we've mistreated her. She has clothing, food, and a place to sleep. The whipping will leave light scars, but she's not in danger of infection. We're not breaking consensus," Boma argued.

"This is certainly mistreatment by Gaiae's standards!" Mimza spat back with rage behind her words.

Mimza's fury scared me. She needed to be smart, calm, and convincing, but not angry. Anger wouldn't let her defeat the King because it was far too impassioned, which the King would cite as hysteria. Everything was about standards, but these standards were subjective and with too many potential interpretations. Men in the Village of Lehom could beat their women until bruised and sore but not maim them. My scars weren't considered being maimed even though they were, unfortunately, permanent. Based upon Mimza's reaction to my whipping, such beatings were illegal in Gaiae, likely Central Village, too.

But, did that help me at all? The legal argument between these Authority members had become too abstract, and I doubted abstractions could free me. I needed to testify about the conditions there, about Belsimi's withering body and the hopelessness of our situation. I met Boma's gaze, so unlike what a woman was supposed to do in this place. "The food isn't nearly adequate. My friend Belsimi is slowly starving. Limcona and I will be too, soon."

Boma was about to reply, but the King held his hand out to silence his legal advisor and spoke instead. "All three of you will receive standard rations once you repent. If you were being mistreated, we would've denied you medical treatment. Again, repent, and you'll no longer be hungry."

How accustomed he was to everyone automatically obeying his commands. Resourcefulness now stood behind him, massaging his shoulders, and Dirmisu remained poised elegantly in her chair, not contradicting a word of his. My former friend focused her eyes on the floor in front of her, though. Perhaps she did feel sorry after all.

Suddenly, Mimza, who had been actively searching the text, smiled. She pointed again to that bothersome section of text and said to the King, "You've misinterpreted the line, '*Criminals may not seek asylum in another village.*' It's about standards. Leilani wouldn't be considered a criminal in Gaiae, so she can seek asylum there."

Not used to being contradicted by a woman, the King shook away Resourcefulness's hands and, barely maintaining a patina of civility, argued, "But she *is* a criminal *here!*"

Mimza neither cowered nor flinched. "That's irrelevant. Leilani's *crime* here is not one in the Central Village or Gaiae, so only *here* is she under your power. She could still seek sanctuary elsewhere."

"No, *your* point is moot. The girl is here, so our standards apply. *If* she were elsewhere, then she could seek asylum." Marit Simi held out his right hand, and Dirmisu, as if a trained spider monkey, scurried up from her chair and quickly brought him a glass of herb-infused waters. He took a long sip and gathered control of his anger. "I won't let her go with you if that's what you're thinking."

Mimza emphasized her next words, wonderful words that inspired such hope in me. "I plan to take her with me."

The King gave her an appraising look before smiling his barracuda smile. "If my authority were breached here, it would violate the *Treaty*. I could then legally withhold our crops."

Her face fell at this threat. "That would be hasty for all concerned."

Being a criminal was, it seemed, worse than exile. At least in exile, I'd be free to make my own decisions and live elsewhere. But the King wasn't giving me freedom. What could he want? I stared at him for a moment, remembering the time I'd thwarted his advances on my first day as virtue.

Then, I understood. He wanted compliance, which to him was repentance. Perhaps if I appeared to make the effort, he'd grant me some privileges, privileges that could get me out of here. I had stupidly missed my chance to leave before, but this time, I would certainly act. Stealthily and surely. "I accept the wisdom of this council," I said, gritting my teeth as I bowed a true bow to the loathsome king. "To aid in my repentance, may I receive more books from the Central Library?"

King Marit tapped his fingers on the armrest of his throne, suspending my potential futures in front of him and toying with them. Instead of answering me, he whispered to Resourcefulness and Dirmisu. They then left the audience chamber without saying a word. He was making me wait, the rotten barracuda. Finally, like the cat who caught its mouse, he smiled. "I must approve of this reading material."

"Of course," I agreed quickly, making sure to keep my voice calm and respectful. "I'll have my grandmother get them if you permit."

The King nodded and yawned. "I consent."

"Speaking of Lady Samilla, good influence that she is, seeing her more would help me repent."

"Under *supervision*," he replied, emphasizing the last word.

I bowed to him again before turning to Mimza, praying she knew about the coded messages. "Would you please tell Lucina that I'd love to read more commentaries on the Ethereal Queen, ones like she sent before?"

For the first time since the King had threatened to withhold his crops, Mimza's defeated expression eased. "Of course. Would you like to write down some titles for me?"

I looked to the King for permission. "If you approve."

The King relaxed back in his chair and gave Boma a nod. How easy that had been. How *frighteningly* easy. The King must've believed he'd won. Boma brought me some lampblack, a quill, a bamboo writing tablet, and some paper, and I slid gracefully to the floor and braced the tablet against my knee. Slowly, I wrote down the names of some book titles, some genuine and some imaginary, making sure to make my slanted letters very subtle. After I was done, the lawyer handed my message to the King, who gave the words a perfunctory glance. "I'll check these texts when they arrive to make sure they're appropriate," the King said as he handed the list to Mimza.

From her smile, I could tell that she understood that this message was coded. "I'll give this to the librarian," she assured me with a wink.

Hidden among my list of titles were the words, *I can swim beyond reef if boat meets me there. Very strong swimmer. Jungle has traps. Ocean escape best.*

I gave Mimza one more covert smile before Uralin, who'd been completely quiet during this whole exchange, provided me with a solemn escort back to the village. On the walk back to my prison, I calculated and planned intensely. I *would* get out of here. Great Pestilence take me, but I'd even swim around the island if it meant that I could be free from the King's reach. I felt light. Hopeful. Alive. This levity shattered, though, when Uralin and I were greeted by a stony-faced Nimec back at the compound. "The one who wouldn't obey her husband got hurt," Nimec said. "She's laying down inside your quarters." Of course, he didn't care to know our names.

Strangely enough, Uralin's face relaxed at this news. Neither of them tried to stop me from dashing into our sleeping hut, where I found Belsimi lying on her palette, her face screwed in agony. Limcona sat beside her, holding her hand. "What happened?" I asked as I knelt by her side.

"I tripped on a tree root outside and hurt my shoulder," Belsimi whispered. The sunlight coming in through the walls highlighted her discomfort.

Limcona looked up at me. She was a wilted flower on the floor, a mess of helpless energy. "I told Nimec to get the doctor, but he said he'd think about it. What's there to think about?"

Thanks to that meeting with the King, at least I had a firm understanding of what constituted mistreatment. Denying crucial medical care to a criminal indeed qualified, so I promised my friends that I'd take care of it. The knowledge I'd gleaned from the meeting gave me the strength to run out of that hut and confront the guards. "You have to get the doctor," I said bluntly. "The *Treaty of Three* calls for humane treatment of all."

"Come now. She's hardly dying," Nimec taunted.

"After what you heard in the palace, you know that's true," I countered, turning to Uralin for support.

Uralin remained quiet for a few moments, but, finally, he sighed in resignation. "I hate to say it, Nimec, but ignoring it could cause trouble with the other villages."

Haughty men don't like to lose, and they hate being humiliated by someone who's allegedly inferior to them even more. I knew Nimec could be volatile, and he first scowled at me, a disorderly woman who didn't know her place and who had set Uralin against him. He narrowed his eyes and weighed his options. He wanted power and obsequiousness from us, but probably not if he caused trouble with the Central Authority.

Eventually, Nimec shrugged. "Fine. I don't care. But you and the other one have to get to work now."

How hard it was to contain my pleasure at winning this battle. I choked back my smugness because I had a part to play, and I'd play it well. It also went without saying that Limcona and I would carry the burden for Belsimi. "Yes, and thank you," were my polite words.

Nimec didn't reply. He didn't even look at me as he left to get the doctor, so I ran inside to tell my friends the good news. Limcona and I immediately scuttled back to the porch and sat down before a huge pile of ground cotilk. The plant's broken cylindrical pods were about half the size of my pinkie nail, and I watched as she extracted the good fibers from the husks and then placed them on separate piles. I followed suit.

As Uralin monitored our progress, our eyes remained focused on our piles. Good, bad, good, bad, we sorted the cotilk fibers from the useless husk material. Limcona's pile of fine cotilk fibers grew larger than mine. I paused and watched her fluid movements, her hands deftly piling up the good material that would make our cloth.

Seeing that I'd stopped working, Limcona gave me a reassuring smile. "Remove the large pieces of cracked husk first, and then swish the rest between your fingers. The good parts will separate from the bad ones."

I remained skeptical but still grasped some ground material within my fingers. Thankfully, with some concentrated effort, the smaller husk pieces separated from the useful fibers. That morning and afternoon remained quiet between us, each of us focused on our respective missions. My pile of fine cotilk fibers grew slowly, and I had plenty of time to think, fortunately or unfortunately. Now that Belsimi was injured, what would I do if the opportunity arose for escape? Could I really just leave them here? I kept working, trying to deny the answer I knew to be true. My pile of bad pod husks grew larger than my pile of good pieces. I knew the truth about myself. Yes, for my freedom and to be with Jenay, I'd easily leave. And I felt such relief that it made me ashamed.

Selfishness can be a virtue, too. How can you take care of others if you neglect yourself? Consequently, I swam for my life when the chance came and promised myself I would help Belsimi and Limcona from afar.

There really wasn't any other choice.

CHAPTER SIXTEEN

L ady Moon will reveal her magic to anyone who opens their eyes to
it. She's the great sentinel in the sky, a companion to the Lord of the
Deep, and has gone by many names in life: Selene, Luna, Ceridwen,
and even the Ethereal Queen, at least by Samilla Ani, the Second Queen of
Lehom. She doesn't care what name you utter so long as you do so with a
pure heart and a kindness towards others. Call on her and see.
    -Gaiae folktale

~~~

The moon is responsible for illuminating the night, controlling the tides,
and regulating a woman's monthly curse. But, like many things in life, curses
can be boons just as boons can also be curses. Any sweet perfume can
become rancid, and some monsters have the potential to shed their menace.
My boon-curse heralded its arrival through a dream five days after I met
Mimza in the King's audience hall.

I stood on the women's beach in my dreamscape, staring at the menacing
clouds that hovered over the sea. Here, the normally lush beach had only
skeletal trees to decorate it. Everything was cast in a sickly green hue,
signaling a storm on the horizon. Far away from me, the other villagers
huddled together and spoke in whispers. Their skin was the color of rotting
flesh. I yelled to them that a storm was coming, but they couldn't hear me or
see my frantic gestures. That meant I was a jungle ghost. The wind began to

pick up, shaking the spindles of the bare, skeletal trees. I couldn't find a building for cover, so I took a deep breath and chose the strongest looking tree, bracing my legs and steadying my body against the quickening breeze and churning surf. The sea was as gray as the sky instead of its typical blue-green hue.

I was merely a ghost in a dream. One about to be consumed by a storm. So I submitted to fate, and my racing pulse calmed when I simply accepted that I'd be carried away in the gusting debris. I watched a great multitude of nightingales, large enough to cover the horizon, fly over us. They squawked like seabirds in lieu of their normal singsong pitter. As the birds passed us overhead, the wind gusted, causing nightingales to drop dead on the ground near my feet. I shrank back, but the villagers remained oblivious to the stricken birds.

Then, suddenly, a figure emerged from the violent sea. I felt terror as her head peeked out of the waves and as her face became visible to me. It was my grandmother. Or, something who had once been her, for this figure's eyes were black, its skin the color of death. Never before that moment had I ever wanted to flee from her.

But, I couldn't even do that. I was stuck against that dead tree as she got closer and hissed on the wind, "Just wait until the water comes."

This was only a dream, I tried to tell myself in my panic, only a dream.

My grandmother was alive.

As my vision suddenly went black, these affirmations calmed me. Even more bothersome than the storm was a persisting throbbing, a deep and powerful ache coming from within my stomach. Then, the raindrops cooled my skin, and I vibrated in time with the rain's pounding, eventually melting into the pain.

I next felt my single sheet tangled around my legs and heard birdsong. Normal song from normal birds. It meant I was awake. I kept my eyes closed so I could gather my thoughts. None of my dream's events had been real, but the pain in my stomach remained, meaning my moon curse would likely come sometime in the next day. I'd have to get something to stem it from Belsimi and Limcona. I sat up, looked through the walls, and watched the palm fronds above dance tranquilly in the morning's zephyr. So different than the wind of my dreams that was strong enough to cast nightingales violently to the ground. Shuddering, I focused on today's lilting sea breeze and tried to ignore what those crushed birds could portend.

Belsimi still slept peacefully on her pallet thanks to the herbs the doctor had given her, but Limcona's bed was empty. The sound of wooden cooking utensils thumping against crockery indicated she was already outside working. I quickly got ready with the dread of that dream still hovering over me. Howling winds, people with skin the color of rotting flesh, churning ocean waves, driving rain, and on, and on.

Limcona gave me a weary smile as I joined her in the pavilion. Thankfully, by that morning, I no longer felt a longing for the sacred fruit. I instead craved Jenay, and thinking of him helped sustain me as we worked. We had an extra load to complete because of Belsimi's sprained shoulder. The doctor had instructed her to rest it for three days, so I boiled the quinoa and fruit while Limcona prepared the coffee. In our silence, I became absorbed by the angry water bubbling with the fury of my dream storm.

"Leilani!" Limcona's earnest tone broke me out of my trance. Startled, I looked up and saw that my grandmother was standing right in front of me, holding a small satchel in her hand.

"What are you doing here?" I dropped the quinoa spoon and ran up to greet her.

After that horrible dream, it felt wonderful to see her in the flesh. Her features, far removed from the tumult of days past, were as calm as those of the Ethereal Queen. She held out a bag made of soft purple cotilk. "I took a nice stroll along the docks so I could bring you something you need."

"Did the King approve?" Uralin approached, his hand outstretched. "I need to inspect its contents."

My grandmother gave him a patient smile as she handed him the bag. "Of course."

Uralin opened the satchel and rummaged around, frowning at the unfamiliar items. "What are these pieces of cloth for?"

"Leilani needs them for her monthly courses," she deadpanned.

"What? Monthly courses? What are you talking about?" Suddenly, the confused expression on his face gave way to revulsion, and he dropped the bag on the compound yard, causing the dust to swirl up in a tornadic cloud. "Disgusting."

I tried not to laugh at his squeamishness as I bowed to pick up the bag. "How'd you know?" I asked my grandmother.

"It was time. You'll find those useful, just as I told you on your day before court."

I stopped, the bag suspended in my hands. My day before court? That day had nothing to do with my moon curse. I scanned my memories to that seemingly long ago time, the day when she'd cautioned me about the banyan tree and also when she'd given me the tokens.

The tokens.

Had she gotten them back from Kimsimi? I discreetly felt one of the cotilk pads and noticed it seemed weightier than usual. My crafty grandmother must've sewn them inside. Keeping my voice casual, I said, "Thank Kimsimi for me as well."

My grandmother nodded when she saw I understood the message. "Inside the bag, you'll also find a new commentary on the Ethereal Queen." She turned to Uralin. "Would you like to read it first?"

He glanced dubiously at the offending bag. "Take it out for me."

Rolling my eyes, I fished out a small folded piece of paper and handed it to Uralin. He scanned it, and finding nothing amiss, he gave me the small folio. "Your grandmother's going to a lot of trouble for you. You'd better repent for her sake."

How simple Uralin was, viewing the world solely through black and white lenses. *Repent*, he commanded, as if that were an easy thing to do. That meant submitting to the King, burying my true self, and forgetting Jenay, all of which I wasn't going to do. However, I had to play the part, so I replied as sweetly as I could, "It'll be my salvation."

"Young man," my grandmother jumped in, "a bath in the ocean would do these girls well."

True enough. As much as I appreciated our nightly showers, I missed swimming in the sea even more than I yearned for decent food. I'd mistakenly thought I'd still be allowed to bathe on the women's beach when I came here, but there were no female guards to watch us. So, showers it was. Limcona seemed to perk up at this possibility too, for she stopped working at my grandmother's suggestion.

"What?" Uralin asked, frowning in confusion. "A bath?"

My grandmother paused and said in a low voice, "It's important for women to purify themselves..."

No doubt envisioning my grandmother's package, Uralin blanched. "Please, stop talking about..."

"When the sun's at its highest point in the sky is best," my grandmother continued and held out a token in her hand. "May I compensate you for the inconvenience?"

At the sight of this money, Uralin's eyes lit up with avaricious delight. "Fine," he replied as he palmed the money. "But from this beach."

My grandmother looked at the shoreline near the docks, empty now since the fisherman had headed out for the day. "This beach is perfect. And the girls will, of course, bathe in their clothes to protect their modesty."

Uralin reddened. Seeing my grandmother exploit his squeamishness brought me joy. She was up to something, though. Why was she bribing Uralin again? The answer to my question was likely hidden in the commentary she'd brought. I needed to excuse myself to read it, so I held up the satchel. "I'll just put this away. Do you want to join us for breakfast?"

My grandmother looked to Uralin for approval. He seemed surprised at her deference. "If you don't mind the basic food."

"All the better for us old ones." She turned to Limcona. "Can I help?"

"A former queen helping me cook? I couldn't ask you to do that!" Limcona said. My poor new friend looked embarrassed. Unworthy of such help.

My grandmother looked at her kindly and then took my place at the quinoa pot. "I don't mind. I need something to do in my old age."

Perfect! I had my excuse to find out what this ruse was all about, so I ran inside our building and saw that Belsimi still slept soundly. I crept into our bathing room to read the commentary, squinting in the filtered morning sun to make out the text. As before, written in slanted letters and hidden among words praising the Ethereal Queen, was a message. It said, *Swim today. Jenay in boat beyond reef when sun highest.*

Oh, my Lady Moon. I now understood my grandmother's motivations for bribing Uralin. How fortunate that only my grandmother knew I could swim well.

I had an escape route. An actual escape route.

Today. I'd always wondered what I'd need to do in order to make the impossible possible, and now that exact scenario was within my grasp.

My mind raced with questions.

Would the tokens weigh me down if I took them? More importantly, could I actually swim that far, sore as I still was from my workload and from the King's punishment? My heartbeat nearly ran away with me, but I closed my eyes and breathed in, letting the morning birdsong and sound of the beach's waves calm me. The jungle was booby-trapped and the roads guarded, so swimming was the only way out. Today, I had an excuse to be on the beach, and I actually had a ride to Gaiae.

There wasn't time to entertain my endless doubts, but I still had to prepare as much as possible. I ripped open half of the cotilk pads and removed the tokens my grandmother had hidden in each. I then placed about half of them in one single pad and secured it between my breasts, anchoring it into the cotilk bindings that protected my modesty. If they fell out when I was swimming, well, then the sea could have them. I left the remaining tokens in the satchel for Belsimi and Limcona.

As I passed my meager cubby on the way out, through the hazy light, I noticed the glint of my grandmother's wedding robe. I couldn't abandon it here, so I gathered the soft fabric in my hands and rejoined my grandmother and Limcona, who had just finished preparing breakfast. "I'm not worthy of it," I said, hoping I sounded meek.

Resting the robe over her arm, my grandmother nodded and let me take her place at the quinoa pot so I could serve the men. "You'll get it back one day."

One day. Such an abstract, indefinite concept.

How and when would we see each other next? Even though the King said he hadn't exiled me the night of my punishment, if I escaped, that was undoubtedly his next action. Because such an escape was so defiant, he'd probably even prevent my grandmother from visiting. My family and I would then be separated forever unless they managed to sneak away. To avoid letting those thoughts distract me, I concentrated on my impending swim as I thumped spoonfuls of plain quinoa into bowls for the men. It was perhaps a quarter of a mile from this shore to the reef. Where would Jenay be waiting exactly? I'd have to scan the sea and orient myself properly before plunging beneath the water.

Not long after, the men had their food, and Limcona, my grandmother, and I sat quietly on the porch and ate our breakfast. Limcona, probably intimidated in the presence of a former queen, didn't speak. Instead, she stirred her quinoa and pretended to be enthralled with its consistency, a process only interrupted when she took a bite.

"There's beauty in uncomplicated things," my grandmother said to break the silence.

I took a sip of coffee, building up my caffeine reserves for later. "There is."

"Speaking of simple beauty, isn't the sea such?" She nodded in the direction of the beach near the docks.

Simple? I laughed to myself and considered the sea's myriad complexities in the teeming life beneath it. And, of course, in how it was now my escape route and the passage to my own Lord of the Deep. "On the surface, perhaps, but I revel in its complexity," I countered.

She smiled, causing the wrinkles around her eyes to crease. "I agree that the things beneath the surface are the ones worth seeing," she continued cryptically. "You should think about that today when you visit the beach."

My grandmother was trying to tell me something. I knew it. But both Limcona and Uralin were within hearing distance, so she couldn't be blunt. Why did she want me to see beneath the ocean's surface? I'd only been able to do that with the mask, which remained hidden in Kimsimi's floor.

I almost dropped my spoon.

What if Kimsimi had given my grandmother the mask as well? She hadn't brought it with her, probably since Uralin would've found it and asked what it was for. Maybe my grandmother had hidden the mask somewhere. Would it aid me in my escape? Maybe if I had to evade someone by going underwater. More importantly, though, I realized that it was one of my grandmother's gifts that I could actually take with me.

I was about to ask Uralin if I could speak to my grandmother alone, when all of a sudden, he plopped his boiled egg in the middle of Limcona's bowl of quinoa. At first, my friend visibly recoiled at the strange gesture. But then she turned lobster red and mumbled a word of thanks before sliding the unexpected gift on her spoon for a dainty nibble. That was the most awkward act of courtship I'd ever witnessed. Uralin looked away in embarrassment as Limcona continued to focus on the egg. I didn't blame her for not offering me any. She'd been here longer than me and hungered more.

With them both distracted, I asked, "See beneath the surface of things? If only. I no longer have the means."

Her eyes sparkling, my grandmother knew that I understood. "The means to seeing the ocean's complexity lie buried near the palm tree closest to the dock."

She buried the mask before she got here, I realized. Ingenious woman. Still, though, I had to devise a way to retrieve it. "How far below the surface of things should I look for meaning?"

She sipped her coffee nonchalantly. "Scratching the surface should be enough."

By now, Limcona had finished the egg, and she stared at us with a perplexed look on her face. "Pardon me, but what are you two talking about?"

My grandmother gave her a patient smile. "Parables, dear. Leilani's repentance depends on her contemplating the Ethereal Queen's essence."

Limcona rolled her eyes. "There's always been way too much work to waste time *contemplating.*"

My grandmother stared at Limcona, pity dawning on her face. Maybe, at that moment, she regretted her earlier warnings to me about avoiding unnecessary contact with lower class people. Was this realization fueled by her abstinence from the sacred fruit? I didn't know.

"You poor thing," my grandmother said before turning to Uralin. "Young man, would you object if I brought these girls some fruit and honey?"

At the mention of honey, Limcona's eyes shone with excitement. "Please, Uralin?"

The guard stopped inhaling his quinoa and shrugged. "If the King approves."

Lady Samilla Ani had by now composed herself. "I'll work it out, girls. In any case, I think it's time you both got to work. Leilani, do you have what you need?"

I gave her a steady look. "Everything."

"Excellent." My grandmother, always the picture of elegance, stood up daintily, her wedding robe draped over her arm. "I'll take my leave, then. I predict I'll be summoned to court at some point today."

Her words struck fear in me. What would the King do after my escape, assuming I succeeded? I didn't want my family to suffer any consequences. Not even my annoying twin. This could also be my last time seeing my grandmother, but we couldn't risk a huge display of emotion that would reveal our plans. I simply said, "Give everyone my love."

"Of course," were her final words to me.

I almost stepped forward to tell her that I'd miss her, and I'm sure she wanted to wish me luck. But again, we had an unwelcome audience. And before I knew it, she'd vanished from the compound of criminals.

The day was very hot, and Uralin told me and Limcona that we'd be grinding mother of pearl, probably the powder for the Queen's robes and perhaps even Dirmisu's new finery. We could tell the hours passed as the sun traced along the palm trees, moving higher and higher into the sky. Even under the shaded pavilion, we wilted in the heat, and our sweaty hands were covered with layers of mother of pearl.

Come lunchtime, Limcona wiped her brow and called to Uralin. "I'm hot! Can we go in the ocean now?"

Thankfully, Uralin was left watching us while the sadistic Nimec patrolled the perimeter of the compound. He gave Limcona a friendly smile. "That sounds like fun."

I studied their interactions. It was now obvious that Uralin had romantic feelings for Limcona. Why else would he be polite to her while simultaneously acting gruff to Belsimi and me? He'd even given her his egg! I'm ashamed to say I wondered how I could exploit Uralin's affections so he could be distracted while I retrieved the mask. Standing up, I said to Limcona, "I'll get ready."

As soon as I entered our sleeping area, I lightened my step to the slightest pitter-patter so I wouldn't wake Belsimi. My friend still slept, splayed across her palette in such a way to minimize the pressure on her injured shoulder. Her deep, even breaths filled the room. Soon I'd be leaving her and Limcona alone here. Abandoning them, really.

Belsimi suddenly twitched on her palette. I held my breath and remained still as the mild wind's rustle threatened to awaken her. After what seemed like an eternity, she settled and resumed her deep, even breaths. Like the sleep of the dead.

I quietly glided into the bathing room, bound my hair extra tightly into a chignon with Jenay's necklace secured inside, and grabbed the piece of cotilk I used for drying myself. My tentative plan was to hide the mask under this small towel and then secure the mask's strap to the cotilk binding around my groin. This plan's success, however, depended on diverting Uralin's attention. Resolved, I left Belsimi to her fate and joined Uralin and Limcona outside.

It was time.

As the three of us walked toward the docks, the dark wood of the small pier was radiant in the white heat of noon. I kept moving one foot in front of the other, struggling to make a path through the sand. For every one step forward, the sand pushed me half a step back, it seemed. Limcona chattered about something beside me, but I could only hear the ocean's waves echoing the sound of surf roaring inside my head. And then I saw the palm tree my grandmother had been referring to. Suddenly, freedom became within my grasp. "Uralin," I said, pointing to the tree. "I think I see some fruit on the ground over there. Can I go get it?"

"That's fine," he replied absently as he focused on Limcona's shapely calves, which peeked out from the bottom of her sarong.

I wanted her to unwittingly distract the guard even more, so I whispered a suggestion. "You can lift your robe up a bit to get ready for the water."

She blushed. "Are you sure? With *him* right here?"

"I'm sure." To help convince her, I adjusted the knot of my sarong around my chest, thereby raising my hemline to just below my knees. My friend shrugged and began to do the same as I veered left towards the tree. Looking back, I confirmed that Uralin was staring at Limcona's legs as she redid her robe's knot.

Thankfully, I noticed a small depression of sand at the base of the tree, so I took my cotilk towel and dropped it over the spot. Then, making it look as if I were about to pick up the towel, I grasped the sand firmly to pick up whatever lay beneath.

The towel caught on something hard, displacing the sand that covered it.

The mask! It simply had to be. I used one hand to slide the mask under my robe, quickly looping the strap to the bands that wrapped around my groin. I got up slowly and felt the mask dangling next to my upper thighs, never happier than in that moment for our loose sarong robes and their ability to conceal.

As I walked back over to Limcona, empty towel in hand, Uralin frowned. "No fruit?"

I sighed in defeat. "A rock, unfortunately."

Limcona tried not to sound disappointed. "Oh, well. I guess we'll have to wait for Lady Samilla's fruit."

I pushed my concerns for Limcona aside and focused on the sea, which was much choppier than at the women's beach. That place, where Meguya had died, was a calm cove compared to here. The reef protected half of this area, too, but larger waves still made their way in through gaps in the coral shoals. Today, the wind also blew stronger than usual, augmenting the ocean's fierceness.

Was I up to the task? Well, if I wanted my freedom, it didn't really matter if I was ready. I had no choice. Shrugging off my fear, I moved forward, took off my sandals, and let the warm water caress my toe.

"Keep your clothes on," Uralin cautioned me, although I'm sure he wouldn't mind if Limcona threw her robe to the wind.

"Don't worry," I called back. "I'm just taking my shoes off."

Limcona followed suit, and we both stepped into the sea up to our knees, letting the water wash over us. I scanned the horizon, where Lady Moon and the Lord of the Deep have their nightly dalliance, and spotted a boat just beyond the reef! I couldn't see who piloted it, but I knew in my heart of hearts it was Jenay.

It was time.

I turned to Limcona. "Look in my satchel in the bathing room. Open up the cotilk pads."

She frowned in confusion, and before she could ask what I meant, I discreetly unhooked the diving mask when I was deep enough, removed my robe, and let the waves carry it where they may. Setting my sight on the boat, I oriented my body in its direction. I turned away from them forever, all of them, friend and foe alike, away from the world of sun and sand. Life is full of many difficult choices, and I was finally making the right one. I placed the mask on my eyes, happy it still fit securely, took a breath, and then plunged beneath the waves. My eyes became enveloped in the golden turquoise of the shallow seas at noon. I swam only a few feet beneath the waves, and even with the current working against me, I made it far on that first plunge.

When I needed air, I summitted and heard Uralin shout, "What are you doing?" and Limcona's devastated shout of, "Leilani!"

I was about to dive again, but a strong hand grabbed my right foot. Someone had me! Probably Uralin. I kicked furiously, enough to free myself and spray water everywhere. Right before I went underwater, I heard Uralin yell, "Whore!"

Thankful for the mask, I didn't dare look back. Only under and ahead.

Again beneath the sea, I noticed the slope of the seafloor, the beginnings of the reef, and the frantic dance of fish hunting and escaping one another. I kicked harder, trying to outpace my captors. I didn't know if Uralin could swim, but it didn't matter, for as the sea got deeper, the closer to freedom I came.

My lungs began to burn. Still, I stayed under the water until my body began to surface on its own. Gulping in a deep breath, I quickly focused on the boat ahead of me. It was closer than before, but I still had a way to swim, especially since the strong undertow kept dragging me back. I plunged beneath the water, kicked my legs, and let the warm sea water wash over me. Emboldened by Lady Moon, I became more tenacious than any current. I continued forward, kicking frantically so I moved toward the darker blue of the sea's depths.

And then the sea embraced me with its rhythms. I would surface, breathe in, plunge down, and watch the world become more sapphire with every stroke. Again, limbs burning, I kept repeating this pattern, lost in time, with one goal only in mind. The bright colors of the reef on the sea floor became bluer, which meant I was getting farther out to sea.

Then I'd surfaced once more.

When I was only a hundred yards from the boat, I stayed on the surface, hoping Jenay would come to my rescue if Uralin were in pursuit. I alternated breaths with strokes, moving closer and closer, thankful the boat wasn't being carried away by the current.

Finally, as my hand struck wood, my arms turned to rubber. Just as I was afraid I'd sink into my beloved sapphire sea, someone pulled me from the water. My body thumped into the boat. Hands, kind and calloused, stroked my face. "You did it!"

I opened my eyes, fluttering them against the white-hot sun, and saw Jenay hovering over me, his silhouette surrounded by a halo of golden rays "Jenay?" I asked weakly.

"Yes, my love," he said before leaning down to give me a kiss.

Velvet soft lips met my parched ones of salt.

At that moment, everything that was meant to be simply was.

CHAPTER SEVENTEEN

L ady Moon, help us. We burned all the maps of this area. Well, except
for one, which I've hidden from everyone, including Rekin and
Chanson. It's not like I think anyone would try to escape. We have
small fishing vessels that fisherfolk can use for a day, but those boats aren't
designed for crossing the ocean. If we ever need to leave the island, we'll
have to build a better boat. Until that day, we simmer in a delicious poison
of our own making. In the Treaty of Three, I've already made some
concessions by ignoring how Rekin treats women. We can't allow ourselves
to upset the balance, or our place of salvation will transform into a prison.
-The Journal of Samsara Ani

~~~

"That's so romantic!" Deanne gushed as she dabbed her moist eyes with
something she called a tissue. She'd returned from her meeting with the
captain in time to hear of my swim and escape. Not that I'd mind repeating
that part of the story.

Blushing, I glanced at the tired figure lying in bed next to me, recalling
what we'd endured getting here on this ship. Sacrifices, concessions, and
trust. "I agree."

"Love gives you the strength to do great things," Tomas added. "I'd swim
ten miles for my girl. I know she'd do the same."

It made me happy to hear that people in Deanne and Tomas's world valued love and commitment to others. Jenay and I could, I believed, flourish in such a climate if we decided to settle somewhere off the island. But everything has a price. Sometimes when you find something great it requires you to surrender something else.

"So what happened next?" Deanne asked.

***

Believe it or not, those moments on the boat after that kiss were the strangest and most tumultuous of my life. Being selected by the King, whipped for trumped-up charges of adultery, and threatened by my twin brother didn't compare to the pain of that moment. For, you see, I felt bliss with Jenay and from having my freedom, but I'd also just turned my back on my family forever. So, I did the only thing I could. There, in Jenay's embrace after his kiss, I inhaled his masculine scent, rested my forehead on his chest, and finally burst into tears.

I felt the muscles in his arms tense. His voice low and angry, he said, "Look what that bastard did to you." I then knew he saw the King's damage.

I pushed back and looked at him through my tears. "I'm crying because I've just left my family forever."

He averted his gaze. "I know."

Lady Moon, please don't let this change things, I begged. Feeling my confidence shatter, I asked, "Does this change anything?"

"What?" His look of confusion was replaced by horror. "Of course not! I just want to stab the man with a swordfish!"

Relief.

I felt blessed relief at Jenay's works, and I actually laughed at the mental image of Jenay, equipped with a swordfish, sparring with the King. I dried my exhausted tears. "Please don't do that. Poor fish! The important thing is I'm free now. So, thank you."

"You are," he said as he helped me sit on a seat at the ship's bow. "We're in neutral waters here beyond the reef, but we'd better leave."

Finally safe, I looked back towards the shore. I couldn't see Limcona or Uralin from this distance, just the dock, the beach's rock formations, and gatherings of statuesque palm trees. But I imagined Uralin's anger and humiliation at being tricked. He was probably screaming "whore" over and over. An adulterer. Whore. Defiler. All words assigned to me by my natal village. They were such malicious words in their intent, but I felt nothing but triumph and joy in the face of them. They meant freedom. I bore the marks of that freedom proudly, much like the King's lashes on my back.

I looked at Jenay. And our future. As he unfurled the sails and let the boat fly, the wind drowned out my past and cooled us in the hot sun. He controlled the ship's rudder while I sat at the bow, breathing in the salt air and watching a new side of the island, one from the vantage point of a dolphin or seabird, appear. Since it was my first time on a boat, I'd never before seen our home as an emerald in the midst of a sapphire. Out of the King's grasp, I reveled in the island's wild beauty. The sea breeze carried my reservations, fears, and guilt away, away to the ends of the earth I never thought I'd visit. I looked back at Jenay and shouted both to him and the unfettered wind, "It's beautiful!"

The docks of Gaiae were about two miles away from the Village of Lehom's docks, exactly on the other side of the island. The journey took about half an hour at our pace. Slowly, the beaches and settlement of Gaiae emerged from the island's lush foliage. I saw the sea huts of the village hovering near the edge of the island. These homes had been erected on stilts about ten feet above the water to allow the tidal waters to flow beneath, and all of them extended about thirty feet from shore and could be reached by a network of covered bridges that connected the shore buildings to the huts over the water. In addition to these fifty or so structures, Gaiae had homes built into the trees on shore. I watched this village grow larger as we got closer, not quite believing I was actually here. When you've been living in a nightmare, it takes courage to believe a dream's come true.

Finally, Jenay hopped from the boat and secured it to the dock. He held out his hand and helped me out of the boat. "We're home," he said, emphasizing that wonderful word. *Home.*

A familiar woman rushed up to meet us at the docks. "You made it!"

"Mimza?" I ran up to hug her. She appeared so different here in her element, much more relaxed than at the palace. "What are you doing here?"

She returned my embrace. "I'll let Jenay explain."

Jenay pulled me close and smiled at the older woman. "Mimza's my aunt."

Mimza was Jenay's *aunt*? Was that the reason she'd gone to such great lengths to help me? "Thank you," I said. "For everything."

She nodded. "I would've still helped anyone from your village, but let's just say that I had extra motivation to get you free."

"She's another friend, Leilani," Jenay said earnestly. "You might have left your family, but you're not alone."

Friends. Family. Such complicated words, tinged by obligation, happiness, and betrayal. And also confusion. I'd heard Jenay's words, "another friend." I felt the sun beat down on my skin and suddenly remembered my lack of clothes. I only had on the cotilk bands that covered my groin area and breasts! "I have nothing proper to wear..." I muttered as I tried to cover myself, quite unsuccessfully I should add, with my hands.

Mimza gave me an amused but patient look. "We're not worried about such things here. Anyway, I have some clothes for you at home."

"Home?" I asked, still embarrassed at my state of undress. Jenay and Mimza had both said the word, so it must've been true. I only owned a diving mask, the cotilk strips around my body, Jenay's necklace, and some tokens. But still, home? Could I trust the comforting feeling that word brought?

"With us," Mimza replied. "You're going to stay with us."

Drained from the day, I simply nodded and let myself be guided along by people I trusted. As we walked, I observed that women wore robes that came down to their knees instead of mid-calf or ankle. Some of the men secured their sarongs around their waists, and others wore the robes over their shoulders. And, despite my meager clothing, people smiled at me as I passed. People also engaged in actual physical contact with one another. I saw a man and woman walking with their hands knit together, and then I saw two women doing the same. I whispered to Mimza, "This place embraces what my village condemns. It's wonderful."

She followed my gaze. "Ah. Understood. Here in Gaiae, we don't punish people for being themselves. So long as they follow the quarantine and health laws, contribute, and don't hurt others, we live freely."

I took Jenay's hand in mine then, interlacing my fingers with his and smiling up at him. "I can do this now."

"And I can do this," he said as he brought his lips to mine again, kissing me longer than he had in the boat. How remarkable. He tasted of mango and sandalwood.

My bare feet relished the warmth of the sun-heated wooden planks of the oversea paths that connected the huts to one another and the mainland. We kept walking until we reached a sea hut with a covered porch that looked directly out onto the horizon.

My home with a view of a sea. Exactly what I'd dreamt of.

"Come in, please, " Mimza said, ushering me inside, where I found a daytime sea garden. The main central room had a vaulted ceiling, three lounge chairs, and a bed. The loosely-thatched bamboo walls were covered with cotilk, which permitted sea breezes and light to filter into the main space. Dried flowers, palm leaves, seashells, and sand dollars lined the walls.

A sea garden.

I spun around, closing my eyes and smiling as I inhaled the fresh air. I whispered to no one, "There's peace here." After a few moments, I stood still and looked around again, noticing two dividers on either side of the main space.

"My wife, Neina, and I have one room, and Jenay has the other," Mimza said. "He's volunteered to sleep here in the main room so you have a space to call your own."

"Thank you. Both." I pulled the bag with the tokens from between my breasts and held it out. "I can pay for my stay."

Mimza pushed the bag back to me. "No, Dear, you keep those. Don't worry about anything right now. Take things as they come. I suggest a shower and some fresh clothes to start." She then turned to Jenay. "Why don't you grab us all some food and drink."

I wanted something strong, something I'd always been forbidden, so I blurted out, "Palm wine?"

Jenay burst into laughter and bowed to me. "Palm wine for the lady it is."

"The shower's there." Mimza directed me to a partitioned area and slid back the door, revealing a bathing room much like the ones I was accustomed to. "In that chest are some robes and anything else you could need."

"How can I thank you?" I asked. My grandmother was the only person who'd shown me kindness without obligation. I wondered if everyone in Gaiae acted in this way.

"Be free. And care for my nephew as he cares for you."

"That I can promise," I replied because it was indeed a vow I could keep. It came from my heart. I only hoped that he cared for me as more than a friend.

What would we do now that the barriers between us had been removed? Freedom can be scary in its own way when you don't know what uncertainty will bring. Prisons have their limitations, but these limitations bring certainties. Too many questions were making my head hurt. "But first, you're right. A shower," I agreed.

Mimza left me alone in the bathing room. I inhaled the serenity of the space, the scent of the lavender mint soap, stored rainwater, and sunlight. As I closed my eyes and let the cool water run over me, the sounds of this new village poured in.

Laughter. They had actual laughter here, so I joined in quietly, dissolving into giggles somewhat like a person who's lost her mind. Maybe I had. I worried all of this was a dream, something I'd be cruelly awakened from.

But no. Those were cowardly thoughts. I had to believe there was some goodness in the world, so I anchored myself in this place through my senses. After I cleaned myself in my artificial rain, I simply stood there for a moment, letting my skin dry naturally. Mimza had even been kind enough to leave bamboo hairpins, so I helped myself to a few, found a dark purple robe in the chest, and availed myself of some cotilk pads. Thanks be to Lady Moon. Finally, I used a thin strip of cotilk that had been in my hair to string Jenay's gift around my neck like a proper necklace.

"Leilani," Mimza's voice called from the covered eating area. "We've got food."

How wonderful. My pitiful breakfast had done nothing to satisfy my needs, especially after that swim. I followed the scent of roasted chicken and came to the porch that hovered over the turquoise shallows.

"Palm wine as you requested," Jenay said as he handed me a glass containing a white cloudy liquid. "Just promise to eat the chicken and pineapple skewers, too."

Eagerly, I sniffed the palm wine and took a sip. Fire coursed down my tongue, causing me to slam down the glass. "Very strong!"

"You've never had this? Be careful," Mimza cautioned.

"I promise." I took another small sip and then devoured the chicken as I stared out at the sea. Who cares if I had slightly unladylike table manners? "Heavenly. I haven't had meat or fruit nearly all week."

Mimza and Jenay told me about village life while we ate. Unlike in the Village of Lehom, in addition to their primary jobs, everyone helped with the harvests when needed. Mimza herself was on the Central Authority, and her wife helped supervise the coconut and soya bean harvests, the agricultural commodities Gaiae controlled. Of course, I knew that Jenay sold clothing and worked as a bamboo architect, but I then discovered that his designs were respected all across the island, which is how he ended up building the Virtues' Annex. I also learned that Jenay had been living with his aunt since his parents died all those years ago. How little I knew about him, but how little that mattered to me right then.

By the time we finished the meal, I was pleasantly warmed by the palm wine. I could see how it could become a problem for some, much like the sacred fruit was in my village. I wouldn't miss that fruit's synthetic bliss because I found something better. Freedom. And love. Well, I hoped it was love. Why would Jenay have kissed me like that if he thought of me only as a friend? He'd also said the words, "my love" out loud.

Tracing my finger along the edge of the wine glass so it sang, I turned to Mimza. "Am I truly *free*?"

She hesitated for a few seconds before replying. "I *think* so. The King will certainly be upset, but the six Central Authority members from Gaiae and Central Village have already deliberated on this. You're not a criminal by our standards. The majority rules, so the King and his other two Authority representatives can't enforce their will. Technically speaking."

I didn't like the tone of those last two words. They spoke of ambiguity when laws should provide assurances. Noticing my wince, Jenay took my hand in his. "Don't worry. You're not going back. Ever."

I took another sip of palm wine with my free hand. "I know. I mean nothing to him."

Mimza stood up. "But Marit Simi doesn't like to lose. He'll come to the Central Authority tomorrow with some outlandish demands, which is why I have to go strategize with the other five *sane* Authority members today." Then, she gave us a conspiratorial wink before she left and said, "And, it's time you both talked."

After Mimza left, we sat side by side and simply took in the beauty of the world around us. Despite the wine and its glowing effect, I felt tongue-tied about what to say. Here I was, finally alone with Jenay, but words failed me as a sandcastle does against the incoming tide. But there in our silence, strangely enough, my real self came back to me. Out in the sea, I saw a glimpse of Elegance swimming through the shallows. I watched happily as she approached the deep sapphire water beyond the coral reef and faded into nothing. With Elegance forever lost in the abyss, the Leilani I knew returned. She appeared first as a glimmer of sunlight at the bottom of a tidal pool. This version of myself showed strength, persevering instead of snapping away at the thought of a cloud. She, no *I*, was free.

Jenay took a deep breath. "Don't worry that I have expectations."

At those words, my heart dropped. Had I been wrong about his feelings for me? Did he think of me as only a *friend?* "But what if I want you to have expectations?" I asked, trying to contain my fear.

His calloused, warm hand touched mine. "Don't worry. That's not what I meant. I have desires, yes, but no expectations. I only wanted to say I won't pressure you."

Well, that was a relief. My last bit of insecurity, of doubt, evaporated. I slapped his arm playfully. "Didn't I swim a quarter of a mile out to your boat? I assure you, desire, not pressure, compelled me."

Jenay joined in my laughter, his low and rumbling like a sunshower's mild thunder. "Well then, what *are* your desires?" he asked, tracing circles on my hand with his forefinger.

"Simple." I looked into his eyes. "To be a scribe again and be with you. What are yours?"

"Be with you, most definitely. Do you have any doubts after that kiss?"

I shook my head. "None now. Can I ask something of you?"

"Of course. Anything."

"I want to savor the quiet sea with you," I said, "savor the laughter of this place while in your arms. Can we just rest and simply *be?*"

Jenay sat back in his chair. "I'd like nothing more."

There was beauty in such simplicity. Jenay took my hand and led me to his room, the one I'd be sleeping in. When we got inside, he looked at me with the kindest expression I'd ever seen, making my legs and vital organs weak. Not the most romantic imagery, mind you, but that's how I felt then. Jenay stretched out on the bed and gestured for me to relax beside him. Although my heart raced then, raced at the prospect of being so close to him, I breathed in the blissfully warm, salt-tinged island air and let myself relax against his strong chest. He placed one arm over me and rested his hand on my hip. I closed my eyes and felt his warm, rhythmic exhales on the back of my neck. And I began to breathe in time with him, in tune to the soft waves that were slapping against the home's stilts, in concert to the wild parrots from the trees, all of which mirrored the joy and kindness that permeated everything here. Joy and kindness, things I'd never experienced in such unreserved quantities.

We spent that afternoon whispering of our pasts, about our motivations for waking in the mornings, and of our hopes for the future. Are such connections regularly forged from only a few meetings? Maybe such abandonment to another is reckless in some circumstances, but for us, it was natural, as natural as the island world around us. More beautiful and mysterious than the sea's unexplored depths.

CHAPTER EIGHTEEN

"The way you describe the island is poetic," Deanne observed.

I pushed my sheet aside and got up out of bed, walking to the porthole so I could gaze out at the sea. The inside of the ship was comfortable with its temperature controls, but at times, I felt stifled by its sterile environment. Deanne needed some plants to enliven the space. Surely, her patients would appreciate a touch of the outdoors. "Well, nature, to me, is poetry. Plants blowing in the wind and the ocean's waves have pulses, sometimes calm and other times chaotic."

The doctor laughed and joined me at the window. "I remember the Queen criticized you for comparing virtues to a chaotic ocean."

"Queen Veluya ignores unpleasantries until she's forced to confront them," I said. Then, I stopped and remembered that despite how much I liked talking about my own happy moments, I still had much of the story, the most painful parts by far, to go.

Deanne must have picked up on my change in mood because she asked me, in a sympathetic voice, "Do you need a break? I've pushed you enough for now."

I took a deep breath and bit my lip, hoping that action would keep my tears at bay. "The next part's difficult for me. I just want to get it done with. But I'll definitely need some time to gather my wits after."

***

The bad news arrived in the late morning, the day after I arrived in Gaiae, when I lay asleep in Jenay's arms, resting better than I ever had in my life.

We'd decided to share the same sleeping space because it felt utterly natural to us. After waking just after dawn in the Criminals' Compound, it was luxurious to sleep late. So, late I slept. That was, until a knock on the door, one that somehow seemed both frantic and tentative, interrupted our morning repose.

My eyes started open. We both sat up, still impaired by the remnants of sleep. Jenay, the gentleman that he is, got up and opened the door. On the other side was Mimza, her face stricken. Afraid of what I'd discover, I asked, "What's wrong?"

"Leilani," her voice faltered. "I have a note."

This seemed serious, so we followed her into the main room. I prayed the Authority hadn't decided to send me back. "W-what does it say?" I asked.

She didn't answer but instead handed me a weighty piece of paper, which was redolent of incense from the palace. News from the King couldn't be good. It was probably my official exile. I opened it and saw Irin's fluid script.

Leilani,

My hands shake with anger as I write this. How could you betray everything you've ever known? You're the evil Lillian Ani reincarnated. The King has, of course, exiled you. You should also know that Grandmother is dead. Come home now and submit to the King's authority, and he'll grant you mercy. You'll be allowed to attend the funeral. Not that you deserve it.

-Irin

The paper made no sound as it settled on the bamboo floor. The room began to sway, and I felt Jenay's arms steady me as he led me to a chair. "What does it say?" he asked.

I remained speechless for a moment, grasping for words that wouldn't come. Was this punishment for something? It couldn't have been. I didn't believe in Lehom or vengeful deities any longer. But still, I had the visceral feeling my grandmother's death was my fault. Somehow. I needed to find out what happened. As I closed my eyes, my grandmother's ghost came to visit me. Her smile reminded me of her wasted moments, like when she'd consumed too much fruit. This spirit, this thing that wasn't really her, remained suspended free from time, the only way it could visit me. For, as an exile, I could never attend her bones in the garden. I wanted to feel pain, then. A pain so hollow that it drowned all other emotions. A pain worthy to mourn her. But, only a numbness came during those seconds of quiet.

Eventually, my grandmother's ghost faded away, and I opened my eyes. Jenay had picked up the paper, and I could tell he'd read it from his stricken face. "I'm so sorry, Lei. What could've happened?"

Mimza came to my side and put her hand on my shoulder. "I'm sorry, too, for her death and because you can't go to the funeral. You'd be under the King's power again."

I'd known that, so I nodded in resignation. Irin hoped my need to say goodbye to our grandmother would make me sacrifice my new freedom, but he was wrong. She was dead, now. A corpse. Corpses don't really need anything from the living. It's the other way around. The living construct rituals around the dead to bring them peace.

"Can't the Authority demand she have the right to attend the funeral and still keep her freedom?" Jenay asked. I could hear the anger in his voice, the helplessness.

Mimza shook her head. "No, unfortunately not." Mimza hesitated a moment before continuing, something that told me more bad news lurked on the horizon. "The King's even demanding that you be punished for interfering in his village's business."

This statement roused me to clarity. "That's *ridiculous*. Jenay stayed beyond the reef, outside of the village's jurisdiction."

Mimza continued, "I know. And six Authority members believe this. Still, the King insists you both attend a meeting. Five days from now. He originally wanted one tonight, but the Authority's convinced him to wait until then. You need time to rest."

"And mourn my grandmother," I whispered, wondering how exactly to do it. Instead of genuine grief, I felt the anchor of my great grandfather's sunken ship pulling me down into the sea with it. Five days until this meeting? Under no circumstances would I be nearly ready to confront him.

But then I remembered Kimsimi's desire to postpone her wedding after Meguya's death. Traditionally, the Village of Lehom granted people a month of mourning upon request. Kimsimi hadn't gotten the full month for her aunt. However, my grandmother been the emissary's own daughter. As an exile, I couldn't make the demand for that mourning period myself, but my family and the villagers *would* certainly want the time to focus on my grandmother's memory instead of my antics. "Make it a month. Our traditional mourning period," I told Mimza, my voice firm. "If the King disagrees, remind him *he* should be leading the village in mourning my grandmother, a former queen and the daughter of Lehom's emissary. She was beloved."

"I can make that case," Mimza said before she left to speak on my behalf, an ability I had absolute confidence in.

Alone with Jenay again, I leaned back in the chair and pondered what a complex series of legacies I'd inherited. The Children of Lehom imposed upon me fear, isolation, and loss, but my grandmother gave me the courage to leave. It was thanks to her sacrifice, too, that I found a precious legacy, the symbolic Coeur that Samsara hid within a story. Irin also assigned me the mantle of Lillian Ani, the cursed one. But, if my interpretation of Samsara's journal was correct, Rekin's hate for his mother, along with the substances he was consuming at the time, is what created Lehom in his mind. Lehom is, therefore, Lillian's legacy, too.

The King's insistence upon a meeting puzzled me, though. Why did he care? Perhaps I'd become a legacy of shame for him, my escape proof of his fallibility. He could've left us alone and condemned us from his high place in the temple, but his own seed of shame propelled him forward on a course of destruction. People like King Marit will even sabotage their best interests if their actions sustain the illusion they have of themselves being divine and infallible. What are legacies but another's baggage that we willingly hoist upon our own shoulders? "I'm sorry for causing such a mess," I said.

Jenay gently took my hands and held them in his. "You didn't cause this mess. He did. And we'll beat him. Together."

"We will." I looked into my ally's eyes and smiled, knowing I'd made it outside of the castle and that Jenay wasn't a useless Laustic. We *would* beat him. Somehow. We didn't have any other choice.

In those horrible moments after receiving Irin's letter, I wished for some physical legacy to connect me to my grandmother. By leaving home and abandoning the Village of Lehom, I was forbidden from the Eternal Spirit Garden in this life or the next. The worry I'd never see her again polluted my heart, so I told myself that because Lehom or the Ethereal Queen weren't real, that any afterlife would allow me to see my grandmother when I died.

To soothe my shattered heart, I had to find some way to mourn my grandmother. In my home village, I would've attended a funeral service in the Ani Spirit Garden, sang as my grandmother was covered in dirt, and cried as the King passed around some fruit from our own garden. Partaking of fruit from our ancestral gardens is the way we consumed our ancestors into ourselves, their matter having gone to feed the fruit trees and then the fruit itself. When we wanted to communicate with them, we could eat the ancestral fruit along with the sacred fruit from the Eternal Spirit Garden behind the palace. That combination was supposed to enable us to see the dead, but I'd never had success.

Instead, Jenay took me to the village's cemetery, which was next to the Temple of Lady Moon and the Lord of the Deep. One carved bamboo marker stood out to me, that of my great-great Aunt Samsara. Using my grandmother's tokens, I purchased some fruit and incense from a vendor and placed them in front of Samsara's grave. Her body served as a conduit to that of my grandmother. That night, I laid down at my great-great-aunt's grave and finally cried for my grandmother, wondering if they were together in death.

***

By the time I concluded that painful section of the story, Deanne's mouth hung open in horror. "Shit. Bloody shit."

Although I didn't know what shit, or bloody shit, meant, they struck me as very unpleasant terms. They were apt terms, though, given how sad I felt at that moment. Heavy, stale air polluted the room, so I looked out the window again at the sea. I wanted to feel the fresh air on my face and smell the sea even if it meant leaving Jenay alone for a bit. "Will you take me outside?" I asked. My voice sounded far away from me. Hollow, almost.

"Of course." Deanne then pointed to the ceiling. "I have cameras installed up there. We can watch your husband on my phone and come back if he starts to wake up."

Frowning, I looked at the ceiling and tried to find the camera Deanne spoke of. The only camera I knew was the King's camera obscura, a large and almost unwieldy contraption. Obviously, I saw no such thing suspended above me, meaning the cameras in Deanne's world had to be smaller. She could explain how it worked later. Right then, I wanted comfort, and first from Jenay. I got out of my bed and walked to Jenay's, giving him the softest of kisses on his forehead so I wouldn't disturb the sleep he so desperately needed. I hadn't told Deanne, but he'd sacrificed his own needs on our little boat so I could rest more.

The doctor's eyes misted a bit as she witnessed my gesture of affection. "Follow me," she said as she grabbed her phone.

Part of me feared leaving the safety of the cocoon that held back the rest of the alien Old World, but that sea-scented fresh air tempted me, so I followed Deanne through the sickroom door and down a metal corridor. For a moment, I felt the walls pressing in on me. However, that feeling ceased as soon as she led me outside, where I had to squint against the blazing white light as my eyes adjusted to the sun.

Deanne stopped under a shaded area that had a collection of chairs. "Let's sit here on the deck."

I nodded and plopped myself down, grateful for the shade's relative coolness. From my vantage point, the sapphire waters glimmered under the sun. The salt air licked my face as a sudden breeze arose, and I inhaled the deepest breath I could and found a measure of sanity. A little piece of calm. The waves looked tranquil, and I felt safe perched up on the deck of this ship. Somewhere far away, my fellow islanders struggled with what to do next. They didn't know a friendly group of people had rescued me and Jenay and that help would arrive soon. Hopefully.

"Would you like one?" Deanne asked as she pulled a long skinny white stick out from her pocket and put it in her mouth. I didn't know what kind of food that was, so I watched in absolute befuddlement as she pressed a button on a red rectangle, an action that caused a flame to spring from it.

"What *is* that thing?" I asked.

Deanne drew a breath from the stick and blew out a stream of smoke. The wispy tendrils rose, only to be blown away by the ocean wind. "I forget, you don't know about cigarettes," the doctor said, chuckling. "It's noncarcinogenous tobacco. I find it helps when I want to forget my feelings."

Forgetting my woes was tempting, but I didn't want smoke near my face, especially not after Deanne coughed a few times with her next breath. Instead, I looked to the sea again. This time, a row of small boats caught my eye. They were strung up to some metal bars close to the edge of the ship. "What are those boats for?" I asked.

Deanne blew out some more smoke, this time in the shape of a ring. "In case the ship sinks and we need an escape."

"A good idea," I replied, thinking of the boat Jenay built for our own escape. My heart began to glow as my mind spun with pleasant thoughts of him and all the work he'd done to complete our little escape ship.

The doctor and I sat for a few more minutes in companionable silence, me staring at the undulating ocean waves and her finishing her noncarcinogenous cigarette, whatever that was. Finally, Deanne stood and threw her stick over the side of the ship. "Don't worry. They biodegrade," she explained when I frowned at that action. "Do you feel better? Ready to go inside and tell me about why you built your own escape pod?"

If pod meant ship, then yes. More than anything, too, I wanted to sit at Jenay's side. "Yes. I'd also like some more bourbon if you have some."

CHAPTER NINETEEN

S ince peace must be maintained at all costs, each village shall set its own rules for governing, but no village may impose its laws on another or deprive its citizens of life, food, or shelter. The Central Authority will settle all differences of interpretation of laws. Their word is final.

-Excerpt from *The Treaty of Three*

~~~

The King's self-destructive tenacity is why Jenay and I feared him the most. Even when both of us were in Gaiae, far from his world of sun and sand, an undercurrent of anxiety plagued me. What would happen at our meeting with the Central Authority? It's funny how nature fostered my sense of reality and also determined it. Boons can be curses and vice versa. After all, the sea gave me my freedom but also formed a boundary since it surrounded the island and kept us here. That anxiety was the genesis of our curious boat.

Five mornings after arriving at Gaiae, while laying by my side, Jenay suddenly sat up and whispered to me. "We need a contingency plan if things don't go our way."

I'd been half asleep and relishing his presence near me. His body felt like my own second skin, an integral part of me that I couldn't imagine being without. Jenay was my *sine qua non*, as an ancient people I'd read about used to say. It roughly translates to "that which I cannot live without." I'd felt his quick, jarring movement, so I turned on my back and looked up at him. "What do you mean?"

His face was rendered violet by purple light from the window as he bowed his head down to kiss my forehead. "In case we have to leave."

I'd just gotten there, though. Was he thinking of coming to the Village of Lehom with me if I got sent back? "Leave *Gaiae?*" I asked incredulously.

"No," he whispered. "The *island*."

My first reaction was disbelief, and I almost burst out laughing at what I thought was a joke. But Jenay's serious expression convinced me otherwise. "Where would we go?"

He sighed and laid back on the bed. "That's the problem. There really isn't anywhere for us *to* go, but anything's better than being separated."

"Separated? No. It'll all be fine," I assured him as I nestled myself in the crook of his arm. I couldn't even entertain the idea of living without him.

"I love your optimism," he replied. "But I still think a contingency plan is a good idea."

I realized then, from both his words and his tense muscles, that he felt the same anxiety I did. I didn't see the point in planning something as impossible as leaving the island, but I played along anyway. "What we'd need first is a boat, obviously. Would the one you rescued me in work?"

"No. The island's boats are for short-range travel. They'd capsize." Jenay twisted his fingers through my hair. "I need to build one that's good on the open seas. I'm just not sure how."

I thought for a moment, wondering what I could do to help. Did we have any helpful books in the library? I'd resumed my job there not two days ago. Then I remembered Lucina's book on Viking ships. Didn't she say these ancient people had sailed across the world in their boats? Excited, I said, "Vikings! Their boats crossed the sea. Does that help?"

"Yes," Jenay replied. "If the book has a design, I might be able to replicate it."

I still hoped we wouldn't need such a ship, but I made a promise I could keep. "Then I'll memorize it."

He bent down to kiss me. "We'll also need provisions, dried meat and fruit, some coconuts, and drinking water."

"My grandmother's tokens can help buy them." I returned his affection with a deep snuggle. We rested there together for a few moments with only the birdsong to soothe our anxieties about the immense risks in this plan. But then I began to wonder. We'd solved some problems, but not all. How, exactly, would we conceal our preparations? Escaping the island was punishable by death, after all. "We can't let people know. Where do we hide everything?"

"Oh, don't worry," Jenay whispered. "I have a place." When I looked up at him in confusion, he explained, "There's a cave near the Gaiae beach that's rarely used. It's safe. No one goes there."

We remained quiet, then, entwined with on one another in the damp, sea-fragrant mornings. With a place to hide our contingency boat, I felt better for a moment but then imagined us drifting aimlessly in that hot blue expanse with nothing surrounding us. "How would we know where to go?"

"That part, I don't know. We all learned how to navigate in case the currents carry us out to sea, but where to navigate to is the question," he said. I could hear the beginning of defeat in his voice.

As much as I doubted we'd need to enact this plan, I also hated seeing him feel so resigned. "I'll see if there are any maps left," I offered. "But what about the Pestilence?"

The uncertainties about the Old World hovered around us. I felt Jenay shrug. "We *think*. But we really don't know. I honestly think people have rebuilt and repopulated."

We *think*. How I hated this uncertainty. But, at this point, everything was still merely a contingency, and Jenay was right. It would be better to leave than be separated. That we both agreed on. There's only one way off an island. By sea. "The meeting's just over three weeks away."

"That's enough time to build a boat. With Baril's help." He sounded so sure of his craft that I trusted him. And Baril, of course, who'd helped us once before by distracting the King.

That morning at breakfast with Mimza and Neina, Jenay and I tried not to make them suspicious of our plans. Jenay and I next went to work as we normally did, him to the clothing kiosk and me to the library, my tokens split between the two of us. I was still getting used to all of the physical affection permitted between people here. A passionate kiss on the lips? No one batted an eye or threatened eternal damnation. People could love who they wanted freely. How thrilling a thing to witness. Despite my happiness in Gaiae, the Village of Lehom still left its marks on me, literally and figuratively. I missed my grandmother greatly. I also hadn't forgotten the promise I'd made to myself that I'd help Belsimi and Limcona from afar. Somehow.

At the library that morning, I asked Lucina for the book on Viking ships. At first, I worried the nervousness in my voice would betray me. I needn't have been, though. She looked so happy to have me back that she let me pick the first book I wanted to copy without hesitation.

Viking ships it was.

As I sat in the sunlit library, inhaling the scent of island-made paper, I perused the book for the most seaworthy vessel. Not that I knew how to distinguish that characteristic, but I did have a good memory, so hopefully that would suffice for an effective contingency boat. I flipped through the pages, and a ship type called a *knarr* jumped out at me. The book's author said this boat could travel on the open seas and that it would be fast with sails, so I memorized the words I saw. *Clinker-built planks, metal fastenings, wide hull, solid beam.* Would Jenay be able to build this out of bamboo, the most plentiful wood we had? Could he use wooden fastenings given the paucity of metal on the island?

I was so focused on the book that I didn't hear Lucina approach. When she placed her hand on my shoulder and said, "I have a surprise for you," I nearly jumped.

"A good surprise, I hope," I replied.

She gave me a strange look and laughed. "Well, of course. What other kind is there? You have some visitors. Follow me. By the way, do you plan on copying that text sometime today?"

My lying lips said, "I want to see if I can recreate the images, too. These words lose meaning without the pictures."

"That's true. Practice drawing before you use the good manuscript paper. See how you do."

She's just given me explicit permission to diagram the boat. How easy that had been! I followed Lucina to one of the manuscript storage rooms, a private place with only clerestory windows. As I saw two people standing in the privacy of the back of the room, I knew why she'd brought me here.

The surprise was perfect.

And completely unexpected, for it was Kimsimi and Gisnen.

"What are you doing here?" I asked in disbelief, pulling my little brother into a hug.

As I released him, he straightened his back proudly. "I escorted Kimsimi here. Irin said I was old enough."

What? Hadn't my twin called me the evil reincarnation of Lillian Ani? Baffled, I asked Kimsimi, "*Irin* let you visit me?"

Kimsimi looked away and blushed. "Not quite. I said we needed spices from the Central Market."

Lucina had chosen our meeting place within this building well. If Irin found out, Kimsimi would be in trouble. Gisnen, too, for chaperoning her. "You lied to him?" I asked. "Why risk the consequences?"

"To bring you these." Kimsimi held out the satchel she'd been carrying, one that I recognized as my grandmother's.

I grabbed that precious object and looked inside, only to find Samsara's journal with its careworn cover, my grandmother's gold bracelet, and her wedding robe. Those gifts blurred as tears filled my eyes. "Thank you, Kimsimi," I managed to choke out. "How did it happen?"

"The night you went missing, my mother found her body in the temple, resting in front of the Ethereal Queen's statue."

The location was suspicious, but so were the lack of details Kimsimi supplied me with. "But *how*?" I had to know. I *had* to. Was it my fault?

"The doctor says from old age. There wasn't a mark on her," Kimsimi replied. Something about her tone, though, also in the way she couldn't look at me in the eye right then, made me suspect she didn't believe that. I needed to believe my grandmother died from old age. The horrible alternative was that my escape precipitated her death.

And with that, Gisnen, who'd been so proud of himself a few seconds before, lost his pride and began crying. "I miss Grandmother. And you, too."

"I know." I pulled him into another hug, realizing that he somehow seemed taller since I left the village. Tears gathered in my own eyes. "But you know I can't come back."

Gisnen shook free and stared at the floor. "It's the *King's* fault."

Kimsimi placed her hand on his shoulder and used her other to tilt his face back up by his chin. "I think it is," she said lovingly. "But that's why we're here. To do something good to make up for his actions."

At these words, Gisnen dried his tears and nodded. My heart swelled with pride for my little brother, that rambunctious, gangly mess of heart and compassion. "We're stopping by the Central Authority on the way home," he said. "To give them a message."

"What message?" I asked.

Gisnen stayed quiet, and Kimsimi patted his shoulder. "Remember, be brave."

"I saw th-he King leave the beach right before Grandmother and Lady Nereno found Meguya there," he spat out.

What? Had I heard him right? "Why were you near the women's beach?"

The poor boy blushed and almost burst into tears again, so Kimsimi stepped in for him. "He was in love with Meguya and wanted to see her bathe."

I looked at him intently, my heart thumping in my ears. If the King had hurt Meguya, it was likely he'd done something to Grandmother, too. "Gisnen. Did you see him hurt Meguya?"

Tears tracked down his cheeks. "Not exactly. I saw the King follow Meguya and then leave the beach without her. I stayed there waiting, and then Grandmother and Nereno went down there. They started screaming next."

My eyes wide open with horror, I turned to Kimsimi. "He hurt Meguya!"

She shook her head in disgust. "It makes sense. My father looked at her funny, just as he's doing with Obedience and Resourcefulness now." Kimsimi reached into her bosoms and pulled out a note. "Obedience gave me this before I left."

I opened it and immediately recognized Dirmisu's handwriting. *I'm sorry. I've told Kimsimi the truth about what the King's doing.*

The final kernel of hate I'd reserved for Dirmisu evaporated just then. My former best friend was awkwardly poised between a lustful king and his jealous, insecure queen, in a place without refuge. The note continued, *I've written a testimony that Gisnen and Kimsimi can give to the Central Authority. In it, I tell them it was my fault you were caught. This is the favor I'd never thought I'd have the chance to give you. Please forgive me. - Dirmisu.*

She did repay my favor, more than she knew. I felt no joy at having been right, for any triumph would be a pyrrhic victory. Dirmisu was in a worse position than I had been as a criminal. "Does Irin know about all this?" I asked.

"No," Kimsimi whispered as she looked down in shame.

I admired her bravery, defying her new husband and therefore going against everything she'd been taught a wife ought to do. I hugged her. "Thank you. I know it was hard for you."

I felt her muffled tears on my shoulder. "I love Irin. Really. But I couldn't do nothing, not when my father possibly killed two people! Doing good is how to emulate the Ethereal Queen."

We stayed in that position for a few moments before Gisnen said, "We'd better go. First to the Authority and then to get the spices."

I released Kimsimi and watched as she rubbed the tears from her face, thereby streaking her makeup. "You should wash your face before Irin gets suspicious." I reached into a pocket and pulled out two tokens. "Buy some more cosmetics and apply them here in Central Village. And get a new satchel. Say the old one broke. Don't let Irin catch you in a lie."

"I'll do that," she agreed. "For all the good it'll do. He'll probably find out everything when the Authority confronts the King. The whole village is talking about how he wants to drag you back there in chains."

This image was so ridiculous that it made me burst into laughter. But then again, his dramatic threats probably meant he was desperate and, therefore, dangerous. "Chains? We don't even have the metal to make..."

"Kimsimi," Gisnen interrupted, looking nervously toward the door. "We have to go."

With all the subterfuge left to pull off that afternoon, they did have to leave.

Quickly.

Even though I couldn't bear to see them go, I pulled each of them into one more embrace and wished them off, grateful for the tangible reminders of my grandmother they'd gifted me. I put the bracelet on immediately, cherishing how elegant it felt against my wrist as it scattered gold light throughout the room. I sat on the floor for a moment, the satchel by my side, trying to absorb Gisnen and Kimsimi's news. The King most likely killed not only my grandmother but also Meguya. I shuddered as I thought about how he'd hurt her, pushed her head against the rock in that tidal pool.

A sinking feeling perturbed me, much like after my and Meguya's parents died. *He'd* been the one to give them permission to use the boat, and they'd all drowned. I had no proof of anything, but the shadow of far too many accidents followed this King. The King's madness was yet another reason Jenay and I needed an escape plan. My heart pounding in my chest and echoing in my ears, I returned to my copying room, where I practiced recreating a beautiful work of deception in the form of a charcoal contingency boat. I secured the best attempt into the cotilk bindings near my breasts, leaving the other copies as proof I'd been working all day. On the way home, I used the tokens to buy dried fruits for our contingency journey, so all in all, it was a productive day of deceit.

When I returned home with my provisions, the house was thankfully quiet. I sat down on our bed and perused the journal once more, focusing on the entry Samsara had written just before her death. I'd read these words before, but who knew what they could yield on second glance. *I hope Samilla remembers the story of the Lady in the Tower. I want her to find the map to Coeur, which means heart, if she ever needs to. Please, Lady Moon, don't let her end up like the nightingale.*

I stared at the words, hoping their meaning would unfurl itself before my eyes. *What* map to Coeur? Did this place have both literal and metaphorical meaning? After all, the Lady in the story found a physical map hidden in the binding of the book. I recalled an earlier entry of Samsara's, one where she said she burned all the maps save for one, which she'd hidden somewhere.

A thought struck me, as quickly and powerfully as lighting does the sea during a storm. Was there something in *this* book's binding, too? In the privacy of our room, I used Mimza's sewing scissors to snip away the corner of the binding on the front cover. Then, I carefully reached down inside, where the durable paper met the wood frame.

Nothing. I was probably ruining this journal for nothing, I thought.

Still, it couldn't hurt to check the other side. I made a similar incision on the back cover, and something on the inside caught on my finger.

Paper. I felt folded paper inside the binding! In the quiet space of late afternoon, I pulled out a piece of paper yellowed by age. I stared at it for a moment and finally got the courage, with trembling fingers, to open it up. Across a great expanse of blue were a series of brown dots of uniform size with coordinates.

Islands.

There were also land masses, rendered as larger dots, on the other side of the ocean. Continents. Names. Forbidden places of the Old World. Including the word *Calabasas* on the coast of a large country or continent. Samsara Ani had hidden the final map inside her journal! The last thing we needed to execute our escape plan! I wondered if Jenay and I should head to Calabasas. Only that specific place-name meant something to me. The impossible was becoming possible, and it made me giddy. I secured the map back inside the binding and hid the journal and the sketch of the boat in a wooden box with my name carved on the top, a present from Jenay. The foodstuff went into the chest we used to hold our clothing.

The setting sun cast the room in golden red, so it was time for me to get the family's dinner ready for the night. I'd begged to do the cooking, having been deprived of it at the Ani home. Amusingly at first, Mimza told me I didn't have to take on that domestic task so long as I contributed somehow, but I assured her that cooking would make me happy. I gathered turmeric, coconut milk, spicy pepper, lemongrass, soya beans, and lime juice and took them to one of the cooking houses near the shore. These cooking areas also came furnished with an assortment of fruits and vegetables that people could select from for their daily meals.

One other person was at the solar stone, a woman of about my age. She smiled as I approached the unused section and asked, "How're you adjusting?"

"Well, I think," I replied as I boiled the coconut milk and added the spices. After my swim and arrival here, everyone knew my name, but I had no idea who most people were. "I never got to cook in my old village. Well, not officially anyway."

This earned me a curious look, but then noticing my embarrassment, she gave me a patient smile. "I'm Amathy."

I returned her smile as I added some sliced peppers and mango chunks to the soup. "It's nice to meet you."

After a few moments of companionable silence, Amathy asked, "So what job have you selected for your work quota?"

"I'm a scribe in the Central Village Library. What's yours?"

The quinoa cakes she was frying sizzled on the solar stone. "I have two. I sew garments, and I'm also a watcher for part of the day."

Again, I was at a loss about the particularities of life here. "What do you watch?"

She laughed at that. "The water, of course. What else?"

"But the waves are always moving," I said, nodding toward the ocean.

"The *waves*?" Amathy looked perplexed, but then her eyes grew as wide as her cakes. "You honestly don't know, do you?"

How wonderful. Another thing I didn't understand, which made me feel rather like a parrot out of its tree. "No," I replied.

"Watchers monitor the water near the seismoscope for distant earthquakes," she explained, frowning. "The Village of Lehom is supposed to have one, too."

How I hated the mention of earthquakes, alleged signs from Lehom, the false god who'd caused me so much pain in life. I stirred the soup. "I understand what earthquakes are, but distant ones can't hurt us."

"Well, if they happen in the sea, they could cause a tsunami, a massive wave."

Her words triggered a memory in me of a historical book I'd once copied. And something my grandmother said about the mountain ledges overlooking our village and the ocean. They were to escape from the ocean! A long time ago, a wave engulfed the eastern side of an island nation after a bad earthquake. Many people died as a result. I had no idea, however, where our island home was in relation to that unfortunate one. A vision of a wave sweeping across the island made me shiver even in the humid tropical heat. "The only place to go is up the mountain path."

"Exactly. The original three Ani siblings had each village clear paths up the mountain to higher ground."

"How horrifying..." my voice trailed off. Why hadn't the King appointed a watcher? The previous King, too? In his sermons, King Marit said Lehom spoke to kings through earthquakes, but we hadn't had any such disturbances in the earth here. Had they been happening elsewhere?

Well, none that we could detect without a seismoscope.

Amathy had by now finished frying her cakes, so she gathered them onto a plate. "I know it's a scary thought, but that's why we have the seismoscope and the watchers."

Preparing. For contingencies. That's what Jenay and I were doing with our boat. I'd rather be prepared than foolish, something that was different from the people I'd grown up with. Why prepare when you've submitted your future to blind faith?

"Thank you, Amathy," I replied, very grateful for this new knowledge.

"It was nice meeting you," she said as she left with her delicious-smelling cakes.

I watched the soup and its ingredients boil, and when I felt it was done, I took the pot off the solar stone, added some lime juice, and let the mixture cool. We'd be trapped if such a wave came. Were our mountain ledges high enough to escape them? Could we get to higher ground in time? I looked up at the mountain and its escape paths and was grateful for their presence. But how useless those paths were in the Village of Lehom with no advanced warning system.

After the soup cooled, I carried the pot of soup back to our outside eating area, which today overlooked a placid sea. Neina arrived first, and she came over to look inside the pot. "This looks delicious. Thanks for making it."

I began portioning the soup into four bowls. "It was my pleasure."

Neina sniffed it and grinned. "Palm wine would go rather nicely with it, right?"

I greatly appreciated Neina's candor and her practicality. Right then, palm wine served a purpose, that of instilling a temporary, occasional numbness that I greeted happily. "Yes, please. The King never let us have it because he said it was intoxicating."

"It is," Neina admitted. "But it's fine in small quantities. That sacred fruit he had you eat was worse."

I remembered the entry from Samara's journal. "A drug."

Neina nodded. "If taken for too long, for too many years, it makes people forget things. It's probably why your grandmother had her dreamy moments."

"That explains her two faces," I said, suddenly remembering how much of it I'd consumed. "Will I have those forgetful moments, too?"

"Not you. That only happens from prolonged, consistent use."

"Our queens and virtues," I whispered. They thought they stared into eternity, but it was all an illusion.

"And they don't even know it." Neina's voice that held pity, thankfully not in reference to me. "Anyway, I'll fetch the wine."

After Neina left to get some blessed intoxicants, I felt a sadness for the death of eternity I'd held growing up. Was there even an afterlife for my grandmother to dwell in? The people of Gaiae believed that everyone goes to a heavenly place under the sea upon their death. As I stared out at the ocean, at its beautiful undulating waves and its expansiveness, I felt a sense of eternity and connectedness, like the one that emerged from within when I looked at the moon. There really wasn't a need for the sacred fruit because bliss was all around us. I'd found it in Jenay's arms, in my work as a scribe, and by communing with the natural world.

Feeling a soft hand upon my shoulder, I turned around to see Jenay smiling at me. He leaned down to give me a kiss. "Hello, beautiful. That smells wonderful."

I returned his kiss, and he wrapped his hands around my waist and pull me closer. "I have good news," I whispered into his ear, into the safe cushion of our embrace. "Gisnen and Kimsimi came to see me at the library today, and they brought me my grandmother's things. Samsara hid a map inside her journal."

He let out a low laugh, pulling me even closer so that my hip bones hit his thigh. "Well done. You've certainly solved a big problem today."

I leaned into his chest and inhaled his sandalwood scent. "That's not all. I found a boat that might work. The sketch is hidden in your room."

"*Our* room," he corrected, kissing my head. "For my part, I gathered some wood and tools and hid them inside the cave."

The location of these caves was still a mystery to me, as we hadn't had time to venture there together. "Are you sure we won't be discovered?"

"Don't worry," he assured me. "The caves are inaccessible when the tide comes in, and I'm the only one who goes there."

Neina came returned with a bottle of palm wine, and she poured a generous portion for each of us just as Mimza stepped onto the porch, her face grim.

Jenay's aunt raised her eyebrow at the wine portions. "You know me well, Neina. It's been a long day."

"Then let's sit down and have a sip. It would also be a shame to let Leilani's food go to waste," Neina offered.

As Jenay and I faced the sea, which glowed red and purple behind the clouds of the setting sun, Mimza savored her first spoon of soup. "Leilani, this is amazing. Thank you."

Strangely, though, her voice sounded dull, and she seemed preoccupied. Jenay picked up on it, too. He'd been quiet since we sat down. "What's wrong, Aunt Mimz?" he asked.

"The Central Authority agrees with both of you, but King Marit made an argument today," she began.

I'd been about to take another spoonful of soup but instead settled the spoon in the bowl before I dropped it. We all stared at her, waiting for what came next.

"He's suggesting that Leilani isn't an official resident of Gaiae and therefore our protections don't apply to her," Mimza said.

Jenay's face darkened. Like me, I felt his enthusiasm about my discovery of the map depart with the vanishing daylight. For the first time, Mimza seemed genuinely worried. And that made us worried. "That's ridiculous!" Jenay said through clenched teeth.

"I know, but the *Treaty of Three* is unclear," Mimza replied. "As I mentioned, the Central Authority agrees with you, but the King is exploiting its vagueness and arguing over what constitutes a resident of a village. He's demanding a vote at the upcoming meeting. There's no way he can get a majority and succeed, but we still need to squash his argument so he doesn't try to make trouble. That's the best way out of this."

Neina refilled our glasses with more wine. "Oh, Lady Moon preserve us! The Treaty didn't need to be so specific! Our ancestors had just escaped a pandemic. They needed to build a new civilization, not argue over trivialities."

Studying everyone's worried faces, I asked, "Is there anything I can do to become an official resident of Gaiae? Doing that seems like the best way to counter the King's argument."

"The Central Authority agrees there is one definite way." Mimza took a long sip of wine and closed her eyes for a moment, thinking before she casually said the words, "You and Jenay could get married."

CHAPTER TWENTY

*I*n the time before time, under a lacuna of silence, a haze of nothingness *separated the skies from the sea. The Lord of the Deep, lonely in his vast oceans, looked up at Lady Moon and sang to her, asking if she'd shine her light on his seas to make them vibrant and happy. She thrust her rays through the void that separated them. This made Lord of the Deep merry. He noticed that her forces changed the rhythms of his waters, and at the same time, the surface of his realm gave her a beautiful canvas on which to display herself. Such it was that the Lord of the Deep became wed to Lady Moon. The humans of the Earth may come together similarly, one entwined to the other. Look out at the sea and up to the night sky for your answers.*

-Gaiae folktale

~~~

"So, you got married to become a resident of Gaiae?" Deanne asked, spraying crumbs on her lap. She'd been sitting on the edge of her chair, eating a snack called crackers that crunched when she bit them. Embarrassed, she swept them right off her lap.

I was about to answer, but a beautiful, dear voice spoke up first. "We got married because we wanted to."

Oh, how I'd missed the timber of his voice. He'd been asleep for fall too long. With tears in my eyes, I spun my head left only to see the figure in the opposite bed sitting up, his eyes scrunched at the light pouring in through the porthole.

Everything was right at that moment. Everything and more.

Jenay had woken up!

I got up from my bed and threw myself against him. He smelled faintly of sandalwood, but mostly of the sea, salt, and the citrus-scented antiseptic that Deanne had decontaminated her ship with. "I'm so happy you're awake," I said. "You'll get to taste frozen water. The pestilence is gone. They found a cure."

"Whoa, Darling," he laughed into my hair, his voice hoarse like mine had been upon waking. "One thing at a time. That frozen water first, please?"

Water. He needed water. Of course he was parched. I knew that thirst, that sandy throat, that deep longing for water. I reluctantly pulled myself out of his embrace and settled beside him on the bed.

"You're the infamous Jenay…" Deanne said, handing him a glass of water.

Nodding, Jenay quickly drained the glass, probably savoring its coolness as I had done. "And you're one of our rescuers?" he asked. How calm he was despite our strange surroundings.

Deanne nodded. "I'm the ship's doctor, Deanne Ambagu."

"Deanne. Thank you." My husband looked around and shook his head. "A ship, you say? It's much larger than I thought possible. Amazing."

"I'll give you a tour later. As a reward for not threatening to kill me like Leilani did when she woke up," Deanne deadpanned.

My husband burst into laughter. "You did what, Lei?"

It felt so good to hear him laugh, too. It was a balm to my soul, especially since we still had part of the story to go, another unhappy part. And, *Lei*. I loved when he called me that. So simple, so endearing, and without my family's baggage. He brought me joy, causing me to laugh as well. "To be fair, she was wearing a scary yellow costume when I met her. I panicked and threatened to kill what I thought was a monster. How can you be so calm?"

"Well, I've actually been awake for a bit. Listening. To see if everything was okay," Jenay confessed. "I figured you wouldn't be calmly telling our story if we were in danger.

Deanne nodded with approval. "Quite right. Leilani's also given me details about the island so we, or someone else, can find it to give your people some supplies."

My husband sighed with relief at that news. "Thank you for that. They need them."

"I am curious. Do you plan on returning to the island with the supplies, or do you want to settle somewhere?" Deanne asked. "Leilani said you were heading for Calabasas."

I looked my husband in the eyes. What a complex question, one we'd discussed in great depth to pass the time our boat floated idly on the still sea. We missed the island, true enough. However, some very unsavory people still lived there. And every time I thought about my home, a sharp pain seared through my heart because of my grandmother's death in that place. Jenay took my hand in his and gave it a gentle squeeze. With that tiniest of gestures, I knew his answer.

"We'd like to settle somewhere, but not Calabasas. We have no real connection there," I finally said. "Are there any places that would take us?"

The doctor smiled. "Well, my home, an island called Virgin Gorda would. I can help you find a place to stay."

Jenay kissed my cheek. "I like that idea. Home's with you, Lei."

Home. I'd heard that word once before when Jenay brought me to Gaiae, to our sea garden with Mimza and Neina. How would this place be different? Could we belong in a world so foreign? Then again, if we were together, any place would do. "Yes, home is you."

My husband pulled away for a second and looked me up and down, again laughing. "Well, now that our future's secure, tell me, love, *what* are you wearing? You look great, mind you, but very different."

Ah, yes. Pants and a hoodie. "Old World clothes. You might get some too, considering the doctor took ours."

Jenay frowned and then lifted his blanket, blushing as he looked at Deanne, who nodded in confirmation. He cleared his throat. "Well, then."

Containing her amusement, Deanne walked over to the cabinet where she'd gotten my clothing and returned with a similar outfit for Jenay. "I'll give you two a minute if you promise to continue the story when I get back."

As soon as Deanne shut the door behind her, Jenay threw back his blanket and rose from the bed. I appreciated the visage before me as he picked up the clothes and studied them for a moment, looking at how I wore mine before he put on the hoodie and pants himself. He shook his head in wonderment. "So many new things."

Although I was used to seeing him bare-chested, I admired how the top garment still clung to his visible musculature. I got closer to him and ran my hands over his shoulders, then moving in closer to kiss his cheek, merely an inch from his lip. "Yes, new things. New things can be good."

He tilted his head so his lips met mine, and I felt the familiar stir of desire drawing me closer towards him and his sandalwood scent. He gently pulled back. "Later, my love. Let's not keep the doctor waiting. We owe her."

I nestled into his chest, laughing. "Yes, I suppose she *did* save our lives."

Jenay held me for a moment longer before settling back onto his bed. I sat beside him and called to Deanne, "You can come back in now!"

The door opened quickly, and a sheepish Deanne reemerged with a sandwich in hand, which she handed to Jenay. "And what happened next?"

I decided to continue the story so Jenay could eat. "As he said, we decided to get married because we wanted to, but at first, Mimza's words stunned us both into silence."

***

Sometimes the event you fear the most ends up being the best option out of many. I'm not talking about getting married here, but the upcoming meeting with the Central Authority where we'd confront the King. It was perhaps the impetus for our decision, and I suppose this impetus helped us get over our fears. Jenay was nervous he'd scare me with a quick proposal while I was afraid he'd regret his decision because I brought him so many complexities. But, while time and space compressed our options, this compression also gave us clarity.

"Married?" I asked, looking back and forth from Mimza's calm expression to Jenay's quiet one. "I couldn't ask him to do that."

Her voice remained steady. "Yes, you can. If you think it's too big a commitment, then think of it as merely a formality. You'd gain official residency in Gaiae, which would sabotage one of the King's arguments."

"It won't be a formality to me," Jenay said, looking directly into my eyes. "I can say I'm sure of this. What about you?"

It wasn't just a formality.

Because of Jenae's words, I felt like Lady Moon spreading her joy across the surface of the sea, glowing blue, and at the epitome of her grandeur. I blushed furiously with both relief and happiness as I confessed, "It's not just a formality to me either."

Our mutual interest confirmed, we got married the next night. Gaiae residents who want to celebrate the joining of Lady Moon and the Lord of the Deep have their marriage ceremony at night when the moon reflects over the sea. As the moon began to rise, we stood under the pavilion of Gaiae's sea temple. The place where we'd first met as children. My grandmother was with me as I wore her wedding robe, and the sound of flutes meshed with that of cicadas and the soft waves lapping on the nearby shore. Departing the world of sun and sand, as I'd promised the Lord of the Deep, I became Jenay's when the sea priestess, Cicara, placed my hand in his. That night, during the ceremony, the rising moonlight shimmered off my grandmother's gold bracelet, the other legacy I'd ultimately inherited from Lillian Ani.

And then afterward.

Wedding nights in the Village of Lehom traditionally involved the woman lying quietly on her back, her legs wide open for her new husband's pleasure. If he asked her to pose alluringly, she should, especially if she faced away from him so he could see her back. Desire on her part was tolerated so long as it wasn't for her own pleasure but rather his. The Ethereal Queen is beautiful and elegant, calm and compassionate, but certainly not coy or wanton. That would make a woman too much like Lillian Ani. This is why Kimsimi's confession about wanting my brother had shocked me at the time.

But me? Well, I decided to be a Lillian on my wedding night, which meant casting the Ethereal Queen's virtues asunder, to the world of sun and sand. Those details belong to me and Jenay alone. Suffice it to say it's much better to be a Lillian, for she gets to enjoy her wifely duties rather than tolerate them or disguise her desire as grace. I'd never realized before how similar our names sounded. *Lillian. Leilani.* I now owned her legacy. Just like Lillian, people in my natal village would remember me as a wretch. The rest of me, the genuine Leilani? *Damnatio memoriae.* The purging from collective memory. An ancient people called the Romans once did that, so I learned from a book.

I still wondered why the King didn't simply let go. I mean, I was exiled, yet he still demanded I be returned to the village. For what? I think Mimza was right. He didn't want to lose, and only the impression of winning would make him relent. To him, that meant compliance. Marrying Jenay gave me legal protection as a citizen of Gaiae, but it didn't make the King feel like a winner. Instead, it applied terrible pressure. I don't have to say that self-involved men with delusions of divinity rarely respond well to pressure.

The next few weeks passed as a repetitive blur of waking up, going to the library, and securing provisions after. Jenay, on the other hand, disappeared during the daylight hours with Baril. Both of them were building the boat in the sea caves, and I must admit Baril was smart. He conjured an alibi for the two of them. Everyone thought they were out securing bamboo for their next project, and they were, to be true, but that project was also a forbidden boat.

I hoped to stay in that blissful holding pattern forever. That's not how time works, though.

The day we had to confront King Marit, a month after I stepped foot in Gaiae, arrived as all days eventually do. Right before that meeting, Jenay finally brought me to the sea caves. My hand in his, my husband led me to the entrance, now exposed at low tide. "Follow me carefully," he said as we stepped over the treacherous, damp rocks.

Holding a satchel with my wooden case, Samsara's journal, my grandmother's wedding robe, and my diving mask, I watched him descend into shadow and followed. I inhaled the damp smell of earth and salt, of green lichens and minerals. Jenay led me through a dark, surprisingly cool tunnel with thick walls that dulled the roar of the ocean waves. "The boat's down *here*?"

"It is," his voice echoed off the walls.

We finally entered a moontrap-lit cavern with a rocky ledge and pool of churning water beneath. I saw a curved, elegant silhouette, about fifteen feet long, moored on the rocks. At the head of the boat, a monster's head glowed in the light. Somehow, it was both fierce and beautiful.

Pointing to the dragon's head in the semi-darkness, I asked, "You made that, too?"

"Out of rosewood, just like the fastenings. The rest of the boat is bamboo. Step inside."

As I rested the satchel in one of the storage cubbies Jenay had built, I noticed a pile of cloth resting on the hull. "What's this for?" I asked.

Jenay got in beside me and pulled on the ropes attached to the cloth. "These are sun shades, and they're different from the sails that will catch the winds." He then pointed to some sacks that were secured into other cubbies. "Our provisions. They'll hopefully tide us over. We'll need more coconuts, though, for water. And then we can use the shells and some oil-treated cotilk to catch rain."

I uttered the only words I had. "Beautiful. And absolutely ingenious. The whole thing is!"

"Does it look like the boat from the book?" He stood behind me, tracing his hands on the sides of my hips as I ran my hands over the smooth contours of the boat's edge.

"It does. How'd you do this so quickly?" I asked in wonderment.

"Bamboo is flexible and strong, a quick wood to build with." His face glowed in the moontrap. "And I had even more motivation for this project."

With Jenay's words, reality again interrupted our happy mood. Uncertain about our future, I asked, "Do you really think we'll have to use it?"

"I hope not. It depends on what happens today at this meeting." He was quiet, then, and the sound of the muffled crashing waves filled the void. After a moment, he continued, his voice a soft echo off the cavern wall. "If the King somehow wins, we'll stall by saying you need to return to the house to get your things."

I nodded. "He won't worry because he won't think I have anywhere else to go."

"Head straight here," he continued. "I'll meet you, and then we'll launch this boat."

"It won't come to that." I pointed to my grandmother's satchel in a nook. "But just in case, the map's in Samsara's journal, which is right here in this bag."

Then, a horrible thought came to mind. What if Jenay regretted leaving with me? Could he really give up his whole life here? Mimza and Neina? Baril? This plan seemed so dramatic, so final, and I wasn't sure I was worth it to him. Remember, women in my home village were supposed to make sacrifices for men, not the other way around. I didn't consciously believe I was unworthy, but I'd still been programmed with such false beliefs. "Wouldn't you mind leaving?" I asked tentatively.

He kissed my forehead and pulled me close. "Of course I'd miss Mimza and Neina. But I've always wondered what's beyond these shores. If we have to leave, we'll make an adventure of it. You're my wife. I've been thinking of you for nine years. Since we were both ten."

"You fell in love with me back then? When we were children?" I asked as I nuzzled into the crook of his shoulder.

"As much as a ten-year-old can. You said the truth and shared an interest of mine, something a girl from Gaiae hasn't done. I felt bonded to you then."

Bliss waxed through me with those words. Love isn't necessarily logical. It simply happens. I'm not saying people should stay together if their love is poison, but when it lifts them up, and when the other person treats them well, why not submit to its gifts? "You helped me too," I replied. "By treating me like a human being instead of the daughter of a prince."

Jenay emitted a contented sigh, one that convinced me of his sincerity. "We'll stay together even if it means departing for the Old World."

I believed in him but didn't trust the environment around us. I didn't trust uncertainty. "Assuming we can make it, though. What if we run out of water in the ocean crossing?"

"There are many ifs, I admit." Jenay took me in his arms as we sat on the boat's floor and reclined against its edges. "But our water supply can last us fifteen days. We can also catch rain with the sails. If we run out of food, we'll catch fish."

Just over two weeks. That's how long our provisions would last. Well, that's how long we thought they'd last. We were wrong, it turns out. "And how far can we get in fifteen days?" I asked.

"It depends on the wind, but the map you gave me shows that it's a thousand miles to the next land mass. We could do it in that time and hopefully get more provisions there if we need them."

"If we need them..." I trailed off and looked around at the hollow space of the caverns. "No one comes here? Why?"

"No one except me and Baril have since my parents died here," Jenay said softly. "They wanted a quiet place away from the world, and one day while they were here, my mother slipped on a rock and drowned. My father, too, when he jumped in. The suction from the tide was strong."

My gasp echoed off the rocky walls. "How terrible."

"The people of Gaiae consider this to be their tomb, my place to commune with them alone," he explained.

And now it functioned as our temporary refuge.

With me in his arms, we listened to the water rushing in and out of the cavernous cave. This same water circulated around the globe. On our way to the Old World, we'd be carried on it by the wind and the sea's currents, hopefully in harmony with these natural elements. My eyes focused on the cave's ceiling, a barrier against the sky. Across it traveled the blue waving nebulas of light from the moontrap's reflection off the water. "How do the stars help you navigate?"

I felt his fingers on my shoulder, tracing invisible constellations on my skin. "The moving patterns in the sky help. Like up there right now."

I looked back at the ceiling and its water galaxies. "It's strange how much smaller that sky is. It's safe in here."

"Safe?" He laughed softly. "The ocean is larger out there, sure, the universe too, but my parents died here. They were trapped, and we will be too if things go wrong."

"You're right," I recognized the cave's dark, deceptive lull for what it truly was. At some point, the moontrap would go out, and the miniature galaxies on the ceiling would die, leaving us cast in suffocating darkness. Illusions, whether of sky, sand, or sea, never last forever. I finally said, "I think it's about time."

"It is." Jenay helped me out of the boat and steadied me on the rocky ledge. "Remember our plan."

I followed him even though part of me still hated to leave the blue, cocooned safety of the sea cave. A temporary refuge is still refuge to the emotionally weary. When we exited, the sun burned brightly on the rocks, exposing every nook and cranny in that world of sand. It took us nearly half an hour to walk from the sea caves in Gaiae's territory to the Central Village Authority's meeting place, the administration building where Jenay and I had met each other again. Unlike that day, there was no rain in the sky. Instead, the sun beat down on us as our feet kicked up the dead, crushed coral. Minute grains of this coral became trapped between my feet and the sandals, causing me pain as I stepped on them.

Trapped. Forced into the same space as the King.

I felt the air in my lungs grow stale, and the kaleidoscopic jungle on either side of me began to sway into a visual cacophony, its flowers melding with the trees and with the sound of parrots. I faltered slightly but then felt Jenay's arms steady me. "He has no real power over you. Breathe for a moment."

We paused, and I imagined the earth beneath the hot sand, made damp through seawater, hold me up with its antediluvian roots. "He has no power," I repeated, whispering both to my husband and the silent multitudes on the island still within the King's reach.

We continued on the road to the Central Village, and before I knew it, my great-great grandfather's home loomed in front of us. Jenay and I, our arms interlocked, walked through the foyer, past our special kiosk, and finally into the room where the Central Authority met.

What a strange political ecosystem that gathering of nine people made, three of them foes and six of them friends, as they sat around a large wooden table. I didn't quite believe they'd let the King take me, but I *did* know that unless we got the King to drop his argument, he'd make life difficult. I knew Mimza would fight for me, but what about the Central Village members of the Authority? The King had three hundred loyal followers, and peace had to be maintained at all costs on this island. I really did understand that even though I'd never sacrifice myself for that ideal.

The sound of our shoes scuffling across the marble floor made the King look up from his book. Sure of his upcoming success, he reclined back in his chair and smiled. "Well, then. The forsaken ones finally appear."

"Let's keep things civil, here," Mimza said with a measured calm before turning to us. "Leilani, Jenay, please sit."

"Thank you." As we sat next to one another, I took the time to look at each Authority member directly in the eyes.

Mimza gave me a reassuring smile before addressing the room. "So, we're first going to hear from King Marit, and then we'll let Leilani and Jenay speak in their defense. Finally, of course, we'll vote. King Marit will need six votes to prevail. But first, I'll introduce everyone to Jenay and Leilani."

Taking my hand in his under the table, Jenay said, "It'd be much appreciated. I still haven't met the Lehom contingent." I loved how he spat out those last two words, making the "Lehom contingent" sound dirty and horrible, a completely accurate assessment on his part.

"Representing Gaiae is, of course, me, our priestess, Cicara, and our doctor, Sametta," Mimza began. She then gestured to the three people who were unfamiliar to me. "The Central Council members are Abato Ani, a relative of yours, Leilani, the grandson of Chanson. There's also Jessip, the tool manager, and Darimy, the quinoa and coffee agricultural manager." Mimza paused for a moment but managed a respectful voice when she nodded to the other side of the table. "And, finally, for your benefit, Jenay, from the Village of Lehom, we have King Marit. There is also his law advisor, Boma, and the King's brother, Prince Addis Simi."

Everyone from Gaiae and Central Village had given me a kind smile when we were introduced, but King Marit and his two minions were positively glowering, first at me and then at Mimza. I could tell the King, in particular, loathed that the proceedings were being directed by a woman. He cleared his throat. "We all have more important things to attend to, so I'll state my case quickly."

The King leaned forward over the table, his fingers interlaced with one another as he continued, "It's really quite simple. Leilani Ani accepted the position of virtue, but she defiled herself with this architect, if not physically, then spiritually. If this had not have happened, she would've been married to a prince or ascended to my royal house as a concubine. We define her actions as adultery, and I punished her according to our laws. Since she escaped *un*lawfully, I demand she be brought back to fulfill her sentence."

I had to clench my jaw shut in order to keep myself from blurting out, *Liar!* But, my success in this bit of theater I'd been forced into depended on me being more level-headed than King Marit. There and then, I realized how much he'd inadvertently taught me about controlling my emotions, about acting deliberately. To distract myself, I focused my attention on the wall of the room opposite me. I noticed that while monolithic and strong, hairline cracks spidered up the wall's coral plaster. How long would this building last in this island's humidity? Certainly not forever. Nothing lasted forever in this place, isolated as it was.

Abato Ani, my relative, spoke next. "Are you seriously asking us to send her back to you for spiritual adultery?" He turned to me and said, "He already punished you rather harshly, we've heard."

Ah, that's right. I was facing the Authority members, and the ones from Central Village hadn't seen the King's damage yet. Suddenly, then, I felt ashamed. Corrupted. Angry the King had forced me on display like this. He seemed way too confident. *Surely* he knew that only the other Lehom representatives would vote with him. Why did he think he had a chance of winning, then?

I stared at the table for a moment and let my thoughts get lost in the whirling grain of the wood. I felt Jenay's hand squeeze mine, a simple, significant act that imparted me with his defiant strength. "The King whipped me seven times," I said as I stood up and slowly turned around to let the Central Authority see the scars on my back. I'd tied my teal cotilk robe low on my back and had worn my hair up so they could see the King's work in its entirety. "And then imprisoned me in the Criminals' Compound."

"And you escaped by swimming away?" Abato Ani asked kindly.

"Covertly and with deceit," the King interrupted in a low voice, pointing angrily at Jenay. "Then, *he* helped her. However, I'll leave his punishment up to you since he's a resident of Gaiae."

Ignoring the King's remarks, I sat back down in the seat and addressed Abato directly. "Jenay picked me up in a boat, but he stayed out beyond the reef, never going into the Village of Lehom's waters."

"That was quite a swim," Abato Ani replied. "I'm impressed."

My distant relative's kindness made me feel at ease, so I said, "It was one of my finer triumphs in life."

"This is all immaterial," the King shouted as he stood up, knocking his chair backward. "Leilani Ani is a citizen of the Village of Lehom, so I demand she be returned to us."

"Well, not quite," Mimza said. "Her name is Leilani Lo now. She's a citizen of Gaiae."

"Leilani Lo?" he spat out in confusion.

"Yes. She's my wife," Jenay replied, giving the King a triumphant smile.

"And spouses of Gaiae residents obtain residency themselves," Mimza added. "We deal with our own criminals, and she hasn't committed any crime according to *our* laws."

As Boma furiously searched his law book, the King thumped his hand on the table. "Women's trickery! You can't prevail because of it."

Mimza didn't flinch as she continued, "You should be careful, King Marit. Do you really want to set a precedent for extraditing someone for alleged crimes?"

The words "alleged crimes" got Boma's attention. He dropped his book and asked Mimza, "Why do you say that?"

"We've heard some alarming reports about the King's proximity to his sister-in-law at the time of her death on your women's beach," Mimza answered. "If we consider sending Leilani back, we'd have to hold the King here while we investigate these claims."

How brilliant Mimza was! She used this meeting as leverage to entrap him. Remove me, hold him. Not a bargain he'd be willing to make.

If Lehom was real, he manifested in the King's eye now, volcano fire spewing forth. "This is ridiculous! We are here to bring this criminal back to justice. I will not tolerate your attempts to distort the truth or her actions!" King Marit turned to the council and demanded, "Vote now. How many will vote to send her back?"

Three arms shot up quickly, those belonging only the King, Boma, and the Simi prince. The King needed to get six votes, but no other hands were raised. King Marit had failed.

Jenay and I were safe! Relief and ecstasy swept through me. We wouldn't have to leave the island after all!

The King trembled with barely contained rage. At that moment, a strange light came in through a window, illuminating the King's soft jawline and the ridiculous luminescence of his cotilk robes. He was accustomed to getting his way. No one had ever challenged him before. On the Authority council, however, he was one voice in nine. Well, three voices in nine since his two lackeys did his bidding, but that wasn't enough. How strange to see him stripped of his power. Of his menacing will.

Finally, an unsettling smile spread across his face as his eyes settled back on me. "This is not the end of it. I will not rest until you, Leilani *Ani*, are dragged back to the Criminals' Compound where you belong. Be careful where you wander in the night."

Although Jenay and I *had* technically won, this victory had stoked rather than quelled the King's resolve. Stunned, I watched him and his entourage get up simultaneously, as a mercenary school of fish, and turn towards the door. It wasn't a good time to panic, so I focused on the murmuring chorus of the remaining six council members to anchor myself in consciousness. These voices sounded supportive, so after a few minutes, I opened my eyes.

"He's mad," Abato Ani declared. "Absolutely mad."

Semetta nodded in agreement. "To think he threatened…"

"I don't even know what his threats *mean*," Cicara added.

Jenay and Mimza spoke quietly together in the corner of the room, and I saw in her eyes a shock and resigned type of sadness. Had he told her about our plans? Left with no other choice, we had to leave now. I was about to ask

Jenay when we should leave, when, suddenly, the sound of a gong pierced through the air.

Everyone stopped talking and looked at each other in horror.

"What *was* that?" I asked.

"Someone's rung the warning gong. The watcher's only supposed to do that when the seismoscope's been triggered. It's never actually happened before," Mimza said. The other council members remained silent when the world should've been descending into chaos.

"A wave," Jenay whispered, his eyes wide with terror.

CHAPTER TWENTY-ONE

I
t's strange what arrives in the mind's forefront when one's struck dumb by fear and disbelief. In my case, after the gong sounded, I envisioned a torrent of dead nightingales at my feet. I didn't know what to do and felt useless because of it. Thankfully, others took action when I couldn't.

"How long do we have?" Jenay asked.

"No one really knows," Abato replied, somehow maintaining his calm. "But, we've planned for this, so let's get our people to higher ground." He turned to Mimza. "Do you need any help evacuating Gaiae?"

"We have a seismoscope, too. They should've already begun the evacuation protocol," Mimza said. I could hear the ambivalence in her voice as she craned her neck to look out of the window in Gaiae's direction. "But I should still head there just in case the watcher didn't see."

"Go along the high ground path in case the main road becomes inundated," Abato cautioned before he and his other Authority members scurried away.

My handsome husband's face was set with determination. "Aunt Mimza, we can warn everyone faster if there's two of us. If you're taking the high path, I'll run along the main road. It's only three minutes to Gaiae at my pace."

Cicara, the sea priestess who'd married us, spoke next. "A good plan. But keep your eye on the sea. If the water retreats, head up the mountain path immediately, no matter where you are. Come, Sametta, let's help evacuate Central Village since Mimza and Jenay have Gaiae under control."

Even though the idea of running anywhere but straight up the mountain terrified me, I had to do something. "I'll go with Mimza. I swam out to meet you, so I have some endurance."

Jenay pulled me into a kiss, his resolve turning into tenderness. "I know you do, but I don't want to have to worry about you. Stay here and follow evacuation routes with everyone else. Please?"

I didn't want him to leave. I wanted to run alongside him, but I knew he'd be more focused on the task at hand without me, so I relented. And returned his kiss, echoing the priestess's words, "Watch the sea. And be careful."

Mimza cleared her throat. "We'd better go. Remember, the objective is to get everyone to higher ground immediately. Leave possessions."

Jenay gave me a final kiss, and everyone dispersed to save as many people as they could.

I, however, was left alone in the building, the home of all three motherless Ani children who'd settled here for a reclusive life. Despite the danger looming, I wondered where Rekin Ani had slept. Samsara? Chanson? As they'd scattered in life, so did the villages now in a time of crisis. The King's ominous threat to drag me back to his domain in the night made me numb. What kind of life would I have always looking over my shoulder? What could the Central Authority do to stop him?

Stop....don't think about that now. There wasn't time. I had to get to higher ground with the other Central Villagers. How lucky that we had the seismoscopes on this island.

Yes, the seismoscope.

Pestilence, curse it! The Village of Lehom didn't have a seismoscope! Had the King and his merry band of yes-men heard the warning before they left? Then again, would they even know what the gong meant?

Perhaps I should've left the Children of Lehom to their fate as they'd forced me into mine, but then I remembered my family and the innocent ones. Gisnen and Kimsimi, who'd risked their own good standing to bring me evidence against their King. Irin, my twin, I even felt sorry for. Belsimi and Limcona, and Dirmisu, my erstwhile best friend whose testimony had helped get Kimsimi to doubt her father's virtue.

I couldn't abandon them. Looking back, I should've asked someone from the Central Authority to go warn them. After all, if I got caught in the village, I'd be under the King's power again. But, there wasn't time for that, and I couldn't live with that guilt if they all died.

I desperately needed a plan that would also protect me from the King. If I snuck into the Ani garden, I could warn Kimsimi or Gisnen, who could tell the rest of the villagers of this threat themselves. Then, I could escape back like a sleek panther or shimmy up the mountain. Hopefully out of the King's reach.

Stealth.

How I wish *that* had been one of the Ethereal Queen's virtues. Tightening my robe and sandals for the one-mile trek, I ran outside and joined the eddy of people carrying children and foodstuffs, but while they turned towards the mountain paths, I sprinted along the road that separated the Central Village from the Village of Lehom, the prison I'd gladly escaped from.

Jenay was going to be mad, very mad when he found out.

If he found out. Today was an entire basket of pesky ifs.

Steam rose from the jungle on either side of me, casting mist ghosts on the road. As the spider monkeys chattered actively among one another, I tried to fly, to move as quickly as I could swim, but my legs began to burn as I inhaled the humid air, the sun burning through the trees on either side of me.

The world of sun and sand.

I breathed in and out, set a pattern, and ignored my burning legs all while thinking of my family. It's amazing how quickly the jungle sped by during my sprint, for my thoughts, my usually rambling internal words, dragged out slowly, making me aware of every thought fragment, every second of the ten minutes it took me to dash through the dense foliage between our villages.

Finally, I saw the border between Central Village and the Village of Lehom. Around the bend in the road, the King's domain officially began. There'd be guards there. I couldn't let those sentinels with the rough-hewn bamboo spears see me. Taking a deep breath, I slowly moved into the jungle, hoping my teal robe would camouflage me enough in the jungle's foliage. I prayed to Lady Moon to help me avoid the traps, so I shuffled my feet slowly in front of me, ready to spring back if I tripped any hidden mechanism.

My plan was to slip through the fence of the Ani Spirit Garden and then go inside the house to find Kimsimi and Gisnen. I kept moving, one foot in front of the other until I reached the fence. Were there loose pieces here? I searched for some and finally found three posts that I could squeeze through. That chink in the fence was a portal to the dwelling place of my ancestors. This would be the last time I could savor it, so I knelt down for the briefest second to feel the Ani Spirit Garden's soft grass. As I closed my eyes and breathed in the hibiscus air, a bird called out, causing me to open my eyes and focus on a mound of fresh dirt.

My grandmother's grave. She was so close to me, only a couple feet of earth beneath my hands. I spent another precious second kneeling and holding my hand on this mound, asking for her forgiveness. For that one second, which seemed to draw on forever, the quiet, tranquil air belied the chaos happening in the other villages, and I believed for one moment in this place's power. In the ghosts of my family members.

"*What* are you doing here?" interrupted an angry voice.

A red-faced, furious Irin stood on that porch. I jumped up and met his gaze, my voice urgent. "The seismoscope went off in Central Village. An earthquake at sea might create a massive wave that can sweep everything away."

He simply glared. "The King's hasn't issued a warning."

Of course, he didn't believe me. "He doesn't have a seismoscope," I argued. "Listen, send Kimsimi and Gisnen up the mountain. Their lives are your responsibility."

A flicker of recognition sparked in his eyes. A mere flicker, but something is still better than nothing. "How sure are you?" he asked.

"We're not," I admitted. "But in the best case, you'll only waste time. In the worst, your hesitancy kills the whole family."

I knew my responsible brother, who was weighed down by his sense of duty, finally relented when the tense muscles of his face relaxed. He turned to the house and yelled, "Kimsimi, Gisnen, Dirmisu, come here please!"

Dirmisu? She was here, too? Why? It took only five seconds, the longest seconds of my life considering the urgency of the situation, for all three to emerge onto the porch. Kimsimi took Irin's arm and looked at me quizzically, Dirmisu stood frozen in place, and Gisnen cautiously approached me for a hug.

"There might be a huge wave coming from the ocean," I said as I quickly embraced my little brother. "You have to get up the mountain."

Gisnen's eyes grew wide with panic, but Kimsimi, to her credit, remained calm. "Oh, dear. Husband, I'll accompany Gisnen, Dirmisu, and Leilani up the mountain while you warn the King."

Irin nodded and gave her an admiring look. "I'll do that. Leilani shouldn't be seen here."

How amazing that my sister had softened Irin toward me. I was about to agree to this plan when I remembered Belsimi and Limcona, as well as the people in the Criminals' Compound. The King probably wouldn't take time to save them. "You three go up the mountain. I need to warn the people in the Criminals' Compound. Irin doesn't have time to get to everyone."

Dirmisu, who'd been silent, raised her head so her watering eyes met mine. "You were right about everything. My monthly course was late this month."

I shuddered, thinking about what she's endured. Just like Meguya.

The King wanted the virtues for visual inspiration? What a lie. Queen Veluya would be furious when she found out. What would Dirmisu do then? I closed my eyes and thanked Lady Moon and the Lord of the Deep that I'd escaped that fate. Now, I could only assure her with an empty promise. I wanted to comfort her, but there wasn't time for anything more. "We'll think of something later," I said with pity.

It became obvious that Irin hadn't known this news until now, for remained stony and wide-eyed. What would my brother do? Support the King or rebel?

Now wasn't the time to find out, though.

We had no time left.

We heard a cacophony in the sky, a flock of seabirds heading for the mountain.

No time.

I looked intently at Gisnen and grabbed his shoulders. "You have to leave, *now*. I made a hole in the fence right there. Take Dirmisu and Kimsimi out that way and find a path up the mountain to higher ground. Don't stop climbing until you find a ledge that's at least a hundred feet off the ground."

My poor little brother blanched and froze in his position, but Kimsimi took Gisnen's hand. "Come, brother. Can you help me?"

He took a deep breath and nodded. "I can do it."

"Those birds know something's wrong," Irin said as we watched the three of them disappear through the hole in the fence. "Can you make it to the compound in time? And what about the guards?"

I saw genuine concern and a dash of fear in his eyes as he asked those questions, something that melted the anger I'd reserved for his role in my disgrace. And he'd made an important point. What *about* the guards? Since it was daytime, Uralin would likely be watching Belsimi and Limcona while Nimec was supervising the men in the fields. Even though Nimec was the meaner of the two by nature, the last time I'd seen Uralin, he'd called me a whore. "I'll worry about the guards later," I said. "As for the wave, I'll run parallel to the mountain's base so I can run up it quickly."

Run parallel to the mountain. *Just as Jenay was doing,* I thought. How I missed him and hoped he stayed safe. My *sine qua non* and I were together in everything we did, connected to one another even more to me than my biological twin.

Irin gave me a kind look that communicated forgiveness. Not acceptance, mind you. We still lived in very different worlds, but I counted that as a small victory. "Good luck, Sister," were his final words as he ran from the garden.

For my part, I moved along the edge of the jungle and avoided the main road until I left the princely section of the village. Irin must've successfully warned the others, for behind me, I heard screams and the frantic pace of frightened people. Yelling that a tidal wave was coming, I ran through the sections for temporary princes and the lowest class. Thankfully, despite their confusion at my words, the villagers fled and warned others to run for the mountain.

The seabirds continued to fly overhead, and that spectacle likely supplemented my warning effectively as I ran as fast as my feet would carry me. I finally burst through the trees to the Criminals' Compound, arriving right in front of the women's pavilion. As expected, Belsimi and Limcona were working on the porch. They dropped their pestles in shock when they saw me. I probably looked like an absolute mess after a run through the jungle, what with my robe soaked in sweat from my run and the day's aggregated humidity and my hair peppered with tropical vegetation.

Belsimi, though just as stunned as Limcona, spoke first. "What in the Eternal Spirit Garden are you doing here?"

Limcona stood up. "Leave quickly!" she hissed frantically.

If the birds I'd seen earlier were any indication, something bad was on the horizon. In rapid-fire succession, I spat out, "The seismoscope in Central Village went off. A tidal wave might be coming. We have to get to higher ground now."

The color drained from Belsimi's face. "Where do we go?"

"At least a hundred feet up the mount---" I stopped when both of their faces suddenly froze in horror. Was it the wave? Were we too late? No, no wave. I felt a familiar cold terror from something lurking behind me. I begged Lady Moon for my suspicions to be proven wrong.

"To think, I stepped out for two minutes to discuss the jungle's traps with the guards," the King crowed from behind me. "And I come back to this wonderful surprise."

I wished it *had* been the wave instead. I could've retreated from that hazard. Fighting my fear, I turned around and saw the King glittering obscenely as the hot sun reflected off his embroidered robes. Uralin was with him, but not Nimec. Was he still guarding the criminal men? Hopefully, my warning would convince them they had more important things to worry about than restraining me. "The seismoscope went off," I began. "There's a wave coming. We have to get to higher ground. Now."

King Marit cocked his head and then broke into laughter. "You came back to warn me of something that won't happen? How stupid of you."

Great Pestilence, curse it. Of course, he didn't believe me. The Sons of Lehom never take women seriously, never on important matters at least. I had to *make* him listen now, so I pointed to the commotion overhead. "We have to evacuate."

He looked aloft and frowned when he noticed the pandemonium of the panicked birds. How had he been blind to them before? Sighing, he turned to Uralin. "To be safe, escort the two women up to one of the ledges on the mountain."

How strange. That made no sense. He wanted Belsimi and Limcona, two nothings to him, to be safe, but he evidently didn't believe me himself, else he'd be heading up the mountain as well, probably demanding Uralin carry him so he didn't have to exert himself.

"What about you? And her?" Uralin asked, pointing to me. At least he called me "her" instead of "whore," an improvement from the last time he'd seen me.

The King's features twisted into a cruel smile. "I'll take care of her."

So *that* was it. He didn't want any witnesses to see what he had planned for me. At that moment, I understood danger as a spectrum of sorts. There's a danger in doing the right thing and in doing the wrong thing, in earthquake-born tidal waves, and certainly in megalomaniacal leaders. However, by taking on these threats one at a time, we can emerge victoriously and prepared for the next challenge life throws at us.

In other words, I resolved to deal with the wave later.

"We should go," Uralin pleaded softly to Limcona, who remained motionless as this scene unfolded.

Belsimi looked at him, disgusted. "You can't be serious! We're leaving Leilani here alone with him?"

I appraised the situation. I could probably outrun King Marit, as out of shape as he was, but I needed my friends to be safe before I could act. I narrowed my eyes at King Marit, dug my sandals into the earth, and poised myself to sprint away like one of the cheetahs that lived on some far-off continent I'd once read about. Thinking women to be inherently weak and unintelligent, he wouldn't expect me to prevail against him now. My hidden strength lay in exploiting these prejudices.

Isolate the threats.

"It's okay," I reassured Belsimi. "Time's running out."

She opened her mouth to protest but shook her head in defeat. "Fine. Let's go then."

Limcona gave me a weak smile and mouthed the word, *run*, and I exhaled with relief as Uralin led my friends away. They slowly began to climb a rough mountain path, moving toward a ledge about seventy feet off the ground. Hopefully, that would be high enough.

Now that they were gone, I focused back on the King. His self-satisfied smile made me more nauseous than the run here had. "So now what?" I asked, for he evidently had a plan in mind.

He inched closer to me, and I shuffled a step back, a parody of the dance we'd done in his audience hall. Only, he now had to deal with a wiser me.

"All the others were easy," he said quietly, studying my face. "But you presented a challenge."

Well, this was unexpected. What in the world was he talking about? "The others?" I asked, not in the mood for his games.

He smiled. "Yes. Those who defied me. Like Meguya."

I'd had my strong suspicions. So did Gisnen and Kimsimi. But we hadn't had any proof. *He'd just admitted that he killed her. With no one but me to hear that damning confession.* I felt a hatred boil inside me, one hotter than Lehom's blood, the magma of the earth. Still, I needed him to admit it. Explicitly. "What did you do to her?"

He inched closer, smiling horribly all the while. "I forced her head onto a rock and then let her breathe in the tidal pool's water until she drowned."

I took a step back, trying not to conjure a dead Meguya, a drowned flower, in my head. I inched away more. "You said *others*." I dreaded his answer but had to know for sure.

"Your grandmother," he said with extra relish. "I summoned her to court. Dismissed the others and offered her sacred fruit tinged with poison from cassava leaves. I watched her gasp and choke."

Do you understand death's knell, Deanne? The one from our family spirit garden rang then, hollow and harrowing in my ears. Due to the timing and location of her death, I'd known he was involved, but I'd pushed that thought down to survive, to permit myself joy with Jenay. Because if the King killed her after my escape, then her death was my fault. How is anyone supposed to live with that guilt? It's impossible, so you push it down, hide it and deny it with everything you have. Why had my poor grandmother eaten that fruit? Was she afraid that disobeying him would make things worse for the family? Had she felt pain from the poison? When the King confronted me with that truth, in that moment where we'd been thrown together by a potential natural disaster, I wanted to scream, call him a murderer, but he'd covet my rage. At least I could deny him his satisfaction. "I pity you," I said, hoping he couldn't detect any anger in my voice.

King Marit relaxed his stance for a moment, looking at me with patient amusement as he continued uttering his legacy of madness. What a ridiculous thing. We were alone in a place soon likely to be inundated with tons of seawater, and all he said next was, "Your parents were also easy. I had their boat sabotaged." He was enjoying this, which made him not only evil but also very sick.

"But *why*?" I'd suspected as much because death followed this King, but I couldn't imagine his motivations for killing my parents. He'd been friends with my father, and my mother was close with Queen Veluya.

"Your problem is that you have no imagination for life's potential. You're limited, afraid to reach for what you want. I suppose it's a fault of women." He inched closer, that sadistic smile still on his face. "Your father and Veluya's father would've opposed me when I changed the laws of kingship. Irin and Veluya's brother, on the other hand, are malleable fools."

I stared at him, somewhat disarmed by this news and unable to understand the root of his motivations. "All for power?"

"Not for power," he corrected me. "For righteousness. The days of shadow are here. No one besides me could bring us closer to Rekin's truth, to Lehom's truth, in order to save us. I saw it all in a dream from Lehom."

Abato Ani was right. The King was mad, mad with blind faith in my great-great-grandfather's extremism. I couldn't hope to rationalize with him. He disobeyed Lehom's own commandments to suit his desires and justified his actions through his infallible political position. The sad thing is that he appeared to truly believe that he was doing what was best for the Children of Lehom. If he felt Lehom gave him legitimate power, then all his personal wants were also legitimized. And, taught not to question anything a King said, these Children followed along. They were too afraid to want an inch of freedom lest the whole system crumble and collapse.

Well, not everyone was afraid to dream or act. My grandmother hadn't been. I've not often been filled with murderous rage, but after hearing his confessions, I could have killed him. I took one step closer to him, staring him down and daring him to hit me. But rage makes people stupid and blind. *He* was blinded by anger when I escaped the village and defeated him in the council meeting.

I needed to regain my wits.

As usual, nature interceded on my behalf by capturing my attention at the necessary moment. I suddenly noticed the world's extreme quiet. The birds and insects had even ceased speaking. In Central Village, we didn't hear the earth move before the gong sounded, yet I now felt a subtle vibration beneath my feet. Turning toward the dock where the boats departed from, I saw a series of exposed pylons because the water's edge had receded to the beginning of the reef.

The sea was gone.

White sand, still wet, lay exposed upon the oceanless shore. Where I'd swum to freedom was now part of the world of sun and sand.

The sea priestess had cautioned us about receding water. Breaking the eerie silence, another flock of seabirds flew overhead and passed over the sandy bottom of the sea to the mountain, crying frantically.

It was time to run.

I heard a slight roar.

And saw movement on the horizon, a dynamic razor's edge of shimmering blue moving closer and closer, a line gaining height, almost gulping up the lowest perimeter of the sky. I looked at the King, whose eyes were wide, and I had to run instead of seek revenge. I bolted across the compound, through the jungle, and towards the mountain. Ahead of me was the rough path that Uralin had led Belsimi and Limcona up. I sprinted towards it, the earth's soil and the jungle's thick foliage weighing down my ankles.

Up.

I had to go up. And quickly. Very quickly if I hoped to survive.

I tried to move vertically, but large stones and unstable gatherings of dirt impeded my path. The last thing I wanted to do was fall, so I inched up, unaware of where the King was. My flinched at the roar's crescendo behind me, but I didn't dare look back and lose a millisecond of escape time.

Up, up, up.

I climbed with my hands and feet until I reached the ledge where Uralin, Limcona, and Belsimi looked behind me in horror. Turning around, I followed their singular gaze, and from this vantage point, poised above even the palm trees, we looked down upon the entire Village of Lehom. A wall of water, a swell of blue, came nearer, eating up the reef again and wetting the sand it had left exposed. The wave barreled towards the docks, roaring louder and louder as white crests developed behind this first wave, themselves also menacing like my devastating nocturnal storms.

At that moment before the first wave hit the docks, time seemed to slow down, an instant growing into a year, a breath yielding a century. I became hypersensitive to the panic of birds, to the hiss of sucking ocean, and, finally, to the sight of the King. He hung upside down, suspended from a rope on a mighty palm tree.

He'd gotten caught in one of the traps he'd set! I wanted the King to see his domain utterly destroyed by the wave before being swallowed up himself. Lady Moon forgive me, but I prayed with all my might that he hung low enough to drown in the approaching torrent. His helplessness empowered me, and I almost felt as if I'd summoned this wave myself with the strength of my hatred. With my lips curled into a self-satisfied smile, I moved back on the ledge I was resting on and stood up next to Limcona, feeling ready for a show, one put on by the Lord of the Deep on my behalf.

Slowly, the wave began to curl.

About to collapse onto the shore, it loomed about thirty feet over the docks.

That eternity of moments ended as the white, angry froth of its crest swarmed onto the beach, pummeled the docks, and reduced the piers to soaring sticks. Beautiful, delicious vengeance flooded my heart as the screaming King disappeared in the rushing waters. The wave's height reached halfway up the palm trees that lined the beach, swaying them cruelly and sending coconuts down into the churn below.

Then, however, I saw movement out of the corner of my left eye.

There were still men working in the agricultural fields, men from the Criminals' Compound and Dirmisu's former section of the village. Located far from the Village of Lehom's princely homes, these fields had been beyond Irin's reach.

Nimec. Nimec was the one who should've warned them, but he hadn't accompanied the King and Uralin back to the compound.

We'd forgotten to warn the agricultural workers.

My cruel glee turned to anguish. By savoring destruction, I wasn't any better than the King. I watched in horror as the mass of water, now tainted a muddy brown color, swallowed up the agricultural fields and the men who worked in them. This monster next devoured the women's and men's pavilions in the Criminals' Compound, covering their roofs, and then cast aside the wooden homes of Dirmisu's old section of the village.

Following that obliteration, the homes for temporary princes were tossed about like a child's toy in the midst of a tantrum.

The swell of water traveled farther down the beach and covered up the men and women's beaches, the one where Meguya had met her end, thus burying the King's sins under a mountain of ocean.

The sea continued inland, unobstructed by Lehom's will or by the King's cruelty. It finally blanketed the princely homes and palace complex with water that reached just below the rooflines. I wanted to laugh again at the destruction of the King's domain, the limits of his power, but when I attempted it, choked sobs emerged instead of triumphant cackling.

Sadness. A numbingly happy catharsis of a madwoman pushed too far, that's what this churning of emotion was.

I didn't see just one wave, but three in total. The two others swooped in and increased the height of the tidal flow. Only the mountain, the great monolith that formed the central backbone of the island, stopped it and cast the water back out, transforming the ocean into a violent assemblage of muddy brown water, bamboo debris, and bits of foliage from the jungle.

I heard a sucking sound as the ocean retreated down the height of the mountain, exposing little by little what remained of my home village. Eventually, when the ocean receded enough, I also saw the King's lifeless body dangling above the churning water. I couldn't see his drowned face from this height, but dead he certainly was. Had this destruction purified Lehom's cursed land? How ironic that an earthquake, an alleged sign of Lehom himself, had instigated such carnage. Of course, I knew that the ocean hadn't enacted justice on my behalf, but that's the way I felt then. Remember, it was the sea that revealed life's meanings to me.

I also felt a sadness for all I'd lost. Friends, family, beautiful garden retreats of my childhood, all gone. And then there was sadness because of those in this village who we hadn't had the chance to warn, the poorest and most exploited of all. They'd been taken advantage of one last time before their deaths. It may have been my fault since I was so caught up in facing down the King instead of insisting we warn everyone. Aside from my role in my grandmother's death, that's the biggest burden I still carry. Thirty-five deaths, numbering the criminal and lowest-class free men. And Nimec unless he somehow escaped. Nimec's potential death, though, didn't upset me in the least.

And after all this, I needed to survive. With Jenay.

My heart yearned for my husband as I surveyed the endless ruin below. Did waves such as this come from all directions simultaneously, or had the other villages escaped destruction? This wave appeared to have hit the Village of Lehom nearly head-on, so perhaps the Central Village and Gaiae were spared. Whatever had happened, there'd be a painful period of rebuilding, one requiring all three villages to work together. We were so divided now. However, with the King dead, we had a chance to survive and set our differences aside. I truly believed that. That was, unless someone like him gained power over the people once again.

While the waters retreated slowly over the next hour, all of us on the ledge quietly watched the remnants of the village emerge from the churning liquid. A post here, a foundation there. But the village was mostly defined by missing homes, muddy debris, with only the tallest, strongest trees remaining. Had everyone, save for the criminal men, Lady Moon bless them, escaped? I'd been so focused on the ruination below me that I hadn't looked for others, so I scanned the mountain ledges parallel to ours and saw clusters of people crying and staring in disbelief.

After many minutes of silence, Uralin put his arm on Limcona's shoulder, and she snuggled into the comfort of his embrace. "Thank you, Leilani," he whispered, his eyes still focused on the destroyed village.

"Leilani is better than a whore," I said, causing Belsimi to burst into nervous laughter.

I wasn't in the mood for levity. None of us were, but laughing was the only alternative to crying. I really needed to get home. To Jenay. I was done with this place forever. "I think it's time I left. For Gaiae. If it's still there."

Uralin craned his neck over the ledge. "Is it safe?"

I shrugged. "I don't think it'll happen again since the ocean's back to normal."

"What are we going to do?" Limcona asked, tears gathering in her eyes.

Belsimi sat down on the ground in defeat. "We'll starve. There's nothing left."

I couldn't leave them so hopeless. There was enough of that misery to go around, and misery was the King's legacy. "I'll tell the people from other villages that you need help," I assured them, keeping the next words, *if they aren't gone as well*, to myself, as uttering them aloud would give them power. "They won't let you starve."

After giving Belsimi and Limcona a final hug each, I descended down the mountain slowly, noting the devastation in more detail as I got closer. I made sure to avert my eyes when I passed the tree the King hung from. I'd gotten my vengeance. And it had come at a horrible cost. Mud covered everything, but the sea stayed back within its normal boundaries. There were no buildings left in the princely section of the village, the temple and palace had washed away, and the statues of Lehom and the Ethereal Queen now lived in the Lord of the Deep's realm. And, of course, the Eternal Spirit Garden was gone. Did that mean the sacred fruit trees were entirely destroyed? If so, perhaps Lehom's hold over the people would wane and there'd be no more visions of paradise on this muddy plain of wreckage.

Where had my old home been? I searched for patterns of trees that looked familiar and finally rested my eyes upon the palm tree trapped by the banyan. Both were inundated with mud at their base, but still present. Scanning the area with my eyes, I found a depression in the earth where my grandmother's grave had been. I knelt before it, my heart lurching in my chest as I closed my eyes and silently asked the Lord of the Deep to take care of her. I'd momentarily forgotten about the King's confessions when the wave came, so frantic was I to get up the mountain, but now the anguish returned because my actions had killed her. Thankfully, the bodies of the men from the agricultural fields must've also been carried away, for no corpses littered the ruined settlement. I asked forgiveness for their deaths, too.

A few moments later, in a world scented with rotten mud, seaweed, and despair, I heard a thump next to me and opened my eyes, only to find a coconut from the palm tree resting beside me. This might sound ridiculous, Deanne, but I took this coconut as a sign that my grandmother was happy where she was. I've found a certain peace with the idea that she's at sea now, free from the confines of our family garden. Perhaps my parents and Meguya are also free. So, I took this coconut, this token of those passed, and vowed to plant it wherever I settled. I planned on establishing my own garden, one without ridiculous limitations. That's why I didn't drink from the coconut you found us with. I wanted to preserve some connection to my family for as long as I could.

It took me about an hour to make my way through the now barren plains of Lehom. When I rounded the bend of the road, the part bracketed by the mountain, I saw the buildings of Central Village emerge. The road at my feet had its graveled coral pavement intact, meaning water hadn't washed it away.

The wave hadn't come here, probably because the shape of the island protected this half from that sea monster. Hope in my heart, I dashed into the village and saw Jenay standing on the porch of the Administrative building where I'd purchased that umbrella. We ran to each other, and the rest is history, as I've read people from the Old World often said.

CHAPTER TWENTY-TWO

D eanne had been listening to the story with rapt attention because she hadn't even bothered to pick up dropped bits of her crackers from her lap. "I'm so glad the wave didn't hit Central Village!" she exclaimed. "What about Gaiae?"

"Spared, too," I replied, leaning back into Jenay's chest. I'd nestled myself as close to my husband as I could. Maintaining contact with him felt almost sacrosanct after all we'd been through. "But the wave still washed away not only the Village of Lehom, but also its crops and cattle."

"Hence the need for supplies," Deanne said, nodding. Finally, the look of mystery in her eyes faded, replaced by satisfaction. She retrieved the map she'd shown me when I first woke up. "Volunteering to get help was very brave."

Jenay pulled me closer to him. "There wasn't any other choice. We couldn't just let people starve. And we already had the boat."

"Can you show me where the island is, Jenay? Reverse engineer your path?" Deanne asked as she sat in a chair next to Jenay's bed and unfolded the map.

I scooted to Jenay's side so he had room to study the map. He stared intently at it for a few minutes, tracing his fingers from island to island as I'd done. Finally, he shook his head and gave Deanne an apologetic look. "We headed east, but we drifted so much. I didn't keep track."

"Don't worry," Deanne assured him. She folded the map back up and tucked it in a desk drawer. "I'm sure there are records of Gerald Ani's purchase of an island in some archive. And we have satellites, too. We'll find it before time runs out."

I stole a glance at Jenay and frowned, mouthing the word satellites. He shrugged. The doctor saw our puzzled expressions and said, "Sorry about that. You wouldn't know what satellites are. They're machines in outer space that take pictures."

At the words "machines in outer space," Jenay's eyes glittered with excitement. "When there's time, I want to learn how those work. But for now, you think these machines take can help you find Ani Island?"

Deanne nodded. "I think so, especially if you tell me more about what the island looks like now. After the wave."

I thought back to the night after the wave hit, of the exhaustion, the despair, and the post-adrenaline crash that left us unable to do anything but drink a bit too much palm wine when we'd finally surveyed the damage. "Well, most noticeably, half the island was stripped of all its buildings and littered with mud," I began.

***

For the first three days after the wave, everyone from Central Village and Gaiae worked to settle the survivors from the Village of Lehom on the undamaged side of the island. The refugees placed their thin palettes on the ground of the administration building, under concert pavilions, and in private homes. And then, of course, people took shifts searching the devastated village for the missing agricultural workers. We found five. A mere five. To my disappointment, though, Nimec also emerged from the shadow of death. He and those five workers had scurried up a large banyan tree at the last minute with the waves licking at their heels.

After the Central Authority finished its tally of the living and the dead, they began the burdensome task of surveying the devastated crop fields and calculating how long the food in Central Village's and Gaiae's storage buildings would feed the island's population. You see, not only did the wave wash away the island's entire quinoa and cotilk crops, but it also salted the soil on that side of the island. The Authority predicted nothing would grow there for years, and only then after dredging the top layers of polluted soil.

Jenay and I didn't fully understand the ramifications of the large crop loss until three nights after the wave struck. With the King dead, we hadn't given a thought to our contingency plan. Mimza, Neina, Jenay, and I sat on our porch, enjoying a light dinner as we looked out at the setting sun, which made the sea burn a fiery red. We were subdued at first, obeying our need for peace and quiet. Then, a knock on the door snapped us out of our stupor. Jenay got up and answered it, and I heard Abato Ani asking if he could come inside.

Abato looked apologetic, almost bashful when he spoke. "I'm sorry for interrupting your meal."

"Believe me, it's no bother," Mimza said between sips of palm wine. "I'm curious about your calculations. And if the news is bad, at least we can get drunk."

Abato sat down, relaxed against the back of the chair, and gratefully took the glass of palm wine Neina offered him. He took a long sip and closed his eyes. "The food in our storage buildings will last one month. What about Gaiae's stores?"

He'd uttered that question reluctantly, so I knew he dreaded the answer. "The same," Mimza replied. "One pestilence-cursed month."

Neina let out a resigned sigh. "We're in trouble. Terrible trouble." Usually, she had the most optimistic stance in the family, but not that night. She stared at her glass of wine as if the answers to the island's problems lay inside it.

"We are," Abato agreed with a devastated laugh.

"What about the crops Central Village and Gaiae are growing now?" Mimza asked. "Will our current soya and vegetable yields be enough? Central Village has fruit and coconuts, too."

Abato shook his head and stared out at the sea. "Those crops, along with the fish we can expect to catch and the eggs from surviving chickens, will give us another two months."

"Starvation in four months," Mimza concluded, lifting her glass in the air. "Cheers to that!"

No one clinked glasses with her, so Mimza downed the rest of her wine and poured another glass. We all fell into a helpless silence, one that comes after you realize fate just shoved your darkest fears right in your path. During those moments of misery, I took Jenay's hand in mind and looked into his eyes. The island was in trouble, and we had a potential solution at our fingertips if we dared mention it. He squeezed my hand and cleared his throat. Our plan at the tip of his tongue, he whispered, "We need help from the Old World."

Mimza and Neina held their breaths. They knew about our contingency plan, of course, because Jenay had told Mimza after the meeting with the King. But saying the forbidden words aloud in front of non-family? Perilous. In the midst of the sound of soft waves hitting the pilings of the house, Abato Ani actually smiled. "Well, then. It seems we do."

There are moments when against all odds, furtively whispered plans utter concrete results. Abato and Mimza decided to propose the plan to the rest of the Central Authority without mentioning Jenay's and my names, just in case people protested. After all, leaving the island used to be punishable by death. How strange the way the wave inverted our world so completely. After it washed away our resources, *not* leaving the island would sentence our people to a painful demise.

***

"So, I assume the Authority approved this plan?" Deanne asked.

I took a sip of water, my throat dry from speaking, so Jenay answered Deanne's question. "Unanimously. Abato also told us he'd heard life from the mainland. Chatter that he sometimes picked up from a radio that couldn't be used to contact the mainland. Chanson Ani stripped away that function from it decades ago. Still, Abato and the other two Central Authority members concealed the radio from everyone. They told us to head east, the direction it came from. Calabasas was also east, so east we headed. The Central Authority members even examined our boat for seaworthiness, supplemented our provisions, and reviewed our navigation plan. We promised to bring back or send help as soon as we could."

I remembered, then, how Jenay and I had been poised with the boat at the entrance to the sea caves, staring out at the expanse of blue that was both our savior and our potential end. One threat, one obstacle at a time. That's how we'd handle life.

Right before our departure, I stood before the sea with my husband and breathed in its humid, salty air. Cicara, who'd married us at the temple, entreated the Lord of the Deep and Lady Moon for our success. What a simultaneously frightening and exhilarating moment that was, again on the precipice of freedom.

"It was a necessary but still frightening choice. We were heading out into the ocean in a boat with limited provisions. Still, I had confidence in this boat." I turned around and kissed Jenay. "This bamboo master built it."

My husband positively beamed at the compliment, returning my kiss.

"How long again were you at sea?" Deanne asked.

I struggled to remember. The last few days had been hazy. "At least eight days."

"Probably a little more than that," Jenay said, giving her a grateful smile. "Thank you, again. We might not have made it without your ship, especially since we underestimated how many provisions we needed."

Deanne blushed. "It was really nothing." She hesitated for a second, and then asked, in a serious tone, "Are you sure you don't want to accompany the supply ship to the island? Serve as a mediator between those people and your islanders?"

Jenay looked to me for my answer. I shook my head. "No," I replied. "That shouldn't be necessary. The Central Authority knows help is coming. No one on the island will refuse it."

My husband gave my hand a comforting squeeze, and I continued with the deeper explanation of why we didn't want to return just yet. "I've always loved the night, Deanne, but I began to feel haunted after the wave struck. When the wind rustled through the palm leaves on a star-filled balmy night, I heard the dead agricultural workers whispering, asking why I didn't run to warn them. I also saw my grandmother's face in the moonlit-filled tidal pools on the beach. She didn't blame me for her death, but I knew her life was the price we'd pay for prevailing over the King."

"I understand," Deanne said. "If you don't think there'll be trouble when the supplies arrive, then we're good to go. I assume the Children of Lehom are living under Central Village's and Gaiae's laws now."

Jenay let out a wry laugh. "For the time being."

I nudged my husband with my elbow and jumped in to explain. I didn't want Deanne to get the wrong impression. "The village is being rebuilt so people aren't crowded together in the other villages," I explained. "But Irin is leading them now. The other princes agreed since he was married to Kimsimi. He's moderated his views a bit. You won't find trouble with my brother."

"Then, I'll contact the authorities on Virgin Gorda and see about finding you a place to stay," Deanne replied.

"We plan on returning to the island someday," Jenay said. "For now, the Old World holds too many wonders."

CHAPTER TWENTY-THREE

My world is no longer hanging on the brink of shadows. I try not to hate the King. We should never hate. What would that accomplish? Only ruin, as we've seen. On that count, the Children of Lehom need to let go of hate, and all islanders need to conquer their fears.

Here I stand at the helm of a great ship, the vivacious blue sea before me, and I see all of its colors and moods. Deanne's told me that her world doesn't crush the will of women into dust. Instead, opportunities will teem and swirl about, ready for the conquering. Jenay and I will seize our futures. We want to get proper educations and use our skills to live in this new place. How strange that the Old World of our ancestors became Jenay's and my New World. When we get to the New World, I'll plant the coconut in a garden, and my grandmother will emerge from her own shadows there. The true Eternal Spirit Garden is the memory we carry of those who have departed. I'll make my own at the back of our home. Jenay's sketched me a small house, a cabin, really, that he'll build us when we get there. It's a simple place with two rooms and many windows. Perfect for our needs. When we departed from the island, I remember the waterfall in the crevasse getting smaller and smaller, eventually vanishing like the false notions that divide people from one another. The Old World fades in favor of the new.

-Addendum to the *Journal of Samsara Ani*, added by Leilani Lo

BEFORE YOU GO

Thank you for reading The Moon Hunters by Anya Pavelle. If you enjoyed the book, please do us a favor and leave a review. It doesn't have to be a dissertation, just a few lines about what you liked. It goes a long way and we'd really appreciate it. You will feel an amazing sense of satisfaction because you're helping new authors to the genre and a publisher that supports them. You can learn more about us, our books, and authors here: https://www.chandrapress.com

If you like free stuff, early access to new releases, sweet deals, discounts, giveaways, and exclusive offers, please join our awesome newsletter. Just follow this link: https://www.chandrapress.com/newsletter

Made in the USA
San Bernardino, CA
06 May 2020